AF268120

Seas of Seduction

Secrets of the Seas
Book 2

Lauren Everly

DRAGONBLADE PUBLISHING, INC.

© Copyright 2026 by Lauren Everly
Text by Lauren Everly
Cover by Dar Albert

Dragonblade Publishing, Inc. is an imprint of Kathryn Le Veque Novels, Inc.
P.O. Box 23
Moreno Valley, CA 92556
ceo@dragonbladepublishing.com

Produced in the United States of America

First Edition April 2026
Trade Paperback Edition

Reproduction of any kind except where it pertains to short quotes in relation to advertising or promotion is strictly prohibited.

All Rights Reserved.

The characters and events portrayed in this book are fictitious. Any similarity to real persons, living or dead, is purely coincidental and not intended by the author.

AI Statement: No AI or ghostwriting was used in the creation of this story, or any story, published by Dragonblade Publishing. All text, structure, content, ideas, and concept are 100% human generated solely by the author whose name appears on the cover. It is prohibited to use this material, or any copyrighted material, for AI engine training.

ARE YOU SIGNED UP FOR DRAGONBLADE'S BLOG?

You'll get the latest news and information on exclusive giveaways, exclusive excerpts, coming releases, sales, free books, cover reveals and more.

Check out our complete list of authors, too!

No spam, no junk. That's a promise!

Sign Up Here

www.dragonbladepublishing.com

Dearest Reader;

Thank you for your support of a small press. At Dragonblade Publishing, we strive to bring you the highest quality Historical Romance from some of the best authors in the business. Without your support, there is no 'us', so we sincerely hope you adore these stories and find some new favorite authors along the way.

Happy Reading!

CEO, Dragonblade Publishing

Additional Dragonblade books by
Author Lauren Everly

Secrets of the Seas Series
Waves of Desire (Book 1)
Seas of Seduction (Book 2)

Dedication

To David. For being my best friend, my everything. My forever.

Acknowledgments

As always, I am forever grateful for Kathryn Le Veque and Dragonblade Publishing for making a home for this series. Thank you for Natalie Sowa for answering my endless questions and navigating all the moving parts of publishing this. To my editor, Cherie Mathis your ability to see the heart of this story and coax it to its best version means more than I can say. Thank you to Dar Albert and the rest of the design team for creating yet another cover more gorgeous than I ever could have imagined. To Alexis Crusher and her sultry voice that brings my words to life in the best way. And to my incredible and talented agent, Christina Miller at Nancy Yost Literary Agency, thank you for cheering these characters on. Even when I doubted myself, you kept me on track and believed in their story. Every day I am reminded of how lucky I am to have you in my corner!

I am so fortunate to have friends who have supported me throughout my publishing journey, and I truly would not be here without them. Livy Hart, you were there from the very beginning—the first person to fall in love with this series. I'm endlessly grateful that our paths crossed, and my life would not be the same without your wisdom and insight. I love how deeply you care and how fiercely you champion the stories you believe in. You'll always be my number one, my favorite partner in this wonderfully unpredictable adventure. To the Llamasquad, thank you for always being there in the chat. To Heather Frances and Kaitlin Stark, I'm so glad to have y'all as agent sibs, Christina has impeccable taste! To my flight attendant friends Patrick, Maren, Marianne, and Brooke and to Marin, Jill, Jen, Kristin and everyone in my close circle, I love you all so much! Special thanks to Alexa for always hyping my work up, even my original ideas when I was still learning how to structure a story. You have no idea how much your enthusiasm contributed to me keeping trying! To Cindy, who inspired me to start writing again after so many years. And to all my fans, especially the ones who sneak into my DMs to share your excitement about my characters, thank you. Your passion keeps these stories alive, and without you, there would be no *Secrets of the Seas*!

Special thanks to my husband, David, who has always been there for me, even when he's not quite sure about all this romance stuff. Thank you for helping me survive late nights and deadlines and for proving that ours is the greatest love story of them all. Thanks to my children for always keeping me on my toes and for reminding me daily what unconditional love truly means. To my parents, who have never once doubted me, thank you for your support and never-ending excitement over my work. Grammie and Bompa, you two are the best grandparents anyone could ever have, and I'm so thankful for how much you love me and my books! Thank you, Aunt Gigi, for telling me a million times I could succeed at anything I set my heart to. You were right. And to my sisters (and Amy,) I am so grateful for how close we are. I know that's not common and I don't take it for granted! Life is simply better with you all in it. For real, I don't think I would survive without our group text.

Finally, none of this would be possible without my faith in God. I'm so thankful for every day I'm given, and for the grace that meets me where I am, allowing me to continue creating and growing.

Prologue

The French colony of Tortuga
July 1803

EVERYTHING HAPPENED FOR a reason.

At least that's what Josephine reminded herself as the mockingbird outside her window increased the tempo of his song. Definitely a he. No reasonable female of any creature would be so rude for so long this late at night. Hours had passed since she'd lost track of the passing minutes. Even opening her shutters and throwing an old slipper at the palm tree where the bird perched hadn't convinced him to take his amorous tune elsewhere.

With a groan, she rolled over and pressed her fingers to her temple. Speaking of birds, Lola slept soundly in her cage, her head tucked tight beneath a green wing. Damn parrot could sleep through a hurricane.

Must be nice.

A loud thump interrupted her thoughts and she went perfectly still. Again and again it sounded. The front door.

Josephine bolted upright, mind racing. At this hour, it must be a true emergency. Living on an island frequented by pirates and smugglers, "true emergency" always meant something dire. She would have heard cannons if two ships had started a fight. So not that. Perhaps a fire? Her stomach twisted at the thought. Almost all the homes in town were wood. A fire would be devastating.

Swinging her feet to the floor, she pulled her nightgown off and struggled into the skirt and blouse she'd laid out before going to bed. The pounding began anew as she found her slippers in the muted moonlight. Heavy footsteps came from the hallway and she opened the door just in time to catch the top of her father's head disappearing down the stairs, bathed in warm lantern light. She followed, pausing halfway down to stay in the shadows.

He opened the door and a man rushed in. "Governor?"

Her father nodded and the man sagged against the door-frame. "First officer, Isaac Caldwell, US Navy. I'm in desperate need of help."

The US Navy? What in heaven's name were they doing here? Though the states made their displeasure well known about Tortuga's relationship with pirates, they had no jurisdiction on the island. Although… A vision of a dark ship flashed across her mind. Captain Thorne had arrived in port last night. The Navy had made it clear the capture of the notorious pirate had become a top priority.

Would they risk a battle in the harbor?

Her father lifted his lantern while the man caught his breath and all thoughts left Josephine.

She blinked to make sure her eyes were not deceiving her. They were not. The most handsome man she had ever seen stood in their foyer. Grateful for the shadows, she let her eyes soak him in. Golden hair fell in messy waves around a chiseled face, and with his shirt sleeves rolled up, tanned muscles demanded her attention. Dirt stained his rumpled clothing, a far cry from what she'd expect for a Navy uniform. She swallowed as her sight dropped to tan breeches, which clung to him in a way some might deem scandalous.

"I'm in desperate need of a ship. It's life or death."

Her father cleared his throat. "A ship?"

The lines on the sailor's face hardened. "My captain is being pursued by Thorne. We were captured by him two days back and escaped tonight."

"Captured by Thorne, you say? I thought he didn't take prisoners."

"Well, he did. By order of the United States of America, I require your assistance."

"I don't understand. Why are you not with your captain?"

Officer Caldwell hesitated the slightest moment. "He departed with another pirate. Thorne's ship left in pursuit shortly after."

"I don't have a ship. At least not one capable of going after the *Reckoning*."

"I will take anything. I must try. You'll be compensated very well, I assure you."

Josephine took another step down toward the men. The stair tread creaked under her weight and she went still as her father spoke again. "And when your rescue mission is unsuccessful? How will I be assured of my funds?"

"Draw up a contract to send to Washington if you must, but be quick about it."

Her father studied the man for a long moment before giving a curt nod. "My daughter, Josephine, will take care of the contract." He waved a hand in her direction. "I will go find you your ship."

Blue eyes fixed on her and she fought back a gasp. They seemed to pierce through her very soul. She stood frozen, her pulse thundering in her ears until he turned back to her father.

"It would be better if I went with you. The rest of our men are waiting at the docks, and will be ready to sail at a moment's notice."

No.

Josephine almost said it aloud.

He couldn't leave. Not yet.

She practically ran down the stairs. "It will be faster if he goes now. Your men can ready the ship while we finish the contract and you'll be able to sail as soon as you arrive."

His jaw twitched, several days worth of stubble running its length in a masculine shadow. When he glanced between her father and her, she could see the war of morals going on in his head. He would be alone with her if her father left. Americans, always so prim and proper with their endless rules.

"Go, Papa. Tell his men he will be but a quarter hour behind you." The sailor's brows rose when she made the decision for him and she gave him a small smile. "If you'll follow me, Officer Caldwell, I'll take you to the study."

She took the lantern from her father and turned, praying the officer would follow. For a few moments, she walked alone. Then, footfalls fell in step behind her.

In the study, Josephine set down the lantern and pulled out a sheet of fresh parchment. While she laid it flat on her father's desk, the officer positioned himself on the other side and her smile wavered. The room suddenly felt very small. In here, with the flame's light dancing off the walls, she could not help being acutely aware she was alone with him. His eyes bore into her and she wondered if he were thinking the very same thing.

She took a quill from its holder and dipped the point into the pot of ink. "How much time will you require?"

"Two months should suffice. If I'm not back by then..." He trailed off.

If he didn't return, it would mean he failed. And failure with Thorne meant only one thing: death. Everyone in the Caribbean knew the name well and made sure to never cross his path. No one had ever done so and lived to tell the tale.

She sucked in a breath. *Don't think like that.*

He was young and fit. A navy man. If anyone stood a chance against the bloodthirsty pirate, certainly it would be him.

Those ocean-hued eyes followed her every move as the ink flowed into words and Josephine struggled to keep breathing. Her hand began to shake, the smooth line going askew.

"Have you done this before?"

The skepticism lacing his voice brought her focus back to the task at hand. "Of course I have. Do you think my father would have entrusted the job to me if I hadn't?"

He didn't answer.

She swallowed and continued. "You must like your captain very much to go through such an effort to save him."

His eyes darkened with intensity. "He is my closest friend. I would die for him. And he would do the same for me."

The fierce and emotional reply left her at a loss for words as a chasm opened within her. She'd never had a friend she felt that way about. That's what happened when one grew up on an island surrounded by pirates and smugglers.

"Well then, I wish you success." She finished and slid the parchment to him. "Would you like me to write out a second copy for you?"

He gave a brisk shake of his head, sending a wave of hair tumbling over his forehead. "That won't be necessary."

With a nod, she handed the quill over. Rough fingers brushed hers and a tingle shot up her arm. She rubbed one hand across the skin there, marveling at the lingering warmth as he scrawled his name in a hasty flourish.

He straightened and moved to the side, motioning her forward. And that was it. Their fleeting time together had already come to an end. She left the contract on the desk and led the way back to the foyer.

Josephine came to a stop in front of the door, but didn't open it. She didn't want him to leave. *Selfish girl.* She didn't care. A few more minutes wouldn't hurt. Besides, she could offer him some extra help.

"If you don't mind waiting a few moments, I can pack some provisions for you. The ship will not be stocked well since it hasn't sailed in a while."

He glanced at the door. "I should go. The sooner we leave, the better my chances are."

She pulled her lip between her teeth.

"But, I would be grateful for anything you can offer. The men have had very few rations the last few days and they will need all the strength they can muster if we are to fight Thorne."

A lightness filled her chest. "Very true. Follow me."

In the kitchen, she took a burlap bag from a shelf. Shaking it out, she handed it to the officer. "Hold this and I'll fill it for you."

A crate of papaya sat on the counter and she grabbed one. The fruit had been delivered that past morning. "How much do you think you can carry?"

"Are you questioning my strength?" Something sparkled in his eyes. A quick flash of mischief, there and gone in a flash.

"Of course not." She couldn't help another look at his arms. He could probably carry ten full bags without breaking a sweat. Maybe more. *You're staring like you've never seen a man before.* With a jerk, she twisted back toward the crate and began to transfer the fruit.

When she emptied the crate, she added a round of waxed cheese. With very little room left in the bag, she glanced around the kitchen. The three loaves of bread she'd made earlier would fit. She pulled them free from the cloth she'd wrapped them in and set them on top of the cheese.

"Did you bake these?"

She nodded.

"They look lovely."

Her pulse jumped at the murmured words. They stood still for several wild beats of her heart before he cleared his throat and took a step back. "I must go."

"Yes." Her throat had gone dry and she swallowed. "Make sure you get fresh barrels of water down at the docks. Even at this hour, there should be someone down there who can get you some. Tell them to charge my father's account."

This time, he led the way to the door and she followed him out onto the porch. He started down the stairs and admiration flowed through her. Here was a man willing to risk everything for his friend, a man who didn't waver in the face of danger. An uncomfortable tightness surrounded her heart. He had no idea what he was getting into.

"Officer Caldwell?"

He paused and turned, those blue eyes locking on hers once again.

"Be careful. Thorne is…Well, he's cunning. Even when you think you're about to win, he'll surprise you. There's a reason he has never been captured."

His face softened. "Thank you, Miss…" He shifted the sack to his other hand. "I'm sorry, I do not even know your name."

Warmth pooled at her cheeks. "Josephine. Josephine Montclair."

"Miss Montclair. And thank you for your hospitality. I will not forget you." His gaze traveled over her as if trying to commit her to memory.

Her heart stuttered as the heat in her face traveled straight through the rest of her body. Before she could form a response, he bowed and turned down the stairs. With several long strides, he passed through their gate and onto the quiet street.

Josephine stood still, waiting until he disappeared from sight before turning back toward the house. The mockingbird's shrill call rang out to break the silence and her lips curved.

Everything most certainly happened for a reason.

Chapter One

Tortuga
Nearly two months later

NO ONE NOTICED the delicate chink of bone dice against glass.
At least no one besides Josephine.

She couldn't fault them. With a grin, she lifted her gaze from the hazard table. No fewer than two dozen pirates had crammed into the tavern. Two dozen very drunk pirates.

Now was her time to shine.

Not with the dice though. She dropped off the mugs of ale she had brought over and made her way toward the back tables where several games of Vingt-et-un had started. Her hips swayed with her best sashay and she stopped at an empty chair between a group of younger pirates.

"Is this spot taken?"

The men about fell from their seats to make room for her to slide in. She took her time settling, deliberately drawing out the moment as she slowly retrieved her money purse from between her breasts. They stared with mouths agape. Just like she wanted them to.

She removed two coins and flipped them between her fingers. "What's everyone betting?"

Several new stacks of coins materialized on the table, and one man fumbled in his pocket and tossed out an onyx sea turtle.

"Turtles are lucky, right?" She reached out and set it upright.

He shrugged. "Not having much of that so far."

She gave a wide grin. "Well, maybe this is the round it chang-es."

He stared at her with a glint in his eye, and she forced her smile to stay in place. Flirting with criminals was a dangerous game, but it helped keep them unaware. After all, she never lost—unless intentionally.

The first few hands passed in a blur. While the stacks of coins moved around the table with each hand dealt, Josephine focused on the cards. The goal of the game was simple enough: whoever got twenty-one, or closest without going over, won. A game of pure chance, they said.

But she'd learned over the years that if she kept track of the cards played, she would have a much better idea of the odds of a certain card being dealt toward the end of the deck and could bet accordingly.

She kept her first few bets small, adding numbers in her head until the odds shifted in her favor. Her fingers tapped the top of her card, a king of hearts. One ace remained in the deck and five face cards.

When her second card came, she lifted the corner. Ace. Years of practice kept her face passive as everyone placed their next bets. She slid all of her coins to the center, her racing heart betraying the calmness she portrayed. One of the men matched her without hesitation. He most likely had double face cards. The others looked at their hands again and two folded with furrowed brows. The last reluctantly added the rest of his coins to the pot and motioned for another card.

Josephine shook her head no when the dealer looked at her and her confident opponent did the same. He flipped his cards to confirm her suspicions and she bit her cheek to keep a smug look at bay.

"Well, hell's teeth!" The other man flipped his cards over with a scowl. A face, a six, and a three.

Though she'd done it a hundred times over, the thrill that came with winning never faded. She turned her face card first, and waited a moment before showing the ace.

The man with twenty looked between her and the pot with narrowed eyes. "What kind of devil's luck do you have?"

She kept her smile bright as she gathered the coins. When you separated a man from his earnings, no matter how ill-begotten, his true character tended to be revealed. And with this sort of lot, one could never be certain how they'd react—especially when losing to a woman.

It's why she never joined high stakes games or played more than one round.

"I guess it's more the luck of the draw. Or perhaps this seat." She picked up the turtle, tossing it once before closing her fingers around it. "Well, gentlemen, thank you for the game."

She stood before any of them could complain further about her winning. "I must get back to work. Next round is on me."

The prospect of free ale wiped any remaining frowns from the pirates' faces.

While Josephine wasn't actually employed at the tavern, the owner of the Golden Lantern was happy to allow her to help out on busy nights. When the ship had sailed in earlier today, she'd headed straight there. The work kept her mind from other things.

Things like handsome sailors.

Correction, one specific sailor.

She slowed and glanced out the window into the inky night.

"You're not still daydreaming about that Navy man, are you?" The voice snapped her attention back to the room as Colette approached.

"No."

Liar.

Colette gave her a knowing look. She was probably the closest thing Josephine had to a best friend. Twenty years older than her, and a thousand times more worldly, the barmaid had taken Josephine under her wing after her mother died.

"Best get your mind off him. You know as well as I do, if he went after Thorne and hasn't come back yet, he's dead."

Josephine's stomach clenched. News of Thorne's capture had reached the island a few weeks after Officer Caldwell had shown up asking for a ship. At first, she had been elated—perhaps her handsome sailor had survived after all. But her relief faded as time passed with no sign of him or her father's ship. Now, only two days remained before her father would assume the vessel lost and send off the contract to collect his payment.

"Thorne?" The drunken slur of a nearby pirate who had just walked in interrupted her spiraling thoughts.

His eyes lit when the two women and half the occupants of the room turned their attention toward him. "Didn't you hear?"

Josephine crossed her arms as a wide smile spread across his pock-marked face. "No, tell us."

The pirate raised his voice. "Thorne has escaped, on the very day he was to be hanged."

The noise in the room dimmed as the news rippled from one corner to the next. Finally, a man at the next table raised his mug. "To Thorne!" Frothy ale sloshed onto the weathered wood. "And damn the Navy! Hopefully the old bastard took out as many as he could!"

That got the rest of the tavern all riled up. Mugs clanked as a chorus of agreement thundered throughout the space.

Escaped.

Josephine's jaw clenched. Could Officer Caldwell have survived the first clash with Thorne only to perish during the escape? *No.* If Thorne had gotten away, the Navy would have thrown everything—and everyone—they could spare into the chase. Yes. That must be it.

Colette raised a red brow. "Don't get your hopes up, Missy. I know exactly what you're thinking."

"Sometimes, I wish I'd never told you about that night." Josephine began filling mugs.

"No need to take offense. Trust me, I've been infatuated with plenty of men in my days." Colette helped her pour the ale. "I know firsthand how infatuation leads to heartbreak. And you don't deserve that, especially not from a man who probably hasn't given you a single thought since that night."

I will not forget you.

She had not told her friend about that particular exchange. He had said it with such sincerity, Josephine could not believe otherwise.

Was she naive? Perhaps he said that to every young woman he met in port.

A cold heaviness snaked through her belly.

Colette was only trying to look out for her.

She gave a small smile and picked up four mugs. "You're right. Here, help me carry these to the table in the corner."

Her friend laughed. "I'm right? Don't think I've ever heard those words out of you before."

Josephine shook her head and headed toward the table where a new game had started. As she set the last mug down, an arm snaked around her waist and tugged her hard. She nearly fell into the lap of the young pirate she'd won the turtle from.

"Looks like my luck has changed." The slurred words sent her skin crawling.

Josephine twisted from his grasp and took a big step back in case he tried again.

"Why don't you head home? I'll distract this lot." Colette winked and sat in the still empty chair. She set a hand on the man's leg and leaned toward him. "There's a private room upstairs, if you haven't gambled everything away yet."

Josephine turned away, a knot in her stomach. Even after spending years watching her friend work, it still made her uneasy. Colette had assured her time and time again not to worry. She picked and chose her lovers each night and charged a hefty price.

While part of Josephine longed for that sort of freedom, she had never dared try. Not that Colette would ever let her. Like any motherly figure, her friend yearned to see Josephine find a good man—which wouldn't happen in the upstairs bedrooms at the Golden Lantern. Not that her chances were higher anywhere else on this God-forsaken island.

With a sigh, she went to the bar and gathered her belongings before ducking into a closet. She made short work of changing from her skirt and blouse into a pair of soft lambskin breeches and a men's shirt. Twisting her hair up, she shoved a straw hat on. Though she lived only a short walk away from the tavern, walking around at this time of night as a woman could be problematic. After being harassed multiple times over the years, she'd come up with the disguise. No one ever seemed to notice a lone cabin boy wandering the streets.

She made her way to the door and slipped outside. A deep breath of humid air replaced the stink of old ale and unwashed bodies. Floral undertones mixed with an ever-present saltiness and she took another appreciative breath. The small size of the island meant one could never escape the smell of the sea.

Josephine kicked at a stone along the dry path leading to her home. Life on a pirate island should be exciting. When they had moved to Tortuga, she'd been ten years old with visions of adventures and buried treasures filling her head. But, as it happened, girls weren't allowed to have any of the fun. And no pirate worth his salt would ever think of hiding treasure on the island. Besides, even with the resurgence of piracy in the Caribbean over the last decade, it was nothing like the swash-buckling days a hundred years back. Back then, the island had been the hideout of some of the most famous pirates of the time.

Her fingers drifted to her pocket and brushed against the cool heft of the onyx sea turtle. She sighed. When her mother had gotten sick and passed, her father promised to send her to boarding school in France or America. But time passed with a different excuse each year and now, at twenty-three, any hope of that had long passed.

If her disguise were truth, she could join a crew and travel the world—feel the sway of a ship beneath her feet, visit ports she had only ever imagined. Instead, being a woman meant she was trapped in the monotony of a life offering little more than domestic routine and evenings spent staring out the window. Marriage prospects hovered perilously close to zero as any respectable merchantmen who passed through never lingered long enough to spark more than a fleeting curiosity. Still, she caught herself wondering what it would be like to sail beside a man whose eyes lingered just a moment too long, whose laugh stirred something in her chest. So she was left to daydream—of distant harbors, of daring adventures, and of a heart brave enough to follow them.

While her thoughts about the Navy sailor had been pleasant, Colette was right, she needed to move on. With a sigh, she pushed open their gate and walked to the steps. At the top, she turned and looked out into the night. Wispy clouds framed the moon and the frogs trilled louder than ever. Whether she got married or wasted away into spinsterhood—whatever happened with her life—the island didn't care. It would continue on as it always had.

Quietly, she opened the door and slipped inside. When she clicked it shut, a scrape came from her father's study and he poked his head into the hall.

"Oh. Hello, Papa." She moved toward the stairs, but he strode forward and blocked her way.

"What did I tell you about the Golden Lantern?" She pressed her lips together as he pointed to the clock. "It's past midnight. You should not be out after dark. And you most certainly shouldn't be wearing men's clothing. You know better."

Heat flashed through her. "Papa, I cannot sit at home my whole life. What else would you have me do?"

"Not work at a tavern amongst drunks and women of loose virtue."

She threw up her hands. "Drunks and loose women? This whole island is full of them if you haven't noticed!"

"Do not raise your voice at me." He crossed his arms. "From now on, I want you to stay home when there are unfamiliar ships in the harbor."

"That's not fair. There are always unfamiliar ships here."

"I've received new reports of growing unrest on the mainland. These ships no longer carry only pirates and merchants." He exhaled. "I only want you to be safe."

"What you want is for me to die of boredom." Josephine pushed past him and started up the steps, tears pricking at the corners of her eyes.

"Josephine."

She ignored the warning in his voice and continued, not stopping until she shut and locked her door behind her. In the dark, she slowly made her way to her bed and lit the candle there. With a groan, she flopped back on the mattress.

Maybe she needed to start paying more attention to the merchants that came through. Because, while she may not actually die from boredom, the thought of staying on the island had become unbearable. If she didn't find a way off Tortuga, her life would never amount to anything. The certainty hit her hard, sinking into her bones.

A shrill whistle came from beside her and she rolled to find Lola giving her a dirty look. "Did I wake you from your beauty sleep?" The parrot ruffled her feathers before turning away and Josephine couldn't help a small chuckle as her melancholy began to ease. "Oh, alright, just give me a moment to get ready for bed and you can have your peace back."

Something dug into her hip when she sat and she shifted to pull the turtle free. She stood and crossed over to a weathered trunk against the wall. When she lifted the lid, the light from her candle glimmered off the collection of mismatched trinkets she had won at the tavern over the years.

"Where should you go?" Her hand hovered over the items, passing a pearl-studded comb, a crystal couple frozen in dance, and a silver teacup. She slowed to a stop above an old brass key. "Here."

After setting down the sea turtle, she picked up the key. The familiar weight of her favorite piece settled in her palm. An ivory carving at its head depicted two skulls facing each other beneath a palm branch with a single Latin word engraved beneath them. *Vita*. Life. She'd won it from an old pirate who'd disappeared before she could ask for more information.

If she were younger, she might daydream about what type of treasure chest it might open. But she knew better. Nothing good would come of fantasizing. Without a matching lock, it was about as worthless as her hopes and dreams about her future. She shook her head. Nothing was worthless. She just needed a plan.

Lola let out a disgruntled squawk, and Josephine carefully set the antique back in place. She blew out the candle and laid back down.

"One day, Lola, we're going to get off this island."

Chapter Two

SOFT DOUGH PRESSED between Josephine's fingers as she folded the elastic mixture over on itself. With a grunt, she threw her weight into her palms and smashed down one last time. She pulled one end over the other to form a tight ball before plopping it into a basket. A strand of hair stuck to her damp forehead and she swiped her hand to push it back. Blasted heat. She leaned in front of the open louvers, willing even a hint of a breeze to bring her some relief.

The glimmer of the sea between two buildings caught her eye and she groaned. A swim sounded lovely. In fact, she very may well kill for one. But with too many new ships in the harbor, it wasn't safe.

Speaking of new, a trio of masts that hadn't been there yesterday towered above the rest. Ships that size were rarely seen in Tortuga. Had Thorne returned? Surely, he wouldn't risk it when on the run from the navy. Maybe a wealthy merchant's ship? She picked up a handkerchief and tied her hair back. With her chores finished, there was ample time to go investigate before starting dinner.

Outside, the sun bore down on her, the heat penetrating her skin within seconds. Probably should have opted for a brimmed hat. With a shrug, she continued. Wasn't like she would take long, only one street separated her from a clear view of the harbor.

A few steps later, the ship came into view and her eyes went wide. A sleek Sloop of War, fully ship-rigged, rested at the docks.

Crisp white sails draped from perfectly straight yards. Out of habit, Josephine counted the cannons gleaming in the sunlight on one side. Eleven Twenty-two guns made her a formidable ship that dwarfed every other boat in sight.

Very few could afford such a vessel, which meant…Her pulse quickened as her eyes flew to the mainmast. Though it draped limp, there was no mistaking the stars and stripes of the United States flag. A naval jack hung at the stern, signaling the ship belonged to the US Navy.

A small schooner floated behind it and her heart stuttered.

The same ship her father had lent.

Could it be? A lightness filled her chest, almost immediately extinguished as she remembered Colette's words from the night before.

Still, she picked up her skirt and turned down a small footpath. It wound down the steep hillside, a convenient yet strenuous shortcut that cut the journey to the water in half. Her feet skimmed over loose rocks and ruts and she drew to a stop when a group of men came into view, standing on the dock next to the ship. A small cry caught in her throat.

The lieutenant.

Standing there in uniform, talking to her father.

He'd survived.

She ran the rest of the way down the path.

When she drew near to the dock, she stopped and glanced down. What was she thinking? Streaks of flour marred her skirt, and her plain blouse clung to sweat-dampened skin. Brushing her hands up to her head, she groaned. Wisps of hair had escaped her handkerchief and stuck out in every direction.

She couldn't face him looking like this.

From where she stood, she could not see the other side of the dock where the men had been standing. If she turned back, she could go home and change. And then what? What excuse would she have for coming to the docks all dressed up? What if the ship left by then? She bit down on her lip. If he left before she got a chance to see him, she'd never forgive herself.

Her gaze slid to the tavern, not far from the docks. Colette would help make her at least presentable. It would only take a few minutes. With a grin, she hurried that way.

"Josephine, what are you doing down here?"

Her father's voice brought her to a stop and she gave a feeble attempt to press her curls beneath her handkerchief before slowly turning. He strode toward her, alone. Thank goodness.

"I came to see the ship." She pointed at the sloop.

"Ah yes. She's a beauty, isn't she? The *USS Tempest*, newly constructed."

With a nod, Josephine started walking again, a curse dancing upon her lips. If only she had finished her bread a little earlier.

Footsteps came from behind her as he caught up. "While you're down here, there's something I need to talk to you about."

She stopped in her tracks.

"I think it's time you get married."

Josephine spun to face him, panic twisting in her gut. "Wh-What do you mean?"

"You're three and twenty. While I have long hoped that Tortuga would become a prosperous island, it has not. And while it has remained outside of the conflict in Haiti, I fear for the future. If the French are overthrown, my position will be in danger."

The revolution in Haiti had been going on for over a decade. Though her father rarely spoke of it, the pirates and merchants at the tavern did. Josephine was not naive. "But what does that have to do with me getting married?"

Her father gave her a tight smile. "If the revolution succeeds, we would have to return to Europe. But that would be hard on you. I have no connections there, no standing. It would be a difficult life. Cyrus Wentworth has just written to me asking for your hand, and I believe he is a good match for you."

Josephine stepped back, a stark coldness sliding through her veins. "Cyrus Wentworth? I don't even know who that is."

"Oh come now, he's the American sugar merchant who has dined at our home many a time."

"That old man?" Josephine recoiled at a recollection of gray hair and a rotund belly. "You can't be serious."

He frowned. "He's not that old."

"He's older than you!" She crossed her arms across her chest, her heartbeat pounding a wild tune against her skin. "I will not marry him. I would rather go to Europe with you."

With a sigh, he turned to face the sea. "I want you to be secure. We have lived a good life here, never in need or want. Cyrus has dined with kings, bankrolled naval contracts, and buried two wives. You'd want for nothing."

"Papa, I can't." Josephine's voice cracked. "I do want to get married. But not to someone three times my age whom I don't even know."

"Well, he'll be arriving here next week on a merchant run, so you'll have some time to become more acquainted with him."

"I said no. This conversation is over." She spun away but he followed.

"Josephine!"

She ignored him and continued, picking up her pace.

"Josephine, don't do anything rash. The newly promoted Lieutenant Caldwell will be joining us for dinner tonight."

Don't do anything rash.

Josephine harrumphed and set the last platter of food on the table.

What did he think she was going to do, elope with the first pirate she met? Not that she could have even done that, as the presence of the *Tempest* had caused the entire island to go dormant.

Of all the men, Cyrus Wentworth.

She shuddered.

He was certainly not whom she pictured last night during her tirade to Lola. Of course, her father would choose an old stuffy merchant. Hell, maybe she *should* take interest in a pirate. Even a smuggler would be better than someone old enough to be her grandfather.

A knock came from the front door and she smoothed her skirt and took a deep breath. The lieutenant. A deep breath filled her lungs. She would not let the discussion with her father from earlier hamper her evening.

Her father had just gone upstairs to change so she approached the door. Once there, she paused and ran her hands over her hair to make sure it hadn't come loose. It rested in a simple chignon with a few curls teased free. Dinner had nearly been burnt as she tried to juggle getting ready and cooking all at the same time. Her pulse raced as she reached for the doorknob.

"Miss Montclair."

The baritone of his voice washed over her the moment she opened the door. Instead of stepping back to let him in, she stood transfixed. A white cravat spilled from a navy double breasted frock coat with gold braiding at the cuffs, and immaculate buff breeches clad to long legs. She jerked her attention up to where a bicorne hat hid the majority of his blonde waves.

Even more handsome than she remembered.

Her breath caught as he returned the perusal, his gaze traveling a slow path from her face to her feet, then back up, pausing for a long moment on her chest, where she'd purposely left a button free on her best blouse. Heat spread through her when blue eyes finally settled on hers.

"I thought of you often."

"You did?" She cringed at her blurted response. "I mean…Well, what I meant…"

A grin spread across his face as her cheeks burned.

"I also thought of you—your safety—while you were gone."

His smile broadened. "Thank you."

"Lieutenant Caldwell, I'm so glad you made it." Her father's voice from behind her made her jump.

The lieutenant removed his hat. "I appreciate the invitation."

She stepped to the side and followed the men to the dining room. Her father sat and motioned the lieutenant to the seat next to him, but he crossed over to where Josephine stood and pulled her chair out for her. She murmured her thanks as her cheeks burned anew.

Once Lieutenant Caldwell took his seat, he gave an appreciative glance across the spread in front of them. "This looks wonderful."

A lightness filled Josephine's chest. Poached snapper, sweetened plantains and steamed greens were all Caribbean staples, but her bread and banana tart brought a French flair to the meal.

They sat and her father poured a glass of madeira for the lieutenant and himself.

Caldwell lifted his glass. "America is in your debt. Because of your ship, I was successful in rescuing my captain and men."

"I'm very interested in hearing the story. I must say, when you said you were following Thorne, I did not expect to ever see you again."

"Had we actually caught up to him, I believe you would have been right." Lieutenant Caldwell took a bite of his fish. "He had shipwrecked them and left them for dead."

Josephine ignored her food, leaning forward as he recounted the story of catching up to his captain and rescuing him from a coral atoll, then returning to Savannah and tracking Thorne to the coast of Florida, where the pirate finally met his match.

When he finished, she sighed. "You're very brave."

He shook his head. "No, I did what any friend would do. Besides, when we finally caught up to Thorne, we had hundreds of men with us. There wasn't even a true battle—more of a skirmish."

She smiled. "Well, I wish I had a friend like you."

Ocean-hued eyes met hers, holding her gaze for a long moment. "I'm sure you have many friends."

Her father cleared his throat. "How did Thorne escape?"

The lieutenant stiffened. "I believe he had inside help. There's no other way."

"What now?"

"Now, we go after him. I have more men and ships being delivered to Savannah as we speak. I'll set sail shortly after returning. Thorne's days of terror are soon coming to an end and he will be brought to justice."

Josephine cocked her head. A very bold and heroic statement. But it sounded too...rehearsed. The small amount of conviction in his voice didn't match the sentiment. Was he scared?

No. Though he downplayed what he had done, she had seen the determination in him the night he came for the ship. He would have faced anything for his friend without hesitation.

"Where do you think he is?" The words slipped from her lips as he took a long drink of his wine.

Her father gave her a disapproving glance at the blunt question, but the lieutenant didn't seem to care. "I'm not sure. It's almost as though he disappeared into thin air. Have you heard anything here? With the number of pirates and smugglers passing through, maybe someone has said something?"

The question was directed at her father but she answered. "No. They only speak of his escape. His ship hasn't been seen since the night you showed up."

This got her a raised brow. "His frigate is in possession of the Navy, currently being retrofitted to become one of our own."

She winced at her mistake. Of course they would have taken his ship when he was captured.

Her father scratched his chin. "I have heard nothing. Thorne is an easily recognizable man; if he had passed through any of the nearby islands, someone would have noticed."

"Precisely. This confirms my suspicions that he's somewhere along the coast of America."

"America? His haunt is here in the Caribbean."

"Not as many people there have heard of him, so he'll be able to lie low with fewer chances of being recognized. I have a feeling he won't be in hiding for long."

Her father arched a brow. "Why's that?"

"Just a hunch. And there's the fact he's a pirate. He won't ignore the thrill of plunder for long."

"Very true. Well, we'll be glad to see him gone. Anytime there's even a whisper of his presence, the port clears out. Bad for business, he is."

The rest of the meal passed faster than Josephine would have liked and the talk shifted to commodities and business. Still, she sat there, transfixed as the lieutenant finished every bite on his plate. He complimented her on each dish and her heart soared.

Her father downed the last of his wine. "Would you like to stay for a glass of spirits and a cigar?"

The lieutenant shook his head and stood. "Thank you, but we leave tomorrow, and there's much preparation to do before we set sail."

"I thought you might say that." Her father wiped his napkin across his lips and he leaned back in his chair. "Josephine, why don't you see Lieutenant Caldwell to the door? I'm going to have another serving of your banana tart."

She smiled at her good fortune. The last minutes had passed with her fervently trying to memorize every angle of the lieutenant's face. Now, she'd won a few more moments with him.

Lieutenant Caldwell bowed. "Thank you for the meal, I mean it when I say it's the best I've had in a long while."

Her father beamed. "My Josephine is the best cook on the island. I'm lucky to have her."

The lieutenant raised a brow. "You did all this?"

With a quick nod, she turned toward the door and away from the question in his eyes. *Why was the daughter of a governor cooking meals?* Over the last few years, the number of servants in the household had dwindled—only one housemaid and a valet remained full time. Josephine didn't mind helping in the kitchen when their cook was away; working with food came easily to her and helped pass the time. He followed her from the dining room and she slowed in the hallway. No need to rush him outside and out of her life.

An ache formed in her chest as she opened the door and he stepped onto the porch. Though she hardly knew him, it felt like saying goodbye to a friend. He turned at the top of the steps when she didn't close the door. He was being polite and waiting for her, but she couldn't do it.

He looked down the street and back to her. "Would you like to join me for a bit?"

Josephine's heart skipped a beat. "I don't want to impose."

He smiled and her stomach flopped. "My men are very capable. A few minutes won't hurt. Besides, I never thanked you again for your help that night. Your supplies were very thoughtful and helped us tremendously."

"It was the least I could do." Her words came out soft and demure. Why, beneath his watchful gaze, did she feel so shy? She took a long breath, the humid night air tempering her dry throat, and focused on the song of the tree frogs.

Pretend he's just another pirate or smuggler at the tavern.

Therein laid the problem. He wasn't *just* another man.

Even so, she'd better start talking before he decided to leave. "What's Savannah like?"

He shrugged. "Same as any southern port city, I suppose."

She pulled her bottom lip between her teeth and fixed her gaze in the dark space behind him. "I've never been to America."

"Of course. I'm sorry. I'm so used to it all...I didn't mean to assume."

"It's alright. You didn't know." She met his apologetic gaze. "I was only ten when we left France, and I can't remember much. I've never left the island since." Admitting it left her feeling exposed.

The lieutenant shifted on his feet. "Sometimes, with as much as I travel, I forget not everyone does the same."

She forced a smile. "Tell me about America and Savannah."

His lips curved. "It's not as cultured as Europe, and certainly not built up as much. We are still such a young country, learning and growing. I grew up in the north, where the cities are larger and more sophisticated. Savannah is, well, it's small. At least the city is. There's a lot of large plantations on the land away from the docks."

"As small as Tortuga's port?"

A rich chuckle broke free. "No. It is larger than Tortuga."

"Do you like living there?"

Silence fell across them for a long moment. "I'm honestly not sure. I spend very little time ashore."

"So, you enjoy being a captain?" She cringed. Of course he did. Why else would he spend so much time out at sea?

"Well, this is my first mission as commander of a ship. I don't hold the rank of captain; that will be a long time down the road. Our navy is so newly formed, right now our captains command the frigates, and we lieutenants are sometimes lucky to be in charge of the smaller ships."

"Smaller?" Tall masts and gleaming cannons filled her mind. "The *Tempest* is one of the most imposing ships I've seen besides…besides Thorne's."

Lieutenant Caldwell's eyes darkened at the mention of the pirate. "Well, hopefully he is at the helm of a much smaller vessel this time."

"I hope so, for your sake."

The edges of his lips twitched in the ghost of a smile. "Thank you."

She took a half step closer, the pleasant scent of sandalwood washing over her. "I will look forward to hearing the news of his recapture, though we often hear about things weeks after they happen."

"I shall endeavor to make it a story worth telling then. The more interesting news always travels the fastest."

She laughed when he winked. "Well, lucky for you, any news of Thorne is considered interesting."

"That's good. Should mean we track him down quicker once he comes out of hiding."

A shiver passed over her. "I hope you're careful, Lieutenant. You're the only person I've ever met that intentionally seeks Thorne out."

He shrugged. "If not me, then who? I'll do it so others won't have to."

"A noble sentiment. But sentiments alone do not win battles."

All traces of amusement faded from his face. "The truest statement I've heard all day." He tapped a finger against his forehead. "This is what wins battles."

She arched a brow. "Good looks?"

His grin returned and a flush of warmth traveled through her. "That, among other things."

Her laugh echoed into the night. "I see subtlety is not a strong suit of yours."

"You'd be surprised." He held her gaze. "As much as I would like to stay and let you inflate my ego further, I'd best get going. Silas, my first officer, will be worried if I don't return soon. I'd rather not disturb the town with a detachment of navy men marching through the streets looking for me."

Though she wanted to protest, she nodded. "I'm glad to have met you, Lieutenant."

"And I, you." His eyes flickered toward the still-open door, then back to her with a quiet intensity. Her breath caught as he stepped forward and took her hand in his.

While she marveled at the warmth of his fingers clasped around hers, he lifted her hand and pressed his lips behind her knuckles. Then he released his hold, leaving her staring at the spot where his touch had seared her.

"Goodnight, and goodbye, Miss Montclair."

Chapter Three

DAMP SAND GRIPPED the soles of Isaac's boots, the hush of the night tide still cloaking the shore. A sliver of sun crested the palm-lined ridge behind the harbor, streaking the sky with thin bands of golden light. Already, heat clung to his neck, heavy and incessant as though the island were trying to hold him back. He folded his arms tight against his chest and scanned the harbor. Beyond the bobbing masts and taut rigging of docked ships, the *Tempest* waited—sleek, formidable…and far too idle for his liking.

They should be underway already, heading north to chase the next whisper of Thorne's whereabouts. Instead, they lingered here, wasting precious hours on cargo they didn't need. The crisp brine of the Caribbean carried on a soft breeze, one that barely stirred the flags drooped above the water. Dockworkers moved with sluggish rhythm, calling to each other in a muddle of languages as crates scraped against the gangplank of a wide brig docked beyond the *Tempest*. The steady clamor grated against the stillness in him, tightening the knot already wound in his chest. Silas and his men should have returned by now.

A burst of laughter rang out from the merchant ship as someone dropped a crate with a splintering crash. Isaac's jaw tensed. He dragged a hand across his face and strode toward the docks, the sand crunching underfoot. This—restless waiting, straining against the leash of his obligations—this wasn't why he'd joined the Navy.

He was built to move. To hunt. To act on instinct.

And yet here he stood, like a ship run aground.

"Let's take on some cargo. It'll give us extra funding for the mission." Silas's suggestion had seemed so reasonable when darkness still cloaked the island and the crew stood idle waiting to sail.

He came to a stop and stared into town with narrowed eyes. How long could it possibly take to procure a few crates of rum and sugar on a spit of land hardly wider than a cannon shot? The longer they delayed departure, the more the island worked its way under his skin—its heat, its ease, especially its distractions.

Unbidden, the curve of a smile flashed across his mind, and his heart gave an erratic thump as memories of the governor's beautiful daughter pressed for his attention. With a scowl, he shook the thoughts free. This wasn't the time to indulge in daydreams about a woman. With a steadying breath, his eyes traced the bluffs beyond town, scanning for any sign of progress, any hint of the cargo's arrival.

A flicker of movement on a hillside caught his eye as a woman climbed a narrow path alone. Deep green skirts clung to her hips, the color vivid against tanned skin where the morning light caught the bare line of her shoulders. She moved like she belonged to the island, barefoot and radiant, a basket slung over one arm, bright flowers tucked behind her ear. Dark hair streamed behind her in a breeze he could not feel. She paused and turned, as if she felt the weight of his gaze, and his breath caught.

Miss Montclair. As if his very thoughts had conjured her. He blinked, half expecting the vision to dissolve into mist.

It didn't.

After a wistful glance toward the *Tempest*, she continued, swinging her basket next to her. Isaac stood quiet as she neared the top of the hill. He took an involuntary step toward her before catching himself. It would be foolish to follow. Irresponsible. Silas could return at any moment, and he needed to be ready to sail the moment the cargo arrived.

Yet, he couldn't draw his eyes from her retreating form. The path she followed curved inland, the same direction his first officer had taken earlier with a group of sailors to visit a sugar mill. Isaac shifted his weight as she vanished from view, swallowed by the trees. His jaw tightened. He could walk a short way. Just far enough to check. If he happened to find Silas—and a reason for the delay—all the better.

His boots left shallow prints in the sand as he climbed the beach and made his way to the trail. The sun pressed higher overhead, heat soaking into his shoulders as he followed the narrow path toward the ridge. Behind him, the familiar harbor sounds fell away, replaced by the hush of the hillside and the dry rustle of palm fronds above.

Isaac reached the crest of the hill and paused. The path split with one well-worn branch following the land as it flattened into a lush valley, the distant silhouette of the sugar mill rising against the hazy sky. The other fork of the trail wound steeply upward, disappearing into thick jungle and rocky outcrops. Miss Montclair strolled just ahead, basket swaying at her side. A few bright blossoms peeked over the rim with what looked like a folded blanket resting beneath them. She didn't hesitate as she began the steep climb of the rugged trail. His gaze travelled up the wild mountainside. This was no simple run for errands. Curiosity drove him forward and he hurried her way. A loose stone shifted beneath his boot and tumbled down the slope with a sharp clatter.

She spun, eyes flashing. They softened a moment later as she recognized him. "Lieutenant! Are you following me?"

Isaac cleared his throat as a hint of heat crept across his cheeks. "No. Of course not. I'm searching for my first officer. He went to a sugar mill and hasn't returned yet."

"Oh." Her voice came out flat, tinged with something close to disappointment. "Mr. Duval at the mill is notoriously slow. It might take him half a day to fill an order. You'll want to take the other path." She pointed toward the valley.

He nodded. "Thank you."

A brief moment of silence stretched between them, neither moving.

He pressed his lips together and lifted his gaze to the steep rocks above her. "Where are you going?"

She flashed him a bright smile. "To my favorite place in the whole world."

He arched a brow. "The whole world? I thought you said you hadn't traveled much?"

Her grin didn't falter. "Have you ever explored a Caribbean island before, Lieutenant?"

He shook his head. "Not willingly. I prefer to keep my feet on the deck of my ship."

"A pity. You're missing out."

He chuckled and wiped sweat from his brow. "I'm skeptical, especially in this heat. Not much can top the rush of wind out on the open seas."

She shrugged. "I guess you'll never know. Unless…" Her eyes sparkled. "Would you care to join me?"

A thread of amusement crept into his voice. "I still don't know where you're headed."

Her smile deepened, warm and enigmatic. "If I tell you, it would ruin the surprise."

"How do I know you're not leading me to a pirate's den?"

She laughed, the sound clear and vibrant among the trees. "Oh yes, the pirates. I forgot to mention them."

A heartbeat passed as he weighed her invitation. He turned toward the valley. "I should really go find my men. Perhaps I can convince Mr. Duval to speed things up."

The playful edge in her expression slipped away, and she gave a single nod. "Of course. I must warn you from complaining to him. He will go even slower if you aggravate him." She glanced at her basket. "I wish I had a loaf of bread to give you; it's his favorite and might have swayed him. I'm afraid you'll have to wait it out."

Wonderful.

At this point, it would be better to cancel the order and leave empty-handed.

He inclined his head. "Thank you for the advice."

"Good luck, Lieutenant." Her gaze lingered on him a moment longer, hesitant and reluctant, before she turned and started climbing.

He frowned as she pulled herself up to the next rock. No woman should be traveling such a precarious route. "Is that safe?"

She twisted her head. "Safer than—" Her words cut off with a sharp yelp as the ledge beneath her hand gave way and she pitched backwards, her basket tumbling to the ground.

He lunged forward, boots skidding on loose rocks as he scrambled up the slope. One hand shot forward to brace against the small of her back, steadying her as she grabbed for a handhold. They stood frozen, her pulse racing beneath his palm.

He swallowed, ignoring the sudden rush of heat through him. "Are you alright?"

She caught her breath, fingers digging into the stone. "Yes. You distracted me, that's all."

"You could have been hurt." He didn't move until her weight was fully balanced again. Then he knelt to retrieve the fallen basket, plucking wilted flowers from the dusty ground.

When he stood, she held her hand out for it. He hesitated, looking back toward the sugar mill. "You shouldn't be alone out here."

Her brows drew together. "And you sound like my father."

"It's a dangerous island. He's right to worry about you."

She snorted. "You forget I grew up here. The pirates stay in town or on their ships and the locals all know each other. It's not as bad as you think."

Visions of his last visit flickered through his mind, sending a shudder down his spine. He should hand her the basket and turn away. He wasn't her keeper, nor her protector. Yet his fingers closed tighter around the basket's handle. If what she said about the mill was right, he had ample time. Knowing that, it wouldn't be right to leave her.

When she reached for the basket, he waved her forward.

"I've changed my mind. I'm coming with."

Her eyes gleamed bronze in the sun. "You won't regret it.'"

They climbed the rocks, Isaac trying to keep his gaze low to avoid staring at her bare feet and the slender line of her ankles. The stone was warm beneath his boots, slick in places with moss, and the sun filtered through the canopy above in shifting, golden shards.

At the top, the trail leveled out again, winding through dense trees. Vines dangled from branches like lazy serpents, and thick ferns brushed against their legs as they passed. He carried the basket while she pointed out plants and called their names— many he'd never heard before.

A flicker of orange darted past them, and Miss Montclair gave a sudden laugh and leapt forward, cupping her hands around the air. When she turned back, she held her closed palms toward him.

"Look," she stepped closer and angled her hands toward a shaft of sunlight until the bright wings shimmered like bits of fire between her fingers.

"Isn't she beautiful? An *Agraulis vanillae*." She slowly opened her hands, and the butterfly lingered for the span of a breath before fluttering free. Long lashes swept up as she met his gaze, eyes shining. "They also call it the passion butterfly."

Passion. The moniker landed in his chest like a spark on dry tinder. He cleared his throat, eyes shifting to the trees beyond her. Here, in the muted light of the jungle, with her so close he could feel her warmth, the word hung between them like a promise.

Or a warning.

Somewhere ahead, the rush of water rose above the hum of insects and the rustle of leaves. She smiled and turned, skirt swaying as she took off down the trail. "Almost there." She quickened her pace.

Isaac lingered a moment before following, drawn by the quiet pull of something he didn't dare name. The forest opened into a clearing after a bend, and he drew in a sharp breath. Before them, a wide waterfall cascaded over a cliff, plunging into a crystalline pool below. The water gleamed azure and sunlit, white torrents pouring like a silken veil over black stone. Mist drifted through the air, catching light in drifting halos while kissing his skin with cool relief. Trailing vines bloomed in wild profusion along the rock face—bursts of pink and white flowers that clung like garlands to the cliffside, softening its edges with color. The canopy above parted just enough for sunlight to pour through, casting the clearing in a golden, dreamlike glow.

He'd never seen anything like it.

"What do you think?"

He stood next to her, taking it in. "It's incredible."

She shot him a smug look and took the basket from him. "Told you." Taking the blanket out, she laid it out on a flat rock overhanging the pool.

"The water comes straight from a spring," she said over her shoulder, already stepping toward the edge of the pool. "It's quite refreshing."

She untied her apron and let it fall onto the blanket beside the basket, then reached behind her back. Her fingers moved with practiced ease. It took him a moment to realize she was unlacing her dress.

His breath hitched. Surely, she wasn't—

She was.

Her hands gathered the folds of her skirts, scrunching the fabric as she lifted them, revealing the pale linen of her chemise. He twisted away so fast he nearly slipped on the mossy rock. "Miss Montclair, this is highly improper!"

"Lieutenant," she called, voice thick with a teasing island lilt, "you're not in America anymore. This is Tortuga. Relax a little."

A beat passed as he struggled to keep his focus on the forest, then her voice came again, softer. "Be grateful. Usually, I don't wear anything at all."

The words struck like a hot brand, searing straight through his composure. A jolt of heat shot down his spine as his mind—traitorous and eager—offered a vivid image of her standing bare and unashamed beneath the sun.

He swallowed hard, throat dry as sand. Eyes still fixed firmly on the treetops, he clenched his jaw and willed the image away.

She chuckled, the sound deep and throaty. "Suit yourself." A moment later, a heavy splash echoed through the clearing.

He clenched his teeth as more splashing came from the pool.

"The water is wonderful today."

How the hell was he supposed to resist? Like a man trapped by a siren's lure, he slowly turned. She had made her way to the base of the waterfall, her dark hair swirling around her in the current. As she reached the shore, she pulled herself up onto a smooth rock, water streaming down her limbs.

He stared. He couldn't help it. Though every shred of discipline urged him to look away, his gaze held fast. The wet chemise clung to her like a second skin, outlining every soft curve, every subtle dip and swell. She turned to face him, water splattering the rock beneath her. A groan built in the back of his throat as he shifted his weight, trying to ease the aching pressure straining against his breeches.

Miss Montclair eased onto the wet stones beside the falls, moving closer to the cascading water. She reached a hand into the rushing stream, droplets splashing across her arm and shoulder. "Are you coming?"

Good God.

The soaked fabric hugged her breasts, revealing the dusky outline of her nipples, dark against pale cotton. Did she realize how much he could see?

Only a saint would turn away.

And he was no saint.

Not today.

His pulse thundered in his ears as he bent to unlace his boots. A moment later, his jacket hit the ground with a soft thud, followed by his cravat and waistcoat. At the edge of the overhang, he hesitated a moment, fingers brushing the collar of his shirt. He shouldn't—hell, he shouldn't be out here at all, but the heat of the day, the cool promise of the water, and the sight of her were too much to resist.

With a swift motion, he tugged off his shirt, letting it fall to the rocks. His bare skin prickled in the shade, goosebumps rising where the breeze touched him. Without a word, he bent his knees and launched himself into the crystal-clear water. The shock of cold seized him, sharp and electric, stealing the breath from his lungs. He broke the surface with a gasp.

Across the pool, Miss Montclair's eyes sparkled like the sun-flecked water around them. Isaac kicked steadily, cutting through the cool water as the roar of the waterfall grew louder. He reached the edge of the pool and braced a hand against the slick rocks, hauling himself up beside her.

"Follow me." She slipped beneath the crashing cascade without hesitation, water streaming over her like liquid silk. Her laughter rang out, clear and uninhibited, carried on the spray.

He hesitated only a heartbeat before following, stepping into the thunderous rush. The water pounded against his head and shoulders, deafening and wild, as if the island was unleashing its fierce spirit upon him. He passed through the cascade and stepped into the hollow behind it.

Miss Montclair's eyes pressed closed, her face lifted, hair plastered to her skin by the spray. For a moment, he simply watched, stunned. There was nothing coy or careful about her— no attempt to shield herself or impress him. Just joy. Wild, radiant joy.

No woman he'd ever met in New York or Savannah or any-where in between had ever looked like that. Had ever *been* like that.

He stepped closer, drawn by something he didn't fully under-stand, until his foot slipped on the wet rock. His hand shot out instinctively, catching her waist. She startled, but didn't pull away. Her eyes fluttered open, lashes beaded with water. For a breathless moment, neither of them moved. The roar of the waterfall wrapped around them, enclosing them in a world of white sound and wild spray.

"Careful," she murmured, laughter still clinging to her voice.

Her face hovered inches from his, her lips parted in surprise—or something else. If he leaned in, just a little more…

His pulse thundered louder than the water.

In another life… another day…

Perhaps here, in this hidden place carved from sunlight and stone, they might have had a tryst. A reckless, breathless surrender to the pull between them.

But this wasn't that day.

He drew back as if the water burned him. Let go of her waist. Took a half-step away. Duty hammered cold and relentless through his veins. He was a naval officer. A man with orders, with discipline. With a mission to uphold and a captain's trust still unearned.

This—whatever *this* was—had no place in the life he was bound to live. He cleared his throat and took another step back, slipping free from the magic of the falls.

"I must return to my ship."

Chapter Four

"LOLA, HE'S EVEN more wonderful than I thought."

The parrot didn't so much as spare her a glance.

"He's the man of my dreams." Josephine strode to the window and leaned out, straining to catch a glimpse of sails in the harbor. "The most handsome, most perfect gentleman in the whole world."

Of course, Lola didn't answer. She never did. But years with nobody but Colette to confide in meant that sometimes, one needed to have a single-sided conversation with a bird.

"Oh, you're so happy for me?" The sunlit sea beyond the ships blurred as the warm haze that had lingered since the waterfall began to fade. "Well, don't be. You see, he leaves any minute. And I'll never see him again."

Saying the words aloud made the reality of it sink in all the more.

It wasn't fair. She'd finally met someone worth pursuing, and he would be gone in the blink of an eye, yet another opportunity slipping away. If she didn't do something, the cycle would continue the rest of her life until she was an old spinster—or her father married her off to the elderly Wentworth. But what could she do?

She began to pace in front of the window. "You know, Lola, maybe I've been doing it all wrong. My whole life, I've been waiting for something good to happen. Maybe that's the problem. Being patient has gotten me nowhere. Maybe I need to take my destiny into my own hands."

Silence surrounded her as she wrung said hands. How did one take control of their destiny? If only she could find a way to spend more time in the company of the lieutenant. Short of sabotaging his ship—which, considering the *Tempest's* size and might, she wasn't sure would even be possible—there were no other options.

Unless…She stopped short.

He said he was taking on more men and supplies once he returned to Savannah. That would surely take the lieutenant several days to organize. Plenty of time, then, for her to make an impression. Her lips tingled at the memory of his searing gaze beneath the spray of the waterfall. They had come so close to kissing while the thunder of the falls echoed the wild rush of her blood. A flush of heat prickled up her neck as she imagined his strong hands pulling her in and closing the distance. A few more meetings, a few more conversations, and she maybe could convince him she was worthy of his attention.

But having the chance to do so meant she had to go to Savannah, and the only way to do that would be on the *Tempest.* She snorted. A military ship would not lightly take on passengers. Finding another ship heading that way that would take her on could take a month or more, and Lieutenant Caldwell would be long gone by then. Not to mention, her father would never allow it—especially with Wentworth's impending visit.

"Blast it." Her shoulders slumped and she turned to her bed and sat with a huff.

So much for taking her destiny into her hands.

She'd enjoyed herself today. More than she had in a long time.

Her fingers curled into fists in her sheets, brushing against a pile of folded laundry she had neglected to put away. The velvety lambskin of her breeches stuck out amongst cotton and linen. She glanced down and picked them up. If she were a boy, she could perhaps get hired onto the *Tempest's* crew. *No.* They wouldn't hire non-American sailors.

But, as a boy, she could walk around the docks unnoticed. And if she were unnoticed, maybe she could get onboard the sloop. Surely on such a massive ship, there would be plenty of secluded spots for one to hide. Her pulse quickened. She was absolutely not thinking of stowing away on a ship.

Or was she?

She stood and shook out her breeches, eyes drifting to the window. From here, the sails of the *Tempest* gleamed in the midday sun, rising above the harbor like silent sentinels. A hush lingered over the town, the usual clamor of Main Street dulled in the heat. Even the gulls seemed quieter, circling lazily above rooftops.

Could she do it?

A nervous laugh broke free. No, it would be too daring—too bold.

And then a familiar sound broke through the sun-soaked silence. The mockingbird's trill. Her heart began to race. Was it a sign?

Everything happened for a reason.

The compelling words she'd thought of the night she first met Lieutenant Caldwell burned through her until she nearly vibrated with the thought. If she stayed, she would have to endure the pursuits of Mr. Wentworth. And if she thwarted that match, who knew whom her father would bring next. If she went to Savannah, she had a chance at something else, something she would never have here on Tortuga. She spun and yanked open the door to her wardrobe. An old leather satchel stuck out from beneath a stack of her straw hats. She tugged it free and gave it a shake, sending a cloud of dust flying. The small interior gave her little space to work with.

She could buy things in Savannah, but should bring at least one nice outfit. Her single ball gown—never used—would take up too much space. Even her day dress, with its ruffles and flounces would be too much. Drat. Maybe just a couple of her newer skirts and blouses then. She folded them and stuffed them into the bag along with stockings and slippers with enough room left to press a nightgown on top. Her reticule, full of coins she'd won at the tavern, followed, hidden between layers of clothing.

At her vanity, she swept a pile of hair pins, some ribbons, and a brush on top of the nightgown and began to pull the drawstring closed. Lola gave a loud squawk and Josephine paused her frenzied packing. "You're right. I can't leave you behind."

She scooped a handful of seeds from a box on her shelf. Dropping the feed into a small pouch, she ran her fingers over the treasures laying there. In light of what she was about to do, they suddenly seemed so small and inconsequential. Yet, she couldn't help picking up the key, the comforting weight a subtle temperance to her racing pulse. Pressing her lips together, she slipped it onto a ribbon and tied it around her neck—a good luck charm for her voyage.

She undressed and pulled on her breeches. A long linen strip was folded with her men's shirt and she wound it tightly around her chest, wincing as her breasts protested the sudden containment. After shrugging into the shirt, she picked up Lola and tucked the bird in the outermost layer of her binding, flipped onto her back. She'd learned over the years that the position would nearly put Lola into a trance. Hopefully, it worked for long periods.

Once she buttoned up, she went to the vanity and used the remaining hairpins to twist her damp hair into a bun at her crown. She used the last pin to fasten one of the straw hats in place and stood in front of the mirror. The shirt hung loose, which might raise some eyebrows, but the one time she'd tried tucking it in, Colette had stopped her and told her if she swayed those breech-clad hips in public, she'd have a whole line of men following her home.

With one last look around her room, she tiptoed out into the hallway and down the stairs. A moment later, she stepped onto the porch, clicking the door shut behind her.

Her throat had gone thick and she forced herself forward.

Don't look back. If she did, her resolve would crumble. Even now, the hot sting of tears pressed at the corners of her eyes. Leaving without saying goodbye seemed so cowardly. She straightened. No choice if her plan was to work. She would write to her father once she arrived in Savannah.

With a deep breath, she hurried down toward the harbor. The sun stood high now, casting sharp shadows across the rooftops, and she quickened her pace. *Please let the cargo still be loading.* She picked her way down the familiar shortcut, heart pounding harder with each step.

What if she was too late? What if the sails were already raised and he was gone—

She broke through the last row of palms, breath catching.

There it was. The *Tempest.* Still tethered to the dock.

Once there, she stopped, catching her breath. The day's heat pressed around her, sweat dripping down her forehead. She craned her neck up. Down here, the ship seemed impossibly large. A wave of nausea burned through her gut.

Turn back.

She ignored the warning thundering through her mind.

Getting onto the dock had been easy enough. But sneaking onto the ship? That was another matter. She shivered, eyeing the multitude of sailors posted along the *Tempest's* deck. These weren't rough-and-tumble pirates—they were some of the new nation's best. Trained. Disciplined. Men who could hunt Thorne and stood a chance of capturing him.

No way she could slip past them.

Lola shifted against her chest and Josephine stilled her with one hand. A group of dockhands carried crates over to a gangplank leading up to the main deck. At the bottom, a uniformed sailor checked off a list as the men carried them onto the ship. She pulled her hat low and made her way closer. This might be her only chance. She frowned as she looked up and down the dock. There were no unclaimed crates left, which meant she had precious little time. She pulled her lip between her teeth as the dockhands walked past—she couldn't just waltz up to the ship with no cargo.

"Stop standing around, boy!" The harsh shout made her jump as a man with two large crates stacked atop each other slowed. "Make yourself useful and take one of these onboard."

A slow smile curved her lips and she patted her shirt. "See, Lola, destiny is already on our side."

She hurried over and took the top crate. Its weight threw her off balance and it slid into her chest, prompting an angry squawk. The man wrinkled his forehead and she coughed, trying to mimic Lola.

Her arms burned as they slowly made their way to the gangplank, and by the time she reached the bottom, her entire body trembled.

"Contents?" The sailor taking inventory held a quill poised over his paper.

She blinked at him. Lead bricks perhaps?

He glanced up when she didn't answer, sharp green eyes reflecting from a nearby lantern.

"We've two crates of sugar." The gruff voice of the man behind her saved her from disaster and the sailor nodded and checked off a line.

When she stepped onto the gangplank, she stumbled, nearly tossing the crate into the water.

"Perhaps someone else should carry that." Those green eyes had followed her progress and she bit back a curse.

"I'm fine."

To prove it, she hefted the crate higher and forced herself to take long strides. It worked and she made it onto the ship without further issue. Onboard, they were directed down to the hold, where all the food was being stored. When a sailor in a crisp uniform took the crate from her, she nearly fell over.

The man behind her gave her a push. "No tarrying, off the ship with ye."

They climbed through a hatch and made their way back

through the berth deck. Once they got up to the main deck, there would be no opportunity for her to sneak away. Even down here, multiple sailors stood guard.

She stopped short. "I…I dropped something. I'll be right back."

The man rolled his eyes but continued. "Better hurry, wouldn't want to make this lot upset." He jerked a thumb toward one of the sailors standing near a shot locker before leaving her.

She hurried back toward the galley. Once in the hallway, she slowed. Nowhere to hide. At the end, a sailor with a crate stepped down into the hatch leading to the hold. *Don't look suspicious.* With her head held high, she followed, resisting the urge to look behind her.

The steps led down into a dark cargo hold, where the man had gone to one side and was tying his crate down with ropes. A lantern sat next to him, the light bathing the cargo with a warm glow. She crept to the opposite end, following the shadows, until she found a space between two stacks to slip into.

Footsteps sounded as another man descended. "Are you finished here?"

After a grunt, the sailor answered. "Last one secure."

"Is anyone else down here?"

"Just me."

More footsteps as one of them climbed the steps. Silence stretched through the room, light still flickering from the walls. Then, the click of boots echoed around her. They grew louder and the light drew nearer. She shrank into her hiding spot and held her breath as he came to a stop mere feet away. Lola shifted against her skin and she reached through the rough linen to stroke the parrot's soft head.

After a long pause, the man turned and the light grew dimmer. She blew out her breath and a moment later, the sailor climbed from the hold. The hatch covers banged shut and Josephine flinched as darkness surrounded her. She blinked, her eyes slowly adjusting until the silhouettes of nearby stacks of crates were visible. *Thank goodness.* A ray of sunlight slanted through a single small porthole, giving the cramped space just enough light to see. At least the journey would not be made in complete darkness.

She flopped her satchel onto the floor and unbuttoned her shirt. "Alright, Lola, this is our home for the next few days." The parrot climbed free, hopped from her shoulder onto a nearby crate, and began preening green feathers. "Now, be a good girl and stay quiet."

Chapter Five

THE BLESSED RELIEF of wind would never grow old. Square sails hummed above while Isaac removed his hat to let the breeze whip through his hair. Though three days had passed since they'd left Tortuga, the memory of oppressive humidity and heat remained fresh. He straightened. Better to remember that part of the island.

Not *her*.

His hands tightened around the spokes of the wheel. Each time he closed his eyes, visions of her beneath the cascading water haunted him. He'd finished undressing her in his mind an embarrassing number of times since their jungle encounter. A fresh wave of desire coursed through him as his body eagerly reminded him how willing it would have been to take it further.

With a groan, he grit his teeth together. *Absolutely not.* She was the governor's daughter, for Christ's sake. Not some doxy in a harbor tavern to have his way with. With her untamed spirit and reckless charm, she was a woman whose magic could threaten attachment. And he was not a man for attachments.

Why would anyone choose a life tethered to commitments on shore when they could have this? His eyes roamed the activity on deck and his heart swelled. The transition from first officer to lieutenant less than a month before had been as seamless as he could have hoped for. It helped he had sailed and fought alongside many of these men over the course of several missions.

Still, he missed the companionship of his best friend, and former lieutenant, Christian Thompson. That friend was the very reason he'd procrastinated returning the schooner to Tortuga for so long. Nothing in the world could have kept Isaac from attending the wedding a few days prior to his departure. He couldn't help his grin. Straightlaced Christian had shocked the entire Navy when he resigned and married a pirate…Ex-pirate.

To this day, his mind almost couldn't comprehend it. Christian, one of the most disciplined and principled men he knew, had fallen in love. He wouldn't have believed it if he hadn't seen it happen with his own eyes. Christian's wife, Samantha, was about as unconventional as they came. She preferred breeches to dresses and could outsail—and outfight—most men he knew. Again, his mind drifted to another unconventional woman.

Unconventional or not, it didn't matter. She wasn't for him. No one was. Not when he had missions to see through, promotions to earn. He would be a terrible husband. So he kept his relationships short and sweet—one night. The constant reminder kept him content, never wanting more.

Isaac replaced his hat. Here he was, in charge of a brand-new sloop of war, with a notorious pirate to hunt down. This was where he belonged, far away from ballrooms and women who expected him to give up everything for them. His palm brushed his sword. He'd much rather fight Thorne than surrender his heart. The thought sobered him as he flipped open his compass to check their course. The winds had been in their favor since leaving Tortuga and they would be arriving in Savannah early. A good thing, because he would have very little time to prepare for his first big mission as lieutenant.

Thorne's escape a few weeks before had sent the Navy scrambling. The government wanted the pirate captured and hanged, to make an example of him for humiliating them. But most importantly, they needed to get the pirate before he cost more lives.

So, he would pick up extra men and weapons in Savannah and set sail as soon as possible. Which wasn't a bad thing. No reason to stay ashore long in the sweltering heat of late summer.

A cough interrupted his thoughts and he turned to find his first officer, Silas Cummings, standing at the top of the stairs leading up to the quarterdeck, his face all hard lines.

Isaac straightened. "What's wrong?"

"We found a stowaway."

Shit.

"How did someone get onboard?" His teeth pressed together. He had posted an obscene number of guards the entire time they had been at port in Tortuga to avoid precisely this.

"It's my fault."

Isaac lifted a brow at Silas's confession. The man was a stickler for doing things exactly the right way.

"When the cargo was being loaded, there was a boy, he was nervous, and something was off about him. I specifically watched for him to come back off and made the error of assuming I'd missed him due to his small size when I didn't see him."

A boy.

Isaac pressed his eyes shut. "Damnation."

Silas stood next to him in silence for a long minute before clearing his throat. "What are your orders, sir?"

Pain radiated along Isaac's jaw from where he held it clamped shut. There was only one order he could give. The rules were very clear. The crime of being caught as a stowaway? A dozen lashes.

"Where was he?"

"Tucked away in the back of the cargo hold. Probably wouldn't have found him, except his parrot made a ruckus when Cook went looking for a missing crate of provisions."

"A parrot?" Isaac blinked. Only one sort of character in this part of the Caribbean would have a pet parrot. What the hell was a young pirate doing on his ship? One would have to be desperate to try their luck getting onto a Navy ship. The question was, did he have nefarious reasons, or was he trying to escape to a better life in America?

A commotion came on the main deck as two sailors dragged

a form out into the sun. Only a head or so shorter than the sailors and sporting a shirt at least two sizes too big, the stowaway must be an adolescent. Possibly older.

Isaac let out a breath. Not that it made the prospect of a flogging any more enjoyable, but at least it wasn't a child.

"Well, the sooner we start, the sooner we can be done with this." He motioned Silas forward.

News had traveled fast and sailors already lined the deck around the foremast, where the two sailors had come to a stop with their captive. Isaac descended the steps after his first officer. With a deliberate slowness in his gait, he made his way to the center of the circle his men had formed. By the time he reached the mast, the crew had fallen quiet. The wind swallowed each intentional click of his boots on the polished deck.

The boy met his gaze and Isaac caught a brief flash of widened brown eyes before the brim of the hat dipped forward to obscure his face. He stared at his boots, unmoving as Isaac came to a stop in front of him.

"What's your name?"

The boy didn't answer.

"Alright then. Why are you on my ship?"

Silence stretched between them.

Isaac set his hand on the hilt of his sword, the warm brass a welcome support. "Look at me."

The boy shook his head and Isaac fought the urge to reach out and yank the youth's face up. He would keep his composure in front of his crew. With a cough, he cleared his throat and lowered his voice.

"Do you know what the punishment for stowing away is?"

"Lashes." The word came soft, almost imperceptible.

"You knew, yet you still thought to stowaway on a United States naval ship? I have no choice but to issue the discipline."

The boy stiffened, but did not protest.

One of his men approached with the whip and Isaac took it. No way to drag it out any further. He nodded to Silas, who pushed the boy to his knees and secured his hands to the mast with a rope.

"Remove his shirt."

Without fabric in the way, the whip would leave cleaner marks, and Isaac would be better able to judge the intensity. He would make sure to keep the damage to the barest minimum.

Bile burned a path up his throat as Silas took hold of the boy's shirt. His first time having to mete out punishment as a lieutenant. He'd known it would happen eventually, but so soon? His gaze lifted to the sails as he filled his lungs with salty air. He could pass the task to Silas, as first officers were allowed to administer lashes.

No. If he were to be a respected lieutenant, and someday, captain, he needed to show his men he was more than capable of performing every aspect of his job, no matter how undesirable. He sighed, bunching the corded leather between his fingers and palm. Would it ever get easier?

"Lieutenant?" Silas's voice cracked. "You're going to need to come see this."

Isaac frowned and strode forward, kneeling when his first officer motioned him down.

Silas pulled the billowing shirt up and Isaac's mouth went slack. He didn't need to see the strip of linen binding. Because beneath it, smooth skin revealed curves that no man possessed.

"Son of a bitch." He swatted Silas's hand away so the garment fell back in place. "Untie her."

The first officer fumbled with the ropes and as soon as they fell free, Isaac grabbed a slender wrist and yanked the woman up. He had half a mind to rip that ridiculous hat free and expose her to all, but he took a steadying breath. It would only cause a scene and that's the last thing he needed.

"Follow me." The words came out in a growl and he didn't wait for a response before starting toward his cabin.

He half dragged her beside him, her feet tripping as she struggled to match his long strides. When he reached his door, he flung it open and pushed her inside. He slammed the door behind them, the sound ricocheting through the room as she took several quick steps away from him.

He followed her, coming to a stop directly behind her. "You've got exactly five seconds to explain what the hell is going on."

She hugged her arms around her midsection, but stood rigid and quiet.

"Do not test my patience." The words rumbled free, laced with warning. Without his crew watching, he reached forward and ripped off the straw hat. Pins went flying and a mess of sleek, dark hair tumbled down. With shoulders straight, she finally lifted her head and slowly turned to face him.

He took a step back, mind reeling as he stared at the familiar face. "Miss Montclair?"

Holy hell. His pulse thundered in his ears. He'd nearly flogged the governor's daughter. The room started to spin. Another step back and he bumped against his door. This was not happening. He shook his head, willing himself to wake from what was surely a nightmare.

And then, she had the audacity to smile at him. "Hello, Lieutenant."

He blinked. It was all he could do.

"I'm sorry I caused a disruption. I hope you can forgive me."

His mouth opened. Then closed. "Sorry? Disruption?"

His blood rushed through him in hot waves. If he'd given her even a single lash...Good God, the thought of hurting a woman was bad enough, but the already poor relations America had with Tortuga could have been jeopardized, putting his job on the line.

Her smile faltered. "Lieutenant?"

His momentary shock dissipated in a flash and he stalked forward. "Do you have any idea what just nearly happened?"

She pulled her lip between her teeth at his growled words.

He stopped directly in front of her, grabbing the collar of her shirt and pulling her close. "When exactly were you planning on revealing your identity, before or after your dozen lashes?"

She blanched. "A dozen?"

"Yes, Miss Montclair. That is the punishment." He loosened his grip. "Why didn't you tell my men who you were when you were found?"

Her shoulders moved up and down with each breath and his gaze dropped to where her breasts swelled above the binding, nearly brushing his knuckles. Damnation. He let go and dropped his hands to his side.

"I-I wasn't sure what they would do to me."

"And what about me, Miss Montclair? You decided it would be better to take your lashes instead of answering me when I questioned you?" His pulse began to pound anew.

"I was going to tell you. And then I saw how angry your face was…" Her voice trailed off and her eyes met his. "Just like it is now."

Double damnation.

He forced himself to take a deep breath and walked past her, stopping at the windows. Blue sky stretched as far as the horizon, the pretty scene doing little to soothe his emotions. He could be angry—was angry—but didn't need to lose his temper.

Too late.

He clasped his hands behind his back. "Do you have any inkling of what it feels like to receive a lash?"

"No." Her voice came out small. "I thought I could endure a few."

"A few?" He spun, trying and not quite succeeding in keeping his voice level. "If I had given you even one…" Another long breath brought his volume down. "I could never have forgiven myself."

The curve of her bare waist flashed across his mind. The thought of marring the perfect skin there sent a cold wave through his gut. If he had hurt her…

She dropped her gaze to the floor. "I'm sorry. I wasn't thinking straight. I didn't think…Didn't think anyone would find me."

The stricken look on her face gave him pause and he pulled his hat free to rake a hand through his hair. "Why are you here?"

Her head remained hung. "I wanted safe passage. If you can imagine, respectable ships do not pass through Tortuga often."

"Why did you not ask? If your father had requested, we would have provided you transit."

She jerked her gaze up. "My father would never have given me permission to leave."

The vibrations in the boards beneath his feet lessened and he frowned. The ship had slowed. While he wanted to ask her to clarify, he needed to get back outside and brief his crew. He pushed his hat back on and walked past her to the door.

"This conversation is not over. You are to stay in here. Under no circumstances will you leave this cabin."

Outside, the sun's heat flooded through him. He jogged up the stairs to the quarterdeck where Silas stood at the helm. "Why are we slowing?"

Silas raised a brow. "I thought you might want to return our visitor to Tortuga."

Isaac weighed his options. On one hand, they could return to the island and deposit Miss Montclair back where she belonged. On the other, such a trip would waste six days. Already short on time, the thought made him cringe. He was supposed to stay on the Georgia governor's good side, and being tardy would not win him any favors. Yet, what did one do with the wayward daughter of a prominent Caribbean official?

His lips tugged up as the perfect solution presented itself. "No, we continue to Savannah. Make sure there's an extra bunk for me, I'll be quartering with you the rest of the journey."

Although Silas hesitated, he did not argue. Instead, he nodded and descended to the deck, shouting orders to continue the course. Minutes later, the sails billowed taut in the wind and energy coursed through the deck as the *Tempest* picked up speed. Isaac fixed his gaze on the horizon, willing his mind to focus on anything other than the infuriating, yet undeniably beautiful, problem waiting for him in his cabin. He made a subtle adjustment to the wheel, aware that a single choice could change the course of an entire life. He had learned that lesson all too well over the past few months.

The spokes beneath his hands vibrated and his skin prickled. Something had already been set in motion, and now, only time would reveal the consequences.

Chapter Six

J OSEPHINE STARED OUT the window, an uncomfortable ache gnawing at her gut. With a sigh, she turned to Lola, whom had been brought along with her bag shortly after the lieutenant abruptly left earlier. Several hours had passed since he had slammed the door behind him and left her alone, but his anger still hung heavy in the air.

"What did I expect?" She stroked the parrot's back. "Of course he's upset."

Upset might be an understatement. Her hands smoothed out the skirt she'd changed into as she bit her lip. She may have ruined all chances at... A bitter laugh broke free—all chances at what? Though she hadn't counted on being discovered, she also hadn't thought through how she would have explained her sudden appearance in Savannah to the lieutenant either. After his reaction today, she doubted he would have felt much differently discovering her ashore.

Still, he couldn't stay mad forever. Perhaps this was better. By the time they got to Savannah, surely he would forgive her. Yes, best to get all misunderstandings out of the way. Turning, she approached his table and poured the rest of the water from a pitcher there into a mug she'd found on a shelf. One thing she hadn't anticipated when deciding to sneak on board was how thirsty she'd become. Her hand stretched out to run over a nautical map and she smiled. The whole room was an insight into how the lieutenant spent his days.

Nothing amiss—which shouldn't surprise her for a ship

commander. Books on the shelf were organized by title, and the sheets on his bed had nary a crease in them. She had opened the wardrobe earlier to find several uniforms hanging in a neat line. Now, she slid open the drawers of the desk, sorting through pages of navy orders, ledgers, and extra tubs of ink. The large white feather quill next to the map begged to be stroked and she did so, running her fingers along its luxurious length.

She took a deep breath and smiled. The woodsy scent he favored permeated the air, drowning out the briny smell of the sea and oiled floorboards. A knock interrupted her and she spun as the door opened. Lieutenant Caldwell stood framed by the setting sun, holding a plate.

"I brought you dinner."

He didn't move and several quiet seconds passed before Josephine realized he was waiting for permission to enter. She waved him in and leaned over the table, sliding the map and compass to the side. After a glance behind him, he stepped inside and brought the plate, setting it down in the space she'd cleared.

"Thank you." Josephine's mind went all jumbled as he looked around the room.

"I need to grab a few things."

"Of course."

He rolled up the map and placed the compass in his jacket pocket. She nibbled on her lip as he took one uniform from the wardrobe and collected a shaving blade from his washstand before walking back toward the door. If she couldn't make small talk with him, it would be a wasted opportunity.

She cleared her throat. "Lieutenant Caldwell?"

He stopped at the threshold, but didn't turn. "Yes?"

"Would you care to join me?"

"I already ate."

Of course. She swallowed. "I...I'd like to properly apologize for earlier."

That got him to turn, but his eyes had narrowed. "And how does one properly apologize for what you did?"

She winced, but stood with shoulders straight. "I didn't think things through when I decided to…stowaway."

It sounded so much worse to say the word out loud.

His expression didn't change. "So you've said."

"I made the decision in haste and overlooked all of the risks I would be taking as well as how it would affect you if things didn't go as planned. I'm truly sorry."

He stood silent, his eyes searching hers before lowering his head in a subtle nod. "Thank you. I believe an apology is in order from my end as well. I should not have been so harsh with you."

A weight lifted from her chest. "So, you forgive me?"

He frowned. "It's not that simple."

Josephine's shoulders sagged as he pivoted to the door. "Oh." The single syllable slipped out so quiet, she didn't think he heard.

His hand tightened on the doorknob. "Tell me, what made you want to leave Tortuga so bad that you dressed as a boy and snuck on board?"

You.

Her fingers drifted up to play with the ribbon around her neck. She couldn't very well tell him that. In retrospect, it hadn't been a wise decision. Yes, she was here on a boat with him. But he was upset with her.

"You wouldn't understand."

He turned again and crossed his arms. "Try me."

Her mouth had gone dry, but she forced the words out. "My whole life, I've wanted something…something different. I don't even know what exactly, but I know whatever it is, it won't happen on Tortuga."

"But why my ship?"

Her hands clenched into the folds of her skirt. "You were kind to me. I felt like…like I could trust you."

He stood silent, a muscle ticing in his jaw, and she sighed.

"At the very least, it would be nice to see another part of the world before…" She trailed off, swallowing past the lump in her throat. "My father is trying to arrange a marriage with a wealthy merchant."

A knowing look crossed his face. "That explains everything."

She blinked. "It does?"

"You don't want to face your future so you've run away."

She bristled. "No. That's not true at all. Well, mostly not." If only he knew how much she'd taken her future into consideration before her decision. "I don't even know him."

"You realize that is how most reasonable people get married?"

Her nose pulled up. "He's older than my father."

"So?" He asked it so nonchalantly, she couldn't answer for a moment.

"So?" She sucked in a breath, a burst of heat flushing through her veins. "So, shouldn't I have a say in my future?

"Do not mistake my lack of agreement for not having sympathy." He exhaled. "It's hard to go against the way things have been done for so long. Maybe someday that will change, but doing what you did put yourself in danger and caused a lot of trouble. Did you at least leave a note for your father?"

She shook her head and he groaned. "He could very well accuse the United States of kidnapping a foreign national."

His eyes locked on hers, and after a tense moment, she averted her gaze. "I'll write him as soon as we get back."

He shook his head. "It could take weeks for a ship to deliver your missive. The damage has been done and I will have to deal with the fallout."

Her throat went tight. "I wouldn't let anyone accuse you of such a thing."

"And what if they didn't believe you?" He didn't give her an opportunity to answer, turning and opening the door. "You will stay here the rest of the voyage."

Though she ached to follow, she stayed seated. She would follow his orders and show him what a reasonable woman she could be.

JOSEPHINE YAWNED AND sat up. Sleeping the night before had proved fruitless. How was one supposed to lay in the very sheets the lieutenant had used, to breathe in his scent, and be able to relax? Hours of tossing and turning had finally given way to fitful dozing once the cabin shone pink with the sunrise. She groaned and stretched, pausing with her arms above her head.

The up and down movement of riding swells had stopped. It had been replaced with a barely perceptible rock. A thrill ran through her. They had arrived in Savannah.

She jumped to her feet and rushed to the windows, pressing her face to a cool glass pane. Another ship blocked the view. Her mind raced as she noted the sun's position high in the sky. How long had they been in port? Had the lieutenant left the ship already?

She snatched up her blouse and skirt and changed from her nightgown. Sweeping her hair up into a bun, she hurried to the door and opened it. Lola squawked from her perch on the lieutenant's chair.

"Don't worry, I'll be right back."

Outside, she squinted in the sun and turned to climb the stairs to the quarterdeck, her bare feet slapping each warm step. Up there, nothing blocked her view. At the railing, she leaned over, her mouth dropping open.

Docks stretched as far as she could see in either direction, lined with a multitude of moored ships. The land rose steeply from the river, with precarious stone stairways snaking up from the thick timber planks lining the water's edge. Buildings of all sizes lined the waterfront and crowds of dockhands bustled about on the docks along with a multitude of men and mules pulling carts full of crates and lumber.

"Why are you out here?"

The lieutenant's curt words cut through her astonishment,

but she didn't turn to him.

"If this is small, what does a bigger port look like?"

He stepped forward so that he stood next to her at the railing and she could almost feel his gaze on her in the silence that followed. Still, she could not drag her eyes from the scene in front of her.

Somehow, she'd expected Savannah to be similar to Tortuga. Unease slid through her veins. How would she be able to cross paths with the lieutenant over the next few days in such a large city? She clamped her teeth together as the impossibility of her original plan fully sank in.

"You've made it to Savannah. Now what?"

She swallowed as he seemed to read her mind. "I'll find an inn or boardinghouse to stay at."

He scoffed. "With all the Navy sailors pouring into town, I'm not sure you'll find lodging of any kind."

If he wanted to see her break down into hysterics, he'd be disappointed. Still, her heart beat wildly. "I'm sure I'll be able to find something."

"And then what?"

She finally swiveled to meet his scrutiny, blinking at the intensity in his eyes. For a split second, she considered how he would react if she told him her plan to conveniently show up wherever he was—a plan currently smoldering in flames.

A ball had formed in her throat and she coughed before she could speak. "Since you seem so keen to know, what would you suggest?"

The smug look on his face had her regretting the question as soon as it left her lips. She already knew the answer—to get right back on a boat and go back to Tortuga.

A voice interrupted them before he could tell her so. "Isaac, there you are."

Josephine spun to find a tall man approaching. Dark wavy hair blew in every direction in the breeze. Green eyes locked on her and widened slightly before he passed her and pulled the lieutenant into a rough hug.

"You made good time."

"Did you expect otherwise?" Fondness shone through Lieutenant Caldwell's grin, and Josephine couldn't help her own smile at the camaraderie. This must be the friend he had risked his life to save.

"I see you've brought a visitor." The man's sharp gaze settled back on Josephine.

"This is Miss Montclair, daughter of the governor of Tortuga. She'll be staying with you."

Was he insinuating…? Her cheeks burned. "I told you I could find my own lodging."

"I would feel much better knowing you were safe with friends. They have plenty of room. Right, Christian?"

His friend's eyes twinkled. "Of course. Welcome to Savannah, Miss Montclair." He bowed. "Christian Thompson, at your service. My wife, Samantha, will be glad to have a guest."

Josephine took a steadying breath. Samantha. His wife. All thoughts of illicit intentions faded and she glanced between the two men. Maybe this would work in her favor. Surely, staying with the lieutenant's closest friend would give her much better odds of seeing him again.

"I…"

Mr. Thompson grinned. "I can't wait to hear how you got Isaac to let you on board his ship."

Josephine dropped her eyes to the deck, careful to avoid the lieutenant's reaction to the statement. "Thank you for the offer."

He clapped his hands together. "Alright, where's your trunk?"

She kept her gaze low. "I don't have one."

"Well, whatever your belongings are packed in, I'll carry to the wagon."

"No need." The lieutenant's dry voice interrupted her response.

Josephine crossed her arms and glanced between the men. "I've but one small bag. I can carry it."

Mr. Thompson gave her a puzzled look but nodded. "Very well, but make it quick. Our cook will need to know about the extra guest tonight before he gets started on dinner."

She spun and hurried back to the cabin, heart racing. With trembling fingers, she pulled on her boots and laced them. She snatched up her satchel and plucked Lola from the chair, carefully setting the bird on her shoulder.

"You stay put. Don't embarrass me by flying off somewhere."

With one last look around the cabin, Josephine headed back outside.

When Mr. Thompson saw her, he let loose a good-natured laugh. "A parrot? Isaac, you failed to mention your guest is a pirate."

She narrowed her eyes. "I'm not a pirate."

He took her bag from her with a wide grin. "I have a feeling you and Samantha will get along real well."

The lieutenant cleared his throat. "I've got many things to do before the day is over. Miss Montclair, you will be in excellent hands with Christian and Samantha."

He turned without even saying a proper goodbye. Josephine blew out a breath as he descended the stairs. He definitely hadn't forgiven her yet.

Mr. Thompson cocked his head. "Usually, he has better manners than that." He strode to the railing and shouted at the lieutenant's retreating back. "Don't forget, five o'clock. Samantha will come fetch you herself if you're late."

Lieutenant Caldwell gave a haphazard wave of his hand and disappeared below deck. Mr. Thompson chuckled. "Wonder what's got him all riled up?" He winked at Josephine and started down the stairs.

She followed him off the ship, trying to take in all the activity on the docks. As she craned her neck this way and that, a cart full of crates rumbled past, missing her by inches.

"Keep a sharp eye. It's all business down here, with little regard to safety." Mr. Thompson offered his arm and guided her up a steep set of stairs between two warehouses.

At the top, she came to a stop. The warehouses along the waterfront had hidden the view of the street and the city itself. Horse drawn wagons and carriages clattered past, and men and women hurried by, arms laden with packages and parasols. Block upon block of buildings seemed to never end.

Savannah was huge.

Josephine's ears began to ring and she took a small step back, but Mr. Thompson set his hand over hers. "A far cry from the Caribbean, isn't it?"

She could only nod.

He led her to a wagon and helped her up. Once settled beside her, he gave the reins a slap and they bumped along over the cobblestone street, a huge difference from the dusty dirt roads of Tortuga.

Each turn they took seemed to offer a new scene. Between mansions with manicured gardens, pretty squares with picnicking families, and tall church towers, Josephine's mouth kept gaping.

She finally turned to Mr. Thompson. "Is Savannah truly a small city?"

He grinned. "For us Northerners, yes, Savannah pales in size. It's not even a tenth the size of Philadelphia or New York. But in the south, it's a respectable city."

They left the city and traded buildings for cotton and tobacco fields with sprawling estates. Eventually, Mr. Thompson turned down a long drive lined by massive oaks, their mossy branches creating a green tunnel. When the house came into view, Josephine couldn't help a tiny gasp. The gray brick manor stretched to both sides of a whitewashed fountain, with wide, stately windows reflecting the sunlight. A broad verandah, supported by large columns, wrapped around the front. They came to a stop and she stared at the wide double doors at the top of the steps.

"This is your home?"

Mr. Thompson nodded.

"It's…" She trailed off, unable to find words.

"It's a bit much, isn't it?" He swung to the ground. "Trust me, I'd much prefer to call a ship home."

Her eyes tried to take it all in. Never had she seen a home like this. Even her distant memories of France held no recollection of something so grand. He cleared his throat and she startled. He'd walked over to her side and stood with his hand outstretched, her satchel slung over his shoulder.

She set her hand in his and stepped down. "I think it's lovely."

"Christian, have you brought a guest?"

One of the most beautiful women Josephine had ever seen descended the steps. Red hair flowed behind her like flames, and bright blue eyes sparkled in the sun. She wore a beautiful periwinkle muslin dress, its high waistline and fitted bodice accentuating her curves.

Mr. Thompson's eyes filled with affection and his face softened as she approached. "Samantha, my dear, I'd like you to meet Miss Montclair, daughter of the governor of Tortuga. She's going to be staying with us for a short visit."

"Oh, how lovely. We're happy to have you." His wife's smile flashed wide and welcoming.

Josephine's throat had gone dry. "Thank you, Mrs. Thompson."

"Oh goodness. Please, call me Samantha. Mrs. sounds so old. Who's this?" She reached a slender hand toward Josephine's shoulder and Lola shuffled over, climbing onto a fair-skinned wrist.

"Lola." Josephine couldn't help but smile. "She doesn't usually like strangers."

Samantha stroked shiny green feathers and glanced up at her husband. "Why didn't I ever think of getting a parrot?"

He harrumphed. "Don't get any ideas."

With a grin, she took hold of Josephine's arm. "Let's go inside and get you ready for dinner."

Josephine looked down. "I am ready."

Samantha laughed. "You just spent days on a ship. At the very least, you should take a bath and change into some fresh clothes."

"I didn't bring much else." The words came out quiet, laced with shame, and Josphine wished more than ever she'd found a way to fit her day dress in her bag.

"Never mind. You can wear something of mine. We're practically the same size."

Mr. Thompson chuckled. "I hope you like the color blue."

Samantha gave him a playful swat on his shoulder and took the satchel from him. "You will find, Miss Montclair, that Americans spend almost as much time socializing as their European counterparts. You best brace yourself for an onslaught of dinners, parties, and house calls. Starting tonight."

Chapter Seven

"This should be good."

Isaac glared at Christian over his glass of brandy. "I'd rather not talk about it at all."

Christian's laugh echoed through the room. "Well, either you tell me now, or I'll get the story from Samantha tonight."

Though his friend was no longer his superior, Isaac couldn't shake the cold weight of failure that threatened to overcome him if he admitted how Miss Montclair had come aboard his ship. He rubbed a thumb along the rim of his snifter. Not that it mattered. One way or another, Christian would find out. No point in delaying the inevitable.

"She was a stowaway."

Christian whistled and tipped back his glass. "How the hell did a woman sneak on board the *Tempest?*"

Isaac ground his teeth together. "She dressed as a boy."

Amusement flashed across his friend's eyes. "And you were fooled?"

"Don't you start. You've no leg to stand on in that regard."

Christian leaned back in his chair with a grin. The very first time he'd met Samantha, she'd been disguised as a boy. She'd engaged him in a sword fight…And won. It had nearly driven him mad and started the hunt of a lifetime.

"Why didn't you bring her back to Tortuga?"

Isaac ran a hand through his hair. "And waste precious time? Besides, Samantha will love an excuse to go sailing on your new ship."

"Ah. So, you want us to return your baggage."

His fingers tightened around his glass. "She's not my baggage."

A dark brow lifted. "But she is very beautiful."

Isaac closed his eyes and was rewarded with the bare curve of her waist—the same vision that had been haunting him the last two days. At least it had replaced the scene at the waterfall. Maybe. A growl formed in the back of his throat as another image rose unbidden: perfect breasts, slick with water, straining against translucent fabric. He took a hearty sip of his drink, welcoming the harsh burn. "What does that have to do with anything?"

Christian set down his glass and stretched, a smirk still etched across his face. "Nothing. Nothing at all."

Isaac sighed. One would have to be blind to miss the reverent look in her eyes each time they crossed paths. "I fear she has an infatuation with me."

"What's wrong with that?"

"You know exactly what's wrong with that. I've no time or space in my life for any of that nonsense."

Christian picked at an invisible spot on his sleeve. "So you keep saying." He grinned anew. "I hope you're not expecting any sympathy from my end."

"That would be too much to hope for." Isaac finished his drink. "It doesn't matter. I'll be setting sail in a couple days and you'll get her back to Tortuga long before I get back."

"Fair enough."

Isaac glanced at the notebook overflowing with pages sitting next to his friend. "Any headway on your research?"

Christian had been poring over all records of ships taken out by Captain Thorne, trying to find a pattern. He flipped open the book and removed a sheet of parchment. "It's been difficult. In the beginning, the only ships he attacked were other pirates, which of course are rarely reported other than word of mouth. But, five years ago, he took out a merchant ship contracted with the Navy. Ever since then, he has targeted a wider variety—

merchant, passenger, privateer, and a few more associated with the Navy. It doesn't make sense."

Isaac's fingers tapped a slow tempo on the arm of his chair. "Has anything about your father ever made sense?"

His friend's lips pressed together. Finding out he was the son of the infamous Captain Thorne had been a life-altering shock. Once a decorated naval captain, Thorne went rogue after pirates killed his wife—Christian's mother—and disappeared, faking his own death. At first, he hunted pirates. At some point, he turned into the very thing he hated. During their recent clashes with Thorne, he'd hinted he was far from finished with seeking retribution. The last time Christian saw him, he'd been shaken to the core by the news his mother had not been killed by pirates after all.

If there was one thing worse than a bloodthirsty pirate, it was a bloodthirsty pirate out for revenge.

The question remained: who was he after?

With brows together, he took note of Christian's set jaw. His friend treaded dangerous waters and risked becoming as consumed with the hunt as his father had. It was a large part of the reason he'd resigned from the Navy. Now, Isaac was the one tasked with bringing Thorne in. It rubbed the wrong way for certain, having to take down the father of his best friend. But it was his duty, and he would do it to the best of his ability.

A heaviness settled over him, as it often did when he thought about the mission. He had kept vital information from his superiors by not disclosing Thorne's true identity, at Christian's request. If it were found out, Isaac could be court-martialed and released from service, a blemish that would follow him the rest of his life. He couldn't help glancing at Christian, who still flipped through the pages in his notebook. For now, he would honor his friend's wishes.

A soft knock came from the doorway and the butler poked his head into the study. "Dinner's ready."

They stood and followed him to the dining room. Of course,

Samantha had made sure a proper feast awaited. The only thing he disliked about being at sea was the terrible food choices. He enjoyed a well-cooked meal and looked forward to the rare occasions he got them. His heart swelled as he took in the various dishes at the table. Having good friends who insisted upon spoiling him also made his time ashore more enjoyable. Samantha entered, clothed in her trademark periwinkle blue and paused just inside the door to wave in Miss Montclair.

Isaac clamped his teeth together. She wore one of Samantha's dresses, the blue silk shimmering over tanned skin. Her hair had been teased into a masterful pile of curls and she wore something tied to a ribbon around her neck, a brooch perhaps. He couldn't tell because it disappeared into her cleavage. Pulse beating in his ears, he yanked his gaze up. Why did she have to be so damn beautiful?

She gave him a shy smile, and all he could do was nod.

Christian slid him a look, that blasted smirk back on his face. "You ladies look lovely." He strode forward and pulled out the chair closest to his spot at the head of the table.

Samantha sat and Christian cleared his throat, spurring Isaac into action. He crossed over and did the same for Miss Montclair. She thanked him, a pretty blush coloring her cheeks, and he took his seat across from the two ladies.

He filled his plate and made sure to keep his mouth full, which meant Christian and Samantha got to lead conversation. As they ate, he couldn't help noticing Josephine's pure delight in trying dishes new to her—which turned out to be all of them. She lifted a spoonful of turtle soup to her nose and took a sniff, a smile pulling at the corners of her lips.

"I've never smelled anything like this before." Bringing the spoon to her lips, she took a small taste and her eyes closed on a sigh. "So lovely."

Lovely indeed. He pressed his teeth together and forced his gaze from her enraptured face. Unfortunately, his quick turn brought him face to face with Christian, who gave him a knowing smile. Isaac shot him a scowl in return and dropped his eyes to his plate instead, taking a sudden interest in his cherry glazed turkey.

A knock came from behind him and the butler walked in with a letter on a silver tray. "I've an important missive for Lieutenant Caldwell."

Isaac frowned as he took it and glanced at the governor's seal. He unfolded the page and scanned the first lines. Re-read them. His pulse picked up as the weight of Christian's ever-sharp gaze settled on him. "Thorne's come out of hiding."

Samantha dropped her fork and turned toward Christian with a worried look. He kept his gaze on Isaac and extended his hand. "What did he do?"

Isaac passed the paper. "He attacked a Naval supply ship off the coast of North Carolina, near Wilmington."

Darkness clouded Christian's features. "Why? Going after the Navy when he knows his recapture is top priority doesn't line up. It's not smart."

"Well, this is the lead I've been waiting for. Now I know where to sail. The rest of my men will arrive tomorrow. We'll be ready to leave by dawn the next morning."

"There were survivors." Christian lowered the page and stared into space, his eyes flitting back and forth as his mind worked. "Is he getting sloppy in desperation, or was there something on that ship worth the risk of revealing himself?"

"Every move he makes is precisely calculated. Desperate is not part of his vocabulary." Samantha set her hand on her husband's forearm. "He's not likely to be anywhere near Wilmington by the time you get there, Isaac."

He nodded. "I know. But hopefully we can find out where he's headed next."

"I'm going with you." Christian's voice came calm and steady from his spot at the head of the table.

Isaac jerked his gaze up. "You know I can't take you on as part of my crew."

Christian shrugged. "Doesn't matter. I'll be taking my own ship."

Samantha frowned. "Christian, I don't think it's wise—"

"I want to interview the survivors. If I can find out what he was after, we may be able to narrow our search."

Isaac chewed the inside of his cheek. He shouldn't allow it. If Christian came face to face with his father again, there was no telling what he would do.

As always, his friend seemed to read his mind. "Never mind. I'm going regardless, even if you won't let me sail alongside you."

The weight from earlier returned in Isaac's chest. "Very well. But I'm giving you strict orders to not engage with Thorne, no matter the circumstances."

"You know giving him orders is pointless." Samantha crossed her arms. "If he goes, I go."

"No." Isaac and Christian said it at the same time.

"Not after what happened last time. He knows he can get to me through you. I won't risk it." A ripple of fear passed across Christian's face as he pleaded with his wife.

She crossed her arms. "If I don't go, you don't go."

Isaac pressed his fingers to his temple. Once she put her foot down, there was no dissuading her. They argued back and forth, Samantha insisting she could hold her own, and Christian reminding her how Thorne had nearly killed her. Multiple times.

A cough came from next to them, and Christian and Samantha both stilled. They'd probably forgotten Miss Montclair sat there, listening to their every word. Isaac hadn't. How could he? She'd been staring at him the entire conversation, the heat of her gaze threatening to break his concentration.

She cleared her throat. "I'd like to come as well."

His head snapped up. Surely, she jested. Her earnest gaze said otherwise, and a curse formed on his lips. This damn mission was on the verge of becoming a circus.

"Absolutely not." He ground out the words.

"Please?"

"This is a dangerous government mission. There's no place for civilians."

She frowned. "But you're letting them come."

He snorted. "They know more about Thorne than the entire US Navy combined. A mere month ago, Christian would have been the one in charge of this mission."

Samantha turned to Miss Montclair. "As much as I would love to have your company, he's right. Dangerous is an understatement. Going after Thorne is a death wish."

Miss Montclair's shoulders slumped. "I suppose I'll have to find that boarding house after all."

Isaac shifted in his seat. She kept her composure remarkably well for all that had just transpired in front of her. Of course, talk of pirates wouldn't faze her, given where she lived. But he'd promised her safe quarters and now that had been yanked away.

"Nonsense." Samantha shook her head. "You can still stay here."

Miss Montclair's eyes widened slightly as she swiveled her gaze around the large dining room and a flutter of pity stirred within Isaac. Alone in this big house, in a new city on a continent she'd never been to before? It wouldn't be fair to her.

"Or..." Samantha had obviously come to the same conclusion. "You can stay with my best friend, Abigail Ross. She would love to have you and the opportunity to show you around Savannah."

Miss Montclair played with the corner of her napkin, her eyes on her plate. "I feel as if I've become quite the burden."

"Nonsense. Abigail is the socializing expert. She's honestly the best person you could be with if you're wanting to get to know Savannah—and to get the people of Savannah to know you."

"Well, that's settled." Christian wore a forced smile. "With all the preparations that are needed, it's probably wise to take her there tonight."

Samantha nodded. "You're right."

"And what of your Caribbean trip?" Isaac gave Christian a hard look.

"It should only take me a few days to interview the survivors.

We'll be back within the week."

Isaac fought the groan forming in his throat. He'd hoped to have Miss Montclair well on her way home by then.

Samantha cleared her throat, snapping his attention back to the matter at hand. "I'm sure you'll be heading down to the docks. The Ross estate is on the way. You won't mind taking Miss Montclair with you, right?"

He avoided looking at the subject of their conversation, the prickle along his neck giving away her stare. Holding in his sigh, he gave Christian a curt nod. With the Ross home such a short ride away, it would be rude to decline.

"Alright. But we should leave now. I need to send word to Governor Milledge about my plans, and get orders to all the new men who've arrived."

They stood and he followed Christian outside while the women went to collect Miss Montclair's belongings. He stretched, mentally making a list of the multitude of things he needed to do before tomorrow night to be able to leave on time. His friend stared out into the distance and Isaac turned to him.

"Are you sure this is a good idea? If we run into your father in Wilmington—"

"Samantha's right. He'll be long gone by the time we get there. I just hope we can figure out why he attacked that ship."

"It could be as simple as him trying to goad us."

Christian shook his head. "No, he wouldn't have come out of hiding without a good reason."

A look of determination had settled across his face and Isaac chewed the inside of his cheek. He couldn't help the suspicion that Christian had not told him everything his father had revealed, but a feminine laugh interrupted his thoughts before they could spiral.

Miss Montclair followed Samantha outside, her satchel slung over one shoulder and that ridiculous parrot perched on the other. As soon as she stepped into the glow of the setting sun, the bird let loose a squawk and took flight, landing on the marble statue of Venus in the center of the fountain.

"Lola!" A flush spread across her cheeks. "She's usually not this ill-behaved."

Isaac crossed his arms. "Now what?"

She blinked up at him. "Now I go get her, of course."

"Of course." He shook his head as she left him on the stairs.

After a minute of pleading to the bird to come to her, Miss Montclair threw up her hands. She sat on the edge of the fountain and pulled her slippers free, tossing them to the ground. Standing, she pulled her skirts up, revealing shapely calves. He pressed his eyes shut. Of course, his mind went to Tortuga—to the waterfall, to her skin glistening with water, to her laughter echoing in the trees.

Not again.

He snapped them open as she stepped into the water and crossed to the center. Using a cherub's wing for support, she climbed onto its head.

Christian chuckled. "Well, that's not something you see every day."

"She's…" Isaac blinked as she stretched her arm toward the bird, who sat unmoving from its perch on the hand of Venus, just beyond reach. She shifted her footing, going onto her tiptoes on the cherub's round head.

Incredible. The thought flitted through his mind, there and gone in an instant. "Out of her mind."

As soon as he spoke, she began to wobble. She jerked her hand down and reached for the wing. Too fast. The movement twisted her and her feet slipped into thin air. With a yelp, she fell backward into the fountain. Her legs flailed, sending water splashing in all directions.

"Are you going to do something, or do I have to be the one to go play hero?" Christian's dry voice cut through his shock.

Son of a bitch.

Isaac unbuttoned his jacket and tossed it to his friend. "I cannot believe this is happening," he muttered.

He strode forward. "Miss Montclair, are you alright?"

She stood next to the cherub, brown eyes wide, water running down her face. His gaze followed a stream to where it disappeared beneath her neckline. A surge of heat slid through him—the periwinkle dress clung to her almost as scandalously as her chemise had on the island, once again leaving very little to his imagination.

"Oh dear." She wrung her hands, her earlier blush spreading from her cheeks all the way down to her chest. Damn. He needed to stop looking there.

With a heavy swallow, he extended his hand. "Come, let me help you out."

She sloshed over, her face tucked down and took his hand. When she lifted her leg to step out, the weight of her sodden skirts caught on the stone and she pitched forward. He dropped her hand and caught her around the waist, his fingers pressing tight against the wet silk and soft flesh below.

With a grunt, he lifted her free and set her next to him, ignoring the thump of his pulse in the most inconvenient place. He released her and took a step back.

A flutter of green appeared in his peripheral vision and he ducked. Something landed on his shoulder and he nearly swiped the parrot off him.

"Don't move!" Miss Montclair edged to his side.

He went perfectly still, eyeing the proximity of a sharp beak to his face. "He doesn't bite, does he?"

"Sometimes." She reached out and gently took the bird, her knuckles grazing his cheek. "And it's a she."

Isaac stayed in place as Samantha ran over with a towel and pulled Miss Montclair toward the house. He lifted his hand and wiped a few drops of water from his cheek as Christian brought him his jacket.

Thank goodness he was leaving, because this exasperating woman threatened complicated feelings. Feelings he didn't have time for.

Chapter Eight

JOSEPHINE YAWNED AND snuggled deeper in her sheets. The plush mattress and soft bedding might be enough to make her decide to stay abed all day. Yes, definitely the bed. Not the embarrassment from yesterday's dreadful fountain mishap. Her fingers drifted down to her sides, where she remained quite certain the lieutenant's handprints had been seared into her skin.

With a sigh, she rolled to face the ceiling, unable to stop the heaviness pressing down on her. He would leave the next morning and shatter all of her ill-formed plans. Destiny, it turned out, did not like being taken in hand. Everything had been ruined, her future no better than it had been back on the island.

No. Though her plans to spend more time with the lieutenant had evaporated, there was still an entire city to explore and new faces to meet. She would make the most of her stay in Savannah.

A knock came from her door and Abigail poked her head inside. "Oh good, you're awake. I came in earlier but you were still sleeping. Figured you could use the rest after your journey. I'm sure you didn't sleep well on the ship." Lola sat perched on her shoulder. "I hope it's alright I took her down to breakfast with me. She was making a ruckus and I feared she'd awaken you."

Josephine smiled. "Of course. She was probably upset about missing her morning meal."

Abigail giggled. "She did steal several pieces of fruit."

"I hope you're prepared for her to think you're now her new best friend. She's highly motivated by food."

A wide smile spread across Abigail's face. "Oh, good, because

I adore her." She reached up and stroked Lola's green feathers.

A flush of warmth spread through Josephine and she knew without a doubt this beautiful woman would become a good friend. She sat up and swung her feet to the floor, stretching.

"Did you sleep well?"

Josephine ran her hands over the sheets. "I think this is the most comfortable bed I've ever slept in."

With a laugh, Abigail went to the window and pulled the curtains aside. "Today's a busy day. I've tea at Mrs. Crompton's. You can stay here if you'd like, but Samantha said you were keen to see Savannah and the Cromptons live downtown."

Squinting against the bright sunlight, Josephine stood. "I would love to join you."

Lola let out a loud squawk as Abigail bounced on her heels. "Good, because I already picked out the perfect dress for you." She pointed at a gown draped over the end of the bed.

Josephine blinked. When had it been brought? She must have slept hard indeed if she'd missed that. Her eyes widened when her fingers brushed against yellow muslin, soft as a sunkissed marigold petal. She lifted the skirt, her eyes tracing the delicate white embroidery along the hem. The fabric shimmered faintly, with tiny glass beads catching the morning light along the bodice. For a moment, she simply stared. Her own best dress was a navy poplin with faded trim. But this—this was a cloud, weightless and unspoiled by the harshness of sea or sun.

"I could never wear this." The words came out in a reverent whisper and she met Abigail's gaze. "I brought my own skirt and blouse."

"Nonsense." Abigail picked it up and held it in front of Josephine. "This suits you very well. You'll want to make a good first impression."

Could she? Josephine took it and stepped in front of the mirror. The golden hue softened her, brightening her bronzed skin and giving her dark hair a richness that belied its unruly nature. This dress belonged in another world, one she had no business in—but for one afternoon, she could borrow it, could pretend she was someone else.

With a deep breath, she smiled at Abigail. "Alright."

Her friend's eyes sparkled as she helped Josephine dress. The gown clung in just the right places, and as Abigail arranged her hair, Josephine caught another glimpse of herself in the mirror. This time, she barely recognized the person staring back.

Once ready, they made their way to the waiting carriage. The door closed with a soft thud, and the vehicle rocked forward in a gentle lurch as the horses fell into a steady clatter. The sun had burned off the thin veil of mist, leaving behind a warm light that bathed the countryside. Josephine kept her gaze fixed outside the open window where the world shifted and changed before her eyes.

At first, it was all familiar—the broad, flat expanse of the riverside where merchant ships bobbed at anchor, their sails furled. The air held the sharp bite of tar and she caught the briny scent of oysters as they passed a fishmonger's stall along the docks. Men in rough linen shirts hauled crates onto wagons, their coarse voices carrying over the sound of hooves. The carriage wheels rumbled over rough cobblestones as the grit of the waterfront gave way to broad streets flanked by oaks casting dappled shadows over all who passed.

Elegant houses of brick and stucco stood behind wrought-iron gates, where climbing roses and jasmine spilled over, their blossoms spilling sweetness into the air. Ladies in pastel gowns strolled beneath parasols along shaded walkways while gentlemen in fine waistcoats and breeches tipped their hats as they walked by. It was all so… civilized. She sat back against the tufted velvet seat as Abigail chatted easily about who they might see at tea.

But Josephine only half listened, her eyes drawn to the passing city. It all seemed too perfect. Too refined. Savannah was a far cry from the wild, untamed edges of Tortuga where vines crawled freely and the sun bleached everything in its path. Here, the beauty felt deliberate and controlled. They slowed at one of the squares where a statue stood at its heart. A group of children in muslin dresses ran around it, their laughter echoing over the street and Josephine's lips tugged into a faint smile.

"Josephine?"

Her gaze snapped back to Abigail, who gave her an expectant look. "I'm so sorry, I was distracted."

Abigail gave a wide grin. "We're here."

Once they climbed the marble steps, a servant opened the door and ushered them inside. They followed the sound of voices to the parlor. Sunlight streamed through tall multi-paned windows draped with sheer muslin curtains, and framed botanical prints lined painted plaster walls. A Turkish rug, slightly faded but richly patterned, covered the wood floor, the faint scent of beeswax polish lingering.

Near one of the windows, an older woman sat at a mahogany tea table, pouring tea from a silver pot into matching porcelain cups. The gilt rims and floral patterns on the china caught the light, but their beauty was lost on Josephine as her gaze lingered on the women arranged about the room in chairs and on the settee.

They sat with perfect posture, their elaborate gowns flowing to the floor in effortless grace. Laughter, soft and deliberate, drifted over the room like the tinkling of chimes. A practiced ease seemed to flow from them—hands delicately folded, even-toned voices, subtle glances around them—as though rehearsed. Josephine's mouth went dry as one by one, gazes flickered her way.

Abigail squeezed her arm and guided her in. "Don't worry, everyone will love you."

Once she finished pouring, their hostess stood with a warm smile. "Oh, Miss Ross, I'm so glad you could make it. And who is this?"

Josephine stood straighter. Was it just her or did the room suddenly go quiet?

"Mrs. Crompton, this is Miss Josephine Montclair, daughter of the governor of Tortuga. She's to be my guest for a short while."

"Oh, how lovely. We've always room for new faces."

They found two unclaimed seats next to each other. Abigail introduced Josephine to the twins sitting to her left, Louisa and Eleanor Bellefleur, and continued around the room. By the time she got to the last girl, Josephine had forgotten nearly all the names.

"Is Savannah very different from Tortuga?" one of the twins asked.

Josephine grinned. "Oh yes. It is so much bigger and so much more refined. In Tortuga, you could cross paths with a smuggler, a pirate, and a merchant all in the span of the same minute."

Their eyes widened. "Surely you jest."

She leaned forward. "It's a wild island, unfettered from the bonds of society. Lawless, you might say."

One of the girls started to fan herself and the others looked away from Josephine, finding a sudden interest in their empty teacups.

"What are we all discussing over here?" Mrs. Crompton sat and began pouring everyone's tea.

One of the girls snickered. "Josephine was telling us how… interesting her island is."

A lump formed in her throat. What had she said wrong?

The conversation turned to the weather and the latest fashion prints.

Louisa held something out. "Sugar?"

She stared at the little bowl with its elegant silver tongs. She never drank anything in her tea or coffee. After everyone gave her expectant looks, she deposited one lump into her cup. Louisa didn't move the bowl and Josephine glanced around the room. *Oh, for heaven's sake.* She took another cube.

The sugar went round the room, each lady taking her portion, and soon the delicate tinkle of spoons on glass filled the air.

Josephine lifted her cup and took a swallow, nearly gagging at the syrupy taste. Abigail gave a discreet cough and raised her cup, her fingers poised lightly on the handle. Josephine dropped her gaze to where her hand wrapped around the cup and sighed, moving her fingers to barely hold the handle. Her next sip nearly sent the cup tumbling from her grasp. How silly to hold something like that.

A servant carried in a tray of petite cakes and bite-sized pastries. She took one with a dollop of fruit spread on top and popped it in her mouth. "This is lovely."

Several of the girls smirked, then made a show of taking dainty bites from their selections. Josephine fought the urge to roll her eyes. Why fashion something so small if not to be eaten in one bite?

Time crawled by, the room bathed in insufferable heat. Josephine shifted back and forth in her seat, trying to find a comfortable position. Oh, how she longed for the airy freedom of her skirt and blouse. Remarkably, none of the other girls showed any signs of discomfort. When the twins suggested they all go stretch their legs in the garden room, she nearly leaped from her seat. But Abigail stayed put as the girls filed from the room.

Mrs. Crompton noticed her longing glance after them. "Miss Montclair, why don't you join the others while I catch up with dear Abigail."

Josephine smiled and stood, her napkin dropping from her lap. With an apologetic smile, she picked it up and placed it on the chair, sending a silent thanks that the other girls weren't there to see her make yet another mistake.

In the hall, she hesitated at the double doors leading to the garden room. So far, every move had felt like a blunder, pushing the girls to dislike her. This moment offered her an opportunity to show them she could belong. She pulled her shoulders back and cracked open the door. The young ladies stood in the center of the room, whispering amongst themselves.

"Did you see how she holds her teacup? Like a sailor clutching a tankard."

The girls tittered and Louisa leaned in. "Governor? I'm sure she was raised among pirates. To think, poor Mrs. Crompton probably has no idea what sort she let in."

"Poor Mrs. Crompton? You mean poor Abigail? She's the one who has to tote her around like a stray kitten."

Heat pressed at Josephine's eyes and she slowly backed away from the parlor door, letting it fall softly shut. She swallowed, looking behind her to where Abigail still sat with Mrs. Crompton. Suddenly, she didn't want to pretend anymore. Her feet propelled her to the front door and she slipped outside without any notice. Once on the wide verandah, she took a deep breath of humid air.

Better.

She stood next to a wide column, facing the square. The children had left, leaving the green grass quiet and bare. A massive oak tree stretched its long branches over a bench, leaving shifting patterns of light and shade. With a quick glance at the closed doors behind her, she started down the steps. Once in the square, she sank onto a bench, closing her eyes to take in the quiet solitude.

A breeze stirred the leaves above her, carrying the sounds of the city. Carriage and wagon wheels clattered nearby, but the lively murmur of distant voices, a few bursts of boisterous laughter, drew her attention. She opened her eyes, her gaze drawn to a side street where the sunlight reflected from colorful fabric. Craning her neck, a multitude of canopies came into view with a crowd milling about. A market.

Her fingers curled around the edge of the bench and she twisted back to the Crompton's house. The doors remained closed. No one had noticed her absence. With a smile, she left the square, her boots clicking against cobblestones. As she neared, the bustling market came into full view—a maze of woven baskets, cloth stalls, and wooden carts. The scent of ripe melons, fresh baked bread, and vibrant flowers swirled together on the back of her palette. One vendor offered bundles of summer herbs, their leaves gleaming in the afternoon sun.

The hum of conversation and the clink of coins blended with the rhythmic calls of vendors, all competing for attention along the sun-soaked street. Josephine's lips curved as a woman next to her negotiated for a bundle of mint. She passed a spice stall, breathing in cinnamon, nutmeg and clove.

Her heart caught as the blue of a naval uniform stood out among the bustling crowd. A small group of sailors haggled with a farmer's wife over baskets of eggs and piles of sweet potatoes. Josephine slowed as they lifted crates carefully into their arms, the early-morning sun glinting off the polished buttons of their coats. The man who had just paid turned, and her breath caught. Lieutenant Caldwell.

His eyes settled on her, widening in unmistakable shock. "Miss Montclair?"

For a moment, all she could think about was the fountain—the way she'd flailed, the splash, the scandal of it all. And from the look on his face, he clearly hadn't forgotten either.

Fire danced across her cheeks. She opened her mouth, then shut it again, words abandoning her as she sent up a silent plea for the earth to swallow her whole.

Taking a deep breath, she curtsied with as much grace as she could summon. "Hello, Lieutenant."

He glanced around, brows drawn together. "Are you... alone?" She nodded and he frowned. "You should not be out unchaperoned."

So many rules.

She sighed. "Seems everything I've done since getting here has been all wrong."

The hard lines in his face softened. "No harm done. The market's fairly safe. Still, I'd feel better escorting you through it." He nodded to one of the men holding a crate. "Bring those all to the ship. I'll be along shortly."

He offered his elbow, and with a swallow, she set her hand upon it.

They made their way down the narrow lane, weaving between stalls. After she'd paused to examine yet another display of goods, he gave her a lopsided grin. "Do you have a market in Tortuga?"

"Yes." She stepped around a basket of squawking chickens. "It's only a few tables though, nothing like this."

She slowed in front of a fruit stand, marveling at the wide variety of produce. Familiar bananas, pineapples, and papaya were stacked next to a multitude of items she'd never seen. The vendor caught her eye and pointed to a pile of round, blushing fruit. It must be fruit. No vegetable could possess such a lovely pink color.

"What's this?" She ran her fingertips over the soft fuzz of the one closest to her.

Lieutenant Caldwell chuckled. "You've never seen a peach before?"

She shook her head as he plucked one from the pile and held it to her nose with a knowing smile. The velvety skin brushed against her upper lip, and she inhaled tentatively. A scent unlike anything she'd known—soft and sweet, with a delicate floral undertone, almost honeyed. She drew in another breath, the fragrance lingering on the edge of her senses, warm and inviting.

"Go on, take it," he urged, his voice low and coaxing, as though sharing a deep secret. "It's just ripe."

Josephine's fingers hovered before gently cupping around the fruit. She lifted it from his weathered palm, the slight give beneath her touch hinting at the truth of his claim. "How much for one?"

The vendor flashed a grin. "For a lovely lady like you? Three cents. Finest peaches you'll find in the entire market."

She pulled out her reticule, but the lieutenant stilled her hand with his. "My treat."

A burst of heat traveled up her arm. "Thank you."

Lifting the peach to her mouth, she took a small bite. The soft skin split between her teeth and a rush of sweet nectar flooded across her tongue. Her eyes widened at the rush of flavor and she took a bigger bite. This time, juice dribbled down her chin and she laughed, leaning forward so it dripped to the ground.

"This is incredible."

Lieutenant Caldwell stared at her, jaw slack, eyes fixed on her mouth as if the world had narrowed to that single, perfect bite.

He let out a strangled cough and pulled a handkerchief free. "Here, I think you'll need this." His voice came out rough and uneven.

She took it, fumbling as the soft fabric brushed her fingers. What a picture she must have made, taking that bite. A new rush of heat blazed across her skin, hot as the sun. Dabbing her lips, she pressed the cloth a little harder than necessary, hands trembling as she tried to steady herself.

He tugged at his cravat and cleared his throat. "Well… Shall we go to the waterfront?"

They crossed the street and came to a stop at a railing near the embankment, trading the hum of the market for the gentle lap of waves against the docks. The sun cast a bright shimmer over the surface of the river, where barges laden with cargo bobbed low in the current.

"It's unlike anything I ever imagined. My father used to talk about Paris and how far its streets and shopping districts stretched, but I never believed him. Seeing Savannah now, I hardly think I could handle a city like that."

One side of his mouth twisted up. "I dare say you, of all people, would find a way to manage it."

"You overestimate my abilities, Lieutenant." A faint smile tugged her lips. "But tell me, how are your preparations coming along?"

"My men have all received their orders, and cargo should be secured by nightfall. I am anxious to set out and see this Thorne matter concluded."

He nodded down the river, where the now familiar masts of the *Tempest* tucked between two merchant ships. A warm breeze stirred off the water, tinged with the musty tang of silt and wet timber. Her eyes drifted closed as the wind tugged at her hair, loosening tendrils from their pins. The distant calls of gulls mingled with the occasional clatter of oars and shouted directions from dockhands. Here, by the water, she could breathe freely. No pretense. No judgment. Just the river, the sun, and the last whispers of the peach's honeyed sweetness lingering on her tongue.

And a handsome man at her side. She opened her eyes to find his blue eyes locked on her, shadowed with something she could not name, intense and unreadable. He jerked his gaze away. His profile, sharpened in the golden light, commanded her attention.

"So—"

"I—"

They spoke at the same moment, and both fell silent, caught in the brief collision of words. After a long pause, she summoned a tentative smile. "Thank you for walking with me."

He nodded, shifting his weight. "Yes... well, it was a— pleasant diversion from a busy day."

"Isaac? Miss Montclair?" Samantha approached, wearing a simple blue day dress. "What are you doing here?"

Lieutenant Caldwell grinned. "I found Miss Montclair wandering around the market on her own. I feared leaving her might lead to another tumble into misadventure."

Samantha raised an eyebrow and stepped between them. "Go on, then. Finish what you were doing. I'll get Miss Montclair back to the Rosses."

"Very well, ladies." He inclined his head in a crisp bow, then turned toward the docks with a purposeful stride.

Samantha's blue eyes glinted in the sunlight as he descended the steps and disappeared from view. "So, how did you end up in the market? I can't imagine Abigail letting you out of her sight for even a moment."

"Well, we went to tea and..." she trailed off, afraid to offend.

Samantha gave her a knowing look. "I did try to warn you.

Let me guess, Mrs. Crompton's?"

Josephine nodded and Samantha sighed. "I can only imagine how that felt for you."

Pushing her toe against the cobblestones, Josephine frowned. "I was so excited to go, but was made to feel quite unwelcome." It was her turn to sigh. "I never thought something as simple as tea could be so… complicated."

Samantha patted her hand. "Don't be too hard on yourself. Those girls live in a world of their own. Their reaction to you would have been the same no matter who you were. Besides, they probably just felt threatened by your beauty."

Josephine couldn't help but snort. "I'm pretty sure that was the last thing on their minds. All they cared about was how different I am from them."

With a wry smile, Samantha gazed out over the water. "You know, it's not our differences that set us apart from the world—it's the courage to embrace them."

Josephine cocked her head. "What's that supposed to mean?"

Grin widening, Samantha took her arm and turned away from the water. "It means there's nothing wrong with being different. Now, let's get you back to tea before anyone gets worried."

Chapter Nine

"I CAN'T BELIEVE you left Mrs. Crompton's house." Abigail broke the silence she'd held the first half of the drive.

"I didn't mean to worry you."

"You could have been hurt, or lost, or any number of things."

Josephine frowned. "Is Savannah a dangerous city?"

"No. Not usually. But it's not proper for one to go out without an escort. People will talk."

Buildings disappeared and the countryside stretched around them. They were getting close to the Ross estate. Josephine sighed. "Are you terribly upset with me?"

Abigail reached out and took her hand, her expression warm yet firm. "Of course not. But, as the person in charge of introducing you to Savannah, please do consult me before running off like that."

The carriage turned up their drive and Josephine gave her friend a small smile. "I can do that."

Moments later, they rolled to a gentle stop in front of the house. The footman opened the door, and Josephine gathered her skirts as Abigail climbed out first. "Not to rush you," she said over her shoulder, "but we need to start getting ready."

Josephine stepped from the carriage. "Ready for what?"

"If you hadn't snuck off, you would have heard. Governor Milledge arrived in town this morning, and he's insisting on a sendoff party for the sailors."

"A party?"

Abigail twirled. "Yes, you know, food, dancing, handsome

gentlemen? Milledge does love his parties."

Handsome gentlemen. Josephine perked up. Would the lieutenant be there? Her heart beat a silly, erratic tune.

Her friend picked up on her excitement. "Let's go pick out another gown for you."

"Another one? What's wrong with this one?" Josephine smoothed the yellow muslin.

"That one is far too plain for this sort of event."

Josephine bit her tongue to keep from saying it was the most extravagant dress she'd ever worn, the scorn from the Bellefleur twins still fresh in her mind. She shifted her weight. "I feel bad borrowing everyone's clothing. I brought plenty of money to buy things here."

Abigail laughed. "I have far too many dresses. Letting you wear them will make me feel better about all the ones I never get to. Besides, you want to look your best, don't you? My modiste has impeccable taste." She took Josephine's hand and tugged her through the door.

Hours later, Josephine exited the carriage with Abigail, her ivory gown a soft shimmer against the night as satin skirts swished around her legs. Overlooking a square in the heart of the city, the pale pink stuccoed home boasted massive Roman columns and ornately carved trimwork.

Once inside, Josephine stared at the gilded molding and massive chandeliers twinkling with hundreds of candles. Flecks of shiny gold studded the floral wallpaper and she had to clamp her hands together to keep from reaching out to touch it. No need to make a spectacle of herself like she had earlier.

"Oh, look, there's Samantha!" Abigail waved her hand wildly.

Josephine followed her gaze across the room and her breath hitched. Lieutenant Caldwell had come. Wearing the same immaculate uniform he'd worn to dinner at her house, he stood next to Mr. and Mrs. Thompson. She couldn't drag her eyes from him as a fluttery lightness spread through her chest. He glanced up as if sensing her perusal and for a split second, blue eyes stared into hers. She held her breath. And then he turned back to his friends.

What did you expect? She shook her head as they made their way through the crowds of people. By the time they reached Samantha, the men had disappeared. Standing along the wall, the trio watched the party unfold. Partners crowded the dance floor, moving so close together, it seemed a miracle no collisions happened. Drinks flowed freely, with servants moving about the room with silver platters full of glasses. The music ebbed and flowed like waves upon the sea.

"Isn't it lovely?" Abigail smiled as Josephine took it all in.

"I've never been to a party like this."

Her new friend let out a happy sigh. "I'm sure someone will ask you to dance soon."

A tenseness slid through Josephine as a couple moved in unison in front of them. She'd learned several dances in Tortuga, but had never practiced with a real-life partner. Also, these dances seemed so much more intricate than the ones she'd tried.

"You have danced before, right?"

"A few times." The words came out thick, and Abigail reached out to squeeze her hand.

"Don't worry. Most of the men here are so used to dancing, they could lead you through the steps blindfolded. I've the perfect distraction while we wait. I used to do this with Samantha. Close your eyes."

With a lifted brow, Josephine followed her new friend's order.

"Now, think about the perfect man." Abigail gave a dramatic pause. "Who do you see?"

Josephine giggled and opened her eyes. "That's easy. Lieutenant Caldwell."

Abigail frowned. "He's handsome alright, but ever since he showed up with Mr. Thompson earlier this year, he hasn't shown so much as a hint at wanting to settle down. Plenty of the ladies have tried to catch his attention, but he gives them no notice. His job is the only thing he cares about. If you're looking for a husband, he's the very last person to chase."

Josephine scanned the crowd until she found him once more, standing next to Mr. Thompson near a pair of French doors. She studied all the men between them and sniffed. Not a single one stood out to her. When she returned her gaze to him, her breath caught. Those deep blue eyes of his were fixed on her. She swallowed, unable to look away until he gave a slight nod and turned back to his friend. With a shake of her head, she spun back to Abigail. Gaping at the lieutenant like a fish certainly wouldn't win her any favors.

"What about you? Who do you see?"

Abigail stilled. "Samantha never asked." She closed her eyes and a wistful smile flitted across her lips. "My problem is every time I try this, I see someone different. Tonight it's Mr. Ainsley. But that's because he's newly arrived in town. I'm sure once I get to know him, he'll turn out to be as dull or boorish as the rest of them."

Josephine grinned. "So, you want someone exciting. What about a Navy sailor? There's plenty of them here."

Abigail went pale. "No. Definitely not a sailor. I can't stand the ocean, especially sailing on it."

"Oh." Josephine tried to imagine such a concept. "Living on an island, every man I've ever met is a sailor of some sort."

"You probably think I'm silly." Abigail hugged her arms around herself.

She shook her head. "Of course not. I'm just not used to all the options one must have living on the continent. What kind of exciting professions do men around here have?"

"Honestly, I don't care what they do. I want someone who is kind and sees me for who I am, not just what I look like. Someone who cares about me more than his bookkeeping or social life. Problem is, every man who has shown interest thus far only sees me for one thing—a pretty placeholder for the title of wife." Sadness laced Abigail's voice, and Josephine understood.

Having one's hopes raised and dashed over and over again would take its toll on anyone, even someone as bright and vivacious as Abigail.

"Well, maybe Mr. Ainsley is the one. Besides, you are so lovely, I cannot believe for a second that you won't attract that kind of man to you."

Abigail's shoulders straightened. "Thank you. I won't give up. I know the perfect one is out there somewhere for me. It's just— maybe this doesn't make sense—but when you have wanted something for so long, and it doesn't happen the way you think it would, it can be discouraging."

Josephine reached out and patted her new friend's arm. "I know the feeling well."

Abigail smiled. "I'm glad to have met you. Now, let's stop being so melancholy, lest the men notice. That's a sure way to keep them away!"

The band started a new song and Josephine perked up. Finally, a familiar tune. She cleared her throat. "Standing alone over here in the corner is another way to scare them off. Come, let's go ask our dream men to dance."

"Josephine, wait." Abigail reached for her arm but was too late. "We wait for them to ask us."

"Well, if what you said is true, the lieutenant will never ask. Where's Mr. Ainsley?"

With a sigh, Abigail fell into step beside her and pointed to the other side of the room. A tall gentleman stood alone watching the dancers. Josephine guided them that way. "Introduce me."

Her friend slowed as they approached, and Josephine slid her a sideways glance. "Are you nervous?"

All she got was a quick nod in return. How could someone so beautiful have any reservations about talking to a handsome man? *Look who's talking.* Between the fountain mishap and the fresh awkwardness at today's market, she wasn't sure she could face Lieutenant Caldwell again.

Mr. Ainsley noticed them and his face brightened. "Miss Ross.

I hoped to see you here."

She giggled. "I never miss a party."

He grinned and turned to Josephine. "Who's this? I don't think I've met you before."

"Mr. Ainsley, this is Miss Montclair. Her father is the governor of Tortuga."

A faraway look crossed over his face. "Tortuga. Where's that, somewhere in Europe?"

Abigail blinked and Josephine bit back a laugh. "It's a Caribbean island."

"Oh. Very nice." He turned to Abigail. "Would you like to dance?"

She beamed and Josephine gave her a wink before leaving the happy couple behind. Dance partners marched and twirled across the floor and as she approached the two men still conversing in the corner, her heart began to beat faster, the small amount of courage she'd gathered fading away. The lieutenant faced away from her, the sound of his voice floating over the music.

"I hired a cabin boy down at the King's Head."

"So, everything is in order to be able to leave by dawn then?" Mr. Thompson noticed her but didn't say anything.

"Yes. Preferably sooner. If it weren't for this blasted party, I'd have pushed to leave tonight." Lieutenant Caldwell stood still for a moment. "Look, I don't mind you putting your foolhardy neck on the line, but I can't stomach the thought of Samantha crossing paths with Thorne again."

Mr. Thompson's hands clenched into fists. "You think I don't feel the same?"

Lieutenant Caldwell crossed his arms. "So, tell her to stay. You're her husband after all."

His friend snorted. "You know as well as I do that she wouldn't listen one lick if I commanded that of her." He swiveled his gaze to Josephine. "Miss Montclair, so good to see you again. You look absolutely lovely."

Her reply was lost as the lieutenant turned and the weight of her recent embarrassments collided with the flutter of nerves his nearness stirred. He stood silent, his eyes traveling over her.

After a few moments passed, Mr. Thompson cleared his throat. "I hope you've managed to stay out of the Ross's fountain." He gave her a good-natured wink, sending heat shooting up her cheeks.

A flash of amusement colored the lieutenant's eyes a darker blue, but he remained quiet.

Mr. Thompson slapped his friend's shoulder. "I had better find Samantha and ask her to dance before she thinks I've forgotten about her. Why don't you two take a spin around the floor as well?"

Lieutenant Caldwell opened his mouth, but Mr. Thompson winked again and strode away, leaving the two of them alone. He shook his head and turned to her once more. "What do you say, Miss Montclair? Shall we?"

Josephine stared at his outstretched hand and her throat went dry. She glanced out at the busy dance floor, her breaths coming shallow. Could she manage in such tight quarters?

"Unless, of course you would rather not?" He looked somewhat hopeful.

She should let him go. Clearly, he didn't want to. But the thought of sharing even one dance with him had her heart soaring. Never mind if she wouldn't see him again. In fact, that made it better. She could fully enjoy herself without wondering what would come next.

With a determined swallow, she set her hand in his. "I would like that."

His fingers flexed around hers as he nodded. "Very well." He guided them out onto the floor.

Abigail had been right. Even if she hadn't known this dance, Lieutenant Caldwell expertly guided her through each step. She fought the urge to close her eyes and lose herself to the magic of it all, instead focusing on each twist and turn, the way the light sparkled from his eyes, and the delightful thrill that shot up her arm each time he took her hand in his. Her lips curved.

When she glanced up at the lieutenant, his face had softened and he wore an amused smile. "You're enjoying yourself."

"I'm starting to feel as though I've been cheated in life growing up on Tortuga. How amazing it must be to go to these kinds of parties and dance whenever you'd like."

His lips pressed together briefly. "Truth be told, I try very hard not to come to these events."

Her eyes widened. "You have no idea how lucky you are to have…" She glanced around them. "All *this* at your fingertips."

"It grows old." They turned and his hand shifted at her waist, sending a shiver up her side. "After a while, they all feel the same."

She lifted her chin. "I don't think the magic would ever fade for me."

"It's easy to say that at your first party." His smile had returned. "I wrote your father today. Luckily, there was a merchant making a run to Jamaica that I was able to convince to make a stop on Tortuga."

Josephine's heart fell and she missed a step. "I wish you wouldn't have."

He raised a brow. "What would you have had me do? It is my responsibility to make sure you get home safely."

"I would have been happy to stay until you return."

His lips tightened as she followed his lead, her skirts swaying with each measured movement. When he reached for her waist again, his touch light but firm, his voice lowered. "And what if I don't return?"

The cloud she'd been floating on evaporated as she stared up at him. "Why would you say such a thing?"

They moved in perfect time, the rhythm of their steps as deliberate as his words. "It's the truth, and you of all people should know it. Didn't you warn me once before how dangerous Thorne is? Do you think that's changed?"

She blinked as a stab of coldness slid through her. "You will be careful, won't you?"

His eyes pressed shut. "I'm sorry. It was not appropriate for me to speak like that. Of course I will be."

Josephine forced a smile. "No need to apologize. I've heard much worse in my days."

The song ended and the lieutenant guided them off the floor. He squeezed her hands and bowed.

She took a deep breath. "I suppose this is goodbye then, isn't it?"

He peered down at her, the seas in his eyes a swirling maelstrom. "Yes."

"It feels a bit redundant to say, but I wish you good luck in your hunt for Thorne."

His lips twitched. "Thank you."

"I'm glad to have met you, Lieutenant."

This time, he did smile. "And I, you. Even if you did cause a lot of trouble."

Her throat thickened, even though his grin held as he said it. "I hope you don't remember me just for that."

His eyes flashed as he locked gazes with her. "I will remember you for many things."

Heat crept up her skin at the intensity lacing his tone. She swallowed, unable to come up with a response, but unwilling to end the conversation.

"Excuse me?" A young gentleman strode forward with a hesitant smile. "Would you like to dance?"

The lieutenant bowed. "Goodbye, Miss Montclair. Enjoy your stay in Savannah."

She dipped in a quick curtsy. "Stay safe, Lieutenant."

And just like that, it was goodbye for real, the man beside her offering his arm and guiding her toward the dance floor.

"Oh, Miss Montclair?"

She paused, turning back with parted lips.

"I must warn you, Savannah's full of fountains. Be careful." With a wink rivaling Mr. Thompson's, he pivoted and strode toward his friend.

Later, in the carriage, Josephine let out a sigh and wiggled her aching toes.

"Did you have fun?" Abigail gave her an expectant look.

"It was a bit like living out a dream. I never could have imagined a party so grand. But my feet do hurt."

"Wait till you go to one of the Montelet's parties. They live just out of town on a grand estate. Theirs are the biggest and most elaborate of them all." Abigail grinned. "And you'll be up past midnight dancing."

A warm glow spread through Josephine's chest. Tonight had been magical—an event she would remember the rest of her life. The rest of the ride passed by in a blur as she categorized and filed away each precious memory.

After Abigail bid her goodnight, Josephine walked out onto her balcony, gazing into the darkness. All the comforting sounds of a Caribbean night were missing; no tree frogs, and all the insect noises had distinct differences. The foreignness of this land wrapped around her, crushing her lungs, until her breaths came quick and fast.

And then, far away, a familiar sound cut through the unknown.

The trill of a mockingbird.

She straightened as the song faded.

Had she imagined it?

She had come to Savannah chasing her destiny, yet now, it seemed further from reach than ever before. Her eyes narrowed as she glared out into the shadows. Destiny be damned. How was it that women like Samantha found partners who allowed them to sail on pirate hunting missions, and here she was, still reduced to the prospect of marrying an elderly merchant?

It's not fair. Though she felt like a child for thinking it, it was the truth. Once her father received Lieutenant Caldwell's message, he would make sure she returned to Tortuga straightaway. She likely would have not much more than a week to even enjoy the company of Abigail. Her lips pulled up in a snarl. So little time.

Why shouldn't she be able to experience the thrill of adventure? Because she was a woman? Hell, she could hold her own against pirates. She knew how they behaved and reacted better than most American men could claim. And they didn't scare her. Well, not in the way most normal people were scared of pirates. Frustration coiled as her jaw tightened. The spray of the sea on her face, the thunder of cannons, the chase of a prize—all denied to her for the sake of supposedly delicate womanhood.

A flutter of wings startled her and she stood still as the mockingbird perched at the corner of the railing, its head cocked to one side as it regarded her. She held her breath, afraid to blink lest it vanish. And then, as she stared into black eyes, a thought hit her so hard, she doubled over. If she wasn't in Savannah, her father couldn't drag her home. Her fingers curled around the stone railing, still warm from the day's sun, and she knew what she had to do.

She hurried inside and picked up the candle next to her bed. Creeping across the hall, she knocked on Abigail's door. A long moment passed before it cracked open.

"What's wrong?" her friend whispered, glancing up the hall toward her father's bedroom before opening the door wider.

Josephine strode in, coming to a stop in front of a window near the bed. "What is the King's Head?"

Abigail scrunched her nose. "It's a tavern down by the docks."

"Have you ever been?"

Blue eyes went wide. "Heavens no. Respectable ladies never go there."

Josephine stared out the window. "Do you think they gamble there?"

"Of course they do. Gambling, and worse."

Excellent.

"Why do you ask?"

Josephine turned with a wide grin. "Because I'm going there, now."

Chapter Ten

*T*HUD.

Josephine's heart gave a lurching beat as she stood beneath the wood sign of the King's Head. Loud music and boisterous shouts pulsed from within.

She pulled her shoulders straight. "Just like Tortuga," she muttered.

But it wasn't. This was a foreign country. The men inside would be a mix of sorts but one thing was certain—there wouldn't be any pirates. Which she was used to.

Never mind. Standing out here wouldn't do her any favors. *Now or never.* She pulled her hat low and adjusted her men's shirt over the breeches she'd brought from Tortuga. With a deep breath she pushed the door open. Larger than the Golden Lantern with tables spaced farther apart, the only light came from primitive sconces hanging along the walls, giving the tavern a private feel. Good. Fewer eyes on her meant better chances of success.

An older barkeep stood behind the bar, scanning the room with sharp eyes and she came to a stop in front of him. He filled mugs while keeping his attention fixed on the patrons and barely spared her a glance. Until she set a coin on the counter.

She lowered her voice to the practiced one she'd gotten so good at on the island. "I'll have an ale. And I'm looking for someone."

He palmed the money and laughed. "Aren't we all."

A moment later, a wooden mug slammed down in front of

her, golden liquid sloshing onto the counter. She picked it up. "I need to speak with the *Tempest's* new cabin boy."

A bushy gray brow lifted. "What makes you think he's here?"

Her heart dropped. Was he already on board the *Tempest*? If so, her adventure would be over before it started. She grasped for words. "I was told I could find him here. It's important."

"It always is." He regarded her for a long moment, then sighed and pointed. "He's over there."

She lifted on tiptoes to find an older boy with an oversized tarpaulin hat hiding half his face. He sat at a table with a group of dockhands. Piles of money sat in front of each of them and her lips curved. Excellent.

"Thank you."

She adjusted her own hat, checking for any wayward curls as she made her way over. While she approached, one man stood, his seat directly across from the boy. Perfect. Without asking, she slid into the empty chair.

"You're not done, are you?" Josephine pulled out her money bag and set a small pile onto the table in front of her. Small, yet big enough to tempt several of the men to place bets, including the boy.

She fell into her familiar routine, making small bets in the beginning of the round, losing more than she won as she counted the cards. Then, toward the end, as the number of remaining cards dwindled, she struck hard, betting big and winning several hands. One by one, the other men dropped out, until it was just her and the boy.

Only a handful of cards remained, and after counting his remaining coins, she set an equal amount out. He scowled, but followed suit. The dealer dealt their first cards.

A nine.

A four.

She pressed her tongue against the back of her teeth. Not ideal. The boy's face hadn't changed, but chances were high he was closer. She would have to risk another card and pray it wasn't the remaining 10 or face.

She nodded and the dealer slid one over.

Six.

Her breath blew out.

He noticed. His jaw ticced, but he nodded for another card. When he lifted the corner, his eyes pressed shut. Josephine didn't need to see his hand. He'd gone over.

"I'm out." He wiped his face and Josephine couldn't help feeling a little sorry for taking all his money. She'd never set out to deliberately ruin someone before. A quick count confirmed she'd likely just swindled him out of more than he would be getting paid for his job. It explained how much he was sweating.

"No, you're not."

He scowled. "I assure you, I've nothing left."

"Sure you do." She let her smile build slowly. "Your job"

His eyes widened. "Hell no."

She shrugged, then pushed all her winnings to the center and nodded at the table. "There are enough cards for one more hand. You and me. All or nothing."

The flame from the nearest lantern glistened in his eyes and he swallowed. The amount there had to be five times what he'd lost. He counted it. Counted again. Shook his head. "I can't"

"Suit yourself." She slowly wrapped her hands around the stacks of coins and pulled them her way. A look of anguish crossed his face as she let one stack topple, the tinkling of coins rising over the tavern noise.

"Wait."

She grinned. Greed always won.

The man dealing pulled her coins back to the center and gave the boy an expectant look. "What can you put down as collateral for your unconventional bet?"

He pulled out a crumpled piece of paper and smoothed it out. Neat handwriting scrawled across it. *Cabin Boy. USS Tempest.*

Josephine's pulse picked up. The remaining cards posed a risk. But it was one she had to take. He would not be staying for another game.

The dealer pushed a card her way and she lifted the corner. A face. She forced her expression to remain unreadable as she considered the unplayed cards. A ten, nine, eight, four and three. From the boy's narrowed eyes, she'd wager he'd gotten one of the lower ones.

The dealer slid another card over, his eyes gleaming in the firelight. An eight.

Eighteen.

She tapped the table, holding.

Her opponent signaled for another. Too quickly. If he held the four and three, nothing left could carry him past her. His lips pressed together as he looked at his card and held. At the dealer's nod, they showed their hands.

She was right,

He turned over the four, three, and ten. She'd beat him by one.

She stood and took the coins and paper. "We can go over details outside."

His lips pulled into a snarl. "If you mean to rob me, I've nothing left."

A snort left her before she could stop it. "Do I truly look like I could overtake you?"

He crossed his arms. "I can tell you all you need to know in here."

"No offense, but do you trust these men to speak freely about a US Navy mission in front of them?" She let her gaze roam over each of the men sitting at the table.

He harrumphed but stood and started toward the door. "Not like I know anything." She followed him outside and once they got several paces away, he turned. "What do you want to know?"

Her heart raced. What indeed? She had no inkling of what a cabin boy's duties would be. "Well, I'll need any information given to you about the job."

"I'm to be a cabin boy. On the *USS Tempest*. It leaves at dawn."

She swallowed at the flippant offer of common knowledge. She needed more than that. "How do you board? Surely this paper isn't the only thing I need? You must have signed some orders."

He looked at her as if she'd sprouted an extra head. "I'm not a navy sailor. The lieutenant asked for a cabin boy, I was available and told him I'd take the job."

"But anyone could say they were you. It doesn't seem like him to be so lax."

Now, he shrugged. "You should be glad. Isn't that the point of you being able to take my position?"

It couldn't be so easy. "So, you just walk up, wave the paper, and say, 'Hello, I'm the cabin boy?'"

"He took down my name."

She sighed. "Which is?"

"Jack Barlow"

"Alright, I board the ship, then what do I do?"

"Have you truly not done this before?" He shook his head and laughed. "You're going to make a complete blunder of this."

She wanted to throw her hands in the air. "Why else do you think I'm asking you?"

"You'll get on and head down to the berth deck where you'll take a hammock. Then, you'll make yourself useful. Usually, I end up helping the cook and scrubbing the decks. It's a navy ship so you'll be doing a lot of that. Of course, your main job is to make sure the lieutenant stays comfortable. Bring his meals, do his laundry. Maybe he'll want you to help dress him like a valet."

Her stomach twisted and heat flamed across her cheeks. Dear God, she hoped he wouldn't. She blew out a breath. It would be fine. No need to keep up the ruse for more than a day at most. Just long enough to be far enough out that he wouldn't return her.

"Why?" Jack frowned at her unease. "Why do you want this job so bad?"

Suspicion filled his eyes and her mind raced to find an answer.

If he suspected her of having ill intentions, he might very well alert the lieutenant's men and ruin everything.

"My father is sick, so I need to work. But, I've no experience. After this job, I'm sure I'll be able to find a ship willing to hire me on full time."

He scowled. "Probably for the best. No one in their right mind wants to go after that pirate they're hunting. Heard he's real nasty."

"Well, the lieutenant already bested him once, so I have faith he can do so again."

With a shrug, he turned. "I'd rather not tempt fate."

Josephine stood still as he walked away. Her palm drifted over her bulging pocket and she chewed her cheek. "Jack, wait." She hurried to catch up, pulling out a handful of coins. While she wished she could give all the winnings to him, if she did, he'd be suspicious.

"Here." She handed them over. "A token of appreciation."

He paused, but relief filled his eyes as he took them. "What's your name, by the way?"

She grinned. "Why, don't you know? Jack Barlow."

A chuckle answered her cheeky response and he dipped his head. "Maybe you'll pull this off after all."

"Oh, one last thing." Her hand remained extended. "I need your hat."

THE WINDOW CREAKED as Josephine climbed in. Her eyes darted to Abigail's bed, only to find it empty. Ice slid through her veins. What if she'd told her father? Earlier that night, when Josephine had walked in disguised in breeches and a men's shirt, Abigail had nearly fainted and tried to make her stay. She cursed having to use the window, but the tree outside made getting in and out of the house easy. A scrape came from the corner and she spun.

"You gave me a start, even knowing you'd still be dressed in that ridiculous boy clothing." Abigail rubbed her eyes from where she stood in front of a plush armchair near the fireplace. "Thank heavens you're alright. I've been worried sick."

Relief rushed through Josephine and she strode forward. "I need your help."

Her friend frowned. "Why do I have a bad feeling I'm not going to like what you're about to ask me to do?"

Josephine waved a hand. "Oh, don't worry, I just need you to watch Lola while I'm gone."

"And where are you going?"

"I'm taking the place of Lieutenant Caldwell's cabin boy."

The gasp Abigail let out could have raised the dead. "Why?"

"Ever since I first moved to Tortuga, I've hoped for an adventure. Going on a pirate hunt would be the adventure of a lifetime. Samantha is going, so why shouldn't I?"

"Samantha has Christian to protect her." After a long pause, her friend's eyes widened. "This is because of the lieutenant, isn't it? You want to use it as an excuse to spend more time in his company."

Josephine pulled her lip between her teeth. Deep inside, her heart betrayed her, thudding in agreement to the accusation. "I don't know. Maybe. My father wants me to marry an old merchant. One I've hardly ever even spoken to. When I met the lieutenant, I felt something. Something I've never felt before."

"Just because you felt something doesn't give you license to act so foolishly. It's a terrible plan. You're only going to make him mad at you. And then you'll be stuck on a ship with him." Abigail shuddered.

"I know, I know." Josephine looked over her shoulder at the open window. "I can't explain it, but I feel certain I'm meant to go."

"Or, you could stay here with me until Lieutenant Caldwell returns and win his attention the traditional way."

"If I wait, I might miss my chance entirely. He wrote to my

father, which means I won't have very long before I have to go back to Tortuga. Besides, didn't you tell me about all the women who have tried and failed to catch his eye the traditional way?"

Her friend threw up her arms. "Why the lieutenant? You danced with several young men tonight that are infinitely better choices than him."

Josephine paused. "If I go back to Tortuga, I'll never know if something could have come from it. It will drive me mad."

Abigail's shoulders slumped in defeat. "Fine. But don't make me say I told you so."

With a squeal, Josephine rushed forward to embrace her friend. "Thank you." She turned and headed to her room. "I must pack quickly, I haven't much time to get down to the docks."

Abigail nodded. "I'll gather some things for you as well."

Josephine made quick work of repacking her things. A pirate hunt. A shiver ran down her spine. She would be safe with the lieutenant. He had over a hundred well trained men and a heavily armed ship. Besides, Samantha had said Thorne would probably be long gone by the time they got there.

Abigail walked in with an armful of items. "Here, if you're going to woo your lieutenant, these might help." She passed over a bundle of ribbons, a pretty yellow dress and a bottle of perfume before looking her up and down. She shook her head. "How is it that I end up with all the unconventional friends?"

Josephine's smile widened as she finished packing and slung the bag over her shoulder. "I hope I get to meet those friends." She walked over to where Lola slept and stroked the soft feathers on her back. "You be good for Abigail."

She hugged her friend. "Thank you. I look forward to telling you all about my adventures."

Abigail gave an uneasy smile. "Promise me you'll be careful."
"I will."

Moments later, she hopped to the ground. She waved to Abigail and slung the pack over her shoulder. The walk back into town took over an hour, and by the time the tall masts of the

Tempest came into view, sweat dripped down Josephine's back.

She pulled out the slip of paper and started down to the docks. Only a few men walked up the gangplank and she quickened her pace. Wouldn't do to be late.

The man at the bottom was not the first officer who had discovered her ruse in Tortuga. Thank heavens. She hurried over and presented the paper to the sailor. He gave her a bored look. "Cabin boy, I suppose?"

She nodded and lowered her voice. "Jack Barlow."

He grunted and waved her on. "Best hurry. We sail within the hour."

Each step up the ramp sent her pulse racing faster. This was it. She was going on a pirate hunt. A thrill ran through her, even as a heavy weight settled within her. Somehow, she needed to convince all these men she knew what she was doing.

Another sailor who had boarded ahead of her headed down a hatch with a rucksack over his shoulder. She followed, climbing down a ladder to the berth deck. Men in uniform secured polished cannons with thick ropes. One more hatch and ladder took her into the berth deck. A whole slew of sailors wrapped their belongings into hammocks, conversing in loud voices. She picked her way over trunks and rucksacks, until she found an unclaimed hammock in the middle.

"A cabin boy?" One of the nearby men approached her. "I thought the lieutenant didn't run a boy on his ship?"

She began to roll her bag into the hammock. "He must have changed his mind."

Another one joined in. "You don't look like you belong on a navy ship."

She shrugged, and they returned to their previous conversation.

"And then, she spread her legs and invited me over. Best night of my life."

Good grief. She bent her head to hide her blush.

"I heard the taverns in Wilmington are full of good doxys."

"Sure are. Plenty to go around for all."

One of the men punched her shoulder. "What about you, lad? Have you put your rigging to good use yet, or are you still green?"

Josephine's eyes widened at the crude question and heat flamed across her cheeks as his meaning hit her. The man laughed at her obvious discomfort. "That's too bad. Mayhap we'll take you to a brothel ashore and we can treat you to your first. It's how most of us gained our experience."

"And still do!" Another voice chimed in, prompting a chorus of laughter.

Good Lord. Men were pigs. Rutting pigs.

She did not—could not—answer and turned her back to them, pretending to unpack some things into the hammock.

As the sailors secured their own hammocks and left to start work on the decks above, Josephine stared at the wood boards beneath her feet. Did Lieutenant Caldwell visit brothels like his men? Her stomach gave an uncomfortable lurch as she pictured him with a busty woman who looked an awful lot like Colette. She shook the image from her head. No, he was a respectable man.

Another image flashed. This time it was definitely Colette, standing with her arms crossed. Josephine could almost hear her voice. *Oh, you poor naive thing.*

Chapter Eleven

THE RIVER LAY like glass, smooth and undisturbed, catching the first pale light of the sun as Isaac lifted a tin mug of bitter coffee to his lips. Dawn held a special reverence in his heart. The sun's unhurried ascent into the sky made the minutes stretch longer than they should, giving the sense one could accomplish anything. Dusk was crueler—the sun racing for the horizon, laying waste to well-intentioned plans before they could come to fruition.

Soon, the deck would be alive with boots and voices, with orders barked and sails snapping. The stillness would shatter. But for now, he let it linger, savoring the fleeting quiet before the day made its demands. And demand it would. His face hardened as he stared out over the water.

Somewhere out there, Thorne sailed. And if Isaac had his way, their paths would cross. Many things would have to fall into place before then, though. The first of which was sailing to Wilmington with great haste. The sooner they got there, the sooner they would be able to find out what the pirate searched for.

Thorne's cold disconnection from the world around him made him a dangerous enemy. He didn't behave like any foe Isaac had ever faced before. Hell, he'd nearly killed his own son without so much as blinking an eye. No matter what drove him to such madness, he belonged behind bars, where he could never terrorize innocent lives again.

For now, Christian remained committed to the same outcome. As long as he wasn't the one making the arrest, he could handle his father's fate. Or so he claimed. Isaac's gaze shifted to the *Red Siren*, Christian and Samantha's schooner. Their efficient crew already had the sails unfurled, ready to tie down.

"We're ready to sail." As if summoned by his thoughts, Christian climbed up the steps to the forecastle and Isaac had to blink.

He'd become so accustomed to calling Christian lieutenant, that the change still shocked him. Gone was the sharp cut of a navy uniform and the crisp posture of a man who could command an entire ship without saying a word. Now, his friend stood easier, his shoulders looser, the perpetual tightness in his jaw eased as though a weight had been lifted. And yet, there were moments—like now, when his gaze swept the deck—that the old lieutenant flickered through, ever sharp-eyed and assessing.

Isaac glanced down to the dock where a wagonful of water barrels had just arrived. "The last of our supplies are being loaded now."

A grin spread across Christian's face. "We've been loaded for the better part of the last hour. What's taking your men so long?"

"Come now, with twice the men, I'd say we're making better time than you."

Christian winked. "We'll see who's faster at sea. Maybe I'll leave you behind and do all the interviewing without you."

Isaac couldn't help his smile. "Well, wouldn't that be great? Just give me the location of Thorne and I won't have to waste any time on shore. Sounds like a dream."

The mention of his father wiped the grin from his friend's face, and he twisted to look back toward the *Siren*. "Jesting aside, I'm glad to sail alongside you. You'll have our unwavering support in all things."

Isaac didn't miss Christian's meaning. The Thompson crew had been one of Samantha's uncle's finest. The merchant had been hiding his involvement in piracy for years, right under everyone's noses. It meant his men were well-trained and disciplined. Having their help during any battle would be invaluable.

"Well, what are you waiting for? By the time you get back on the *Siren*, we'll be pushing off."

With one more wink, Christian left him, and Silas jogged up the stairs. "We're ready, Captain."

Isaac stood at the quarterdeck's railing, staring down the expanse of the main deck. A sharp edge of anticipation curled within his chest as he gripped the rail with steady hands. Beneath the surface calm, his gut tightened, same as it always did when taking to sea. Part reverence, part exhilaration—a primal thrill he suspected would never fade.

"Cast off the bow and stern lines!" His command carried through the heavy morning air. "Ease her off the dock!"

At once, the crew leapt into action. Ropes slapped against the timbers as the dock lines were freed and heaved aboard. The *Tempest* drifted slightly, vibrating with her new freedom.

Isaac turned toward Silas, who stood at the wheel. "Ahead slow. Bring her into the current."

"Aye, sir." His first officer handled the wheel with practiced ease.

The sails snapped free and billowed in the slight breeze, and the ship caught the wind, her bow slicing through the dark water as she pulled from the docks. Gradually, their speed increased, and he couldn't help looking back. Even with their head start, the *Siren* followed closely in their wake. Moments later, she passed them in the narrow channel. Christian gave a cheerful wave from his spot at the helm.

"Not so fast," Isaac muttered. He lifted his eyes to the yards, where crewmen still fastened lines. "More sail. Shake out the topsails!"

"I certainly hope the entire trip is not made into a race." Silas's dry comment brought Isaac's attention back.

He clapped the first officer's shoulder. "That, officer, is not a bad idea."

To port, the city gradually fell away, replaced with wide

expanses of reeds and sawgrass. As they passed Hutchinson's Island, the sluggish current tugged at the hull. Silt and sandbars lurked beneath the surface, shifting with every tide. Isaac scanned the water for telltale swirls hinting at hidden shoals. Beyond Elba Island, the waterway widened, most of the threats disappearing, and he let out a breath, fixing his eyes on the horizon where the river gave herself to the sea. The wind, unshackled by the narrow banks, filled the sails and the *Tempest* surged forward with new purpose.

Once they passed the Tybee Island lighthouse and the *Tempest* cleared the last of the sandbars, Isaac went below to his cabin. With effortless precision, he unbuckled his sword belt, gently setting the leather scabbard on his desk. Sinking into the chair, he spread a navigational map out and retrieved his instruments from a drawer. His fingers traced up through the inlets of the Carolinas. With practiced precision, he measured the distance, using his brass divider to mark the nautical miles. He marked the spot they should be by midafternoon and charted their course from there—a steady northeast tack hugging the coastline, where they would benefit from the prevailing winds.

Leaning back, he pulled his sword free, the steel glistening even in the dim light of the cabin. He ran his thumb lightly along the edge, testing its sharpness. A whetstone lay in his top drawer and he removed it, drawing it across the blade in a familiar rhythm. Back and forth, each pass smoothed invisible nicks away.

A soft knock came from his door and he paused as the cabin boy entered with a tray of food. The boy kept his head down and approached in silence. He extended the tray and faltered, silverware clattering while water sloshed over the edge of a full goblet. Isaac bit back a curse as some dripped onto the map.

"I'm sorry, sir." The slightest hint of an accent laced the boy's soft words as he used his sleeve to wipe up the mess before it could soak into the linen-backed paper. Something familiar, yet he couldn't quite place it.

"Jack, isn't it?"

All he got was a quick nod in return as the boy turned and hurried from the cabin. Shy, then—or perhaps had worked under harsh captains before. No matter, after a few days, he would come out of his shell. Isaac turned back to his sword, wiping it with an oiled cloth before sliding it back into its scabbard.

His gaze drifted to the window, where golden sunlight filtered through the panes. His mind wandered—back to the island, to the wild beauty beneath the waterfall's rush. To a peach pressed to supple lips, juice flowing down bronzed skin. Her image came unbidden, an unwelcome visitor to his thoughts, yet in the solitude of his cabin, he found himself unwilling to cast her out. A silent surrender to a temptation he dared not name.

ISAAC STRETCHED HIS arms above his head after he climbed from the main hatch. His rest had done him well. Now for four hours at the helm. He glanced off the port side, where the *Siren* had taken the lead a few hundred yards out. Close enough for him to see copper hair billowing from behind the wheel. Though most men would scoff at the idea of letting Samantha captain a ship, Isaac knew better than anyone how adept she was at it. Hell, she could probably outperform half his men—on the water and with a blade.

He slowed as he passed a group of men polishing the deck, brushes sweeping rhythmically against the planks. The new cabin boy hunched over a spot, scrubbing with a desperate fervor. The boy seemed smaller, frailer, than he had come across in the tavern the night before. Now, he struggled under the weight of a simple task. Isaac's brow furrowed. The kid had probably lied about his age—and experience.

He nearly stopped to question him, but after a sigh, continued. Even if the boy admitted it, what option was there? Wasn't like he would toss the lad into the brig. Up on the quarterdeck, he took the wheel from Silas.

His first officer flexed his hands, rubbing them on his breeches. "She's under too much strain. Best to slow our pace."

Isaac glanced up at the sails, billowing in the rushing wind. The massive canvas sheets stretched taut, humming under the pressure. Still, considering the steady breeze and calm surf, she would be fine—was built to withstand much worse.

He shook his head. "Let's take advantage of these conditions and make as much distance as we can. I'll have the men shorten the sails before my watch is up." Silas gave a single nod and headed down to take his rest.

Isaac fixed his eyes on the horizon, but his thoughts refused to stay on course, despite his best efforts. Each time he closed his eyes, he saw *her*. Though his palm rested against the spoke, he could almost feel the subtle tremble in her fingers as he had led Miss Montclair around the dance floor. The light scent of her hair, something floral, clung to him like a ghost. He'd meant to keep his distance, meant to follow Christian away. Yet something about her had tugged on him, like the pull of a full moon's tide. And he'd asked for the dance.

He shouldn't have.

The shape of her waist beneath his palm, the pulsing warmth of the curve there, all burned into his memory. Something about the wonder in her eyes as she experienced the party, her unfettered enjoyment, had softened his usual disdain for such events. She hadn't wanted to say goodbye. Truth be told, he hadn't either.

He exhaled sharply, forcing his grip on the wheel to tighten, the rough wood biting into his palms. It didn't matter. She was back in Savannah now, far removed from this deck and foolish thoughts. He had left her behind, just as he should have. And yet, the memory clung to him like sea mist, refusing to drift away. With a scowl, he turned his eyes back to the sails, determined to let the wind carry her from his mind.

His skin prickled, the weight of someone's gaze pressing on

him, and he turned. The cabin boy ducked his head, returning to his work, his face cloaked in the shadows from his brimmed hat. The wind gusted across the deck, pressing Jack's shirt around his frame, highlighting a curved waist. Isaac gritted his teeth and dragged his gaze away. Ridiculous. Now he was seeing things.

A sudden crack echoed across the ship and Isaac's heart leapt to his throat, his hands tightening around the spokes. His gaze darted to the deck just in time to see a young crewman knocked off his feet as a thick line snapped across the deck like a whip, striking him hard across the chest. He tumbled, landing hard against the railing, his body crumpling in a heap.

"Damn it!" Isaac spun hard starboard to take pressure off the sails.

The wheel groaned under the force, the ship's heavy rudder straining against the current. A heartbeat later, the vessel heeled sharply, tilting as the bow swung to the right. An odd silence fell over the deck as the rushing wind slowed. The crew stood in shock as crimson blossomed across the sailor's chest. Tightness clawed at Isaac's gut as the man lay motionless.

"Get the surgeon's kit!" he barked, but before anyone could respond, a small figure darted across the deck—a blur of motion amid the chaos. The cabin boy. Jack dropped to his knees beside the injured man, reaching for the wound. His hands were steady, his focus unshaken, even as blood pooled beneath the sailor.

Isaac gritted his teeth as tension vibrated through the wheel, the ship already fighting his sudden change in course. "Steady," he muttered, willing her into submission.

The crew scrambled, one pulling a bucket of fresh sea water up, another darting below deck. Jack had torn a strip from the prone sailor's shirt and pressed hard on his chest. The doctor appeared at last, moving quickly toward the scene, though the cabin boy had already done much to stem the bleeding. The sailor's arm lifted, grasping at the wound.

Isaac finally allowed himself a breath, but his mind didn't settle. Jack still knelt, his hands working with a confidence that struck Isaac as… odd, considering his interactions with the boy thus far. He loosened his grip on the wheel, letting the ship slide back into the wind. Two crew members carried the wounded man down below, while the cabin boy stared after them, wringing his hands. After a few moments, he returned to his spot on the deck, picking up a brush and scrubbing the boards with fresh vengeance.

Isaac couldn't help but chuckle. Maybe he had been wrong. Awkward or not, Jack at least had a steady head. And that would serve him well on board the *Tempest*.

Chapter Twelve

BEING A CABIN boy was hard.

Correction: being a cabin boy was one of the worst ideas Josephine had ever come up with. Her back ached from lugging buckets of water and scrubbing the already polished deck on her hands and knees. Her nose burned from cleaning the head, where not one, but three men had taken a piss in front of her. And her eyes still stung from spending an hour chopping onions in the galley—at least she could use that as an excuse if anyone asked why they watered now.

She shielded said eyes from the sun as she stared high up into the rigging, where she was expected to go up and replace a line that had come loose from its pulley. Easy, the sailor next to her had said. Just climb up to the topmast yard and put it back. Never mind the pitch of the ship on the swells along with the whipping wind or that the pulley was at the very end of the yardarm. She scowled. Jack hadn't mentioned this particular part of the job.

"Any day now, boy." The sailor untied a clewline and gave it a slap. "Can't adjust the sail until it's fixed. Wind's changing and the lieutenant won't be happy if we waste time."

Her eyes darted to the quarterdeck where Lieutenant Caldwell and his first officer stood at the wheel. If she delayed much longer, he might come down to investigate. With a deep breath, she set a hand on the shroud and pulled herself up. Hand over hand, she ascended using the ratlines, trying to ignore the wind pushing against her. After what seemed an eternity, she passed the main yard.

A few more minutes of careful climbing and she reached the topmast yard. The *Tempest* tipped down a swell and her heart leaped into her throat. She kept her face averted, but her body still went tense.

The wind hummed through the rigging around her and she tightened her grip. From this angle, she couldn't even find the pulley amidst the maze of ropes. Which one was the clewline? The sailor below shouted something, but the rushing air blurred his words. He slapped the line again and she followed its length to where it came to the yard. There. It flopped against an empty pulley. Her gut twisted. How in heaven's name was she supposed to reach it?

Earlier, she'd watched sailors unfurl the sails after they climbed out on narrow footropes swinging below the yards to release the sheets. With a swallow, she reached out to grab a guide rope and slowly extended a foot. She had to swing herself off the ratline and her stomach hit the yardarm with a solid *thump*. Once both feet balanced on the footrope, she began edging out.

She had made it a few steps out when a strong gust of wind whipped against her and swung her feet out, nearly making her lose her grip on the yardarm. *Don't look down. Don't Look down.*

She looked down.

Her stomach gave a violent lurch and she wrapped her arms around the yardarm. She'd never been this high above anything in her life. Tears sprung to the corners of her eyes, pinpoints of wet heat that dissipated almost instantly in the wind. She couldn't do this. Damn what anyone below said.

Though steps away, the mainmast seemed impossibly far. Panic clawed at her gut and everything around her began to spin. She took one small unsteady step toward the mast. Another. Her hand slid along the top of the yardarm, reaching for the next handhold of rope just beyond reach. She blinked to try and steady her swirling vision. The ship shuddered as it crashed down a swell, the impact vibrating through the wood beneath her fingers, and she lunged for the rope.

Her fingers closed around thin air. For an agonizing second, her nails dug into the yardarm, trying to stop her wild movement. But the smooth wood didn't yield and her hand slipped free.

A scream wrenched from her throat as she pitched backward. With arms flailing, she fell, the world around her flipping upside down. A horrible dizziness filled her as she plummeted. She pressed her eyes shut, but her body jerked to a stop when her ankle somehow twisted in the footline, the thick strands of the rope biting into her flesh.

She swayed with the movement of the ship, muffled shouts from the deck barely registering in her mind. Her foot began to slip and she whimpered. She was going to die.

"Hold still!" A commanding voice floated above the roar in her ears.

Lieutenant Caldwell.

As if she could do anything other than hang, helpless. Would he curse her name when he examined her broken body? She bent her neck to find him and her foot slipped even more. With a squeak, she held her breath as pain radiated through her leg. Any second now—there'd be no saving herself.

"Quickly. Grab ahold."

She blinked as a rope fell in front of her face. How had the lieutenant climbed so fast?

With blood pounding in her head, Josephine wrapped her fingers around the oiled cords, and he began pulling her up. As soon as his grip closed around her wrist, her muscles went slack. He guided her hand to the yardarm and it took her a moment to make her fingers work enough to grasp the rope handhold. She sucked in several deep breaths, willing her racing heart to slow as he bent to untangle her foot.

"You're lucky, Jack."

He hadn't recognized her.

Yet.

A few expert twists of his hand and her throbbing foot slipped free. She shimmied to the mainmast, keeping her face turned from him. "Thank you," she mumbled, twisting to grab the shroud.

"Wait."

She ignored his order and started down, sending up silent thanks her pins had somehow held her hat in place. Faster than she could have thought possible, she scrambled down the ratlines, missing a few and burning her hands on the ropes. When her feet hit the deck, a tendril of hair fell from her hat alongside her face.

"Boy!" The lieutenant's voice sliced through the air only a few feet above her.

Oh no. She couldn't face him, not on the main deck. Spinning, she ignored the stabs of pain shooting up her leg and darted toward the main hatch. Sailors stared from their cannons as she flew by and flung herself down the ladder to the berth deck. She didn't make it far before a loud thump announced the lieutenant's arrival.

"Stop!"

She grimaced but obeyed his shout as he strode over in several long strides. "What happened up there?"

With her face down, she shook her head. What happened indeed. She wasn't even sure. The panic she'd felt earlier began to return as a vision of the deck swaying far below flashed across her mind.

"On shore, you assured me you had experience. It's clear you were lying. By doing so, you put more than just yourself at risk."

She nodded.

"Look at me and give me a proper answer. This is a naval ship and you will behave accordingly." He barked his words out, each one laced with authority.

With a swallow, she lifted her head until his face became visible beneath the brim of her hat. "Yes, sir."

"That's better. Now..." His voice trailed off and his eyes narrowed as a flash of recognition crossed his face. "So help me God."

Josephine took a step back as he reached for her. Another. Her back bumped into the wall and she spun to flee. Strong fingers clasped her arm, yanking her to a stop. Drat. She'd hoped to make it until nightfall before revealing her identity. Surely, he wouldn't turn back now though. Not with the information he had on Thorne's attack propelling the ships forward at breakneck speed.

He grabbed her hat and threw it to the floor, the pins finally meeting their match.

She swallowed as a flurry of different emotions ran across his face in quick succession—lips parted in shock, furrowed brow of confusion, then the ice of anger coloring his eyes.

"God's blood." He pressed his lips together and stared hard at her. "Where is Jack?"

"I didn't kill him, if that's what you're asking." Josephine mustered a shaky smile. "Please don't be angry."

He blinked. Opened his mouth. Closed it when a strangled laugh bubbled forth. "Oh, don't worry, Miss Montclair, I'm not angry."

Despite knowing better, lightness filled her chest. "You're not?"

"No." His fingers tightened around her arm. "I'm furious."

Understandable. "I'm really sorry—"

"Sorry? You nearly killed yourself!"

She winced. "I didn't mean to."

He pulled his hat free and dragged his fingers through his hair, an incredulous look etched onto his face. "I highly doubt anyone goes up into the rigging meaning to die."

She chewed on her bottom lip, trying to find something to say that would soothe his temper.

"Why?" He pressed two fingers to his temple. "Why are you here?"

Josephine retrieved her hat and pulled out the pins holding her hair up. "I wanted to join your adventure."

His gaze burned like a brand, unblinking and cold. "Adventure? You think that's what this is? It's a naval mission. A dangerous one with no room for civilians—something I thought I made abundantly clear the other night."

"I promise I'll stay out of the way. You won't even know I'm here."

He shook his head. "You're right. Because you're going over to the *Red Siren*. Now. And you will stay there until Christian and Samantha can take you home."

"But—"

He lifted a hand. "Don't say another word. I'm in no mood to argue right now, Miss Montclair. Get your things."

She retrieved her rolled up hammock and followed him up to the main deck where he barked orders to his shocked first officer to call the *Siren* over. Minutes stretched by as curious crew gathered round. She pushed her hair behind an ear and refused to make eye contact with anyone, especially the man standing rigid next to her.

Mr. Thompson guided the schooner close, his lips twisted in wry amusement. Josephine took a few steps toward the railing. The slap of waves between the hulls drew her gaze down and she swallowed. How was she supposed to get over to the *Red Siren*? Her eyes scanned the deck, but her heart fell when Samantha was nowhere to be found.

A shadow flashed across the deck, accompanied by the whistle of a rope cutting through the air, and a thump came from behind them. Josephine spun with a gasp as a form rose from a crouch.

"Samantha?" The name came out in a croak as she stared. Gone was the periwinkle dress. Instead, Mr. Thompson's wife stood in skintight leather breeches with a ruffled white blouse tucked in, showcasing curves any woman would be envious of. Her flaming hair blew loose in the wind under a cavalier hat with a jaunty red feather. A rapier hung from a belt at her waist.

Josephine blinked. Samantha looked like...

She looked like a pirate. Her lips curved as she set a hand on her hip. "I knew I'd like you, Miss Montclair."

With eyes still wide, Josephine stepped forward. "You…" She glanced toward the *Siren*, where Mr. Thomspon stood, overseeing his crew as they fastened ropes between the two ships. "He… How?"

"I prefer dressing like this while at sea. It's much more practical, especially in that it allows for more movement in battle."

Isaac scowled. "Do not give her any ideas, she's troublesome enough as it is."

"Of course, Lieutenant." Samantha winked at Josephine. "Let's get back to the ship before we upset him further."

The crew had slung a rope ladder across the gap between the vessels and Josephine gulped. Lieutenant Caldwell waved her forward. She paused at the railing, panic rearing in her once more.

He cleared his throat. "Make it quick, Miss Montclair, we must be on our way."

She reached out and took the rope but as soon as her fingers closed around it, she froze. A hand settled on her shoulder and she jumped as Samantha pulled her back.

"Good heavens, Isaac. No need to be a bully after what just happened." Samantha shot him a dirty look and stepped past Josephine out onto the rope ladder. "Take both sides and follow me. As long as you hold on to the ropes, you'll be just fine. I'll be right here to help you."

Josephine swallowed, but Samantha's ease helped her take the first step. Though the ladder swayed with the ships, she held tight and focused on getting her feet on each thin wooden rung. Samantha stayed one step ahead of her, encouraging her, until toward the end, a small smile tugged her lips. Not so terrible after all.

Once her feet landed on the deck, the lines were swiftly untied, and the sails unfurled. The ship eased into motion as wind filled the sheets, the mainmast creaking as the schooner turned to open sea.

Mr. Thompson strode down from the quarterdeck. "What were you thinking going up into the rigging? You could have been killed."

Josephine winced and Samantha swatted his arm. "Oh, don't be crabby. I'm sure Isaac already gave her an earful."

Mr. Thompson glanced behind them, where the *Tempest* had begun to catch up. "Twice in a row. I dare say you've put him into quite the mood."

Josephine rubbed the toe of her boot into the wood decking. "He's quite upset."

Mr. Thompson chuckled and glanced at Samantha, his eyes softening. "Wounded pride will cause people to say things they normally wouldn't. If it makes you feel better, I can vouch for his character. He's a good man."

Josephine couldn't help a small smile. "I knew that the day I met him. Unfortunately, I'm fairly certain he never wants to see me again."

"I'm sure he'll come around." Samantha patted her shoulder. "Let's get you into my cabin. I'll move Christian's things out and you and I will share it."

"Oh, please don't do that. I don't want to inconvenience you two."

"Don't worry yourself. You'll be safest there." Mr. Thompson dipped his head. "And please, call me Christian."

Samantha led her to the main cabin. "I'm going to go help. Why don't you get yourself situated? Feel free to change, or not." She winked.

Josephine paused with her hand on one of the carved doors. "You help out on the ship?"

Samantha's lips curved. "But of course. It is my ship after all."

"Yours?"

"It was a wedding gift from Christian." With another grin, she spun and headed toward the quarterdeck.

When the door shut, Josephine dropped her rolled up hammock. Sunlight streamed through windows along one wall of the spacious room, glistening from oiled floorboards. The pleasant scent of lemon filled the air and she walked over to a wall of built-in shelving. An extraordinary collection of shells lined two of the shelves, and Josephine couldn't help reaching out to pick up a few.

The carved desk in the center of the cabin drew her attention and she stepped over. Two large chairs were pushed in, one on either side. A double set of maps and navigational instruments were laid out. Her lips parted. Samantha didn't only own the ship, it looked as though she and her husband split captaining duties. Fascinating.

She grinned at the differences between both sides of the desk. On one side, items laid in disarray, the bent corners of the topmost map weighed down by shells. The other, everything lined up neatly, maps crisp and flat. Her hand drifted forward to brush the cool brass of a weathered compass. A stack of paper, tied together with twine, sat directly in the middle of the maps with a single word scrawled across it: *Thorne.*

She glanced between the desk and the doors. Snooping in the Thompsons' paperwork was the last thing she should do. Still, the chance to know more about what they were heading into pulled at her. *Not now.* With a swallow, she turned to her hammock and began unpacking her things. Plenty of time to learn more during the rest of the journey.

Josephine leaned against the railing on the quarterdeck where the lights of Wilmington stretched before her. She glanced up to the crow's nest, where Samantha had climbed as soon as they had tied up to the dock. With a shudder, she lowered her gaze. Not a spot she would ever be inclined to visit.

Masculine voices floated up and she edged toward the rail overlooking the main deck. Her heart skipped a beat when the lieutenant came into view, standing next to Christian.

"I want to go ashore now, before word spreads that the Navy has arrived. If there's any smugglers or pirates around, they will clear out by tomorrow." Lieutenant Caldwell strode to the railing. "I know you want to interview survivors, but if we go to a tavern without announcing who we are, we may be able to glean important information from those sorts. The attack happened right off shore here, so it's possible Thorne or his men visited the town."

"I suppose it won't hurt. I'll have to change into something more casual." Christian looked the lieutenant up and down. "So will you."

With a nod, the lieutenant turned and headed toward the gangplank. "I'll meet you in a quarter hour."

After Christian descended below deck, Josephine gave one last look up the main mast, then made her way to the cabin. If the last day and a half had given any indication, Samantha would stay up there for over an hour. Watching her captain the ship had been a treat. The men listened to her as well as they did Christian, and Samantha knew everything about the *Siren*, never faltering in her instructions to the crew.

In the cabin, she passed the hammock she'd hung from the rafters and sank into a chair at the desk. The stack of parchment from yesterday had disappeared when Christian had retrieved his things. Should have looked when she had the chance. Never mind. Tonight, while the men were ashore, she'd ask Samantha to tell her everything.

Meanwhile, she should get to work on the letter she'd decided to write. If the lieutenant could send her father a missive, so could she. Perhaps she could convince him to let her stay with the Ross family longer. Not likely, but she had to try.

She eased open a drawer, looking for fresh parchment. Nothing but a knife and logbook. The next drawer revealed a few blank sheets and she grinned. As she lifted the top one, her fingers shifted the stack and a string of twine peeked out. She paused.

Could it be? Pushing the sheets back, her pulse jumped. It was.

Pulling the stack free, she set it on the desk in front of her. With a hurried look behind her at the closed doors, she leaned forward and untied the string holding it together, shuffling through the pages within. Some had ship names and crew manifests while others had hastily written notes about eyewitness accounts of Thorne.

Brutal. Cruel. Merciless. No survivors.

She shivered at the words that seemed to repeat themselves over and over again. Another page had a sketch of a man— middle aged, prominent eyebrows, and a well-manicured beard. Handsome in a rugged way. She blinked at the words scrawled below the portrait.

Captain Thorne.

She'd never seen him in person. Anytime his ship had sailed into the harbor in Tortuga, her father refused to let her leave the house. Not that it mattered. He rarely came ashore, sending his giants to do his business instead. Colette said she'd seen him once, that he was good looking until you saw his eyes. Soulless, she'd said—the eyes of a monster.

With a shudder, Josephine turned the page over and sucked in a breath. "What in the…"

Her fingers trembled as they slid over the paper, tracing a drawing there. She fumbled with the ribbon around her neck and pulled it over her head. The key slipped from her grasp, falling onto the page with a hollow clink. A cold dread spread through her veins, settling like a stone in her heart.

The drawing matched the carving at the key's bow.

She shook her head as her eyes darted back and forth between the drawing and the key. The palm fronds. The skull. The Latin inscription. All of it the same.

An address had been written neatly below it.

15 Queen St.
Norfolk

Another line, this time words blending together with splotches of ink.

Dead end. Nothing but an empty building.

The sheet had wrinkles from being crumpled up at one point. Perhaps Mr. Thompson had meant to throw it away, but had changed his mind and returned it to the stack. Her key had something to do with all this—she could feel it in her bones, though what exactly, she had no clue. If she could find out more information, and prove she was more than just a burden, perhaps she could finally win the lieutenant's favor. With a thundering heart, she took the piece of paper and folded it, tucking it into a pocket in her skirt.

Voices came from outside and she crossed to the open window. The lieutenant and Mr. Thompson walked down the dock, and she watched them until they melded with the night's shadows. She sighed, imagining the very proper lieutenant strolling into a tavern and trying to get information. The men inside would see through him without hesitation.

People always assumed pirates were stupid. In some ways, yes, they were. But one thing was certain: a pirate would do anything to save their neck—in other words, expertise in identifying and avoiding the law practically ran through their blood.

Too bad she wasn't going along.

Her gaze settled on the wardrobe and she opened the door. Inside, Samantha's blouses hung next to a stack of haphazardly folded breeches. Stretching her hand out, she ran her fingers over the supple leather of the closest pair. A slow smile spread across her face and she pulled them free.

Chapter Thirteen

DAMNATION.

Isaac glared back at the tavern doors before setting off down the road. He hadn't gotten a single bit of information from the men inside. In fact, he'd been rather rudely escorted to the door and told to leave.

Three men stood between him and the next tavern, arguing over something. As he got closer, he realized they had surrounded a woman. A wench from the tavern perhaps?

"Leave me alone."

The words rang out over the boisterous heckling and Isaac stopped dead in his tracks.

Son of a bitch.

He knew that voice.

A sudden scuffle followed—boots scraping, a grunt, the thud of someone hitting the wall.

Then a yelp.

"Get your hands off me!" Miss Montclair's voice rang fierce but strained.

"Come now," one of the men jeered. "Join us in the alley. 'Twill only take a few moments of your time."

Isaac surged forward as the man pulled her toward the dark shadows between buildings. Moonlight reflected off the man's leering face. "She's mine first, boys."

The hell she was. Isaac flew toward him with his fist pulled back, barely coming to a stop before cracking it into the man's jaw. The satisfaction of seeing the limp body hit the ground vibrated through him as he spun to face the remaining assailants.

"What in tarnation?" One of the fallen man's friends leaped toward Isaac, shoving him violently toward the alley.

He threw his weight onto one foot and pivoted, grabbing the man's shoulder as he came at him. With a grunt, he used his attacker's momentum to propel him face-first into the brick wall of the building. He crumpled, limbs collapsing in a heap against the wall.

This was too easy.

The remaining man put his hands up. "We was just trying to have some fun. No harm."

"No harm? You were accosting a lady."

The man snorted. "She ain't no lady."

Isaac lunged toward him and the coward spun and took off running.

"Are you alright?" A hand settled on his shoulder and he spun to find Miss Montclair blinking up at him.

At least he thought it was. He fought to keep his mouth from dropping open at her transformation. *Damn it, Samantha.* Clearly she'd had a hand in this, as Miss Montclair stood in tight breeches, her blouse open in a deep V down her chest. Her hair fell in voluminous curls past her shoulder with a red canna lily tucked behind one ear.

"What the hell are you doing here? And why are you dressed like that?" He kept his eyes on her face to avoid the cleavage on full display.

"I was looking for you," she said brightly. As if it explained everything.

"My God, Miss Montclair, you could have been hurt."

Or worse. The men who had been harassing her had made their intentions clear. He shook his head to clear his mind.

"I didn't know there would be more than one tavern." She pulled her bottom lip between her teeth. "I thought you'd be inside. I was halfway through the room before I realized you weren't there."

"Do you ever stop to think things through?"

Her eyes widened at his accusation, but instead of lingering, the hurt quickly faded. She crossed her arms and opened her mouth.

He raised a hand to stop her rebuttal. "Never mind. Let's get back to the ship."

"No."

"No?" He blinked at her.

"I came to help you."

"You…" He couldn't help his strangled laugh. "Help me? Dressed like that?"

Her eyes narrowed into slits. "Yes, Lieutenant. Because while your mind cannot seem to fathom it, I assure you I am better equipped than you to get information from these sorts of men."

"Really? You could have fooled me. Because last I checked, you were about to get…" He couldn't say it aloud.

Her face paled yet she stood straight. "Nevertheless, once inside a tavern, I can find what you need."

"Miss Montclair—"

She turned and walked away. Straight to the tavern door.

"Don't even think about it." He strode toward her.

With flashing eyes, she yanked the door open and walked inside.

"Blast it." He hurried to catch up, weaving between patrons before reaching her side. Taking hold of her elbow, he pulled her close. "You've got a lot of nerve."

She beamed up at him. "Thanks. Now, stop looking so… murderous. You'll blow our cover."

"Cover? Miss Montclair, hear me well. There's no cover. We are going to turn around and head straight back to the ship."

With a shake of her head, she flipped her hair over one shoulder and turned toward the bar, a wave of jasmine washing over him. He followed, refusing to loosen his grip on her. When they reached the tall wood counter, she lifted herself on tiptoes and leaned into him, the soft weight of her hair settling on his forearm. "We are here, don't waste the opportunity to get your information."

He swallowed as a shot of desire hammered through his frustration. Every nerve in him screamed against it—and yet... She was right. By the time he got her back to the ship and returned, many of these men would be gone. He sighed. "Alright. But let me do the talking."

With a shrug, she lowered herself back to her feet but stayed pressed to his side. The barkeep arrived before he had the sense to take a step to the side to relieve the burning heat coming from where their arms touched.

He shook his head. *Get it together.*

"I'm looking for information about a pir—" A sharp jab came from his ribs. He rubbed the spot where she'd elbowed him and lowered his voice to a whisper. "What was that for?"

She ignored him and leaned over the counter. He followed the barkeep's gaze and bit back a curse at the perfect view of cleavage she'd offered the man. "What my..." she slanted him a glance. "Partner was trying to say is, he'd like two mugs of your finest ale."

"I was n—" She stomped on his foot and he coughed. What was she up to? "I mean... Yes, I was."

He pulled out several five cent coins and set them on the counter while the man filled two mugs. "I thought you wanted me to ask questions?"

She smiled as the barkeep set the ale in front of them and took the money. "He won't give you any information." She headed into the room and scanned the tables before pointing. "There."

In the back corner, a group of especially rough looking men sat with cards laid out in front of them. Surely, she didn't mean to... She did. He followed her to the table and hesitated when she gestured to the only empty seat.

Miss Montclair faced the men. "I do love a good game of vingt-un. Who's winning?"

So much for letting him do the talking.

A gruff man tilted the brim of his hat and she swiveled to Isaac. "You do play, don't you?"

He shifted on his feet. "Not regularly."

A pout fell across her mouth. "A pity."

She leaned in, her lips grazing his ear, and every nerve in his body shot to life. "If this is going to work, I need you to play along, no questions asked." Her words came on a whispered breath that sent a shudder through him.

"What say you?" She raised her voice and arched a dark brow before tilting her ear to his mouth.

His pulse jumped as he leaned into her. "I say you play a dangerous game."

She reached between them, her fingers setting on his pocket, and his throat went dry. Dangerous indeed. With a laugh, she twisted her hand and lifted a money bag. One that had certainly not been there before.

"He says I can play. You gentlemen don't mind, do you?" Crooked mouths twisted into smiles and he marveled at the power a pair of shapely breasts could wield. She gave him an expectant look and waved her hand at the chair. "Don't take all day, my dear."

He pressed his lips together, but sat. No sooner had he got situated, she lowered herself into his lap. He sucked in a breath and his entire body went rigid as her soft curves pressed into him. Hell. This was going to be a long game.

She pulled a few coins free and made her first bet as the dealer passed out the first cards. He craned his neck as she lifted the corner but missed her card in the brief flash she offered. Same with her second card. She nodded for a third. Lost.

The next hands passed in a flurry, as she bet small amounts, winning some, losing some. She fell into a rhythm, laughing and engaging with the men, until they seemed at ease with her.

She'd done this before.

He took a hearty drink of his ale and leaned back in his chair.

If she was going to enjoy herself, he may as well try to as well. His lips curved. Who was he fooling? With her supple bottom wiggling in his lap, he already immensely enjoyed this.

As the cards in the deck dwindled, she became more aggressive with her bets, and won two hands in a row. The next hand, she pushed her entire pile to the center. Risky.

She turned, her bottom twisting against the part of him that had sprung to attention. "How about a good luck kiss, dear?"

His eyes widened. No. He began to shake his head and her smile wavered. Damnation. His gaze flitted past her to the expectant stares of all the men there. If he didn't, he would be telling them she was fair game.

"Miss—" He flinched when she gave his shoulder a playful swat.

"I'm no miss." She shot him a sultry look.

With a growl, he leaned into her, his lips claiming hers in one swift action. His hand lifted, tangling in her hair to hold her in place as he ran his tongue over her bottom lip. So damn soft. Her hands twisted in his shirt and her mouth opened in a gasp.

The other players hooted and Isaac forced himself to pull back. Miss Montclair stared at him, her eyes glazed and lips parted. He shifted his weight. If she kept looking at him like that, he was going to kiss her again.

"Was that lucky enough?" His words came out hoarse and he cleared his throat.

Her fingers lifted, touching her lips briefly before she turned back to the table. "Let's find out if his kiss is as lucky as he says."

When the cards were turned, she let out a little squeal. She'd won.

Astonishing.

The deck was passed and while the next man shuffled it, Miss Montclair leaned forward, placing both elbows on the table. "I heard there was a pirate in town."

The men sniggered and one spoke up. "Plenty of pirates here."

She arched her back and Isaac couldn't help an appreciative glance down to where her bottom rested in his lap. "I'm looking for a very specific one. One who doesn't play by the normal rules. One you're probably glad has left."

It took a moment for Isaac to realize what she was doing and he quickly scanned the men's faces for any glimmer of recognition, cursing himself for nearly missing the chance.

But Miss Montclair had already focused her attention on an older seaman with deep wrinkles on his weathered face. "What do you think?"

He glanced around the table. "Was happy to see him go. Something dark about that one."

Isaac straightened, a tingle running up his neck. Not a quarter hour in and she'd already made headway. He rubbed his aching knuckles as she leaned even further forward.

"Did you see him?" She gave the man her rapt attention. In fact, now he had the attention of the whole table.

He nodded. "He was at the Eagle Tavern a few days ago. Looking for men sympathetic to his cause. I've no desire to go up against the Navy, but a good friend of mine welcomed the chance and joined his crew."

Isaac's pulse quickened as Miss Montclair's nose scrunched. "His cause? Didn't he find what he was looking for on that naval ship he sunk?"

Now, he fought the urge to lean forward with her, and forced himself to look down at the pile of money in front of them, pretending to count it while he waited for the answer.

"Heavens no. And he was right mad about it."

She nodded and flipped a coin between her fingers. "I imagine he was eager to get on his way and try again. Do you know where he sailed?"

His brow furrowed. "Now, why would a girl like you want that type of information?"

Her laugh rang out, echoing across the room and turning heads their way. "Let's just say, I've a bone to pick with him."

The man glanced around and leaned forward, this time speaking in a much lower voice. "My friend said they were sailing north."

She smiled. "What a coincidence. We also sail that direction."

"Well, I would recommend changing course. No telling what he would do if he got his hands on you."

With a shrug, she settled back into Isaac's lap. "He doesn't scare me."

The man straightened. "It's time I leave." He shook his head, pale eyes flicking to hers as he gathered his money. "I wouldn't tempt fate if I were you."

Miss Montclair stiffened at the warning and Isaac leaned over her shoulder. "What do you think, dear, have you won enough yet?"

She gave a single nod and stood, shoving her stack of coins into the money bag. Isaac rubbed his palms over his thighs, trying to ignore the sudden lack of warmth where her bottom had rested, the space between them an unwelcome reminder of the distance he should be keeping from her.

The man sitting next to him grabbed his elbow. "Come, friend, why don't you share your pretty piece with us?"

Heat surged through Isaac and his fist curled. Miss Montclair set her hand over his and gave the man an apologetic look. "My lover is a jealous man. Perhaps next time."

Isaac gave the smuggler one last glare and followed Miss Montclair outside. They walked in silence until they rounded the corner. He stopped and she followed suit. "Your lover?"

Even in the darkness, the blush across her cheeks stood out. "It's what they all assumed."

"They expected a lucky kiss as well?"

She swallowed and dropped her gaze. "I'm sorry. I shouldn't have."

He shifted his weight to take pressure off his erection. Blasted trousers were too tight. Part of him wanted to shake her for her foolishness, but the rest of him? He had half a mind to pull her back into his arms and kiss her senseless.

But he wouldn't. He pulled his shoulders back. "What you did in there, that wasn't your first time playing like that. Where did you learn to cheat at cards?"

She lifted her eyes to meet his. "Who says I was cheating?"

He chuckled and closed the distance between them, bending his lips to her ear. "You hid it well with all your flirting, but don't think you can fool me."

After a shaky breath, she took a step back. "I sometimes worked at the tavern in Tortuga."

"Your father let you?" He frowned as he imagined all the men she would have used the same tactic with. How many laps she'd graced.

"He didn't like it." She stared out over the bay, where the *Tempest* and *Red Siren* docked. "I would sneak out when pirate ships were in town and go to the tavern to listen to their stories. The owner let me help on busy nights."

Her shoulders rose and fell and her gaze turned distant. Growing up as a high bred girl on the island could not have been easy. He cleared his throat. "Well, I am grateful for it."

She spun, eyes wide. "You are?"

His lips curved. "Because of you, I got more information than I could have hoped for."

"So, you're not mad at me?"

"Am I upset you disobeyed me and got yourself in trouble? Yes. But you proved an invaluable asset tonight with your... skills. In light of that..." He extended his hand. "I'm willing to call a truce, if you are."

Her lips curved and she set her hand in his. "A truce."

He ignored the heat of her palm and forced a stern look over his features. "That means no more deceptions."

"So, no more sneaking aboard your ship?" A slight pout twisted her mouth.

"Especially that." He hadn't released her hand yet and tugged her closer.

Her brows lifted, but she followed his pull, her intoxicating scent washing over him. Jasmine. He hadn't been able to place it earlier with the immense distraction of her on his lap. His gaze traced her lips, dropped lower to where her blouse barely contained the swells of her breasts.

"Isaac!"

Christian's voice cut through the charged silence and he dropped her hand, coughing to clear his thickened throat.

"There's a party being thrown, right now, in honor of the fallen sailors. There's sure to be survivors in attendance." Christian jogged over. "Oh, hello, Miss Montclair."

As if it were the most normal thing to see a woman dressed the way she was.

"If we hurry, we can still make it and interview survivors. Will make our job a whole lot easier." His friend's gaze raked over the two of them. "Of course, we're going to have to change. All of us."

—❧ ✦ ❧—
Chapter Fourteen

THANK HEAVENS FOR Abigail. Specifically, Abigail's dress.

While Samantha quickly twisted Josephine's hair up, she stared out the window. Two times now she'd been warned to not tempt fate. She pulled her key free and rubbed her thumb over the skull. Each time she replayed the old man's words in her head, the hairs on her neck lifted. What did it mean?

She shivered, even though the heat in the cabin bore down on her. For all her talk about destiny, it seemed she should have worried about fate instead.

"What's that?" Samantha nodded toward the key.

Josephine tucked it back below the delicate lace trim of her squared bodice. "Just an old relic I won from a pirate." She'd swapped the ribbon for a yellow one that matched her dress.

Samantha grinned. "I'll have to hear the story sometime." She pinned the final locks of Josephine's hair into a loose chignon. "You look ravishing. Leave it to Abigail to choose the absolute perfect dress for you."

A grin tugged at Josephine's lips as she took in Samantha's empire dress, the blue silk shimmering in the lantern light. "Speaking of ravishing, I can see why you favor that color."

With a scrunched nose, Samantha smoothed the dress. "I despise the constriction of skirts. They sure aren't handy if you need to climb into rigging or sneak out of a window. And they are especially cumbersome if one has to fight." She winked. "I'm sure you understand."

A blush heated Josephine's cheeks. Samantha had been abso-

139

lutely delighted when she'd seen Josephine return wearing her clothing. "Have you truly fought before?"

Samantha pointed to the rapier hanging above her bed. "I don't carry it around for nothing." Her face had sobered. "I almost killed Christian with one just like that."

Josephine's eyes widened. "Surely you jest?"

When Samantha shook her head, Josephine leaned toward her but was met with a raised hand. "Another time. I'm sure Christian and Isaac are waiting for us now. Meanwhile..." She lifted her skirt. "One can never be too prepared."

A leather sheath hugged her ankle, the hilt of its dagger resting against her calf. Josephine blinked and Samantha chuckled. "I think it might be good to give you some basic swordsmanship lessons. We can start tomorrow if you'd like."

A thrill ran through Josephine at the thought of learning to wield a real sword. She nodded and Samantha dropped her skirt and motioned toward the door.

"Do many women in America have this... knowledge?"

This time, Samantha's laugh rang through the cabin. "Heavens no. At least no one respectable."

Josephine frowned. "Then why do you?"

Samantha opened the door and slid her a sly look. "Who ever said I was respectable?"

Out on the deck, Josephine fell a few steps behind Samantha with a wide grin. No wonder Abigail had mentioned unconventional friends.

"What took so long?" Christian leaned against the railing near the gangplank wearing a deep blue tailcoat. "We'll be lucky if the party isn't over by the time we get there."

Samantha lifted on her toes to plant a kiss on his cheek. "Precisely."

Lieutenant Caldwell stood several paces away with his back to them, his attention fixed on the lights of the city beyond. When he turned, his gaze found Josephine at once. Heat pooled in her chest as scenes from earlier flashed through her, the ghost of her bold kiss still lingering on her lips. A slow, knowing smile tugged at the corner of his mouth, and his eyes raked over her as if recalling every moment.

The ship rocked gently beneath her feet as she lifted a hand to adjust the ribbon at her neck as he stepped forward to meet her. He came to a stop, too close, the scent of salt and sandalwood settling over her.

"You look…" He leaned back and took her in once more. "Incredible."

She managed a breathless laugh and dipped into a curtsy, hoping he wouldn't notice the tremble in her hands. "Abigail picked out the dress. It is lovely, isn't it?"

He offered his arm and his voice dipped low. "I wasn't talking about the dress."

Heat blazed through her as her thoughts tangled with the way his gaze lingered. Instead of replying, she lifted her chin and set her hand on his arm, focusing on the soft wool beneath her fingers. Definitely not the man at her side.

Once settled in the waiting wagon, they jolted forward, iron-rimmed wheels creaking over uneven cobblestones. Josephine sat next to the lieutenant, hands folded neatly in her lap though her pulse still hummed. The lantern hanging from the driver's perch swung, casting shifting shadows across his profile—highlighting the strong cut of his jaw, the quiet control in his expression. The streets grew livelier the closer they came to the heart of town. Music floated from open tavern doors, laughter spilling into the night air. Carriages rumbled past, their occupants draped in silks and velvets, many bound for the same gathering. The wheels dipped into a rut, sending a jolt through the bench. She grasped for the side of the wagon, but the lieutenant's hand caught her elbow.

"Careful," he murmured, the backs of his fingers brushing against her skin before he withdrew.

Her stomach tightened and she stared straight ahead, willing her heart to behave as they came to a stop in front of the grand columns of a large manor. They climbed the front steps with a crowd of other people, and once inside, Christian kissed Samantha's forehead.

"You two stay together while we see who else we can talk to. Hopefully, it won't be long."

Samantha and Josephine chose a spot near a potted palm to wait. Minutes stretched into an hour and though she yearned to dance, Josephine stayed put, forced to observe only. Samantha kept one eye on the dance floor, constantly scanning the room.

"Are you looking for someone?" Josephine raised onto tiptoes to see over the tall hat of a man in front of her.

"I don't like being in a room full of strangers. Any one of these people could be a foe."

Josephine cast her gaze over the crowd and the hairs at her nape pricked. "Are you worried about Thorne? I thought you said he would be gone."

"I'm always worried about Thorne." A faraway look had come over Samantha's face, and she gave a quick shake of her head. "No, he's likely long gone with his new crew. But he's smart enough to keep ears on everything going on. Especially if he knows we are on his trail."

A thread of unease curled through Josephine. "So, he could have spies? Here?"

Samantha gave her a reassuring smile. "Probably not. I've just learned to never let my guard down where he's concerned."

Josephine couldn't help thinking back to the argument at the dinner table the other night, how Christian had brought up multiple times that Thorne had nearly killed Samantha.

"I think it's best we change the conversation." As if reading her mind, Samantha set a hand on Josephine's forearm. "What are your intentions with Isaac?"

Josephine blinked at the forward question. "What do you mean?"

Samantha set her hands on her hips. "Come now, I'm not blind."

A flush spread across her chest. "I... I was lamenting my future when he showed up in Tortuga and took it as a sign that there might be a chance of falling in love." Her shoulders fell. Saying it out loud made it all seem so silly. "It was foolish."

"Maybe it wasn't such a farfetched idea after all." Samantha nodded toward her husband and the lieutenant who stood across the floor, conversing with a man with his arm in a sling. "He seems different around you, especially after your little foray into town."

Josephine gave a rueful smile. "Probably because I exasperate him."

Samantha's laugh caused several guests nearby to turn their way. She lowered her voice. "You should ask Christian how I made him feel at first."

"He must have fallen in love with you right away, how could he not?"

A wry grin spread across Samantha's face. "Hate might be a better word. But we are not talking about Christian. Tell me, did something happen earlier?"

Another blunt question. "Well, I had to pretend we were lovers." Her face burned as Samantha laughed again. "I had to. He was about to ruin his chances at getting any information from the men at the tavern."

"I'm sure he didn't know how to react to that."

More heat rushed to Josephine's cheeks. He'd reacted alright.

After a knowing look, Samantha returned her gaze to the men. "If not for him, Christian and I would likely be dead."

Josephine turned. "How so?"

"We were shipwrecked together and Isaac rescued us."

Her eyes widened. "You were with him?"

When Samantha nodded, Josephine's mind began to race and snippets of memory flooded back. How Lieutenant Caldwell had shown up that night and told her father his captain had left with another pirate. Samantha's shocking clothing choices. Her comment that breeches were better for fighting. That she'd nearly killed Christian with her rapier. *Who ever said I was respectable?*

"You're a pirate?" Her voice came out in a squeak.

Samantha's lips parted, then curved. "You *are* good at investigating. Maybe I should send you over with Christian to help with their interviews."

"And you're good at deflecting." Josephine crossed her arms. "Is it really true?"

"Ex-pirate, if you must know." Samantha gave a half curtsy. "I'm positively reformed."

"Does Abigail know?"

Samantha jerked upright, face paling. "No."

A thousand questions pressed to the front of Josephine's mind. But before she could ask a single one, someone cleared their throat behind her.

"Do I want to know why you look like you've seen a ghost?" Christian stood there, frowning.

Samantha laughed. "Oh, it's nothing. I was just surprised by Josephine's perspicacity. She's sharper than you think."

He raised a dark brow. "Doesn't surprise me. Now, I've interviewed everyone here I can find. How about a dance before we head back to the ship?"

Josephine smiled as the couple strode out onto the dance floor.

"Miss Montclair?" The lieutenant's baritone voice rumbled from just over her shoulder.

She spun. "Has anyone ever told you it's rude to sneak up on people?"

He grinned. "Yes, but I wanted to ask you to dance."

"I thought you didn't like dancing?"

"What can I say? You've inspired me to try to change my mind."

She snorted. "Very funny." The music rose in a graceful swell, the lilting rhythm of a waltz—a dance Josephine had definitely never learned. "Unfortunately, I don't know how to waltz."

"There's a first time for everything."

She swallowed, her pulse quickening, as he took her hand, the warmth of his fingers steady against hers, his other palm settling at her waist with practiced ease. He tugged her toward the dance floor but she hesitated.

"This is the part where you move with me." Amusement laced his voice.

"I told you, I don't know how." The words tumbled out in a paralyzed whisper.

His thumb brushed lightly over the back of her hand, a fleeting reassurance. "Follow my lead, and I'll teach you."

The way he said it, full of command and assurance, gave her no option other than to agree. He moved with effortless confidence, each step measured, while she fought to match his lead, her muscles taut with the strain of keeping pace. The steps were unfamiliar, the movements too fluid, too close. She concentrated on her footing, wary of tangling her feet with his, but he kept his hand steady at her waist, his fingers a silent guide.

"Trust me." His voice came soft and her fingers curled slightly against his shoulder, though whether in agreement or unease, she wasn't sure.

As they glided through a turn, he drew her close and the heady scent of sandalwood unraveled what little reluctance remained. The music grew louder, and he increased their pace, his hold never faltering.

"Better," he murmured. His breath stirred against her temple, sending heat curling low in her stomach.

She decided in that instant that she very much liked the waltz.

The music carried them through another turn, her steps growing steadier. A happy sigh escaped her as the room blurred around them, the flicker of candlelight and murmur of voices fading beneath the steady rhythm of their steps. She focused on the movement, on the warmth of his hand at her back.

"Were you able to find any more information to help you in your search for Thorne?" Her voice came thick and she drew in a steadying breath.

"The ship carried archived naval orders. The survivors we talked to said Thorne and his men took them off the ship before sinking it." Another turn loosened their hands and separated them by an arm's length.

"What do you think he was looking for in them?"

He drew her back in, his hold steady, his gaze unwavering. "We're not sure. Thorne used to be a navy captain, so it may have been he's searching for records of an event that happened during his service. Maybe something that happened to cause his wife to be targeted."

"His wife?"

He pressed his eyes shut. "Pretend I didn't say that."

Josephine swallowed, thinking back to all she knew about Thorne. It wasn't much. But no one had ever mentioned a wife. She filed the knowledge away. "Perhaps retribution for a ship he captured?"

"Perhaps." He didn't sound convinced.

The music began to wind down and the lieutenant slowed their steps, guiding them toward the edge of the dance floor. The last notes echoed softly in the room, leaving a quiet stillness in their wake.

His ocean-hued eyes stayed locked on hers. "Care to join me for a stroll outside? We may be in the city, but I'm sure they've got a garden out back."

She nodded and slipped her hand into his elbow. Outside, they took a turn around the busy verandah before he led her down the stairs. A stone pathway led them between tall hedges and the sounds of the party began to fade. They came to a stop in a small clearing, moonlight reflecting off a statue in the center.

Lieutenant Caldwell's gaze lingered on it before dropping to her. "Did you enjoy your first waltz?"

The intensity in his eyes sent her pulse racing and all she could do was nod, her throat tight, the air between them suddenly thick. He stepped closer, just enough to feel the heat of him, and a shiver that had nothing to do with the night air slid all the way down to her toes. Time seemed to slow, each beat of her heart thumping against her chest as he slowly leaned down.

His fingertips grazed her neck. Her jaw. A sweet shudder passed through Josephine as his mouth paused a hairsbreadth from hers. And then, the softest touch, a barely there brush of warmth against her lips. Her breath hitched as her eyelids fluttered shut.

The faint scrape of a boot against stone came from nearby, and Josephine's eyes snapped open. A shape materialized in the shadows behind the lieutenant and she gasped. His hand dropped to his side and he spun.

"I wouldn't do that if I were you."

The metal point of a blade pressed beneath the lieutenant's chin and he slowly released his grip on the sword he'd drawn, dropping it to the ground with a clatter.

Josephine's heart went cold as the man stepped into the light and she recognized him from the drawing in Christian's papers.

"What do you want, Thorne?" Isaac ground the words out.

The pirate laughed, the hollow sound sending a shiver up her spine. "So sorry to interrupt your romantic moment, but I needed a word."

Isaac glared at him, shifting his weight to position Josephine behind him.

"I'd like to give you the same offer I gave my son. Join me, Lieutenant."

Lieutenant Caldwell sucked in a breath.

"Choose your response carefully. Remember, I've no reason not to slit your throat."

His hands clenched into fists. "Are you insane?"

Thorne chuckled. "Perhaps."

"This isn't a game, Thorne."

All amusement faded from the pirate's face. "You're right. It's not. I could use your help. In return, I'll give you anything your heart desires."

"Never." Isaac spat the word out and Thorne drew his lips into a snarl.

"Very well. But hear me and hear me well. This is the only warning I'll give you. I intend to finish this. Keep prying and I will kill you."

"Not if I kill you first."

"Bold words for someone standing in your current position." Thorne slipped the sword to the side of Isaac's neck and stepped to the side, his dark gaze settling on Josephine. His lips curved into a predatory smile when she lifted her eyes to meet his. "I heard you've a bone to pick with me?"

She sucked in a gasp as he repeated her words from earlier.

"Don't touch her," the lieutenant bit out, his voice a low growl.

The pirate arched his brow. "Or what?" His blade swung toward her. "You know what I do to those my enemies hold dear?"

"She's not...I don't..."

A numbness crept over her and the cold laugh rang out once more as her jaw tightened. "Now, now, look at what you've done."

Sharp steel pressed against her cheek. "You've gone and hurt her feelings. Not very gentlemanly, I must say."

Her chest heaved with each ragged breath as the weapon brushed down her jaw, grazed the skin of her throat, and came to a stop at the ribbon disappearing below her neckline.

"What do we have here?" He twisted the sword and lifted the key from its hiding spot.

His eyes narrowed before flicking up to meet hers. The darkness in his gaze made her breath hitch as a coldness began to twine within her. After a long moment, his lips drew into a thin line and he returned his attention to her chest. "What an interesting piece. Where did you get it?"

She swallowed and reached up, her hand closing around the key. "I've had it a long time."

His gaze sharpened as she spoke. "What's a girl from the Caribbean doing here in North Carolina?"

"Thorne, leave her alone. She's got no part in this." Isaac had edged toward the pirate's side.

Thorne whipped his weapon back toward Isaac with a snarl. "Don't do anything stupid, boy. She's not worth dying over."

Somehow, the words cut her worse than the blade could have.

The pirate began to back away, keeping his sword level. "Remember what I said, boy." A few more steps, and he disappeared in the shadows.

Lieutenant Caldwell took her arm. "Come." They rushed up the stairs to the verandah. Once the light from the open doors washed over them, he paused and turned to her.

"Are you hurt?" His thumb grazed the skin at her neck, where moments before, Thorne's blade had rested.

No.

She swallowed past the lump in her throat as warmth spread from the spot he touched her. "I'm fine."

His eyes searched hers for a brief moment, and he dropped his hand to her elbow. "Let's get inside. I need to alert my men."

She followed, heart still racing. "Lieutenant, perhaps you should listen to him. He said he would kill you. Is this mission worth dying for?"

He twisted his head and continued toward the doors. "Do you take me for a coward, Miss Montclair?"

Her steps faltered. "Of course not."

"Then don't think for a second I will let him bully me."

They passed into the light of the ballroom, and she slowed, forcing him to as well. "He could have killed you out there, but he didn't. It would be wise to heed his warning."

"Thorne is an enemy of this country. His actions have sealed his fate. It is my duty and honor to track him down."

Her throat thickened and she clamped her mouth shut. No use arguing with him at this point. They crossed the dance floor, dodging twirling couples, and headed straight toward Christian and Samantha.

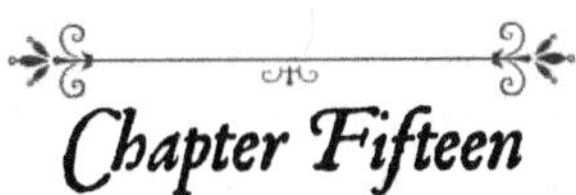

Chapter Fifteen

ISAAC GRABBED CHRISTIAN'S arm and tugged him toward the front of the room. "We need to get back to the ship right away."

His friend didn't miss a beat, falling in step next to him. "What's happened?"

"Thorne just paid me a visit in the garden."

Christian's gaze flew to the open verandah doors, his hands closing into fists. "Here? That's bold. What happened?"

"He tried to warn me off the hunt. Gave me the same spiel about joining him as he did you."

Christian snorted. "As if you would listen."

Samantha frowned next to him. "It doesn't make sense, risking all that just to tell you something he knew you'd never agree to. What if it's a trap?"

Miss Montclair shifted at his side and he could almost feel the weight of her accusing gaze.

I could use your help.

Thorne's words rang through Isaac's head. "I think, whatever he's looking for, he needs someone on the inside. Someone who could get access to the archives he wasn't able to steal. I wonder if he's sailing to Washington?" A new certainty buzzed through him. "I think we need to take a closer look at the archives from the year your mother died."

Christian shook his head, his eyes flicking to Miss Montclair and back. "Would be a waste of time. It was the first place I went after Thorne escaped. Nothing in the records stood out as suspicious. Not to mention, I'm sure Thorne has seen all of it. He's had years to find a way to see them."

Isaac clenched his jaw. "There must be something we're missing."

The wagon sat ready and waiting for them, and within moments, they sped off. Silence stretched thick and oppressive between the group as they bumped along the cobblestones. The hairs on Isaac's neck lifted, a tingle of warning he couldn't shake. He scanned the darkened road ahead of them, his hand hovering above his sword.

As they approached the docks, Christian cleared his throat. "Why don't you sail ahead of us? Samantha and I will stay and finish interviewing the survivors. One of the men in charge of the archives was badly wounded and is recovering in the countryside. He'll know more about the contents. If we can find out what Thorne is looking for, it will narrow the search."

Isaac nodded. As always, Christian was one step ahead in his reasoning. "It may also throw him off if only one of us follows him, perhaps it will make him bolder."

Christian nodded. "We'll be less than a day behind you."

The wagon rumbled to a stop and Isaac swung to the ground. He helped Miss Montclair down and offered her his arm while they waited for Christian and Samantha to come around from the other side. A cough came from behind them and he spun.

A man stumbled their way, waving his hand. Isaac frowned at his tattered clothing and unkempt hair. A beggar, from the looks of it. Sunburned and blistered, a wild look blazed in his eyes. Miss Montclair took a half-step back, and Isaac set a steadying hand on her elbow. His other eased around the hilt of his sword.

"Are you Lieutenant Caldwell?" The man's words came out weak and hoarse.

Isaac nodded, his grip tightening on his weapon. "Are you in need of assistance?"

The man stepped forward, into the light of the nearest lantern and Isaac's eyes widened. The torn and filthy jacket the man wore was a navy issued one.

"My God, sailor, what's happened?" His hand left his sword and he strode to meet the man as he fell to his knees. Christian hurried to the sailor's other side and they helped him back to his feet.

"Able seaman James Burke, sir, of the *USS Reliant.*"

The ship Thorne had sunk. Nearly a week ago.

"Where have you been all this time?"

"I've been adrift at sea, clinging to a piece of wreckage. I thought I was on my last breath—thought I was hallucinating—when I saw a fishing boat coming my way. They rescued me and brought me here. Told me the Navy had arrived."

He'd been floating for almost a week. A true miracle he'd survived. "Christian, hurry and fetch a doctor."

They stood in silence while Christian drove the wagon away. Samantha bent to one knee, adjusting her slipper. All a ruse. If he knew her, she had her fingers wrapped around the hilt of that fancy little dagger she kept there. Once a pirate, always a pirate. She lifted a brow at his perusal and he turned his attention back to the shipwrecked sailor.

She didn't have to worry. He could take this man down blindfolded with one hand tied behind his back. "What can I do to ease your discomfort? Have you been offered food? Water?"

With a nervous glance between the two women, the sailor cleared his throat and lowered his voice. "There's more I must tell you. As we sailed into the harbor, I saw the very ship that attacked us sail away."

Isaac exhaled. "Not surprising. We had an encounter with him less than an hour ago."

"I know where he sails."

Isaac gave a curt nod. "He sails north."

The man's eyes blazed in the lantern light. "He sails to Norfolk."

"Norfolk?" The hairs on Isaac's arm prickled. "How do you know?" Not a single man they had interviewed had been able to give them any clues pointing to Thorne's next destination.

"When he brought the last of the crates onboard, I heard him say to one of his thugs that even if it wasn't there, they would still go to Norfolk."

Straight into the hornet's nest. Home of the Norfolk Navy Yard, a key naval base, entering the city would be a death wish for the pirate. Only one reason would drive him there. He was going after someone in the navy. Isaac's chest constricted. Could someone in uniform have had a hand in Mrs. Thompson's death?

Isaac shook his head. *No.* There had to be some other reason. It had to be why Thorne had tried to get him to join his crew. He would have been a great asset to gain access to information guarded by the base. It made the most sense.

"Let me join your crew."

Isaac jerked his attention back to the man. "You need medical attention; a ship is no place for you right now, Burke. Don't worry, I'm leaving immediately and have plenty of men fit and ready to fight."

The seaman lunged forward and grabbed Isaac's forearm. "You must let me. I thirst for justice for the crewmates I lost. I'm willing and able. Besides, I know what his ship looks like. I've got the image seared on my brain. I'll be able to spot it a mile away, far before any of your crew could."

Isaac wavered, weighing the advantage the man could offer and the sailor smiled. "Besides, I trust the doctoring I'll get onboard much more than anything on shore."

Spoken like a true navy man. "Alright. But you will take a bunk in the sick bay and stay there for the duration of the trip to recover. If there's any fighting, you will stay out of it."

"Yes, sir. Thank you."

"Lieutenant, is that you?" Silas's voice came from down the dock.

Isaac waved, thankful for his first officer's sharp eye. "We require assistance." He turned to the sailor. "My first officer will take you onto the *Tempest* and get you situated. We will be sailing immediately."

Once they walked away, Samantha stood. He met her worried gaze. "Did you catch all that?"

She nodded.

"He's looking for something in Norfolk. Probably something guarded by the Yard. That's where the ship he sank had sailed from. My guess is he was hoping it would be in the archived records. See if the man he interviews tomorrow knows anything about what that could be."

They made their way to the *Siren*. At the gangway, Samantha turned. "I don't think it's smart to allow that man to join your crew. Something seemed off about him."

He gave her a tight smile. "He's suffered a heavy ordeal. People aren't themselves after going through that sort of thing, as you well know."

Her blue eyes flashed but she did not push the issue. "Keep your guard up. We will see you tomorrow. Hopefully sooner than later."

Miss Montclair shifted at his side when Samantha started up the gangway, slender fingertips brushing his forearm. "If you don't mind, I need to have a private word with the lieutenant."

Samantha turned and a soft smile played across her lips. "I'll wait on deck."

Miss Montclair stood still and silent in the lantern light, her brows furrowed, eyes flitting side to side as she worked through something in her head. One hand lifted, playing with the yellow ribbon descending into her neckline, while the other slipped into a pocket in her skirts.

"There's something I need to show you."

She pulled a folded piece of parchment free and handed it to him. His own brows pressed together as he scanned the drawing. "What's this—" His eyes darted to where her fingers still hovered at her chest. "Your key."

She nodded and pulled it free, moonlight reflecting from the ivory skull. He reached for it, warmth flooding through his fingers from where it had rested against her skin. It matched the drawing on the page perfectly.

He frowned as he read the scrawled notes and recognized the handwriting. "This is Christian's. Why do you have it?"

She cleared her throat. "I borrowed it. I'll give it back."

"You can't be going through his things."

This time her voice came quiet. "I know. When I saw the sketch matched my key, I couldn't help it."

He sighed and lifted his gaze to meet hers. "You think this has something to do with why Thorne is going to Norfolk?"

"It has to. He recognized it as soon as he saw it. And I could tell he wanted it in a bad way."

He nodded, turning the key over in his hand. What the hell could it be to? The carving had been done with expert craftsmanship, edges still crisp and sharp. It wasn't an antique, yet she'd told Thorne she'd had it a long time.

"Where did you get this?"

"I won it off a pirate."

A pirate wouldn't own such a nice piece unless it was stolen or plundered. He wagered it had once belonged to someone very wealthy. He looked at the address on the parchment again, and his pulse quickened. If whatever Thorne was looking for was there, he could finally piece everything together.

"I need to go. The quicker I can get to Norfolk, the better chance I have at getting answers before Thorne."

"Let me come with you." Her words came out soft yet determined.

"Absolutely not. Thorne will be there. He could come after us at any time."

Her hand closed around the key and she tucked it back beneath her neckline. "What's the difference? Samantha and Christian will be right behind us. On a smaller ship. Isn't the *Tempest* the safest place to be if Thorne attacks?"

"The *Siren* is faster and could get away from an attack."

Her lips twisted into a half-smile. "No offense, Lieutenant, but I don't think your friend would leave you behind."

She was right.

Didn't matter.

"Everyone seems to keep forgetting that this is a military mission. I can't just take on civilians and write it off. I answer for every action I take, every decision I make, Miss Montclair.

Her smile widened and a thread of unease wound through him. "Precisely. But, at this point, I'm no longer a civilian, am I?"

He needed to walk away from this conversation. Take the key. Leave her here. "What are you talking about?"

"I'm an informant."

He blinked.

"Anyway, I'm not giving you the key unless you take me." She took a step back as if to prove her point.

"I could order you to hand it over."

Her smile didn't waver. "But, you won't."

He wouldn't. Damn it.

He could go without it. Anything locked with a key could be opened if one had the right tools. But time could be of the essence, especially if Thorne was after the same thing.

A groan rumbled in the back of his throat. "One day. And when Christian and Samantha catch up, you go back to their ship."

She nodded.

"Very well." He pressed two fingers against his temple. "Go get your things. Quickly."

ICY RAINDROPS PELTED Isaac's face. "Hold fast!" The wind ripped his shouted orders from his throat and he cursed, tightening his hands on the wheel as the *Tempest* shuddered down a swell, a foaming wall of water crashing over the deck.

The storm had come upon them not long after they left. At first, a mild nuisance, it had built into a menacing force over the last hour. One he didn't have time for. He fought the rudder with a growl as the wind threatened to blow them off course. The aggravations on this trip continued to build.

Silas had barely spoken to him since they left, making his disapproval of their newest passenger clear. "Ain't right," he'd said.

For the last few hours, he'd had plenty of time to make excuses for why he'd let her come. Knowing her, she'd have tried to stowaway a third time. So, he was just trying to save himself the frustration of dealing with that. Had nothing to do with their almost kiss earlier.

Damn Thorne for interrupting.

He glanced down to the main hatch, mulling what exactly the blasted pirate was after now. Last time, it was a map to a buried treasure. And Miss Montclair hadn't been wrong. Her key had certainly caught the pirate's attention. Enough so that he'd almost gotten the jump on Thorne while he examined it.

But why hadn't Thorne taken it? Christian had taught him there was no such thing as coincidence. A heavy weight shifted in his gut, one that had been there since they set sail. Water streamed into his eyes and he swiped it away, staring into the gnashing waves ahead of them.

He'd had enough interaction with Thorne to know that what the pirate wanted, he would get. One way or another. If he wanted the key, or more importantly, whatever the key unlocked, he would stop at nothing to get it.

A bolt of lightning struck nearby, and Isaac flinched at the blast of thunder. He could use her as bait to draw the pirate out. The thought sent his stomach roiling. *No.* He shook it away. Too risky. Thorne didn't play by the rules and would kill an innocent without blinking.

It had been a foolish move to bring her. If Thorne found out she was with him, he would absolutely use her against him. He shuddered as the memory of how the pirate had nearly killed Samantha to get to Christian flashed through his mind. With a swallow, he returned his attention to maneuvering the *Tempest*.

She thought she'd be safest here on this ship. But the truth was, Thorne had already proven he wasn't keen on killing his son. Which meant she would have been infinitely safer on board the *Siren*. His shoulders tensed as another rumble of thunder vibrated through the ship.

He now had two jobs. Capture Thorne. And protect Miss Montclair. His pulse quickened when he closed his eyes and saw her parted lips, smelled the ghost of her jasmine scent. Ever since her charade back at the smuggler's den, he couldn't stop thinking of her. Mostly of how her bottom felt in his lap. But also, her reckless kiss. Even now, his body stirred to attention.

"Lieutenant?"

He snapped his eyes open. Silas stood in front of him. "You should take a break. The wind is shifting. Worst of the storm has passed."

Isaac stared out over the water, and the next several flashes of lightning confirmed his first officer's observation, the rolls of thunder taking slightly longer to reach them. He nodded and let his first officer take the wheel.

"I'm going to change into something drier."

"Best check on your guest as well."

Again, Isaac's gaze drifted to the hatch and a thread of guilt bubbled up. He'd meant to go down and reassure her before the storm hit its worst, but it had grown so fast, he hadn't wanted to risk leaving the helm.

A lamp hung near the main hatch and he took it on his way to his cabin. Once below deck, the movement seemed worse, and he ran one hand along the deck above to steady himself. It was no coincidence a captain's quarters always rested in the aft portion of a ship where there was the most stability. Hopefully, it hadn't been as bad in there.

At his door, he knocked. No answer. "Miss Montclair, I'm coming in."

When the *Tempest* crested a wave, he opened the door and stepped inside the dark room. A few things laid strewn across the floor, casualties of the waves. He swept the lantern in front of him as he took in the rest of the cabin. A form huddled on his bed and he stepped forward.

"Are you alright?" He lifted the lantern, the flickering light reflecting off her pale face. His breath caught. She'd changed into nothing but a shift, rumpled and disheveled from the storm. The thin fabric clung to her curves, the swell of her breasts pressing softly against the material. One shoulder had slipped free, exposing smooth skin beneath.

He quickly averted his gaze, heat creeping up his neck. He should turn around. Leave her. Yet the storm howled outside, the walls of the cabin creaking and groaning. She slumped against the wall with her knees pulled to her chest. He couldn't just walk away. Couldn't leave her to her fears.

"Miss Montclair?"

She gave a barely perceptible nod, her silence almost as loud as the storm outside.

"The peak of the storm is over, it will get better from here on."

Another quick nod.

He crossed the room to his wardrobe, and opened the door, trying to recall his first storm at sea. He'd been keen to show his bravery and had performed his tasks with enthusiasm. But no amount of bravado had prepared him for the way the ship had bucked and groaned with each plunge down a wave or the deafening crash of water against the bow. Each roar of wind in the sails had sent his heart plummeting, a knot of fear twisting deep in his chest.

Over the years, he had come to understand the rhythm of a ship in stormy weather, to trust the timbers beneath his feet. A well-built vessel reacted to the storm's rage—absorbed its power. Now, when the winds howled and the waves rose, he faced the fury with the same steady resolve as he did the calm.

He cleared his throat. "I know it seems frightening, but I promise, all will be well." Water dripped from his sodden clothing as he collected a new shirt and coat. "You should try to get some rest."

She pulled her knees closer to her chest, still mute, but gave him one more nod. He sighed. Not much he could do. She'd have to weather the storm and make it out on the other side before she realized it wasn't so bad. With a reassuring smile, he turned to the door. He almost reached it before she finally spoke, her soft words barely reaching him.

"Don't leave me."

Chapter Sixteen

L IEUTENANT CALDWELL PAUSED, his hand resting on the doorknob and Josephine tightened the grip around her knees, her pulse mirroring the pounding rain against the window. Sitting alone for the last few hours had been agonizing. Anything not secured went clattering to the floor as the ship violently rolled back and forth, each crash making her tense. After extinguishing the lantern for fear of starting a fire, she'd sat in darkness, flashes of lightning casting their ominous glow through the windows.

Every story she'd ever heard told at the tavern of storm-wrecked ships played through her mind, and as the storm grew worse, her imagination created a wide range of scenarios that either ended with her clinging to a piece of wreckage or being pulled into the dark depths of the sea. Unable to keep her balance, she'd retreated to the lieutenant's bed, the sandalwood scent of his sheets providing little comfort.

He stood still, the light from his lantern reflecting from a puddle forming at his feet.

Please.

She repeated it in her mind, again and again.

Or perhaps she said it aloud. She wasn't sure.

He turned, his hand dropping from the door, and her muscles slackened, causing her back to sag against the wall.

"Alright."

That one simple word might be the sweetest one she'd ever heard.

He reached up and clipped the lantern to a hook in a rafter, where it swung safely. Raising the bundle in his arms, he gave her an apologetic smile. "I need to get out of these wet clothes. Do you mind if I at least change my shirt?"

"No. Of course not." She shook her head at her hoarse voice and turned toward the wall.

Silence fell around them, punctuated by the wet slap of clothing hitting the floor. Her pulse quickened at the thought of him standing there, bare from the waist up. The need to put a picture to the thought warred with her sense of propriety.

To hell with propriety.

Ever so slightly, she tilted her head to the side until he came into sight. Her breath caught. He stood with his back to her, his coat and shirt lying in a wet heap at his feet. Lantern light shimmered off drops of water running down the smooth valley between his shoulders, and honed muscles wrapped around his sides, disappearing into his breeches.

He lifted his arms, rubbing a towel through his hair and her ability to breathe ceased to exist. Oh, glorious biceps. She stared as they bunched and corded with each movement he made and her mouth went dry. He twisted his head her way and she jerked her gaze back to the wall. A soft chuckle reached her and heat shot up her cheeks. She'd been discovered.

The rustle of cloth over skin came and a moment later, he spoke, amusement lacing his words. "You can look now."

She turned, grateful for the shadows hiding her face. He had not put his coat on and stood with a plain white shirt untucked. Damp curls framed his face, still mussed from the towel.

"Alright, Miss Montclair. How can I ease your fears?"

Slowly, she stretched her cramped legs out, wincing as blood began to rush back through them. "I'm not sure you can."

"Nonsense. Fear is like a shadow; it nips your heels when you try to run from it. You must face it before it will shrink away."

"Easy for you to say. I can't even stand up."

"Well then, maybe that's the first step. It takes a while to get true sea legs, but come, let me show you."

She gave him a skeptical look. "This is going to end up just as embarrassing as my mishap in Christian and Samantha's fountain."

He grinned. "I promise, it won't."

She waited for a slight break in the near constant up and down movement before swinging her feet to the floor. Standing, she wrapped a blanket around her shoulders while keeping one hand on the bed.

"No cheating." The lieutenant motioned her forward. "See how I'm standing? Right now, your feet are too close together, which makes it easier for you to lose your balance. Try moving them apart."

The ship pitched to the side and Josephine's hands curled into fists. "I'm not… I've never…" She took a steadying breath and widened her stance to match his. "It doesn't feel like the ship can withstand such wild movements."

He nodded. "I know it feels that way, but you must think of the waves as if they were a solid landscape. Picture a road traveling over rolling hills. A carriage will go up and down with every little change along the route."

The ship shuddered and she pressed her eyes shut. "But the sea is not solid."

"To the *Tempest*, it is. Her shape allows her to cut through some of the smaller swells. But in a storm, if she passed through towering waves, she would be overcome. Just as the carriage would crash into pieces if it tried to go through the hill instead of over it."

Visions of splintered wood brought her heart racing again. She took a deep breath. "You must think I'm a coward."

A warm weight settled on her shoulder and she startled. Her eyes snapped open as his thumb rubbed a comforting circle. "You're not."

She searched his gaze, but it hid no mirth or condemnation. Tension slowly began to drain from her as he took a step back.

"You look much better already, almost like you're starting to get used to it."

A shaky laugh escaped her. "I wish. I think it's only because you're distracting me."

As soon as she spoke, the ship rolled on a swell and she gasped, her stomach lurching. Her feet lifted slightly, slipping on the wet floor. The sudden movement threw her off balance, and she staggered forward, tripping on the blanket. It tangled around her ankles as Lieutenant Caldwell jumped to meet her, strong hands closing around her waist. She grabbed at his arms, trying to slow her momentum, but it didn't help.

"Oof!" Her face slammed into his chest.

One of his arms slid behind her back and the other lifted to brace against the ceiling. He held her tight against him as the ship finished its descent and began the next rise. "I forgot to tell you to bend your knees when that happens."

Sandalwood filled her nose as she breathed in, her cheek resting on the soft linen of his shirt. Beneath it, his heart beat in her ear, the strong thrum reverberating against her. In slow succession, the rest of her body began to react to being plastered against him. Every inch of him was hard muscle, from the planes of his stomach all the way down to where one of her legs twined with his.

With awareness humming through her, she lifted her face. "I told you this wouldn't end well."

His eyes burned into hers, like they had in the garden earlier. A rush of warmth spread through her and her breath caught as his lips parted. The lieutenant didn't move, his arm still holding her tight. She pulled her bottom lip between her teeth and his gaze dropped to her mouth.

"I rather like how this ended." His voice came out hoarse, each puff of his breath brushing across her forehead.

"Oh." She swallowed as his eyes met hers once more.

"Our kiss in the tavern..." He trailed off, his grip loosening just enough for the movement of the ship to rock her back a half step. "It wasn't proper."

"I…" Her gaze dropped as a pressure built around her heart. "I'm sorry."

She tried to take a step back, but his arm remained in place, fingers splayed across the small of her back. "I meant I didn't get a chance to properly kiss you. It ended too soon."

Her face jerked up. "Too soon?"

The intensity in his gaze sent a shiver through her. "I thought to make up for it in the garden, but we were interrupted."

Each beat of her heart hammered in her ears as he lowered his head, his mouth separated from hers by a sliver of air. "May I?"

Yes.

A roll of thunder reverberated through the ship. She opened her mouth to answer, but no words came out. He held his position, eyes searching hers, his breaths coming slow and steady against her cheek. A thread of panic coursed through her as he waited. If she didn't do something, the moment would pass.

With her voice still trapped, she gave a breathless nod.

The hand at her back tightened, pinpoints of heat spreading from his fingertips as his head dipped, lips brushing hers.

A pulsating warmth curled in her belly and her eyes fluttered shut. Earlier, in the tavern, with all the distractions, their kiss had passed in a blur. Not now. She wouldn't let it. This kiss, she would sear every bit of it into her memory. The soft weight of his mouth covered hers, and all thoughts evaporated.

She stopped trying to balance, letting her body fall into him once more. A low groan rumbled from the back of his throat and a moment later, the slick heat of his tongue pressed against her lips. Her own parted in a heady gasp and he groaned again, louder. He flicked his tongue forward, meeting hers in a brief exchange before retreating.

Her hands lifted, fingers tangling in his shirt as he repeated the motion—this time, in a languid stroke, tasting her with deliberate, aching sweetness. She met him with a tentative brush of her own, every nerve in her body drawn to where their mouths met. The sharp brine of the sea lingered on his lips, mingling with the warmth of his breath.

A thrill ran through her as the *Tempest* plunged down another wave, the vibrations running through their bodies where they pressed together. Lieutenant Caldwell shifted his stance, his hand sliding up her back. Strong fingers wrapped behind her head while his thumb grazed a path below her ear. A fire began to burn inside her, spreading from his touch. The dance between their tongues slowed and he pulled his head back.

Her eyelids lifted, heavy with need and she met his burning gaze. He brushed his thumb over her swollen lips, sending the most delicious tingle straight to her toes. Her breaths came in quick pants as his fingers slowly curled in her hair.

Somehow, she found her voice. "Was that proper?"

"Mmm… Far from it." His voice rasped over her in a rough caress laced with promise, sending her already frantic pulse spiraling higher.

Emboldened, she lifted on tiptoes and leaned into him. This time, his mouth claimed hers with a raw, unyielding hunger. His tongue tangled with hers with a fervor she couldn't hope to match. Her knees weakened and she sagged against him, swaying in time with the ship, her hands balled into fists in his shirt to keep herself upright.

Without breaking their kiss, he started moving toward the wall. Rafter by rafter, his arm held them steady as the ship's movement became an afterthought. The backs of her knees hit something. The bed.

His forehead pressed to hers and he grinned, lips still pressed against her own. "That. Was a proper kiss."

He lowered the hand at her neck, and with the sudden loss of support, Josephine fell back onto the sheets. Her hands remained tangled in his shirt and he followed, hovering over her on his hands and knees.

He dropped his lips to her ear. "Would you like more?"

The words sent a molten barb to her core. She'd never wanted anything so badly in her life. "Yes."

He closed his teeth over the tender skin of her neck, and Josephine jerked at the searing contact, the back of her hands brushing his soaked breeches.

"You're going to get the bed wet." The words came out in a breathless whisper as his teeth grazed the skin above her collarbone.

He pulled his head back with a devilish grin. "What would you have me do?"

Take them off.

Her eyes widened. She'd almost spoken the shocking words aloud.

He chuckled, his mouth continuing its path of sweet torture, stopping when he met her shift. He nibbled the linen, tugging down as her chest rose and fell in an erratic rhythm. The fabric moved with agonizing slowness, stretching until he uncovered the dusky pink of her areola.

With an appreciative growl, he gave a sharp tug and her nipple sprang free. He hooked a finger below the neckline, dragging it further, until her entire breast was bared.

"Mmm…" He stared at it with a quiet reverence before he began planting small kisses around her nipple, each one bringing him closer to the hard point. Soon, he hovered above it, hot breath caressing her skin. She squirmed beneath him, arching to push herself straight into the heat of his open mouth. With a groan, he clamped around her.

He sucked, the warmth of his tongue enveloping her nipple, interrupted here and there by the rough drag of teeth. Josephine's head fell back at the exquisite feeling—too much and too little all at the same time.

"So perfect." He nuzzled the valley between her breasts, shifting the fabric to bare her completely.

While his mouth closed over her nipple once again, one hand cupped her other breast, his rough palm alternating between squeezing and rubbing as his mouth worked its magic. Torture.

Sweet torture. Her back arched and her mouth fell open, words forming and dissolving in the span of a second.

Finally, when she thought she could bear it no longer, he lifted his head, eyes dark with desire. He grinned and let his fingers trace the hem of her shift. Slowly, deliberately, he gathered the fabric, lifting it inch by inch. Gooseflesh rose in its wake, her breath catching as he exposed more of her to the lamplight. When it bunched at her waist, he sat up, straddling her. Aching heat coiled low in her belly, mingling with the warmth that pulsed quietly through her. She shifted beneath him, seeking relief, but the motion only deepened the sensation.

He sat in silence, his gaze burning into her as he took her in, thumbs tracing lazy circles at her sides as he waited. For what? What did he want her to do? Bare him as he had done her? She almost growled her frustration at her lack of knowledge.

With shaking fingers, she unbuttoned his shirt, letting it fall open. Even cloaked in the shadows, the muscles of his chest stood out, each one carved and honed. Her mouth went dry as she feasted on the sight. She lifted her hands and laid them flat against his skin, marveling at the solid heat and strength beneath her palms. Men in Tortuga often worked shirtless, so why did seeing him affect her so? Her fingers flexed outward, skimming over soft blonde hairs. The faint matting grew thicker, forming a trail that arrowed down toward his waistband. She followed it, and his breath hissed out.

With a soft growl, he leaned down and captured her mouth once more. This time, he kissed her slowly, soft lips teasing hers open. He shifted his position and her eyes widened. The thin linen between them did little to disguise the bulge pressing against her.

Was it...? Her cheeks flamed as she remembered the very same protrusion pressing against her bottom at the tavern. Tentatively, she reached between them, her fingers brushing the rigid warmth there. Her pulse jumped. He rocked his hips, grinding himself fully into her palm and she gasped. *So hard.* She gave a tentative squeeze. He groaned into her mouth, the sound low and rough, reverberating through her like a spark to dry tinder.

She fumbled with the buttons at his waistband, the sudden need to feel his flesh against her skin consuming her. He didn't stop her when she slid her hand inside, her fingers tangling in coarse curls. And then, the smooth heat of his manhood bumped her knuckles. He sucked a harsh breath in when she turned to hold him.

She slipped down his length, her lips parting as she explored him—velvet soft, yet forged like iron.

"Be careful, or I'll be finding my release in your hand, love." He reached between them and caught her wrist, pulling her from his pulsing heat.

His palm settled on her ankle, cool flesh tempering the fire raging within her. But the relief didn't last as he skimmed it up her calf, pressed it to her thigh. Heat spiraled from her core as his fingertips eased closer and closer to her most private place. Somehow, she knew if he would only touch her there, the pressure would ease.

"Please." The word tumbled free at the same time as she lifted her hips, bringing him agonizingly closer.

He pushed through her curls, one finger flicking out to touch her, there and gone in a flash. But that minuscule touch sent her senses spiraling, giving a split second of blessed relief. A sound built in the back of her throat, and when he touched her again, a moan broke free. This time, he kept the contact, rubbing a slow circle.

Josephine's eyes fluttered shut as something fierce and unfamiliar began to twist and curl behind his finger. Her back arched, hips colliding with his, and his growl rumbled through the room. He moved, the solid weight of his knee parting her thighs. A moment later, his other one followed, spreading her legs to either side of him. She lifted her head, but couldn't see over her bunched shift. Even the thought of being open before him sent molten awareness rippling through her.

The ache between her legs verged on unbearable, throbbing with a need she could not name. Her thoughts fractured as his length settled there, nudging her with blunt heat. His breath hitched and he dropped his head, lips grazing her neck. She shivered and he groaned.

"So wet. So soft." The barely decipherable words sent a thrill through her.

He shifted, his flesh slipping up and down her most private spot. Each movement sent tendrils of exquisite pleasure radiating through her, each one stronger than the last as he pressed closer and closer to her core. With a subtle rock, the very tip of him pushed there, and the throbbing ache in her core seemed to bunch up tight. He went still and she nearly cried out.

"May I?" his voice came gravely, between pants.

She might die if he didn't.

"Please." The word came on a gasp. "Yes."

His hands closed around her hips, holding her in place as he thrust forward. A splinter of pain burned from where they joined, wrenching a sharp gasp from her.

He froze, his breathing hoarse and fast. "I'm sorry. I thought…at the tavern…the way you…" His eyes pressed shut as he trailed off.

A thread of shame twisted in her belly—he'd thought she was a lightskirt. That the easy laughter and boldness had meant she had experience. Seconds passed as he hovered motionless above her and the uncomfortable tightness began to ease.

"I…" She couldn't form words. Couldn't form a rational thought as an all-consuming need gripped her—the need for more. More of him. More of this.

"Tell me to stop." He began to pull free, the movement sending an explosion of feeling radiating from her core. She gasped again, this time from the pleasure. If he stopped, she might never experience anything like this again. The thought sent a chill nipping at the edges of all the warmth throbbing through her body and her fingers curled, digging into his back.

"No."

"Miss—" She lifted a finger to his lips before he could address her formally and his brows pushed together. "You don't understand."

"I do." Her breath came out on a shudder. "I understand I want this. More than anything."

He pressed his eyes closed, a silent battle etched in the lines of his face as he remained motionless. Damn man was going to stop himself. So, she did the only thing she could think of—she tilted her hips up, making him slide a little deeper.

He groaned, brows furrowed. She did it again. And this time, he moved with her, in a slow glide that filled her. "Is that…?" He searched her eyes and she nodded.

"Yes."

His head dropped forward and he repeated the movement. Every fiber of her body thrummed as the slick slide of their bodies together sent fingers of sharp pleasure radiating outward, each one stronger than the last. The ache at her core returned, hot and heavy, somehow accentuating the pleasure.

"God, you feel so good." His eyes squeezed shut, his features taut with intensity.

His lips found hers once more, the primal groans vibrating from the back of his throat sending new waves of fire shooting straight to where they joined. He moved with deliberate care, pulling nearly all the way out before plunging deep inside. Her hips moved with him, the fullness of each slick thrust wrenching a small moan from her.

He adjusted his weight onto one hand and reached between them with the other in a jerky movement. When his finger found her sensitive spot again, she cried out. The intensity of that touch mixed with the friction of his shaft within her sent her teetering on the edge of a precipice—one she didn't know existed. At once, all of the sensation became too much. Too unbearable.

She tried to pull away, but he pressed harder, his fingertip moving so fast, she cried out. Her hands twisted in the sheets as she wriggled under him, hips bucking.

"Please." The word came out in a desperate whimper.

"Shh…" His mouth moved to her ear, lips brushing her skin. "Just let go."

Let go.

He made it sound so easy.

"How?"

With a groan, he seated himself fully within her, and slowed his finger, rubbing lazy circles. With the torment eased somewhat, she tried to focus, her breaths coming in quick gasps.

His heavy eyes locked on hers. "Close your eyes." She obeyed and he slowly increased the tempo. The intense sensation tightened in her core, every inch of her on fire with need. "Don't fight it."

She let her head fall back, tense muscles slackening.

"Yes, that's it."

The encouragement was all she needed. With one last gasp, the pent-up sensations exploded outward, almost numbing in how they laid her body flat. A fractured scream tore through her throat, echoing from the rafters above as wave after wave of energy poured through her. Moments later he grunted and yanked himself free, his body shuddering over her.

Chapter Seventeen

A SOFT GRAY light filtered through the cabin as Isaac's eyes fluttered open. For one disorientating second, he forgot where he was. There was only *her*. Curled against him, one leg tangled with his, she shifted with a happy sigh. Dark hair fanned from where her head rested on his shoulder, tangled around the arm draped over his torso. Her scent—jasmine and something uniquely her—rose with each breath she took, and he drank it in, a warmth blooming unbidden in his chest.

He closed his eyes. He could almost believe he was someone else. Someone who had the right to hold her. But as quickly as that fragile contentment came, it vanished—burned away like mist beneath a rising sun. Reality returned in a brutal rush. He'd gotten carried away. Let himself forget.

Fool.

The word rang like a warning bell in his head. His hand rose, fingers pressing his temple. He'd forgotten every rule of copulating. Hell, he'd nearly completed within her. He'd taken her to bed like some tavern wench he could forget in the morning.

Only he wouldn't forget.

Not her.

His breath caught as images from the night before crashed through him. Of skin against skin. Of her bold touches, her sweet cries. *Damnation.* A growl rumbled in his throat. He didn't have the luxury of thinking like that. He had obligations—his commission, his crew, capturing Thorne. She had no place in any of this. Not on his ship. Not in his heart. He began to pull away, gently lifting her arm from his chest, but before he could rise, she stirred with a soft moan and stretched against him. He froze as her eyes fluttered open, dark and languid.

"I'm sorry. I didn't mean to wake you." His whisper sounded abnormally loud in the silence.

Lips curved against his chest and her hand drifted lower, fingers splaying against his stomach. Desire flared low in his spine before he crushed it with practiced resolve. He couldn't afford to want her—he needed to remember that. Still, he didn't move.

A few minutes longer wouldn't hurt. Besides, she didn't deserve for him to jump up and run off, leaving her alone after her first time with a man. He settled his hand over hers. It was all he could do—if he touched her anywhere else, he doubted his ability to control himself. Even now, her breath stirred his skin like fire.

He let his head fall back. If she were any other woman, he would take her again, get his fill and go on with his duties without a single look back. But she wasn't just another woman. She was Miss Montclair—a lady who deserved so much more than he could ever offer. A low groan escaped him. Everything had changed last night.

"Is everything alright?" She tilted her face toward him, lips still swollen.

"Yes."

A lie.

Still, he didn't want to give her hope of something that could never be. His lips brushed her cheek. "Last night—"

"Was incredible." Her eyes met his as she spoke, warm browns catching the morning light.

He kissed her forehead. "It was. But it can't happen again."

Her expression faltered and she drew back with furrowed brows. "What do you mean?"

"Miss Montclair, I don't expect you to understand this, but my life is bound by duty. First and foremost, I'm a military man. I have a mission to complete, and I've already stretched the limitations of every rule I know by allowing you to come with us.

I bent those rules for one reason—to keep you safe. To see you returned to your father."

Her body went rigid against him and she gave a tight smile. "Of course."

He tried to squeeze her hand, but she pulled it away. So much for not ruining her morning after. With a shake of his head, he turned to keep himself from capturing her mouth with his, from telling her it wasn't true—that he very much wanted it to happen again. He stood, facing away from her so she couldn't see the physical proof of how she affected him.

"I need to get to the helm. I'm late for my watch." The excuse fell flat as he picked up his pants and pulled them on with jerky movements.

But what was there to say? That last night hadn't meant anything? That it had? He raked a hand through his hair, jaw tight, as his resolve deepened.

He didn't turn back to her until he had fully dressed. She had already begun to dress, movements quiet and careful, as if the wrong sound might break whatever fragile thing still hung between them. She didn't look at him directly, but he didn't miss the pause in her hands, the slight stiffening of her spine. Without a word, she turned her back to him and finished buttoning her blouse.

Shame coiled in his gut and he jerked his gaze away. He cleared his throat and crossed the room. At the doorway, his hand hovered over the latch, the thud of his heart a steady beat in his ears. Behind him, silence settled heavy and absolute. He didn't dare look back. If he did, he might not leave. He pushed open the door.

Cool morning air swept in from the corridor. It cleared his head, but not his heart. His boots echoed as he climbed the steps up the main hatch. Wind rushed him once he stepped onto the deck, snapping at the loose ends of his shirt. He welcomed the merciless sting of salt spray. It brought him back—reminded him where he belonged.

This was his world. A place of order. Structure. Command.

Not softness. Not sweet sighs in the dark.

And yet… she'd crept in like a tide he hadn't seen coming. He exhaled sharply and bowed his head. He should've known better. *Did* know better. But that didn't stop the guilt gnawing at him like rats in the hull. Not for what they'd done—no, part of him would burn in hell and still not regret touching her—but for what came next. For what he couldn't give her.

Isaac stared out over the waves, the sky above beginning to bloom with the faintest pinks and golds. A new day. The chance to right his path. He squared his shoulders.

"Lieutenant?"

The single word sliced clean through the wind and his thoughts. She had followed him out onto the deck. "Will you teach me to use a sword?"

He went still, the image of her fingers wrapped around him flashing through his mind. Damn it. Now was not the time to be thinking of *that*. With a tight smile, he turned. "Learning to swordfight takes time. Time we don't have. You will not be involved in any fighting."

She blinked, hands wringing together. "But what if I do find myself in a situation where I need to defend myself? I would like to have a chance."

Her tangled hair had been pulled into a loose braid, and the wind had already pulled several tendrils free. The wild look suited her.

He cleared his throat—and mind. "You'd be better served learning to run and hide."

"You think I should run?"

He threw his hands out. "Yes."

"On a ship?" Her eyes swiveled slowly from one side of the deck to the other. "What happens when I can run no further— when there's nowhere left to hide? I don't want to go to battle. But I don't want to be helpless either."

He met her steady gaze and his retort dissolved on his

tongue. She was right. He blew out a slow exhale. "Alright. But very basic moves, defensive only."

Opening a chest near the railing, he picked up a light training blade, flipping it in a circle. Probably still too heavy for her. Handing it to her, he frowned when she dropped the point to the deck. "Don't ever hold it like that. This isn't like picking up a rapier in a parlor for sport. When you hold it, life and death are at stake."

He settled a hand on the hilt of his sword, the familiar comfort of the weapon grounding him. Already he regretted his decision. From the corner of his eye, he caught Silas's gaze from the wheel. His first officer's eyes had narrowed, face carved with disapproval. Isaac didn't need to hear it aloud to know what he thought—*send her back to the cabin. Do not indulge her.*

"So?" Miss Montclair waved the blade in front of him, pulling his thoughts back. "How should I hold it?"

"First, don't hold it so tight. You'll tire yourself out before you get your first swing in." He reached out, hands closing around hers, guiding her fingers into position.

"Here." His palm brushed the inside of her wrist as he adjusted the angle of the blade.

She didn't move. Didn't breathe.

Neither did he. The softness of her skin beneath his—warm, familiar—sent his pulse racing. He pulled back, clearing his throat. "That's better."

With a swallow, he drew his sword, the soft rasp of steel ringing across the deck. "Keep your stance light. Feet apart, knees bent. Just like last night." Again, memory tugged at him. He shook his head.

She mimicked him, brows drawn in concentration.

"Good. Now, we'll start with the simplest guard. Blade up. Angle it to glance the blow aside. The trick is not to catch the blow, but to deflect it."

She raised the sword and he stepped forward, bringing his blade down in a smooth arc toward hers. Steel clanged and she winced.

"You're holding it too tight again. If I strike hard, you'll jar your arms out of the socket."

Her grip shifted and she gave him a determined look. "Again."

He repeated the blow, harder, and the clash of blades echoed across the deck. Muffled voices came from the rigging as men swung down to watch. Isaac's jaw tightened. A woman on board was already enough to stir unease among the crew. But a woman being trained with a blade, by their commanding officer? So much for earning their respect.

He kept his voice low. "Next move is a sweep. If someone comes in low, this is how you stop them. Drop your blade. Here." His hand came to her hip, the heat of the brief touch igniting his senses. "Don't twist your spine. Let your knees absorb it."

Her breath hitched, and again, he put space between them. He swung his sword toward her, keeping it low, and she blocked it. Raising his arm, he forced her into the first block he'd shown her, walking a slow circle around her. "One of the most important parts about a sword fight is the movement of your feet. Keep them moving. If you stop, you give your opponent an opportunity."

With a nod, she twisted to the side, circling with him. They danced that way for minutes, blades rising and falling, and he slowly increased his speed and intensity. Soon, her curls stuck to her sweat-dampened forehead, shoulders rising and falling in quick breaths. After a heavy blow, she stumbled to her knees. In a blink, she pushed herself back up and leveled her blade at him. Her gaze met his, flushed and fierce, and something dangerously close to affection stirred in his chest.

He lowered his sword. "Enough."

She frowned, swiping a lock of hair from her face with the back of her hand. "Already?"

He didn't answer. Instead, he reached to his belt and pulled his dagger free. He held it loosely, the worn leather grip familiar against his palm. A much different weapon than his sword—personal, meant for close quarters. The kind of fighting that happened when all other options had run out.

"You won't win a fight with a sword. But…" He flipped the blade in his hand and offered it to her. "This could save your life."

He moved behind her. "Imagine someone grabs you. One arm around your waist, pulling you back." His arm wrapped around her front—not touching—but close enough to let her feel the idea of it. "Don't panic. Drop your weight and drive the blade back. No warning. No hesitation."

She turned the dagger in her palm, and nodded once before turning to face him. "I can't take this." Her fingertip grazed his engraved initials at the base of the blade, and she offered it back to him.

He closed his hand around hers, wrapping her fingers firmly around the hilt. "Keep it. I will feel better knowing you carry a capable and well forged blade."

She stared at it, running one slender finger along its length. Again, heat coursed through him and he chewed on a curse. After last night, he wouldn't be able to look at her without remembering… remembering it all. He twisted, staring out over the sea behind them.

He didn't like complications. They clouded judgment. Fractured focus.

Got men killed.

"She's a dangerous distraction."

Isaac jerked his gaze from the main deck, where Miss Montclair had just walked out into the midday sun. Silas gave him a level look, daring him to argue. Truth was, he couldn't. His first officer was right.

"I know." His gruff retort had Silas raising his brows. "By the end of today, she'll be back on Christian's schooner. No more distractions."

"You say that as if having a civilian ship—one captained by a woman who looks like a blasted pirate—alongside us isn't a distraction in and of itself."

Silas had joined Isaac's crew a month ago, which meant he hadn't witnessed Christian's and Samantha's skills. The men who had sailed under Christian's command and had aided in his rescue held a healthy amount of respect for both him and his new wife. Those weren't the ones he had to worry about.

"I assure you, having their help greatly increases our chances at success." Isaac kept his gaze fixed forward.

"You have a lot of faith in a former lieutenant." Silas stepped forward and took the wheel. "It's no secret you were good friends before you served together. I just hope that doesn't cloud your judgment—or hamper your duties."

A thread of unease wormed through Isaac's gut as his first officer voiced the very concern that had been lingering on his own conscience all along. *No.* He straightened his shoulders. Christian had been his friend since they were boys. They had gone through their entire lives together. He trusted him. Wholeheartedly.

Didn't he?

Isaac clenched his jaw and turned his eyes toward the horizon, willing a smudge of land into view. A gust of wind tugged at his coat, and movement on the deck caught his eye. Miss Montclair had moved to the railing, her posture graceful and unguarded as she leaned into the breeze. The way she stood, skirts whipping around her legs, she looked like a regal princess yearning for a glimpse of a faraway land. She twisted to face him and he quickly dropped his gaze.

Not quick enough to miss her knowing smile.

And damn him, he nearly smiled back.

Whatever passed between them—whatever *this* was—it

couldn't matter. Not now. He had his duty. She had a home to return to. He tilted his head her way again and his pulse jumped. She had moved. Was moving. Toward him. His throat went dry. He forced himself to stand still, hoping his expression remained neutral, though his mind still raced.

She passed by Burke, the shipwrecked sailor who perched on a barrel in the sun, sharpening his dagger. His condition had markedly improved overnight.

"Miss Montclair, isn't it?" he drawled, raising his head, eyes dragging over her like she was something for sale.

Isaac's jaw clenched as she slowed.

"Oh. Hello." She took a slight step back as Burke openly stared at her. "You look much better already."

"I am, thank you." He picked something from under his nail with the point of his blade. "What I want to know is why the lieutenant gets to bring his paramour on board during a mission."

Her cheeks went pink. "I'm not his—"

A grating laugh burst free. "Come on now, you don't think the rest of us are stupid, do you? Everyone knows you two spent the last night together."

Before he knew what he was doing, Isaac vaulted over the railing and dropped to the main deck, his boots slamming the boards. The crewman barely had time to turn before Isaac closed the space between them and grabbed him by the collar, hauling him upright.

"You watch your mouth," Isaac growled, voice low and lethal.

Burke raised his hands in mock surrender, but the smirk remained. "Didn't mean no harm, Cap'n. Just making conversation—"

Isaac's hand tightened, twisting the sailor's shirt until the man choked for breath. "This is *my* ship." His voice came sharp as drawn steel. "You don't speak to her. You don't *look* at her. You forget she's aboard, or I'll toss you overboard myself and let the sea decide your fate."

The seaman stared at him for a long moment, sails flapping overhead. Finally, he nodded. Isaac released his grip and Burke took off, rubbing his neck. After the sailor descended the main hatch, he turned to Miss Montclair, who stared at him with wide eyes. A gust of wind swept across the deck, and the moment stretched between them like a taut line.

Footsteps creaked behind them, and Silas called down from the helm, "Land ahead!"

Isaac turned instinctively. Sure enough, the gray silhouette of Norfolk rose from the horizon, hazy but unmistakable. He exhaled, grateful for the distraction.

"We'll be docking within the hour." He climbed back up to the helm and she followed, keeping her distance.

The crew hurried into action, readying the ship for their arrival. While activity bloomed around him, Isaac watched her from the corner of his eye. Tried not to notice the flush still high on her cheekbones—the storm she kept so carefully locked behind her eyes. Her hand moved, slow and deliberate to her neckline. She tugged the ribbon there. The key slid free like a secret, catching the morning light before she curled her fingers around it, holding it close to her chest.

After a long moment, she turned to him. "Please—"

He lifted his hand. "No need to convince me. You're coming. With Thorne in town, I'm not taking my eyes off of you until Christian and Samantha catch up."

Chapter Eighteen

"**A**RE YOU READY?"

Josephine turned from the cabin windows, her breath catching when she met the lieutenant's gaze. He leaned against the doorframe, the brass buttons of his navy jacket gleaming in the light.

His eyes dropped to the ribbon around her neck and she patted her chest. "Don't worry, I've got the key."

He jerked his head up. "Of course. I didn't think otherwise."

They left the cabin, silence trailing after them like a shadow. The gangplank creaked beneath their boots, the wood slick with seawater and salt. Norfolk's harbor sprawled before them, bristling with masts and sails, the air thick with tar and brine. Dockhands shouted over the groan of ropes and the rumble of carts, and gulls wheeled overhead with sharp cries.

Beyond the piers, brick buildings crowded narrow, uneven streets, their windows thrown open to the heat. A church spire rose in the distance, cutting a clean line against the blue sky. Josephine tugged her shawl tighter around her shoulders as they stepped off the gangplank and into the chaotic rhythm of the city. The noise, the motion, the sheer size of it all set her nerves on edge—but not nearly as much as the man beside her.

Each time she slanted her gaze toward him, her pulse jumped and heat pooled low in her belly. She scowled at her traitorous body. The sting of his comments from the morning still rubbed raw. She'd barely awoken, still wrapped in the afterglow of the most glorious night of her life, when he'd shattered it by mentioning her father. He may as well have thrown a bucket of ice water on her.

Still, her heart fluttered as they walked together. Last night, she'd truly become a woman. She walked a little straighter at his side on the dock, as if the memory itself could shield her from uncertainty.

At the street, he offered his elbow. "I must warn you, there was a fire in Norfolk during the Revolutionary War. Most of the city burned down. That building may no longer be there. Could be why Christian felt it was a dead end."

She smiled, the pulse in her throat quickening as her fingers drifted to her neckline to touch the ribbon. "There must be something. Why else would destiny allow our paths to cross?"

He slowed, fixing her with a piercing look that sent her skin tingling. "Why, indeed?" Heat laced his voice as his gaze dipped to her lips and her pulse jumped for a different reason altogether.

Lieutenant Caldwell raised a hand and a passing hackney slowed, iron-rimmed wheels creaking as the mismatched horses tossed their heads. Sunlight gleamed from the black carriage as the driver swept off his hat in greeting. The lieutenant stepped forward. "We'll take a ride to 15 Queen St."

"Queen? Are you sure?" The man's face scrunched when the lieutenant nodded. "There's no such street."

"Are you sure? We've an address." Lieutenant Caldwell unfolded the paper and squinted at the writing.

The driver huffed. "Then you have the wrong address. Been driving these streets for over a decade and there ain't no Queen St."

With tight lips, Lieutenant Caldwell thanked him and turned to her. "Looks like Christian was right after all."

Josephine frowned. "I don't understand." She took the sheet from him and traced the angry line beneath the address. "It says empty building, not no building."

"There's no way to know. Let's get back to the ship." He offered his arm as he glanced around. "Not a good idea to stay out in the open."

She pulled her lip between her teeth. Unless Christian had gotten the address wrong in the first place, it didn't make any sense. *Queen Street.* It must be a common street name. So why wouldn't a city the size of Norfolk have one?

Her hand drifted up and pulled the key free, her stomach sinking. The lieutenant kept his gaze straight ahead, his jaw set. Now what? The question hovered on her tongue but she pressed her lips together. In theory, Thorne could be walking the very same streets as they were.

The thought of the dreaded captain sent a shiver skimming down her spine. She saw him again—half-swallowed by the garden's shadows, as if part of the darkness itself. Colette had been right about his eyes. Even now, the ghost of that piercing stare lingered on her skin. She tightened her grip on the lieutenant's arm, willing the memory to dissolve.

A group of sailors walked toward them and they moved to the side. Josephine's hand brushed over the rough stones of an old wall. She slowed as her palm passed over a blackened area, her fingertip pressing into a worn groove. She squinted. *105.* Perhaps an old address marker.

"When did you say the fire was?"

"1776. British forces bombed the city."

Josephine tried to recall what she'd learned about the American Revolution. Very little. She glanced back at the retreating wall.

"When they rebuilt the city, is there a possibility they may have renamed any places that reminded them of the crown?"

Lieutenant Caldwell came to a stop, turning to her with a thoughtful expression. "You might be on to something. Sentiments against the British run deep to this day." He pressed his lips together, nodding. "I know where we can find out. But we'll have to hurry, it's getting late."

He started again, this time at a brisk pace and they veered down the next street, heading away from the docks. They pressed deeper into the city, keeping to the edges of the cobblestone streets. The lieutenant pulled her close as they overtook a group of elderly ladies. When they passed them, he came to a sudden stop. Josephine bit back a cry as he seized her arm and dragged her into a small alleyway between two buildings.

The damp scent of stone clung to the heavy air around them, their bodies pressed together in the dimness. Josephine's heart slammed against her ribs, each frantic beat quicker than the last. She opened her mouth, but Isaac's hand shot up, his fingers pressing to her lips.

"Quiet," he murmured, breath warm against her ear. "I think we're being followed."

She nodded and he dropped his hand, settling it low on her back. His fingers splayed wide, holding her away from the moss-covered bricks behind her. Which meant the entirety of her front rested against him. Her cheek rested on his chest, where the steady thrum of his heart reverberated through her. Though her stomach had gone knotted, heat crawled up her neck. His sandalwood scent filled the space between them, and with each measured breath she took, her panic began to ebb.

After a tense minute passed, his muscles slackened and he twisted his face toward hers. His lips grazed her ear and for a moment, she couldn't move. Her fingers curled in his shirt. When had they gotten there?

"I must have been mistaken." His voice came in a low whisper against her skin. "There's no one. Let's go."

Still, when they edged from between the buildings, he kept his head down and retraced their steps back to the nearest street. They cut across it, moving with purpose, and a few blocks later, he pointed ahead. "The courthouse. If there's any old maps of the city, they will have them."

The building loomed before them with columned porticos framing an arched doorway, their white stone contrasting against warm brick.

They entered, the soft jingle of a bell announcing their arrival. It took Josephine's eyes a moment to adjust to the dimness, the only light coming from a few flickering lanterns along the walls. She sniffed, pulling her nose up at the eclectic scent of old paper, beeswax, and mildew. Tall shelves lined the walls and jutted out in several rows across the floor, their weighty contents sagging the wood. A large central table bore ink spills, strewn with haphazard stacks of documents waiting to be sorted. In the corner, a writing desk sat beneath a small, clouded window that let in a sickly shaft of afternoon light.

A young clerk sat at the desk, his quill scratching away at his paper. He glanced at the clock, then back to his work. "We're only open for another half hour."

The lieutenant approached him. "Lieutenant Isaac Caldwell. Do you have any maps of the city before the great fire?"

"If we do, they will be in the records room." Without looking up from his writing, the clerk frowned. "Why don't you look in the naval archives?"

"The courthouse was closer and time is of the essence."

After a long sigh, the clerk dropped his quill and stood. "Very well." He opened a drawer and pulled a key out. "Only one person is allowed in at a time, and no women."

Lieutenant Caldwell straightened. "Certainly, an exception can be made."

The man stared at him as if he'd suggested treason. "Rules are not made to be broken. If that's not satisfactory to you, feel free to make the trip to the naval yard to do your research."

A muscle ticced along the lieutenant's jaw, but he nodded. "Very well." He turned to Josephine. "Will you be alright?"

She set a hand on his forearm, ignoring the instant burst of heat the touch sent through her. "Of course. I'll see if I can find anything helpful out here."

The clerk walked him over to the records room, leaving Josephine alone. She swiveled and meandered to a row of bookshelves in the back packed with leather-bound ledgers, bundled papers tied with string, and wooden document boxes.

She pulled her key free and rubbed a thumb over it. Who was she fooling? With no clues about its origin, she had no idea where she would look for any information that could help in the slightest. Not like the courthouse would have a ledger of most wanted pirate artifacts.

With a sigh, she tucked the key back and ran a hand across a stack of land grants. She turned toward the records room. A bench sat beneath a small window looking into it. May as well wait there.

As she started over, the bell rang again. A man entered, his hat pulled low. She frowned. Something about him pricked familiar. He spoke to the clerk, voice too hushed for her to make out. Satisfied with whatever the clerk had told him, he adjusted his hat and for a fleeting second, his face caught the light. Her blood chilled as she recognized Burke, the shipwrecked sailor.

Samantha's warning about trusting him rang like an alarm in Josephine's head as his gaze swept the room. She dropped to the floor and shimmied back between two bookshelves, heart slamming against her ribs. Why was he here? Worse, had he seen her? With mind racing, she straightened and found a gap between two stacks of papers. Holding her breath, she peered through.

He was gone.

She sucked in a breath. *Don't panic.* The ship Thorne had sunk had come from here. This could be his home. It could be as simple as a friend or family member that worked in the library. Her breathing slowed. Still, she stayed put. After their altercation earlier on deck, she wasn't taking any chances.

Click.

The echo of a boot heel struck the wood floor just on the other side of the bookshelf she hid behind.

Click.

She held her breath as he stopped directly opposite her. He coughed, and the ledgers near her face shifted as he adjusted them. Her throat went dry. If he pulled them free, he would see her. After an agonizing moment, he started walking again.

Though her muscles slackened, she stayed perfectly still, her chest squeezing. Once he made it to the end of the aisle, one single step would put her in his line of sight. Slowly, she backed up, until she reached the end of the bookcase. She would have to time it perfectly.

With heart pounding, she waited until his shadow fell into her aisle, then eased herself around the back of the shelf, into the aisle he'd just left. It worked. Her breath rushed out as a tremor wracked her body.

Burke approached the window of the records room and peered inside. He didn't move. He simply stood there—watching. Waiting. She narrowed her eyes. Why was he snooping on the lieutenant? He lingered a moment longer, his posture too still, too focused. Then, with a final glance toward the clerk, he turned and strode out the door.

Only when the bell jingled again did Josephine let out the breath she'd been holding. She waited—counted to ten, then twenty—before she stepped into the open, heart still thudding in her throat. Burke hadn't seen her. But the unease remained, curling cold and tight in her belly.

The door to the records room creaked open. Isaac emerged with a triumphant glint in his eye. He strode across the room and caught her elbow, leaning in with a whisper.

"You were right. After the fire, some of the streets that had been named after British roads were renamed. Queen Street is now Church Street." He hurried toward the door. "And, it was in an area of town unscathed by the fire."

Her heart soared. Finally, good news. But she needed to tell him what she had seen. She chewed on her cheek. If she told him, he might decide to go back to the ship. Nevertheless, he needed to know.

"Lieutenant, while you were in the records room, Mr. Burke came in."

He frowned. "What did he want?"

"He didn't see me. But he watched you in the records room

for a while, then left."

With a shake of his head, Lieutenant Caldwell continued across the room. "Earlier, he had the nerve to ask if he could come along. I told him to stay on the ship." A scowl twisted his lips. "He's proving more trouble than he's worth."

She shifted her weight, crossing her arms around her middle. "Something about him feels off."

"He's letting his anger toward Thorne cloud his judgment. I'll have a stern talk with him later."

But it wasn't just grief or rage. Josephine could feel it deep in her bones—the crawling unease she felt around him, how her instincts had screamed when his gaze swept past. There was something more in him, something dangerous.

She took a steadying breath and forced a smile. They had an address to hunt down. Later, after they had their answers, she could worry about Burke and his spying.

"Let's go find our answers." Lieutenant Caldwell guided her out into the afternoon sun. He unfolded a sheet of parchment and pointed to the rough sketch of a map he'd drawn. "It's not far from here."

The air hung heavy around them, clinging to their skin as they walked in silence. As the blocks passed, the sounds of the city faded beneath the weight of her thoughts. Her key may very well unlock the information the lieutenant needed to capture Thorne. The possibility quickened her pulse.

"This is it."

He'd slowed and Josephine jerked her head up. She wrung her hands together as she stared. "Are you sure?"

The house loomed like a hollowed shell, set back from the narrow street. Choked by creeping ivy, its shutters hung crooked on bricks faded by wind and rain. Josephine's skin prickled as she took it in—the slanted roofline, the shattered panes, the over-grown grass hiding the path. It looked forsaken. Her fingers curled into fists at her sides as they stepped onto the sagging porch, weathered boards groaning under their feet. Above the door, a Latin inscription had been carved into stone.

Societas vitae umbrarum.

She squinted at it. "The Society of Shadow Life. Or perhaps Life in Shadows."

He gave her an appreciative glance. "Someone was paying attention in school. Good thing because I never bothered."

She gave a shaky laugh. "This is about the only time in my life it's proved useful."

"And I'm glad for it." Warmth flowed through his words and her pulse jumped again. He reached for the doorknob, giving it a shake. "Locked."

Josephine's hand rose to the ribbon at her neck. "My key?"

He shook his head. "No, it's a different type of lock. Stand back." With a grunt, he threw his shoulder into the door. It flew open, sending him tumbling inside, his arms flailing.

Rubbing his shoulder, he raised a brow. "Well. That was a lot easier than I expected."

She couldn't help a giggle. "Or maybe you're just that strong?"

He shot her a lopsided grin that sent a flutter through her chest. "I like that theory."

"Wait here." He ducked inside, leaving her alone on the porch. She twisted, eyes scanning the empty street and jumped when he popped his head out. "All clear."

She hurried in, eyes adjusting to the dim light. The scent of mildew and dust hung heavy in the air, and she fought back a reflexive cough. Blinking, she took in the room. The wallpaper—once patterned in elegant swirls—peeled in long, curling strips, exposing raw plaster beneath. At the far end of the room, an ancient fireplace, choked with soot and cobwebs, held a pair of abandoned candlesticks, their wax melted and hardened into twisted stumps. But it was the mirror that drew her attention. It dominated the wall across from her, its silver backing speckled and faded. Her reflection stared back, ghostlike in the dim light, and unease curled low in her belly.

Something was wrong.

A moment later, the lieutenant put it to words. "There's nothing here." He dropped to his knees, rubbing a finger across the dusty floorboards and pointed to a bare spot. "Someone's been through before us."

She bent. Though several footprints were visible, a fresh layer of dust had already gathered. "Not recently."

He lifted his head to meet her gaze. "You're right."

Together, they moved deeper into the house, their steps stirring motes of dust into the thin shafts of light filtering through the grimy windows. Each room they checked yielded the same result—stripped bare. No furniture, no papers, no hidden compartments or signs of recent life. Only shadows and silence.

"This can't be it," Josephine whispered, her voice nearly swallowed by the empty air. She turned slowly in the center of the big room they'd started in, the key suddenly cold against her skin. "There has to be something."

The lieutenant moved with purpose, knocking along the walls, running his hands along the stone of the fireplace. Jaw tight, his frustration simmered just beneath the surface. "I think someone made damn sure there was nothing left to find."

All the work today. All for nothing. Tears stung Josephine's eyes, threatening to unleash a torrent of emotions. She came to a stop in front of the mirror, the tarnished surface distorting her image. The lieutenant stood behind her, his reflection a mere shadow.

"I wasted so much of your time." A heavy ache wrapped around her heart. "I'm so sorry."

He stepped forward into the light, his gaze locking with hers. "I'm not."

Chapter Nineteen

ISAAC TOOK ANOTHER step toward her, eyes on the clouded glass.

A tightness wrapped around his heart as disappointment etched Miss Montclair's face. She was upset. Not for the lack of answers. Upset for him, for *his* disappointment—spurred by a genuine care for him. The warmth of her concern settled in his chest, something he hadn't felt in a long time—perhaps ever.

He swallowed, the sound echoing through the room. He should turn away. She deserved better than stolen moments and second thoughts.

And he…

He didn't deserve her at all.

Yet he wanted her more than anything. More than whatever that blasted key unlocked. More than finding Thorne.

As the thought materialized, it unlocked something inside him. All afternoon, he'd wrestled with the urge to touch her again. To pull her into his arms. He'd fought a multitude of battles in his head, rationalizing all the ways she didn't—couldn't—fit into his life, how she deserved so much more than he could offer. He'd reasoned, resisted, reminded himself who he was.

To hell with reason.

Another step. She stood still, her eyes unblinking in the mirror's depths. He eased closer, until the warmth of her scent curled around him. If he stretched his arm just right, he would be able to touch her. Could he? If he did, the line between duty and desire would blur for good.

As if in a trance, he reached forward, curled one finger until it brushed the inside of her wrist. A shock coursed through him at the simple contact, the sharp current of heat sending his pulse jumping. He eased his hand back, but she twisted her arm to follow his movement, bumping against his knuckles. The barely-there touch shattered his restraint and he closed the space between them.

She started to turn, but he shook his head, holding her gaze in the mirror. He positioned himself directly behind her, his hands hovering on either side of her waist. Her breath came out in a shudder as he closed his hands around her hips. With the searing contact, his last chance to walk away evaporated.

He leaned in and nuzzled behind her ear. "I've wanted to do this all day."

His teeth closed on her earlobe and her needy gasp sent a thrill coursing straight to his groin. Both hands skimmed up her sides until the heavy weight of her breasts rested on them. With a soft groan, he cupped them, never taking his eyes off hers as her nipples hardened beneath his palms, straining against the thin fabric. Emboldened, he unbuttoned the top button of her blouse, baring the silky skin at her neck. Another button and the swells of her breasts teased him, promising him so much more. He shifted his weight, his erection already thick and hard. One more button.

He growled his appreciation when the blouse parted, baring her to him. Even in the shadows, the dusky pink of her nipples pebbled beneath his gaze. Her lips parted when he rolled one between his fingers, and his body answered with a surge of possessive hunger. With slow precision, he traced the outline of the key where it rested in the valley between her breasts.

Her chest rose and fell beneath his touch and he fanned his fingers out, running them in a whisper-soft circle around each perfect globe. The need to turn her became an overwhelming urge, to claim each nipple with his mouth. Gritting his teeth, he resisted, instead closing his hands over them.

Her body melted into his hands, her back arching as if pulled by some magnetic force as the soft curve of her breasts yielded to his touch. He groaned. So damn perfect. A frantic pulse raced beneath his hands, each beat drumming against his palm. He kneaded, firm and demanding, and the air around them crackled with tension, the weight of her desire matching his own. With a shaky gasp, her breath caught as he let his hands fall away and reached for the hem of her skirt.

Muslin twisted in his hands as he inched it up, baring the softness he yearned to claim. His knuckles grazed the smooth skin of her thigh when he pulled the fabric higher. No drawers. God help him. With a shuddering breath, he continued his path up, inch by agonizing inch. The soft brush of curls stilled him, the heat of her searing through him like flame, and he paused for the briefest moment.

"Tell me to stop."

Her gaze found his in the mirror, steady and unflinching. "Don't stop."

The simple words, spoken with conviction, snapped his controlled movement. His palm settled over her center, her gasp lost beneath the roar in his ears. She was his. Not in a way that could be measured or explained—not yet. That clarity could come later. For now, all that mattered was the undeniable truth of it, pulsing between them like a shared heartbeat.

His finger dipped between her folds, and he groaned at the slick warmth that met his touch. Her hips shifted as he circled gently, then pressed deeper. She rewarded him with an aching cry that sent his cock throbbing.

"Look at us," he rasped against her ear, his voice frayed and low.

Her gaze locked on the mirror. Her blouse hung open, her flushed chest rising and falling with every breath, his hand hidden beneath her skirt, working her with relentless purpose. While she stared *there*, he found the entrance to her womanhood, slipped his finger inside. Her legs trembled as he curled it, stroking her from the inside.

With one last tug, he lifted her skirts to expose her. The sight sucked the air from his lungs and he plunged deeper, burying his hand in her dark curls. She cried out again, louder, and desire crashed over him in a wave so fierce, it nearly took him to his knees. The wild want, the way her body writhed, all of it branded into his memory.

"Have you ever touched yourself?" The shocking words tumbled free before he could stop them.

Her lips parted. He held his breath. And then she nodded.

"Show me."

Even in the old surface of the mirror, her blush shone. "I—"

He caught her hand in his and guided it toward the junction of her thighs, coaxing her fingers alongside his. Pressing them between her curls, he held her hand cupped over herself. For a long moment, she didn't move. And then, a slender finger shifted. He followed the movement with one of his, into the pulsing wet between her legs. She gasped.

"Feel how ready you are for me?" he growled into her ear.

She nodded, breathless.

He trapped her finger with his, dragging it up to her swollen nub and settling it there. "Show me." He repeated his command, his voice strained with the consuming need to see her, to feel her.

With a jerky movement, she rubbed herself. Her breath sucked in and her knees sagged. He tightened his arm around her waist, lifting his hand from hers for a better view. Her head fell back against his shoulder, eyes closed, mouth slack as she moved her fingers.

Holy hell.

The sight alone might be his undoing.

Slowly she increased her speed, parting her thighs for a better angle. His breath hitched as her back arched into him. Not much longer. A soft moan escaped her and he dropped his hand, tangling his fingers with hers as his blood pumped hot and heavy. Her eyes fluttered open in question and he leaned into her ear. "I want you to find your release while I'm inside you."

With a pout, she strained to touch herself again and his lips curved. "Patience."

He dragged her hand away, baring herself to the mirror. From this angle, she was all curves and softness. Pure perfection. Every muscle in his body coiled tight, desperate for more. He reached between them and unbuttoned his trousers, freeing himself from the tight confines.

Brown eyes followed his movement and she pulled her hand from his, twisting it behind her back. With a growl, he rocked forward into her searching touch. Her fingers faltered, and he caught her wrist, pinning it gently as he leaned in, letting her feel the full weight of his desire. A soft groan shook through her as she moved her hand along his length.

His breath quickened as she worked him, the sensation of her delicate hand wrapped around him nearly driving him to madness. Each stroke, each gentle pull, sent waves of heat rushing through him. He clenched his jaw, willing himself to stay composed as her fingers moved with purpose. Each touch pushed him closer to the edge, the raw need between them building with every second. He fought the overwhelming urge to thrust into her hand, to spill his release then and there, but he took a breath, steadying himself.

He jerked his hand down and stilled hers, pulling it from his aching member. She trembled, her shoulders rising and falling as he used his feet to pull her legs apart, opening her to him in the most delicious way. With one hand, he guided himself between the pale crescents of her buttocks, until he dipped into the silky pool of wetness between her thighs. She whimpered as he hovered at her entrance.

"Isaac."

He stilled, the sound of his name on her lips tethering him to her like an anchor to a storm-tossed ship. Her voice, soft and trembling with need, ignited a fierce ache within him. He tilted his hips, nudging until he slipped just inside her. The sensation was almost too much, every nerve in his body sparking with fire.

"Isaac, please," she pleaded, pushing herself against him.

How could he say no? With a grunt, he plunged forward. Her answering cry echoed through the room as he seated himself fully within her. Pleasure crashed through him, a hundred different bursts of feeling spreading along his length. So wet. So tight.

His hands moved to her hips as he pulled nearly free before burying himself again. She stumbled forward with the force, her hands darting out to brace against the mirror. He followed, his body pressing against hers, breath hot against her neck. She clutched the frame of the mirror, hips tilting instinctively into each wild thrust. He groaned as her body moved with his, welcoming him deeper. A blinding pressure began to build at his core, threatening to unleash at any moment.

She shifted against him, urging him on with soft, breathless sounds that sent fire licking through his veins. He found a rhythm, powerful and unrelenting, each thrust pushing her closer to the edge—dragging him right along with her. His gaze locked on the mirror as she bucked against him, her skin flushed and glistening with sweat. All for him. The slick rhythm of their joining mingled with her gasps—a symphony that could drive him to do wild and reckless things.

With a sharp exhale, he reached one hand around her front, pressing his finger into her curls until he found the slick and quivering nub of her sex once more. She jerked, crying out as he stroked her with deliberate, unrelenting pressure. Each gasp she gave him, every frantic shudder, fueled the storm in his own blood as she unraveled in his arms.

Her fingers curled, her lips forming a soundless *"Oh."* Her body stiffened, her head jerking back against him, as she clamped around him in delicious pressure. A moment later, a throaty scream echoed through the room.

Yes.

A savage satisfaction coiled low in his belly as she continued to writhe beneath his hand. His own climax built to a crescendo and he increased the speed of his thrusts. Her knuckles went white as she hung onto the frame of the mirror, her legs beginning to give out. One slender hand slipped.

Josephine.

Her name burned on his tongue, swelling like a shout at the back of his throat. His body surged toward release, unstoppable, as the entire world narrowed to their joining. And then—*click.* The sound, small and sharp, echoed around them. A moment later, the entire mirror shifted, swinging out on hinges to reveal a sliver of dark space behind it.

No. No, not now.

"God above." He ground the words out between gritted teeth, willing his release to back off, to obey him just this once.

His breath sawed from his lungs, harsh and uneven. The pressure clawed at him, insistent and brutal, but he shoved it down with a growl of frustration. He forced himself to think—*focus*—but all he could feel was her, still hot and trembling around him. With a strangled grunt, he pulled free, every inch of his body raging at the loss. *Later*, he swore to himself.

Josephine still clung bonelessly to the frame, her breaths ragged. He eased her skirts down with care, the backs of his fingers grazing the soft curve of her buttocks. She shivered, and the small, involuntary reaction stole his breath. He leaned forward and planted a kiss at the crown of her head as he tucked himself back into his trousers, the strain of restraint still humming through every muscle.

One breath. Two.

"Seems we have a knack for interruptions." His voice came out low and rough-edged.

Her hands dropped as she stepped back, confusion flickering in her eyes. She tugged her blouse back into place, fastening the few buttons with slow, deliberate movements. One hand lifted to her lips, wiping gently before falling to her side. "What just happened?"

"You've discovered a cleverly hidden compartment." He took hold of the mirror and slowly swung it the rest of the way open.

A single lock box sat within. He reached in and pulled it out, blowing the thin layer of dust from it. Grasping the lid, he gave it a tug. Locked.

"Your key."

Her hand closed around the ribbon and pulled it free. With trembling hands, she slid the key in. It fit. His heart pounded in his ears as she turned it and a loud click echoed through the room.

She gave a shaky laugh. "You open it."

Isaac hesitated a moment as something uncomfortable twisted in his belly. Once opened, whatever was inside would change his life. The certainty rang through him. But it had to be done. With one deep breath, he yanked the lid free.

Her face fell. "It's just a bunch of papers."

He frowned and lifted the stack, reading the top page. "Not just any papers. Naval orders."

> *Confidential Directive*
> *Naval Office, New London*
> *Dated: August 12, 1779*

He pointed to the date on the yellowed parchment. "This is from after the fire. Clever. They used the old address so no one could discover them."

She leaned in as he flipped the paper. As his eyes scanned the page, the words seemed to betray reality.

"No." The single syllable came out in a hoarse croak and he fell to his knees, pain splintering up his legs as he reread the faded ink, willing himself to be wrong.

> *You are hereby ordered to execute the removal of the subject at the Thompson residence on the evening of August 14. Ensure the scene reflects the work of pirates—no witnesses. Should resistance be encountered, act swiftly and decisively. Mrs. Thompson is to be delivered to our associates offshore for further transport. Be advised our benefactors expect the matter to be*

concluded with discretion. Captain Thompson is a threat to our livelihood; his investigation into our operation must not be allowed to continue.

This mission is to furthermore remain unrecorded. Report directly to me upon completion.

He stared hard at the signature, shaking his head as his stomach threatened to empty itself.

C. Ross

"Lieutenant, what's wrong?" Josephine's hand settled on his shoulder.

Treason.

The word cut through him like a blade, leaving a cold chill in its wake. He stared at the papers in his hands, unable to focus. Behind it all… Ross. The very man he had tried to leave Miss Montclair with in Savannah. His gaze flicked to her.

"This changes everything." He returned the pages to the box, his movements stiff as his thoughts raced, the implications unfolding too quickly for him to grasp all at once.

Thorne had been right all along. Pirates hadn't killed his wife. The damn government had—and not just any government officials, but the very ones that had sailed alongside him, ones he likely had considered trusted friends.

He rose abruptly, hands clenched tight around the box as the fog around his mind cleared. "We need to get back to the ship. Now."

A hollow emptiness settled in his gut as he swung open the door, stepping into the blinding sunlight. He hesitated for a moment, staring out into the open street while his heart churned. Before he could take another step, a shadow passed over him, slicing through the daylight. He instinctively took a step back into the safety of the house. But it was too late.

Crack!

Chapter Twenty

J OSEPHINE SCREAMED. IT was all she could do as Lieutenant Caldwell fell to the floor and Mr. Burke stepped over him. "Hello, Miss Montclair."

She stood frozen in place, staring at the lieutenant's prone body, searching for any sign of life while the seaman bent and picked up the box that had clattered to the floor.

"Many thanks for doing the hard work in finding this."

Her jaw clenched as his palm flattened on the lid, fingers drumming a slow, deliberate tap, the sound echoing like a gavel in her chest. Her heart gave a hollow drop, sinking lower with each pat. Samantha had been right about him after all.

Run.

Every muscle in her body thrummed. She needed to get out. To warn someone. She pivoted and sprinted toward the back of the house. Heavy footsteps followed as she turned down a hallway. He closed the distance and she flung herself through the nearest opening in the wall.

There.

An outside door.

She fumbled with the lock and jerked it open as his hand closed over her shoulder. *No.* She twisted, the fabric of her blouse tearing in his closed fingers. It was enough. Her feet flew down the stairs into a small alleyway between buildings. His curse followed her as she forced her legs to run faster than she ever had before.

When she burst onto the street, she didn't slow and turned

right, feet pounding against uneven cobblestones. At the next intersection, she dodged a mule and cart while crossing and making another turn. Each time she turned down a new street, she chanced a quick glance behind her. But no one followed. Still, she pressed herself forward, garnering startled shouts from passersby as she weaved between crowds. Finally, with her side burning, she sagged against a brick wall. She could go no farther. And was lost.

Pressing her hand below her ribs, she struggled to catch her breath. She tipped her head back against the wall, tears welling. She'd left Lieutenant Caldwell. He could be dead. But if she had stayed, she would probably be in the same position. She straightened her shoulders. If she could get to the docks, she could warn his men, get a doctor. Bending, she eased the dagger from its leather binding at her calf.

She stepped from the shadows and lifted her gaze to the sky, trying to get her bearings. The midday sun did her no favors. With a huff she started down the street, the muscles in her legs screaming their protest. At the next intersection, she did a slow pivot.

There.

The glimmer of water shimmered at the end of the street. She hurried that way.

"Not so fast." A wagon clattered to a halt and Burke jumped down.

She spun, but his fingers tangled in her hair, the sharp tug yanking her to a stop as pain rippled across her scalp. "Don't think the boss would be too happy to have you running around raising the alert."

With a grunt, she drove the dagger back, aiming for his ribs. Somehow, he twisted, the blade grazing his side. He snarled, his free hand catching her wrist before she could strike again. She tried to pull away, but he gave a vicious yank and took the dagger.

He clenched his fist in her hair, jerking her head down, and backed up to the wagon, the searing pain forcing her to follow. "You'll be coming with me."

A heavy coldness slid through her, and she dug her heels in. "I won't go with you."

He grinned and flipped her dagger in his hand. "Then I'll have to kill you."

Nausea rolled through her as he lifted the lieutenant's blade. "Get in the wagon. And don't you even think of making a noise. If you scream, I'll slit your throat and dump you in the ditch."

He let go of her hair and she stood completely still. Surely someone had seen and would stop him. But no one even looked their way. Business as usual. The knife's point jabbed into the small of her back, and she jumped.

"I'm going to count to three and if you're not in there…" He pressed a finger to her throat and dragged it across sideways. "One."

Josephine's entire body trembled. Getting in that wagon was as much of a death sentence as the knife at her back. The only difference? Time. But time meant hope.

"Two."

With a heavy swallow, she climbed up. Moments later, he sat next to her and cracked the reins. The mule jumped forward and Josephine dug her fingers into the wooded seat. She stared at passersby, willing someone, anyone, to meet her frantic gaze.

A mother with two young children stood at the curb, waiting to cross. No luck. An empty hackney with a lanky driver. Again, nothing. She may as well not even be in the wagon.

As they got closer to the waterfront, her desperation built, eyes darting back and forth. A young dockhand walked up the street, hands shoved in his pockets, not paying attention to his surroundings. The mule nearly ran him down, and he jumped out of the way last second.

"Watch yourself!" Burke shouted.

And blessedly, the man looked up, eyes flashing. He started to yell back, then saw Josephine. *Finally*. She locked eyes with him and wagged them toward her captor, mouthing *help*. For a second his brows furrowed. Then, a salacious grin spread across his face and he winked at her.

The damn man thought she was flirting.

Just like that, the opportunity passed and he continued on his way. The wagon clattered down to the docks and her heart clenched as they headed in the opposite direction of The *Tempest*. They stopped in front of a run-down Chebacco boat. Two small masts with fore and aft sails rose from the small fishing vessel, the canvas stained and patched.

Josephine frowned. "This is Thorne's boat?"

"You've got some humor. Of course not." He chuckled as he hopped to the ground. "You gonna get down on your own or would you like me to drag you off?" He gave her a slow perusal, eyes glinting.

With narrowed eyes, she clambered from the wagon. "Don't touch me."

With a grin he shoved her forward and they boarded the boat, the heavy stench of fish making her nose scrunch. Two men sat up from where they had been resting, the sun beating down on weathered faces. Another man sat toward the bow, a hulking mass of sinewed muscles.

He stood, towering above the other men. "I presume this means you got what we came for?"

Mr. Burke grinned and held up the box. The giant grunted and strode toward them, hand extended. Once he had it, he held it up in the sun. "Thorne will be pleased." His gaze dropped to Josephine. "She was not part of the plan."

The seaman shifted on his feet. "Well, she was there. I would have killed her, but there were too many witnesses by the time I got my hands on her."

The big man shrugged wide shoulders. "Suppose we can do it once we're out of the harbor. Fish will take care of her."

Josephine's eyes widened and she made a lunge for the gang-plank. Burke's hand closed around her arm. "No. She had this."

He held up the key.

The giant took it, examining it.

"It fits the box. No sense throwin' away a chance at more information for him."

With a scowl, the big man shrugged. "Very well. But if he's not happy, you'll be the one to blame."

The other two men threw the lines free and the boat drifted from the dock. When the sails were unfurled, they caught the afternoon breeze and they cut through the harbor. Sunlight glinted from the water, making her squint. The city faded from view, its docks and warehouses shrinking into a hazy line of gray against the sky. Burke began to hum a shanty as they made their way down the river. Soon, the broad expanse of the Chesapeake Bay stretched before them.

The chebacco rocked unevenly, its shallow hull bobbing over the choppy waves in the harbor. Silence had fallen over the men, the slap of water against the hull echoing between them. Josephine eyed the murky water, then glanced to shore. Mr. Burke noticed and gave her a toothy grin. "If yer thinking about jumping in, think again. This bay is full of sharks."

She gritted her teeth. Not that she could have outswum the boat anyway. As they made their way from the sheltered waters, the swells increased, the pitching sending Josephine's stomach into tight knots. Gulls swooped overhead, dipping and swirling in the wind. Josephine's eyes followed their erratic patterns, a lump building in her throat. If only she could sprout wings.

They rounded a point and a ship rose before them. Her heart seized. A frigate. How had he gotten another one? A dark figure stood at the ship's forecastle with a spyglass tracing on them, and the hairs on Josephine's neck lifted. Tears bit at her eyes as the hopelessness of her situation fully hit her.

One of her captors stood and waved a black flag in the wind, and the men turned the chebacco into the waves, cutting out toward the larger ship. Salt spray stung Josephine's cheeks as the massive ship loomed ever larger with each swell they rode.

Finally, they bumped against the frigate's hull, the thud of wood against wood reverberating through her bones. A moment later, a rope ladder tumbled over the side, worn and fraying at the ends.

Burke gestured her forward. "Ladies first." Her boots slipped on the weathered oak planks, and she didn't have time to recover before rough hands yanked her forward. When she stood still, he nodded to the ladder with a raised brow.

With a swallow, she took hold of one smooth rung. Pulling herself up, she began to climb, the ladder swaying with the ship. The breeze whipped her skirts around her legs, threatening to get her caught up in the ropes, and as she yanked them free, a loud whistle came from below her. Heat shot up her cheeks when she looked down. Burke stood directly below her. Gritting her teeth, she climbed faster, putting as much space between her and him as she could.

Worn planks shifted with the faint roll of the sea under Josephine's feet when she clambered over the railing. She forced her chin up, schooling her expression as her eyes darted over the crew on deck. A man crouched by a coil of rope, running a whetstone over the blade of his dagger with slow, deliberate strokes. The edge gleamed sharp in the sunlight as he stared at her, unblinking. With a shiver, she turned away. Nearby, two pirates leaned against the rail, speaking low in a guttural dialect. One spat over the side, then glanced her way, his mouth curling into a leering grin showcasing a row of broken teeth.

The acrid scent of gunpowder and oiled ropes filled her nose. An eerie silence wrapped around her, sending a thread of dread curling in her belly. The quiet glances, the slow, measured movements. No bawdy laughter or drunken shouting, only the faint creak of the hull and the rasp of blades being honed. They were all waiting.

She swallowed, her throat heavy and thick. The measured click of boots came from the quarterdeck behind her and her heart began beating like a caged bird.

Breathe.

But she couldn't.

Her eyes pressed closed as the footsteps descended the stairs and crossed the deck in a slow, deliberate percussion.

"Miss Montclair. What an unexpected surprise."

The smooth baritone of his voice echoed across the ship, the sudden sound making her flinch. Josephine's hands clenched into fists and she turned to face the dreaded Captain Thorne.

He wore a dark navy frock coat, the wool fabric cut to perfection, and his bicorn hat looked new. A well-trimmed beard, shot through with silver curved around his jaw. In the sunlight, he looked… normal. Until she dared gaze into his eyes. She shivered as he stared at her, unblinking. In the garden, the shadows had hidden the true depth of them. Forest green, a color some might call striking. Not on him. The green faded into darkness without depth, sharp as shattered glass. No warmth, no mercy.

In an instant, those eyes flayed her, stripping away what little courage she had. She swallowed and dropped her gaze to his hands, where several gold rings glinted in the sun.

"Well, men? I certainly hope you brought more than a pretty piece to feast our eyes upon." At his dry words, the giant handed him the box and key.

Thorne held it to his chest. "Well done." His gaze swiveled to Josephine and his eyes burned into her. "Such commendable effort, Miss Montclair. One might almost think you enjoyed fetching it for me." A cold smile tugged at his mouth. "Even brought me the key, how thoughtful."

Her eyes narrowed as he flipped it between his fingers.

"Weigh the anchor and make for open water." He stood still as the crew jumped into action. As men climbed the rigging, he turned to Josephine. "Follow me."

She stood frozen as he strode toward the main cabin doors, her heart pounding within her ribs. He paused halfway there. "Unless, of course, you prefer to stay out here with my men?"

Burke caught her gaze, his hungry eyes sending a chill up her spine. With a swallow, she hurried after the captain.

He opened his door and waved her into the shadows. A heavy pressure closed around her chest as she stepped inside and he followed, the door closing with a soft click. Her breaths came fast, each one bringing notes of cedarwood and leather. When her eyes adjusted, she blinked.

The spacious cabin was neat as a pin, not a single item out of place. A heavy oak desk sat bolted to the floor, its surface clear except for a logbook and a single feather quill and inkpot. Not a single wrinkle marred the sheets on his bed, folded with military precision. Above it, a single cutlass gleamed from a rack—identical to the one at his side.

He pointed to the ornately carved chair at the desk. "Sit."

She hurried over as he crossed to the stern windows and positioned the box into a ray of sunlight.

"I've been looking for you." A hard glint filled his eyes as he inserted the key and turned it.

Instead of opening it, he ran a hand over the lid, his fingers skimming it reverently. Tension filled the air, thick and oppressive as he stared hard at the box. Though she already knew the contents, Josephine couldn't help holding her breath as he lifted the lid and pulled the stack of papers free. His hand shook, his breaths coming sharp and quick.

After a moment of hesitation, he lifted the top sheet. As he scanned the words there, his knuckles went white, his jaw tightening.

"No." The word came out in a whisper, laced with disbelief.

A crackle filled the room as the sheet crumpled in his hand and his legs buckled, the box clattering to the side. The thud of his knees hitting the floor reverberated through Josephine's feet. She sat rigid in her seat as his forehead dropped to the floor. He didn't make another sound—just knelt there, his body hunched. Broad shoulders rose and fell, a tremor rocking through him.

For a brief moment, her fear dissipated, replaced with... sympathy? She shook her head. *Never.* Not for him.

After a long moment, he lifted his face, eyes wild and nostrils flared. Gone was the raw vulnerability that had just laid him bare, replaced with a fury so sharp it seemed to split the air. Whatever sorrow cracked him moments before had passed. He pushed to his feet and stalked to his shelf, rummaging through the stack of tubes there and grabbed one with a snarl. She shrank back in her chair as he approached. He yanked a navigational map free, smashing it to his desk hard enough to send the bottle of ink tumbling to the floor. The delicate glass shattered, thick ebony fluid splattering outwards. He ignored it, smoothing the map flat.

With jaw clenched, muscles pulsating with barely leashed fury, his eyes raked over the map. "Looks like we're sailing back to Savannah."

Chapter Twenty-One

"I SAAC?"

The voice came from far away. He cracked his eyes open and winced as pain sliced through his head. Planting his hands on the floor, he slowly lifted himself to a sitting position and the form in front of him came into focus.

A frowning Samantha came into focus while the rest of the room swirled at the edges of his vision.

He tried to shake the fog from his head and a fresh burst of throbbing pain flooded his skull. "What the hell happened?"

"I could ask you the same." She reached out and touched his temple, yanking her hand back when he let out a curse. "Looks like you took a blow to your head."

He blinked, trying to remember. "How'd you find me?"

"Your first officer told me the address."

He groaned and pressed his fingers to his head. "It wasn't the right address though."

"Yes, that was a hurdle. But I asked one of the old timers down at the docks and he told me where it used to be."

"Wish I'd thought like that. We wasted over an hour going to the courthouse and looking at the old maps."

"We?"

"Jo—Miss Montclair." He swiveled his head around the room, willing all the blurred lines to come together. "Where is she?"

Samantha's face paled. "I thought she was on the ship."

The room snapped into focus and he sat straighter. "Son-of-a-bitch."

She stood and offered her hand but he ignored it and jumped to his feet. He pushed past the lightheadedness that rushed through him and scanned the floor. No box. A single ribbon lay there, minus the key.

"He took her." The chill rushing through his extremities had nothing to do with his injury. His hand curled into a fist. "You were right to be suspicious of that shipwrecked sailor. I believe he was planted."

Samantha's eyes pressed together. She didn't need to ask him who the sailor worked for. "Let's get back to your ship."

He staggered to the door. "Where the hell is Christian?"

"He stayed in Wilmington."

A growl left him as they walked outside, the sun searing his eyes, sending fresh pain blinding through him. "Explain."

"Your sailor wasn't the only one. Another of the rescued men turned out to be one of Thorne's who had fallen overboard during the battle. He was pulled from the water and decided to try and blend in with the survivors. Christian thought it would be worth staying and pressuring the man for information."

Pressuring. She almost made it sound pleasant. Isaac pressed his eyes shut. No longer in the Navy, his friend didn't have to honor any unspoken rules. "Why are you here, then?"

Samantha set her hand on his forearm. "He found out what Thorne was looking for and told me to come ahead and tell you. Isaac, he's hunting for naval orders from the war. Specifically, ones from before the kidnapping. That's what the ship carried."

"I know. We found the ones he wanted."

She jerked her gaze to his, her mouth opening, then closing on unspoken words. They crossed to a waiting wagon. Isaac lifted a hand to the rough wood and turned. "Samantha, these orders… they're worse than any of us could have imagined. And when Thorne gets his eyes on them, all hell's going to break loose."

With tight lips, she vaulted to her seat. "Do they have to do with Christian's mother?"

He nodded and climbed next to her. "It was an inside job."

She stared straight ahead as the wagon lurched into motion. A full minute passed in silence. Finally, her shoulders dropped. "We've little time to spare if we hope to catch up with Thorne."

He stared ahead. She hadn't asked for more information. And for now, he was glad to not have to tell her that her best friend was about to become Thorne's next target. If Ross truly was the one to give the order to kidnap Thorne's wife, there would be no mercy for his daughter, Abigail.

She snapped the reins, urging the mule faster, and the wagon rattled over the cobblestones, each bump driving spears of pain through his head. He gritted his teeth and tried to take even breaths as buildings passed by in a blur, a single word ringing through him. *How?*

Ross had been a senior commander in the Navy. He had retired years ago, a decorated war hero. Respected. It didn't make sense.

They turned off the road to the docks, and he frowned. The *Tempest* sat alone at the main dock. "How did you get here?"

"I caught a ride on a merchant ship."

He nodded, lips tight as the wagon pulled to a stop. It would have been nice to have the support of the *Siren* and her men. They raced up the gangplank and onto the main deck. Silas jogged down from the forecastle, concern in his eyes. "What's happened?"

"Never mind that. Cast off the bowlines—now!" Ignoring the pain, he barked orders for the sails to be set, then turned back to his first officer. "You'll take first turn at the helm. We sail for Savannah."

Silas nodded and climbed up to the forecastle. Sailors rushed into action around him as they prepared the ship. Samantha stood in the center of the main deck, arms crossed as she stared out to sea. With a sigh, Isaac strode to her.

"You don't need to come."

She shook her head. "Of course I do. Besides, I'm hopeful we can intercept Christian before we catch up to Thorne."

"Lieutenant?" Silas frowned from the wheel. "She's not responding."

Isaac's jaw clenched. He charged up the stairs and wrapped his hands around the spokes. Sure enough, the wheel spun freely, as if detached from the ship.

"Son-of-a-bitch." He twisted, dragging a hand through his hair, wincing when he hit the raised bump there. "The rudder's been sabotaged."

He strode to the railing. "All hands, BELAY! BELAY!"

Samantha's face had tightened with unease when she caught his eye. "Repairs will take hours. We'll never catch up to him with that kind of lead."

"We need another ship." Mind racing, he gazed down the docks. Of course, no suitable warships were docked.

"There." Samantha pointed to a patrol schooner.

He squinted. Smaller than he would have preferred. At least she had a row of cannons gleaming on the main deck. Her size would make her agile and give them the speed they needed to overtake Thorne. At the same time, he would be able to fit fewer than half his men. Would it be enough to win a skirmish with the pirate?

Doubtful. But it might be their only chance. So, he would take it.

"Silas, I need a lean and capable crew. Only the best and most experienced. Quickly." He pointed to the schooner and his first officer nodded.

A few minutes later, they filed from the *Tempest* and made their way down the dock. Isaac's boots clicked along the dock's weathered oak planks, his stride purposeful as Samantha broke into a jog to keep up. As they approached the schooner, a man wearing a crisp navy jacket strolled to the railing and crossed his arms as the group approached.

Isaac didn't stop at the bottom of the gangplank. He boarded the vessel, Samantha and Silas flanking him.

Now, the man frowned. "What's all this?"

Isaac extended his hand. "Lieutenant Caldwell. Commander, I need this ship."

The man glanced between Isaac and Samantha, his brows lifted. "I'm afraid you're mistaken, Lieutenant. This schooner is on patrol duty. She's not yours to take."

Isaac's hands curled into fists. "I'm not asking."

The commander laughed. "And I guess you're expecting I'll just hand it over?"

"I've been tasked with capturing Captain Thorne. He's just left Norfolk, and sabotaged my sloop-of-war. Time is of the essence. He's kidnapped the daughter of a foreign national as well."

"It doesn't matter. You'll still need to get it approved. You can't just take any boat you please from the yard. Until you produce orders, you're not taking this vessel anywhere." With chest puffed, the commander looked down his nose at them.

Isaac groaned. That could take longer than repairing the *Tempest*. "You don't understand—"

The man's eyes narrowed. "I understand you don't seem to be capable of listening to a superior."

He grimaced. "I didn't—"

A flash of blue skirts passed him and before he could react, Samantha held her dagger to the Commander's throat. "We don't have time for approval." Her voice rang with authority.

Oh God. He should have known she'd do something reckless. The sailors around them jumped to attention, drawing swords and Isaac's men responded with their own weapons.

Shit.

"Call your men off, Commander." She lifted the blade until it dug into the soft skin below his jaw.

Sweat beaded on his forehead and a few tense seconds passed before he nodded. "Arms down."

The sailors backed away, but Samantha kept her dagger pressed to his skin. "Lieutenant, make sure your men are ready to board."

The commander frowned at her as Isaac gave the order. "Who the hell are you?"

She gave him a cheerful smile. "Someone you don't want to cross. Now, get your men off this ship."

He grimaced, but gave the order. Once his crew vacated the schooner, Isaac's men raced up the gangplank. His heart swelled as they clambered up the rigging and began unfurling the sails. Not a single one questioned this insanity. Loyal to a fault.

Samantha waited until the last of the sailors from the *Tempest* had boarded before loosening her dagger's deadly grip on the commander's throat. She guided him to the gangplank. "Go on."

He took a step, but once free of her blade, he spun with flared nostrils. "How dare you!"

She nodded to the men holding the lines and they tossed them free. The ship began to pull away, the gangplank sliding along the dock as the commander swung his arms for balance. "You won't get away with this!"

A grin spread across her face as the sails billowed in the breeze and the schooner surged forward. "I just did."

His eyes widened and he turned toward the dock. It was too late. The gangplank clattered off the thick boards and dropped from below his feet. With a high-pitched scream, the commander splashed into the water.

Isaac stared, his jaw slack, until Samantha jabbed him with her elbow. "You better get this ship sailing, and fast."

He raced to the helm and spun the wheel. "Get her moving. Full sail, now!"

The men already up in the rigging adjusted the sheets and the schooner headed into the harbor. The commander had been fished from the water and stood at the edge of the dock, his face beet red. "You'll answer for this, you bastard," he shouted, shaking his fist.

Isaac groaned as he adjusted the wheel. "I'm going to lose my job."

Silas nodded. "We all are."

Samantha had climbed the stairs to the quarterdeck and gave them a tight smile. "Nonsense. Catch Thorne, and all will be forgiven. Besides, that man was all pomp. He needed a good setdown."

"SHIP AHOY."

Isaac's pulse jumped as Samantha's voice rang down from the crow's nest. A moment later she swung from the ratline and landed gracefully on the deck.

She handed him the spyglass with a grim look. "I think we found him."

He strode to the forecastle and trained the glass ahead. There. On the horizon, the dark smudge of sails. Three masts. His breath caught. The bastard had found himself a frigate.

Wind whipped through his hair as the schooner practically flew across the ocean's surface. With no cargo to weigh her down, and a light crew load, they made excellent time. His sailors went about their duties, tense but sharp, sensing the fight ahead. Samantha gave a longing gaze toward the dim haze of the coast. He didn't blame her. Would have been a hell of a boon if they had Christian at their side.

Isaac returned his gaze ahead. Nothing to be done for it now. He couldn't hope to match Thorne in firepower, but perhaps they could gain an advantage by using the schooner's speed and maneuverability.

"Double shot the charges—let's make every shot count. Aim for crippling hits. We need to take her down by taking away her offensive edge. If we just try to sink her, she'll take us out before we can do enough damage."

The men were quiet, boots pounding the deck as they hurried to their stations. Isaac pulled the looking glass back to his eye. Thorne stood at the helm, hands steady on the wheel as the pirates readied their weapons. With each passing minute, the frigate loomed larger. Soon enough, he could read the vessel's nameplate. The *Avenger*. It certainly matched the captain's lust for revenge. And followed a trend—his last ship had been named the *Reckoning*.

When they were close enough to hear the muffled shouts of Thorne's men, a puff of smoke blossomed from the pirate ship's hull. The shot splashed harmlessly ahead of them, sending a clear warning—*come closer and feel our wrath*. Without flinching, Isaac steered straight ahead, the schooner surging through the waves with deadly intent. The powerful vessel ahead of them began to turn, and Isaac's knuckles tightened. For the second time in about as many months, he stared down the barrels of Thorne's cannons. An unnatural silence stretched across the sea—the calm that always came before battle. Isaac counted down in his head as the two ships barreled toward each other. *Three. Two. One.*

"Now!"

Thunder filled his ears as the guns fired, black smoke billowing across the deck. At the same time, the deck below his feet shook, the ear-splitting cracking of wood piercing the air as Thorne's men fired. The ship shuddered as she took the broadside shots, each one splintering through the hull. Isaac grimaced. Too much damage. He swung the wheel as fast as he could, battling the steady force of the water against the rudder.

"Haul her over! Keep her off their guns!" He aimed the ship across the *Reckoning's* stern as the men above adjusted the sails.

Salt spray stung his eyes as his crew fired another round of shots down the deck of the pirate ship, making the crew dive for cover. Good.

Still, the pirate ship turned with them, lining up for another attack. The schooner listed, already taking on water. They couldn't take much more. His heart pounded as the chaos of the attack thrummed beneath his feet. The ship bucked under him, every movement sending a pulse of pain through his chest. If they didn't make it to the windward side of the frigate, they were done for.

Before he could shout the orders, another round of cannon fire came, the deafening boom ringing in his ears. A horrible crack split the air as the top half of the mast sheared, men screaming as they plunged into the sea with the rigging. Still attached to the schooner, the lines went tight, dragging the ship to a near standstill, her bow swinging port. Splintered wood and fallen sails littered the deck. Isaac's teeth ground together, his eyes darting over the damage. The pirate ship closed in fast, and his crew were scrambling.

"We need to move! Get those lines cut—NOW!" His voice came raw, the urgency cutting through the chaos, but in the back of his mind, he knew it was already too late. Thorne had his ship pointed straight at them.

Isaac closed his hand around the hilt of his sword. "Ready your weapons!"

The crew pulled their swords free, all the while clearing debris from the deck, kicking it to the side and heaving it into the rolling swells of the ocean.

He caught Samantha's arm as she yanked her rapier out. "If things go poorly, you need to know, Thorne's target is the Ross family."

Her eyes widened. "Surely, you jest?"

He gave a grim shake of his head and spun, drawing his sword. The *Avenger* approached, sun glaring from soot covered gunports. Men crowded her deck, armed with cutlasses and grappling hooks. Isaac spread his feet in instinct, moments before the frigate crashed into them broadside, wood groaning as the two ships locked together.

Hooks arced through the air, biting into the schooner with sickening crunches, and the first wave of pirates swung over, boots hitting the deck with solid thuds. Isaac leapt from the quarterdeck, meeting the charge of a cutlass-wielding foe. The clash of steel rang out as Isaac's sword met his opponents in a shower of sparks, the impact sending a tremor up his arm. He barely had time to recover before the pirate struck again, a savage thrust aimed for his ribs. Isaac twisted, narrowly avoiding the blow.

His grip tightened on his sword as he parried, using an underhanded jab to knock the pirate off balance. With a swift thrust, he sent the man sprawling to the ground, the pirate's last breath escaping in a ragged gasp. Isaac barely had a second to recover before the next man closed in—a broad-shouldered brute, eyes wild with bloodlust.

Isaac dodged a heavy slash, the air shifting where the blade passed—too close. He countered with a low strike, aiming for the pirate's midsection. The man grunted in pain but pushed forward, throwing Isaac off balance. A fist collided with his jaw, sending him stumbling back, but he recovered quickly, spinning to face his opponent once more. With a deafening roar, the marauder charged. Isaac sidestepped, the man's massive arm grazing his shoulder. The impact knocked him back a step, but he twisted his sword, steel meeting steel with a clash that rang through his bones.

The man lifted his cutlass for another strike, but Isaac slid under the brute's guard, his blade slicing upward, catching ribs with a spray of blood. He struck again, his sword biting into the pirate's exposed side. His opponent's eyes widened as he staggered backward. Isaac pressed the advantage and spun, his blade driving into the pirate's chest with brutal precision. The hulking form crumpled, crashing to the deck with a thud.

A pistol cracked somewhere behind him and a man screamed, but Isaac had no time to look back as yet another pirate engaged him. His arms burned from the constant movement. Sweat poured down his face, and he swiped the stickiness of splattered blood from his brow in a furious motion.

Body after body fell, too many of them his own men. They were outnumbered—losing ground with every passing minute. The fight wouldn't, couldn't last much longer.

Enough.

"Thorne!" Isaac bellowed the pirate's name.

He sprinted down the main deck, twisting around fighters and knocking blows aside. There. On the forecastle, the silver-shot hair of his target. The captain had engaged with a young sailor, looking bored as he deflected each frantic thrust. As Isaac raced up the steps, Thorne's face changed, and he rained a series of heavy blows on the unsuspecting sailor. The pirate twisted the man's blade free and it clattered aside. Lips curled in a wicked grin, his sword plunged down. With a guttural growl, Isaac dove forward, his blade taking the impact meant for the sailor. The force of the blow rang up his arm and he clenched his jaw.

Thorne's grin widened. "There you are." He slid his sword back and swung it at Isaac's side, the movement quick and calculated.

Isaac twisted, the blade missing him by a hair's breadth. He met the pirate's next blow, a heavy downward arc, steel vibrating as their weapons clanged against each other.

He threw his weight into keeping the blades pressed together. "Call your men off."

The captain's eyes gleamed as his blade slid down Isaac's. "Do you surrender?"

"Yes." The word hissed out between his gritted teeth.

"A pity." Thorne didn't relent, his sword sliding closer to Isaac's hands. He locked his forest-hued gaze on Isaac as his arms trembled beneath the weight of his sword. Finally, with a flick of his wrist, the captain disarmed him.

Holding the blade to Isaac's throat, Thorne pushed him to the railing overlooking the main deck. "Hold! They yield!"

Somehow, his voice carried over the din of the fighting, and slowly the clanging of swords wound down. Isaac raised his hands, signaling his surrender to his men. His jaw clenched as the pirates began leading his crew to the deck, forcing them in a tight group around the broken main mast.

Isaac swung his gaze over to the frigate. "Where is she?"

Thorne's brows rose. "Who"

"I'm not here to play games, Thorne."

"What do you call this?" The pirate chuckled as he swept his hand across the blood-stained deck, littered with fallen bodies. "War is always a game, Lieutenant. One you chose to engage in, if I must remind you."

"Only because you refuse to give up this foolish crusade."

The sharp edge of steel jerked Isaac's chin up as Thorne answered, his voice deadly soft. "I won't give up until every last person has paid for their sins."

Isaac held the pirate's steady gaze. *And I won't stop until you're behind bars.* A muscle twitched in his jaw, but he kept the words to himself. Only a fool would dare goad the man pressing a blade to his throat.

Thorne lowered his sword and gestured to the two pirates nearest him. "Go retrieve my guest."

While Thorne's men did his bidding, Isaac scanned the deck, his eyes searching for Samantha's familiar red hair. If she was hurt… He squinted in the sun. There. She stood flanked by two pirates, blue eyes flashing, her blood-stained rapier cast at her feet.

Her safety confirmed, he turned back to Thorne's ship, where the men dragged someone from the main cabin. Isaac's heart pounded when they turned and Josephine's dark hair billowed in the wind. A gangplank had been lowered between the two ships and they dragged her across it.

Isaac started forward, but Thorne lifted his blade. "Not so fast."

Chapter Twenty-Two

"LET GO OF me!" Josephine struggled against the hands gripping her arms as the two pirates dragged her across the deck.

Her pulse slammed through her, the thunder of cannons still ringing in her ears. After Thorne had locked her in his cabin, she'd been hopeful for rescue. But when the boards shook beneath her and the sound of splintering wood filled the cabin, that hope quickly turned to a grim fear—even if the opponents won, she could very well be blown to bits in the process.

So much for rescue. Thorne's men had quickly overtaken the other ship. As the pirates guided her toward the rail, her heart sank. The smaller ship had been gravely damaged with its main mast cracked in half. Its surviving crew had been rounded up in a small circle near a mess of rigging and fallen sails. Bodies lined the deck, pools of blood glistening in the sunlight.

Her stomach heaved as she averted her gaze. Thorne stood at the helm, his dark coat whipping in the wind, like a fallen angel lording over the ruin before him. He held a crimson stained sword at the ready, vaguely pointed toward the man standing next to him.

Blue eyes locked with hers and she let out a strangled cry. *Isaac.* He stared at her, jaw clenched and hands curled into fists. He was alive.

For now.

He took a step toward her and the pirate swung his sword up to his throat before shouting across the water separating the ships. "Bring her over."

The men pushed her onto the gangplank. This one didn't have any rope guidelines. Just a narrow board with nothing between it and the rolling swells below. She swallowed, her throat thick. One foot edged forward. As soon as her fingers left the rail, her body pitched, swaying precariously over the water.

The pirates behind her laughed and she pulled her shoulders back. *Breathe.* She bent her knees like Isaac had shown her and stepped farther out. Better. Her gaze flitted up to him, and her heart stuttered. His eyes had not left her, and concern filled them. She took another steadying breath and started across, rising and falling with the pitch of the waves.

Once her feet hit the solid planks of the ship, she nearly collapsed at the steady comfort. But she didn't have time to savor the feeling. One of the brutes had followed her across and grabbed her arm again. He gave her a shove toward the captive crew and a glint of copper caught her eye.

"Samantha!" Relief crashed through her as she rushed to her friend's side and pulled her into a hug.

Samantha's hands were bound, but a rueful smile touched her lips. "Sorry we were unsuccessful in rescuing you."

"Tie her up." Thorne's cold voice sliced through the air, jerking Josephine's attention back to the reality ahead. They were all at the pirate's mercy—which she knew didn't stretch any further than the edge of his blade.

Rough cords bound her wrists, pulling them tight together in front of her. Thorne watched until the last knot had been tied, then jabbed his blade between Isaac's shoulders. "Go join your crew, Lieutenant."

Isaac kept his gaze on her as he descended the steps. He walked past the group, his eyes searching, counting. When he finished, he pressed them shut. Her own heart squeezed as the weight of his losses hit him. Squaring his shoulders, he turned and strode to the front of the group.

Captain Thorne made his way down to the main deck. His

steps echoed across the ship, deliberate and slow. Josephine slid her gaze to Samantha. "What happens now?"

Samantha didn't look at her. "Now is when he kills us."

Josephine's heart pounded at the words, spoken so matter-of-factly. A chill slid through her as the pirate paused at the gangplank, then turned to face the captives.

Isaac stood perfectly still, his fists clenched at his sides. "Spare them."

Green eyes flashed. "And why would I do that?"

"If you do, I will join you."

"Isaac, no!" Josephine snapped her mouth shut. Too late. The name was already out—desperate and unmistakably intimate.

Thorne's eyes gleamed as a smile played at the corners of his mouth. A shiver trembled down her spine as his gaze traveled up and down her length, and she fought the urge to step back.

Isaac stepped forward and went down on one knee. "Their safety, for my allegiance."

Josephine's hands balled into fists at her sides as her heart twisted at Isaac's rough voice.

Thorne's laugh came cold and calculated as his gaze never left Josephine. "I got what I needed. I've no need for your help anymore, boy."

"You've got one name. What about the rest?"

Thorne swung to face him. He ran a thumb over his blade, his grin growing wider. "Ross will squeal like a pig by the time I'm done with him. He'll give me all that I need."

"And if he doesn't?"

The question hung in the air. For the first time, a sliver of hesitation slid across Thorne's expression. Those green eyes sharpened, but the pirate didn't answer.

"It can't hurt to have a naval lieutenant working for you." Isaac's voice had lowered, sliding the offer out like a dare.

Thorne ignored him and walked past him to the group, each footstep reverberating through the deck. He stopped in front of Samantha and grinned. "I hear congratulations are in order."

She set her jaw, staring straight ahead, her eyes fixed on the sea beyond the pirate's shoulder.

"Come now, is that any way to greet your father-in-law?"

Josephine's mouth dropped. *Father-in-law?* The words echoed, hollow at first—then struck their mark. Her mind flashed back to the orders she and Isaac had found. *Mrs. Thompson. Captain Thompson.* The truth aligned, sharp and merciless, knocking the air from her lungs. Thorne was Christian's father.

Samantha's gaze flitted to her for a brief second before returning to the captain. "You'll never be family to me." The words ground out through clenched teeth.

Thorne chuckled. "I see you're feisty as ever."

His gaze leveled on Josephine for a moment, before he turned to Isaac with pursed lips. "Alright, Lieutenant. I accept your offer."

Josephine didn't miss the way Isaac's shoulders curved inward. Offering to work alongside the very enemy whose capture his entire career hinged on... Her heart squeezed. For someone who had fought so hard—had made it his goal to take the pirate down—the sacrifice would cut him deeper than any wound, something akin to a preacher selling his soul to the very devil he sought redemption from.

Thorne nodded toward the gangplank. "After you."

Isaac turned to Josephine. "Are you alright?"

She nodded, tears pricking her eyes. "Don't do this."

He glanced behind him, then leaned in, voice low. "This is the only way. It's not his nature to leave survivors." His fingers lifted, brushing a wet drop from her cheek.

Thorne cleared his throat behind them. "Go, boy. Before I change my mind."

A muscle ticced in the lieutenant's jaw, but he dropped his hand and turned. Once he made it to the pirate ship, two men took him by the arms. They tried to drag him from the railing, but he dug his feet in, twisting to face Josephine and his surviving crew.

They stood silent as the pirates combed the bloodstained deck, picking up fallen weapons. Josephine dropped her eyes to her feet as they tossed the bodies overboard, each heavy splash making her flinch. Once satisfied, the men filed onto the frigate.

Captain Thorne waited for the last of his crew to file across before he lifted a foot to the gangplank. He paused midstep, turning back to Josephine and Samantha, his lips twisting into a grin. "I've changed my mind after all."

Isaac surged forward, but the two brutes grabbed his shoulders, holding him back. "Don't you go back on your word!"

A hollow laugh rang out between the two ships. "You should know better than most, a pirate's word is good for nothing." He started toward the bound crew and Josephine shrank back.

Isaac thrashed against his captors, muscles straining as they struggled to hold him tight. "Don't you dare hurt them."

"I wonder…" Thorne slid his sword free and pointed it between the two women. "Which one you care the most about?"

The pirate set the blade below Samantha's chin. "This is awfully familiar, don't you agree? Really, we need to stop meeting this way."

"Go on." Her eyes narrowed and she leaned into the steel at her throat. His brows lifted as he adjusted his stance, his arm easing back to keep his sword from piercing her. "Why don't you finish the job you started? Lucky you, your son's not here to stop you this time."

His gaze darkened, blade steady in his hand. "Don't worry, daughter, I'll have my pound of flesh yet."

Thorne glanced behind him at Isaac's stoic form and raised his voice. "You're not making this game very fun, Lieutenant." Isaac didn't answer and stood straight, his face like stone.

The pirate frowned. "What do you think, ladies? If he had to choose, would it be the wife of his best friend?" He reached out and ran the back of his knuckles over Samantha's cheek before swinging his weapon toward Josephine. "Or his new lover?"

Her pulse roared in her ears as the tip of the blade settled against her neck. The metallic tang of drying blood filled her nose and she swayed, the deck spinning around her. A hand closed around hers with a reassuring squeeze. *Samantha.*

Her breath shuddered as she focused on the planks beneath her feet, the hum of the wind in the rigging—anything but the man in front of her. The moment seemed to stretch into eternity, the steady thump of her pulse slowly bringing her back. Finally, Thorne shrugged and flicked the blade down, the razor-sharp edge slicing through the bindings at her wrists. She glanced at him, brows twisted as the ropes fell to the deck.

He waved her forward. "I think your dear lieutenant would enjoy some company during our trip."

When she hesitated, the pirate captain gave her a push toward the gangplank. "Go on."

Her heart beat wildly at the prospect of going back to Thorne's ship. But when she raised her gaze, Isaac stood there, still flanked by the two pirates. She wouldn't be alone. *He* wouldn't be alone.

So, she leveled her chin and stepped back out onto the precarious board. This time, her steps were even. She made it halfway across when the wood trembled beneath her feet.

Thorne stepped out. "A Caribbean girl such as yourself does know how to swim, right?"

Josephine froze as he closed the distance between them.

"Leave her be, Thorne." Isaac's voice rang through the air, heavy with command.

"Calm yourself, Lieutenant. I'm not always as heartless as you think." Thorne scratched his chin. "Though, it's been a while since I've made someone walk the plank. I've forgotten how very much I like this."

"Damn it! I had your assurance of her safety."

"And here she is, alive and safe." The pirate drew a circle in the air around her with his blade. "You didn't specify *where.*"

Isaac jerked his arms, twisting from the grip of the brutes holding him. He swung, fist crashing into the jaw of the nearest one before two more jumped forward and held him back.

Thorne grinned. "That's more like it. I was beginning to think I'd pegged you wrong." He lifted his sword and pressed the sharp point between Josephine's shoulder blades. "Go on now."

She hurried the rest of the way across, vaulting over the railing to stumble onto the deck. As soon as she regained her footing, she flew straight to Isaac and threw her arms around him. His heart slammed against her cheek, the wild thumps betraying his rigid posture. The pirates dropped his arms and he folded them behind his back.

"Steady, Miss Montclair." He murmured the words so only she could hear.

With a swallow, she released her grip and stepped back. His blue eyes looked over her shoulder, deliberately ignoring her while Thorne strolled across the plank and stepped onto the deck. He stopped short of them and met Isaac's gaze. An uneasy silence stretched while he regarded them with sharp, calculating eyes.

Finally, the pirate's lips twitched. "Welcome to the *Avenger,* Mr. Caldwell."

Isaac's lips drew into a thin line, but he didn't respond to the captain's intentional slight. He'd been demoted.

Thorne walked past him, nodding to his men in an unspoken command. They burst into life, climbing the rigging and setting the sails. "I apologize we don't have a cabin for you on such short notice."

Isaac followed him to the stairs leading to the quarterdeck. "Well, maybe you should have thought that through before dragging her back on board."

Thorne's eyes narrowed and he waved the two pirates back over. "Take them to the brig then. If they want privacy, they can have it there." Without another look, he climbed to the helm, his silhouette dark against the setting sun.

One of the brutes grabbed Isaac's arm and dragged him forward. Josephine swallowed and followed them to the main hatch. Down the narrow steps they went, into the bowels of the ship where the light faded and the stink of sweat and gunpowder grew thick. Another hatch and the brig loomed below—iron bars bolted to beams carved in the hull. The door creaked open on rusted hinges, and the men pushed them in.

After locking them in, one of the men hooked a lantern onto a crooked nail, and they both climbed up. The hatch cover banged shut and Josephine flinched. Dim light pulsed with each sway of the ship, breathing unease into the narrow cell. Every creak of the hull, every gust of wind through the planks, and the walls seemed to close in a little tighter.

Isaac stood with his back to her at the door, his head leaning against the bars. She stepped forward, but he lifted a hand. "Give me a moment."

The lantern flame flickered, casting shadows that danced across the walls, painting his face in shifting hues of grief. She didn't move. Couldn't.

The silence between them stretched—thick, suffocating—wrapping around her ribs like iron bands. The cost of what he'd done haunted the damp air, heavy and unspoken. They stood that way for what seemed like hours, breathing in the same heavy silence, as though a single movement, a single word, might shatter them both.

The thud of boots came from above.

Josephine stiffened as the hinges groaned again and the hatch door swung open. He descended the stairs like a shadow given life, each slow step tugging the darkness after him. He didn't speak as he approached, eyes gleaming in the low light like a cat watching cornered mice. A crystal glass rested in his fingers with several fingers of amber liquid that caught the light like fire. A key dangled in his other hand.

The captain studied them both for a long moment, then finally spoke, his voice low. "You joined me. Not as a prisoner, but as a member of my crew. I don't intend to keep you locked up. You'll work for your freedom."

He slid the key into the lock, the cold metal scraping as he twisted it. For a heartbeat, he stared at Isaac, his eyes nearly black in the shadows. Then, with a click, the door swung open.

Isaac strode from the cell with purpose and stopped in front of the pirate. "Tell me, Thorne, now what? You sail to Savannah, cut down Ross, and walk away? When does it end? Will you ever truly find peace?

Thorne swirled his glass, staring into the liquid depths. "There is no peace for a man such as me. I've accepted that fate."

"How? How does a man whose life was bound to uphold the law, to do what is honorable and right, end up like this?"

A terrible calm filled Thorne's eyes, like the sea before a storm. His fingers tapped the side of his glass in slow succession. "Don't try to play my past against me. It's a game you'll never win. Besides, there are monsters much worse than myself walking free." A slow smile spread across his face. "Who are you to decide what's right and wrong?"

"It's my job. Just as it used to be yours."

Thorne threw back his drink, then leaned forward. "Precisely."

A shiver ran through Josephine at the icy calm in the pirate's voice, the weight of his words settling in her chest like a stone. Isaac stood rigid with jaw clenched as the captain rubbed his thumb along the rim of his empty glass.

After an uncomfortable pause, he extended his hand. "I'll take your uniform jacket, Caldwell. You won't be needing it here."

After a long pause, Isaac shrugged free of it.

The captain crumpled it in his hands before he turned and climbed to the hatch. At the top, he paused, his figure dark against the faint light from above. He looked down at Isaac, his eyes cold and calculating. For a moment, he said nothing, the weight of his gaze hanging in the air.

"I'll tell you this once, and once only. If you disobey a command—if you step an inch out of line—you're dead. There are no second chances on my ship."

Chapter Twenty-Three

T HE WARMTH AGAINST Josephine shifted, pulling her from sleep. She blinked, her eyes adjusting to the dim light that filtered through the lone porthole. The soft sway of waves tugged at her eyelids as if trying to woo her back to sleep. With a smile, she brushed her fingers across Isaac's chest.

A dull ache throbbed through her back and her smile faltered. A wall. In a brig. Tension crept into her limbs as fragments of the previous day's chaos rushed back. With a quiet sigh, she eased her arm away and pushed upright, wincing as stiffness tugged at her muscles.

When she lifted her head, her breath caught. Storm-blue eyes stared at her, unblinking. After a silent moment passed, he groaned and pulled his arm from around her, rolling his shoulders. He pushed to his feet, hooking his hands behind his neck and stretching. His shirt lifted, baring a swath of skin and she forced herself to look away.

"Now what?" she whispered, more a question to the empty air than to him.

He lowered his arms. "Right now? We wait. That's all we can do."

She frowned. "I feel like we should be doing something."

A blonde brow lifted. "Like what? Convince Thorne's men to form a mutiny? Take the ship by force? There's just the two of us. Waiting may not feel right, but it's all we can do." Truth rang through his words.

One of his hands stretched out, skimming along the wall's

rough planks. "She's listing to starboard, which means she's taking on water faster than they can purge it. We're sailing slow. If Christian and Samantha can follow us…" His fingers flexed against the wood. "They may be able to catch up."

She pulled her lip between her teeth. "Do you really believe that?"

Isaac's gaze drifted away, following the flickering shadows cast by the dim lantern. "We weren't far from Wilmington when we caught up with Thorne. It's possible Samantha and my crew could have limped to shore and made contact with Christian… if he was still there." She didn't miss the hitch in his voice, the way it softened at the end—not just with doubt, but with the heavy drag of hopelessness pulling at every word.

"I'm sorry." He set a hand on her shoulder and gave a gentle squeeze. "As long as we are alive, there is hope. We won't reach Savannah until the middle of the night at this rate. I'll figure something out by then."

She stood and smoothed her rumpled skirts before pushing a lock of unruly hair behind her ear. Salt clung to her curls, sweat beaded on her brow, and her nerves strained at the seams. Heat flared beneath her cheeks—God only knew what a wreck she looked like.

Her gaze slid to the shadowed stubble along his jaw, the blond curls falling in tousled disarray. He looked both undone and unshakable. Still impossibly handsome. Something about it tugged at her—an echo of that very first night in Tortuga. Her heart gave a quiet lurch.

The shadow of a bruise stood out on his temple, darkening against pale skin. She took a hesitant step closer. The sight of it brought everything rushing back—the hilt of Burke's sword cracking against Isaac's head, his sudden collapse, the cold terror she had felt. She reached up, brushing her fingers lightly against the dark spot. He flinched at the touch, but didn't pull away.

"Last night, I didn't get a chance to…" Her voice faltered, and she caught herself before the words could tumble out too quickly.

He raised a brow as she traced the outline of the mark. "To?"

"I'm so sorry." Her voice came out barely above a breath. "I tried to get away. Thought I had. But I—" She stopped herself, the guilt sinking deeper with each passing second. "I put you in danger. If I hadn't been there… none of this…"

Isaac's expression softened, his hand coming up to catch hers. He gave a gentle squeeze, the pressure steady and grounding. "You didn't make this happen. This was never your fault."

Her chest tightened at his reassuring words. But deep down, a part of her still couldn't let go of the feeling that she was to blame. The weight of everything that had come before, the trail of danger that followed her from the moment she made her fateful choice back on Tortuga, pressed down on her.

If only she hadn't—

No.

Her fists clenched at her sides. If she hadn't, then she wouldn't have known what it was to know true passion. And even if it all ended tomorrow, she wouldn't undo it. Not if it meant losing what she'd found in him.

"Isaac…" She hesitated when his gaze sharpened at the use of his name. It felt too intimate, too charged—but "Lieutenant" no longer fit, not after what they'd shared. She wanted to say more, but her words caught in her throat, too tangled to make sense of.

I love him.

The knowledge hit her like a sudden rush of cold water, and she sucked in a breath, startled by the force of it. Not because of her silly convictions back on the island. Not because she'd chased him across continents. Because he made her feel. Feel *alive* in ways she never had before. He'd come after her without hesitation, had offered himself to secure her safety. Warmth curled in her chest as she met his blue gaze.

He dropped her hand and reached forward to brush a lock of hair from her forehead. The touch sent a jolt through her that settled somewhere deep inside. "Have faith. We will make it through this."

Her heart stuttered. She wanted to tell him everything—about the way his presence anchored her, how his strength pulled her through these dark moments. To confess she'd never realized she could feel so much for someone. How, for the first time ever, she was starting to believe that someone might care for her in return.

Instead, she nodded.

He stepped back, his hand falling away. "Besides, there is one good thing about all this."

Her head tilted, brows drawn together as his eyes brightened.

"My mission was to find Thorne." He waved his hand toward the deck above them and gave her a wry grin. "I'd say I succeeded."

A small smile tugged at the corners of her mouth. "At least I'm good for one thing."

He stiffened, eyes cutting like ice. "Don't say that."

She blinked, caught off guard by the sudden shift in him.

His gaze searched hers. "You're good for more than you know. For your courage. For your wit. For the way you never back down." He hesitated. "For making me feel there's more to life than duty."

Without another word, he reached for her, his hands framing her face and pulling her to him. His mouth crashed against hers, consuming, unyielding. She gasped against him as she leaned into the kiss, hands twisting in the front of his shirt. For a few glorious moments, the world narrowed to the press of his body, the heat of his lips, the way her heart stuttered like it might never right itself again.

Then, the dull thud of boots on the deck above broke the moment like glass. He pulled back, his forehead brushing against hers for a beat before he straightened and glanced at the closed hatch, breath ragged. "I need to get above and put some work in. Don't want to upset the captain."

Her entire body burned, breathless and aching for more. "I'm coming with you."

He frowned. "You should stay here. You'll be safer."

Alone. Where no one would hear her if she cried for help. She shivered, wrapping her arms around her. "Will I?"

His lips drew into a thin line as her meaning sank in. "Alright. But stay close."

They climbed through the hatch onto the gun deck. Muffled light filtered through the open gunports, casting long, slanted beams across the rows of cannons that lined each side like silent sentinels. Chains clinked with the sway of the ship, and a low groan rose from the wooden hull with each shift of the waves. Shadows moved at the edges of her vision—pirates, mostly silhouettes in the gloom, casting predatory glances as they passed.

When they reached the foot of the steep companionway ladder, Isaac went first, climbing with practiced ease before pausing to glance down. His eyes softened at her hesitation. "You don't need to come."

She shook her head and grabbed the first rung, lifting herself up. He caught her wrist and guided her out onto the main deck. Dawn's soft gray spilled across the deck, the creak of rigging and slap of waves rising to meet her. The morning breeze pressed into her lungs, a welcome respite from the stale air below.

Men moved about the ship, their motions methodical and efficient. They lined the rails, lounged near the ropes, crouched on barrels. Their gazes crawled over her skin, sinking into her like cold fingers. Isaac's hand brushed the small of her back, a silent reassurance, grounding her in the face of the scrutiny. She kept her head high, but her heart beat faster with every step they took.

Isaac reached for a loose clew line and pulled it taut, fastening a knot. He strummed his fingers across the rope, testing its tension. The wind tugged at the sails above as he stepped back, his eyes scanning the deck.

"Caldwell. A word with you."

Isaac's back stiffened at the sound of Thorne's voice, and a chill raced through Josephine's blood. She turned toward the captain, who descended the stairs from the helm with a deliberate, measured pace. All eyes shifted to him, drawn by the gravity he carried like a storm front rolling in. His eyes flicked briefly to her, ever sharp and unreadable, before focusing solely on Isaac.

Isaac didn't move at first, his posture taut, but then he gave a slight nod. "Of course, Captain."

Thorne motioned to the carved door beside him. "Join me in my cabin."

With a sidelong glance at her, Isaac strode forward and ducked into the shadowy cabin. Josephine began to follow, but the captain lifted his hand.

"A private word."

Her pulse quickened, and she halted mid-step as Thorne pivoted and stepped through the door. It closed with a soft click, leaving her standing alone, the quiet of the deck pressing in on her. The pirates loitering nearby gave no comfort, their laughter low and rough, beady eyes flicking over her with calculating interest.

She took a deep breath but the salty air did nothing to calm her nerves. A stack of crates had been secured in place against the wall and she reached for the nearest one and perched on the edge, her knees pulled up to her chest. The murmur of voices reached her and she frowned, looking to both sides. The cabin itself had no windows facing the deck to speak of, only a small vent at the top of the wall, narrow and wrought with rust.

With a swallow, she moved to a crate just below it. Leaning her head back, she tilted her ear closer to the opening. Her heart pounded in her chest as she strained to hear, every creak of the ship suddenly deafening in the silence. Still, she focused, desperate for any fragment of information that might shed light on what was happening inside that cabin.

"Tell me about Ross's involvement." Isaac's voice came low, warped by the timber and rusted metal.

She stretched her back, adjusting her position. There. The scrape of a chair. The heavy footfalls of boots pacing.

Thorne cleared his throat. "He came to me during the war.

Said he had found a way to double our salary, but he needed my assurances of secrecy."

More silence.

"I asked him if it involved anything illegal," Thorne continued, his voice low, almost a murmur. "He refused to answer me."

The rustle of paper came and Thorne's voice cracked. "All this time, after all the men I've hunted down and made pay, and it was him behind it all. That bastard took her from me."

"There's better ways to do this, Thorne." Isaac's voice cut through the air, sharp and frustrated. "Killing him doesn't—"

A fist slammed against wood and Josephine jumped, the sharp crack echoing through the vent.

"Do not try to hamper me, Caldwell," Thorne's voice came dangerously quiet, his fury palpable. "If you get in my way again, I'll make sure your woman doesn't see another day on this ship."

Isaac let out a low chuckle, the sound rough and humorless. "You'll have to find another way to threaten me."

A pause, then Thorne's gruff voice. "What are you on about now?"

"Look, you were right about Christian and Samantha, but there's nothing between myself and Miss Montclair."

Josephine leaned back against the wall as the words sank like stones in her stomach. A suffocating pressure wrapped around her lungs, her heart stuttering, her thoughts tangling. Surely, she had misheard him.

Thorne's disbelieving laugh rang through the cabin. "Don't waste your time trying to convince me otherwise."

"She's nothing more than a passing fancy, a whim indulged. I mean, look at her, who could resist?" The cruel words cut her, each one deeper than the last, and his easy laughter fell over her like a blade she couldn't deflect. "She's not my woman. Never will be."

Ice slid through her veins, a sharp pain twisting in her chest like a knife. Her spine pressed harder against the cold timber, hands trembling as they clutched the edge of the crate beside her.

She wanted to scream, to call him a liar through the vent. To demand he explain why he would say such a thing when only minutes ago, his mouth had found hers like it was the only truth left in the world. When his hands had held her like something... like something that had mattered.

The silence that followed in the cabin was worse than any sound. It rang in her ears, hollow and final. Her chest heaved as she bit back the sob clawing its way up her throat. She wouldn't cry. Not here. Still, hot tears burned at the corners of her vision.

The back of her hand swiped across her traitorous eyes and she turned her face toward the shadows, wishing she could rip his words—rip him—from her memory.

"Well, hello, Miss Montclair."

Her spine went rigid at Burke's drawled words. She refused to look his way in an effort to get him to move on. He didn't.

"Where's your protector?" he murmured, stepping in too close. Rough fingers slipped through a lock of her hair.

She jerked her head back and swatted his hand away. "Leave me alone."

He laughed. "You wound me. Just think what good *acquaintances* we could make."

His arm snaked out, fingers digging into her flesh. She tried to twist away but his other hand slid around her waist, fingers splaying across her hip as he leaned in, breath hot and foul.

"You've got spirit," he said, dragging her from the crate and a half-step toward him. "That'll make it more fun."

She stiffened, bile rising in her throat. The ship went still as conversations faded and footsteps slowed. But no one stepped forward. Why should they? They were pirates. She was nothing but an object in their eyes. Her limbs trembled as he twisted toward the main hatch.

"Get your hands off her." Isaac's words came from behind her, low and lethal.

Burke yanked her against his chest. "Guess what, sailor?" He spit the last word like an insult. "You don't get any special privileges on this ship. This pretty little doxy's no longer yours alone—any of us can have a turn."

A fist blurred past Josephine's face and crashed into Burke's jaw. The pirate stumbled back with a grunt, releasing her as Isaac surged forward, teeth bared. Burke retaliated with an elbow into Isaac's ribs. But Isaac didn't falter. He sidestepped the next punch and struck again, his fist splitting Burke's nose with a crack. Blood sprayed, and still they kept swinging at each other. Josephine couldn't move, couldn't breathe. This wasn't a fight either man intended to lose.

She scrambled out of the way as the scuffle spilled across the deck. The two men grappled like animals, slamming into barrels and rigging, boots scraping over the planks.

With a roar, Burke drew his cutlass, the steel hissing through the air. Isaac ducked the first swing and caught Burke's wrists, wrenching the blade wide. After a vicious twist, the weapon clattered to the deck between them. Isaac drove his shoulder into the pirate's chest, shoving him back into the railing. While the man fought to keep his balance, Isaac's hands wrapped around the pirate's throat and forced him down to the deck.

Veins bulged in Isaac's forearms as he bore down, muscles straining. Burke thrashed beneath him, gasping, face darkening as Isaac pressed harder. Josephine's breath caught as the pirate's eyes began to roll back in his head.

A shadow moved. Another pirate. Sunlight flared off a drawn dagger—aimed straight for Isaac's back.

"No—!" Josephine lunged forward, diving for the fallen cutlass. Her fingers closed around the worn hilt, swinging the blade up to block him. Not fast enough. Fire lanced through her shoulder as the dagger grazed flesh.

She cried out but didn't fall back. Didn't let go. Arms shaking, she held the cutlass high and glared into the man's eyes. The pirate hesitated, eyes flicking next to her.

Isaac stepped forward, his gaze locked on him. "Back off," he growled.

The man looked left and right. Narrowed his eyes. He shifted his weight, readying for a strike.

"Enough!" The deep voice cracked like a whip.

Thorne stood outside his cabin, his eyes hard as iron. Every movement on deck stilled as the captain strode forward. The crew fell silent, eyes darting between the pirate and the combatants.

"Damn it, Thorne, control your men. I thought you ran a tight ship." Isaac snarled the words as Burke groaned and staggered to his feet.

Thorne marched over, his eyes narrowed. "I do."

His arm snaked out, lightning fast and Burke doubled over, his mouth gaping open in a wordless scream. When the captain yanked his hand back, a dagger gleamed in his hand. Blood dripped from it, splattering to the deck in fat drops.

Josephine's eyes widened as a red stain spread over the sailor's shirt. He raised his hands, clutching his chest as he wheezed. He staggered back one step. Another. Hit the railing. Thorne followed him and twisted his hand in the man's shirt collar. He leaned in close and muttered something in Burke's ear before giving him a violent shove.

Josephine twisted away, but a heavy splash rang in her ears. The sea swallowed Burke without ceremony. No one moved. No one spoke.

A gull cried overhead.

Thorne wiped the blade on his trousers and slid it away. "As I said, I don't tolerate disobedience."

Josephine's heart pounded at the chilling calm in his voice. She took a step back, but her knees buckled, sending her to the deck.

"You're hurt." Isaac knelt and tore a strip from his shirt. He pressed it to her stinging shoulder and she bit back a gasp.

"I'm fine." She gritted her teeth. "It's just a scratch."

He stilled, eyes locking with hers. "You could have been killed."

"Why do you even care? I thought I was just a passing fancy."

His eyes darkened. "It isn't what you think, Jo—"

"I don't want to hear it." She lifted her hand. "Just leave me alone."

Chapter Twenty-Four

I SAAC GRUNTED AS he pulled a line tight, the oiled cords slipping against his calloused palms. Night settled thick and heavy over the frigate, wrapping everything in shadows and hush. The wind had died to a gentle breeze across the sails, leaving only the creak of the rigging and slap of waves against the hull.

His shoulders ached from hours of labor under the watchful eyes of men who would just as soon slit his throat if Thorne gave the word. Ever since the scuffle with Burke, the crew had given him a wide berth on deck. That suited him just fine. Meant they couldn't see all the little ways he helped slow the ship further.

Nothing too obvious. Just a loose knot here and a slackened line there.

He pulled the rope harder—too tight—and tied a knot, securing it fast to the pinrail. Stepping back, he flexed his fingers, the ache in his joints a welcome distraction from the storm within him.

His gaze wandered to the forecastle deck, where Josephine sat perched on top of a stack of crates. The light from a single lantern cast its dim glow over her, shimmering from the dark braid over her shoulder. He sighed. Even as night fell and the majority of the crew slowly descended to their berths, she stayed above deck. Though his feet itched to stride over to her, he held fast.

She'd told him to leave her alone. And he had.

Even if every bone in his body ached to do otherwise.

He'd replayed his conversation with Thorne a hundred times over in his head. How much had she heard?

Enough.

A vise-like grip took hold of his chest. He welcomed the pain. Urged it to quell the knot tightening in his stomach. Damn his mouth. But also, damn her for hearing—and misunderstanding.

He knew better than most how quickly Thorne would wield the bonds of affection against him. How the pirate would run her through without hesitation if it suited him. She'd called out his name in front of the captain on the schooner's deck earlier.

A mistake.

Because as quickly as Thorne would use her against him, he would do the same to her by leveraging him and his life. Could force her to do terrible things to try and save him. A precarious position. He'd thought to downplay it. To make the captain believe he was wrong about how much she meant to him.

He was wrong.

Wasn't he?

Isaac.

The way his name had wrenched from her throat earlier had nearly undone him. Almost as much as it had watching her gasp it in the mirror as she pleaded for more. As he claimed her as his own.

His own.

He gave a shaky laugh and took hold of the next line. He had no claim on her. Not when oceans separated their homes. Not when her father was the blasted governor of Tortuga—one who would skin him if he found out what had already happened between him and his daughter. And especially not when she was promised to another man.

Though his heart stirred and dared to hope, he smothered it. Foolish thoughts. He'd accepted his lot as a solitary soul. Had done a damn good job at keeping it that way. He studied the curve of her jaw in the flickering light and cursed the way she made him want things he had no right to want.

Marrying the merchant would be better for her. She would have stability. Could sail with her husband whenever she wished.

Wouldn't be left behind by a man bound to duty, to danger, to a life that could never truly be hers.

After a long moment, he turned from her and gazed into the blackness stretching as far as the eye could see. They had passed Charleston as the last rays of light streaked the sky, a few hours prior. Which meant…

He squinted ahead.

There.

A faint light glimmered ahead—the Tybee Lighthouse.

They would make it to the docks in Savannah in less than six hours. Unless Thorne decided to anchor in the river and launch his attack from there. He pursed his lips as he stared over the sea. It made sense. Would shave off over an hour of sailing and make for a clean getaway with fewer eyes on the ship. He gave a grim nod. That's exactly how the pirate would do it.

A gust blew, and the groan of strained ropes came from next to him where the longboat hung. His pulse stirred, a restless thrum beneath his skin as the shape of a plan took root. He swung his gaze across the ship, counting, strategizing. A helmsman, the lookout in the crow's nest, and two men on night watch. Only four men on deck. A barebones crew as the fighters below rested before battle.

He pushed off from the railing, walking with purposeful steps toward the forecastle. When he was a few feet from the crates she sat on, he stopped at the railing. He didn't look at her directly, keeping his gaze pointed toward the horizon.

"Miss Montclair?"

She stiffened, keeping her back to him. "Go away."

He edged closer, leaned in enough for the soft scent of jasmine to wash over him. "Listen to me carefully. We are going to escape."

That caught her attention. She spun toward him but he shook his head. "Don't look at me. They can't know we are talking."

He didn't wait to see if she listened; instead, he unfastened the knot in the sheet line tied to the cleat nearest him. "When the ship enters the river, we have a slim window of opportunity. The lookout will be preoccupied with keeping us off the sandbars, and the night watch will be standing by, ready to adjust the sails. They won't be watching us."

Silence.

After giving the sheets too much slack, he yanked a bowline knot as hard as he could. Not many men could undo one that tight without slicing the rope with a knife.

"I'm going to cut the longboat loose. If they don't notice, we'll jump in and use the boat to get to shore. There's a place not far from the lighthouse, Miller's Rest. An older Revolutionary War veteran and his sons run it. If we make it that far, we can secure horses. With luck, we'll make it to the Ross estate before Thorne."

He swallowed and pretended to inspect the knot. "See that light ahead to your starboard? It's the lighthouse. We've about an hour until we reach it. As soon as we draw even with it, meet me near the longboat. It's a blind spot for the helmsman."

Time passed like a slow match burning toward a keg of gunpowder. He moved with care, each action crafted to look routine. As the lighthouse loomed larger, he made his way back to the longboat. With a quick glance around, he made short work of one of the knots holding it. With a groan, the boat shifted, then swung down to dangle from the remaining line. One step closer to freedom.

Josephine drifted over, floating across the deck like a shadow. She leaned over the railing. "Won't they see us?" she whispered, glancing up toward the crow's nest.

Isaac nodded toward the sky. "The clouds are covering the moon. They'll have a hard time spotting us in the shadows." He began to untie the remaining knot, cursing as it didn't budge, cemented together with years of salt buildup and the tension of the boat swaying from it.

"Would this help?" She waved a dagger in front of his face. His dagger.

"Where did you get that?" He grabbed it and began to slice at the rope.

"During the battle yesterday, Thorne locked me in his cabin. I found it in his desk."

Clever girl. He grinned and slowed his movement. "Crouch down."

She ducked behind a barrel as the blade slid through the last oiled strands. The longboat plummeted and hit the water with a heavy splash. Isaac held his breath, one eye on the quarterdeck. A few moments passed and he let out a slow exhale, eyes flicking to the helmsman—still watching the horizon, oblivious. He wiped a hand across his face, sweat trickling down his temple, his heart drumming in his chest.

"Alright. Follow me. If we jump farther back, it won't be as dangerous." He stayed hunched down and hugged the railing.

One of the men on watch began climbing the ratlines on the port side of the deck and let out a whistle. They froze as he shouted to the other watchman. "Go get the rest of the men. It's time."

Isaac's pulse jumped. In less than a minute the deck would be swarmed with pirates. His gaze shot toward Thorne's closed door and he glanced over the railing. This spot would have to work.

He caught Josephine's waist and hoisted her over, his heartbeat thundering in his ears. "Jump as far out as you can to keep from getting pulled beneath the wake."

She nodded. Took a deep breath.

He caught her wrist. "You can swim, right?"

She flashed him a sharp look, eyes burning. With a scowl, she yanked her hand free and leaped into the night.

His heart caught as she disappeared into the frothing waves below. With one last glance over his shoulder, he dove after her. A rush of air whistled in his ears as his stomach lurched with the fall. A heartbeat later, the cool bite of the sea swallowed him whole. Dark water pressed around him in a thick, choking weight, muffling the sounds of the night and pulling at his limbs with relentless force. He plunged deep, kicking away from the looming hull sliding above him. Though he couldn't see it, the water trembled, vibrating with the passing of its massive frame as it sliced through the waves.

The currents tangled around his legs, fighting him, but he kicked harder, struggling to move faster through the darkness. His lungs burned, the need for air growing desperate, but still, he pressed on, fighting against the pull of the sea. Finally, the raging water stilled and he surfaced, swiping at the sting of salt in his eyes. He spun, searching for her dark hair.

Nothing.

Damn it.

He forced himself to calm, gritting his teeth against the panic that clawed at his throat. With broad, desperate strokes, he pushed himself through the water. He divided the river ahead into quadrants, searching each one before moving to the next.

There.

Far ahead, a shadowed shape cut through the water, her form almost swallowed by the low swells. *Thank God.* He glanced toward the retreating ship and after confirming no one had raised the alarm, kicked after her.

They reached the longboat at the same time. He grabbed the side of it, muscles burning, and pulled. It rocked with the weight of his effort, tipping dangerously close to the water.

He let go. "I need you to go to the other side and hold it steady while I get in."

A wordless nod and she disappeared. She popped up on the other side and held on tightly, her knuckles white against the wood. With a series of strong kicks, he pulled himself up and hefted one leg over the edge. One more heave and he swung his other leg over and rolled in. The boat settled, and he sat up.

He grasped her hand and hauled her from the water. She collapsed onto her side, breathless and shivering. Without a word, he turned to unfasten the oars. By the time he dropped into his seat, she had taken the one opposite him.

His throat went dry and he averted his gaze. Thank goodness for the cloud coverage, because her clothing stuck to her like a second skin. With a swallow, he forced the sudden heat in his core to retreat.

Focus.

Teeth clenched, he threw his weight into the oars, the rhythmic pull of them through the water grounding him, forcing his mind back to the task at hand. Several minutes passed, a tense silence settling over them. Not much farther. Between the splashes of his paddles, the lap of waves against the shore punctuated the night air.

Movement caught his eye. A pale column of light stretched across the water, sharp and sudden, creeping toward them with unsettling speed.

"Damn it," he muttered, rowing faster. As if he could outrun it.

A moment later, the water glistened around them, the moonlight's reach turning the dark swells silver, exposing every ripple, every shift in the waves—every board of the longboat.

He cursed again, keeping his eyes on the dark shadow of Thorne's ship. His arms trembled as he threw his all into the oars, slamming them through the water. He grunted with each stroke, the longboat cutting through the river like an arrow shot into the night.

A clanging pierced the stillness, sharp and jarring. His muscles tensed, eyes pressing shut for a heartbeat. An alarm bell. Their absence had been noticed. He cast a desperate glance at the sky, silently pleading for the clouds to smother the moon. Instead, the stars burned cold and relentless above them.

Returning his focus to the *Avenger*, his heart lurched. She had slowed. Only a few hundred yards separated them. Too close for comfort. Lanterns swayed on the main deck, casting long shadows as the bell's toll lingered like a death knell. And then, a small flash of light, there and gone in an instant.

Shit.

He dropped the oars and grabbed Josephine's arm. "Overboard, NOW!"

His feet slipped on the wet boards as he jumped up and threw her. He followed, pushing off the boat in a sloppy dive, grimacing as a high-pitched whistle filled his ears. As his face smacked the water, the world behind him erupted in a blinding burst of light. A crack like thunder split the sea as a wall of heat punched through the air. The shockwave slammed him underwater in a violent surge that drove the breath from his lungs.

The sea churned around him as glowing bits of flaming wood splashed down like falling stars. A ringing filled his ears and the pressure in his chest built into a scream. Kicking hard, he clawed his way upward through a dark maze of bubbles and debris. He broke the surface and sucked in a breath, gunpowder and ash choking his lungs.

"Miss Montclair?" He twisted, kicking in a frantic circle, eyes scanning the wreckage strewn across the waves.

No answer.

He dove, hands blindly combing through the murky water. Something brushed his leg—seaweed? A shred of clothing? He couldn't tell. His hands grasped for it but it had already swept away in the current. As he fumbled forward, his vision narrowed, lungs already screaming for air. Every instinct demanded he keep searching, but his body gave him no choice. With a furious kick, he tore upward and broke the surface in a ragged gasp.

"Josephine!" This time he shouted, voice raw as her name tore from his throat.

A faint cough broke the deafening silence.

He spun.

"I'm here." She floated next to an overturned section of the hull, hair plastered to her face, eyes wide as she gasped for breath.

Relief crashed through him so hard he nearly choked on it. His feet kicked hard, his arms slicing through the water as he swam toward her. A splintered plank bumped against his shoulder and he swatted it aside. "Are you hurt?"

She shook her head and angled away from his extended hand. "I'm fine."

Before he could say anything else, she began paddling for shore. With a tight jaw, he followed, keeping one length behind her. The shallows crept up quickly, and soon his feet dragged against silt. It clung to each step, sucking at his boots as if the river itself meant to hold him back. Josephine staggered forward, and he reached for her elbow, steadying her.

Once they made it to dry ground, he pointed ahead. "There, just up the hill."

A building sat there, its silhouette dark against the night sky. A single candle flickered from a window, casting an uncertain glow into the surrounding darkness. They trudged through the long grass, the solid earth beneath his boots a welcome contrast to the murky water behind them.

When they climbed the embankment to the road, her gaze slanted toward him. "Is he going to kill Abigail?"

Isaac's shoulders tensed at the question, but he didn't answer. A shadow passed over her face, quick but unmistakable as the weight of his silence settled between them. She nodded and yanked her skirts up, picking up her pace. They pushed open the gate and climbed the steps, shoulders heaving. He lifted a shaking hand and pounded hard on the door.

As the scrape of boots inside reached them, he turned toward her. "Have you ever ridden astride?"

She let out a small huff. "That's all I've ever ridden. We don't have fancy side saddles on Tortuga."

His lips twitched, a brief flicker of a smile twisting his face. "That's the best thing I've heard all day."

Chapter Twenty-Five

"JUST A LITTLE farther." Josephine ran her hand down the soaking-wet flank of her mount. "If you only knew how kind Abigail is, you would understand."

They had pushed the horses to their limits for over an hour, alternating between a brisk trot and ground eating canter. Foam flecked their bits and their sides heaved, but slowing was not an option. All the stories she'd heard of Thorne, every heartless tale, and now she found herself in the middle of one. Her heart constricted with each pounding stride, bringing her closer to... To what, she didn't know. A nightmare already come to pass? Face to face with the pirate again?

She took a steadying breath. *Don't give up.* Isaac had told her as long as they were alive, there was hope. So she held onto that, clinging to the words like a lifeline fraying in a storm—thin, uncertain, but still holding.

The humid night air had dried her clothing to a damp cling, the fabric sticking uncomfortably to her skin with every movement. Sweat mingled with salt and dirt, itching along her neck and arms. She'd long given up on her hair—most of it had worked free from her braid, curling in wild, frizzy tufts that clung to her cheeks and tangled at her nape.

Finally, Isaac pointed ahead, his voice tight. "Their drive."

He kicked his gelding into a canter, its hooves tearing up the earth in a spray of dirt. Josephine clutched the reins, her fingers slick with sweat. She pressed her heels to her mare's sides once. Twice. The horse let out a labored snort, then lurched forward in an uneven gait. It would have to be enough. One last stretch. One last hope.

The trees blurred past in dark streaks. Her thundering pulse drowned out the pounding hooves beneath her as they turned through the gate. The house came into view—pale in the moonlight, shadowed and still.

"Wait!" Isaac yanked back on his reins. His gelding reared slightly, then stopped. Dust clouded around them.

Josephine mirrored him, and her mare skidded. She gripped the saddle horn to stay seated. "Wha—"

He jerked a finger to his lips, his other hand pointing toward the porch.

A cluster of figures stood in the shadows.

Her stomach dropped.

Too late. The pirates were already here.

She frowned as heavy pounding floated through the night air. Only a handful of silhouettes, fewer than she expected. Thorne must be awfully sure of his men's skills. The front door opened, light spilling out to reveal their forms in sharp relief.

Her heart soared. "It's Samantha and Christian!"

Isaac squinted through the haze of dust. "By damned, you're right."

He urged his horse forward and she followed, racing up the drive. Gravel flew as the sweat-drenched horses tossed their heads. A moment later, they jerked to a stop in front of the fountain.

The ring of steel floated through the courtyard as the group on their porch drew their swords.

Isaac jumped to the ground. "For heaven's sake, put your weapons down."

He helped Josephine down, her feet barely touching the ground before they were rushing up the steps.

"Bloody hell, am I glad to see you." Relief laced Christian's voice, but his gaze flicked behind them. "I don't want to ask how much time we have, do I?"

Isaac set a hand on his shoulder. "Minutes. At best. Where's the rest of your crew?"

"We went ahead of them, they'll be here soon. Maybe a quarter hour."

Isaac didn't respond, his eyes already narrowing toward the door, where a flustered butler stood, blocking their way. "Let us pass."

The butler sputtered something about the hour being improper for visitors, his voice high and uncertain. As he rambled, Samantha yanked Josephine into a quick hug, the warmth of it a brief comfort. "You're safe, thank God."

They turned as the butler shouted. Isaac had twisted his hands in his collar and yanked the man out onto the porch. With the doorway cleared, they all surged inside.

"Ross!" Isaac bellowed. He released the butler, whom he had dragged back in with him. "If you value your employer's life at all, you will wake him and his daughter immediately."

A door banged open somewhere upstairs. "What the hell is going on? I'll have you all arrested for this!" Abigail's father stormed down the stairs in his nightshirt, the hem flapping around his bare ankles, hair disheveled and face flushed with indignation.

"No time to explain, Ross, but you must leave immediately. Captain Thorne and his men are on their way here right now."

The man scoffed. "What the hell do I care about a pirate?"

Abigail appeared at the top of the steps with her arm hugged around her waist. "What's going on, papa?"

"Nothing to worry yourself over, dear. Go back to bed."

"Abigail!" Samantha's shout made her friend's eyes open wide.

"Samantha?" She hurried down the steps. "Josephine?"

Samantha spun to face her father. "You must go to New Orleans. Find my uncle. He'll be able to help."

Mr. Ross shook his head. "This is preposterous. I'm not letting some blasted pirate scare me from my home."

Isaac stepped forward with a growl. "Thorne is not any pirate, you fool."

"Are you saying you men are incapable of fighting him off?" Ross laughed. "That the United States government can't even handle one pirate? This is absurd."

Isaac grabbed the man's nightshirt and jerked him forward until they were nose to nose. "Listen to me real close. Thorne has an entire ship full of mercenary pirates. We'll be outnumbered ten to one. He's likely minutes behind us, maybe fewer. When he gets here, the first thing he's going to do after overpowering us is slit your daughter's throat in front of you."

Abigail let out a whimper and Josephine squeezed her hand. Mr. Ross opened and closed his mouth as the color drained from his face.

Samantha took Abigail's other hand. "If you won't take her to safety, I will. Come on, Abigail, let's quickly grab some things." She tugged her toward the stairs and Josephine followed.

"I… You…" Mr. Ross took a shaky step after them. "If you really think it's necessary, I will go. But we need to change, and properly pack."

Christian pulled out a pocket watch. "You have exactly five minutes to gather what you can carry. I have a wagon ready behind your kitchen. Get in, and cover yourselves with the blanket. The driver will take you out the servant's entrance and deliver you to Augusta. You'll need to secure a carriage from there. Do not linger. Thorne will follow you once he's done with us."

"Go!" Isaac's barked command made Josephine jump and she rushed up the stairs with Samantha and Abigail.

Samantha threw open the door to Abigail's bedroom and flung a satchel onto the floor. "Only what fits in here," she snapped, voice sharp with urgency. "Jewelry, silver—anything you can use to trade for supplies along the way."

Abigail stood frozen in the middle of the room, her eyes wide, lips parted, chest heaving like a startled doe. Samantha grabbed her shoulders. "Snap out of it."

In a daze, Abigail turned to her vanity and pulled open a drawer with trembling fingers. "My jewelry's in here."

Josephine hurried over and began scooping handfuls of glittering bracelets and gemstone-studded necklaces into the satchel. Gold clinked against silver, strands of pearls tangling with brooches and rings as she hurried. Snatching up the lantern, she pushed through the door into Abigail's dressing room. Rows of dresses lined the walls, silks and muslins in every color. How could she possibly choose?

She didn't. With a frustrated huff, she grabbed the nearest two gowns and flung them over her arm. She hooked a pair of soft kid leather boots with her fingers and turned back, skirts brushing her legs. As she knelt beside the bag to shove the clothes inside, a shrill squawk made her head jerk up.

Lola.

The parrot blinked at her from her perch in the corner of the room, feathers puffed, eyes gleaming. Josephine's throat tightened. "No time," she whispered. "Later."

"Time's up, let's go." Isaac's bellow echoed up the stairs and the girls hurried out into the hall. The door to Mr. Ross's room hung open, the glow of a lantern casting shadows on the wall.

Samantha pushed Abigail forward. "Josephine, take her downstairs." She flipped her dagger out and ran into the room. "Mr. Ross, you need to leave."

A muffled curse reached them as they rushed down the stairs, dragging the heavy bag behind them. Abigail twisted to look over her shoulder and tripped, nearly sending them both tumbling down.

"Damn it, you she devil!"

A moment later, Mr. Ross appeared at the top of the steps, with two large bags slung over his shoulders. His face had turned a bright shade of red. Samantha stood behind him with her blade pointed between his shoulders. Before he took a step, the crash of breaking glass shattered the air around them. Someone had broken a window in the parlor.

Abigail screamed as another window shattered.

Isaac drew his sword. "Get them out back. We'll hold them off as long as we can."

Josephine grabbed Abigail's wrist. "Come on!"

Samantha had already seized Mr. Ross by the elbow, dragging the stunned man through the servants' hallway. The corridor was narrow and dark, lit only by a single lantern casting shifting shadows on the walls. Their quick steps echoed in the silence, the faint creak of floorboards beneath their feet punctuated by more breaking glass behind them.

"This way!" Samantha hissed as they burst through the back door. The humid night air slammed into them, wrapping around their bodies like a damp cloak. Josephine followed, her heart pounding in her chest. The darkened yard stretched ahead, the moon casting an eerie halo around them as they rushed to the waiting wagon.

Samantha yanked down the rear gate as the horses pawed the ground. "Get in. Now."

"I, I can't—" Mr. Ross stammered, turning to look back at the house.

Samantha shoved him toward the wagon bed. "You *will*. Get your daughter to safety before it's too late."

Josephine helped Abigail climb into the back, her hands trembling. "Lay flat. Stay out of sight."

"I'm scared," Abigail choked.

"I know," Josephine whispered, brushing a strand of hair from her friend's face. "But you have to do this, it's the only way."

Mr. Ross climbed in behind his daughter, finally shaken into motion.

Samantha turned to the waiting driver. "Make haste. Don't stop until you reach Augusta."

He nodded, pale and determined, and with a slap to the reins, the wagon jerked forward. Wheels crunched over gravel, then mud, vanishing into the shadows just as shouting erupted from the far side of the house. A crash came, the unmistakable clatter of furniture toppling. Josephine spun, her heart in her throat.

Samantha's eyes narrowed, her expression hardening with determination as she drew her rapier. "Stay here," she ordered, her voice low and commanding. Without waiting for a response, she spun on her heel and disappeared into the darkness of the house, her figure swallowed by the shadows.

Josephine stood paralyzed, her heart hammering in her chest as the clang of steel rang through the air, sharp and jarring. A wave of panic surged within her as she glanced down the empty servants' road. In a matter of minutes, she could slip into the night and escape the nightmare unfolding within the house. Her hands trembled as she clenched them into fists.

But then another crash, louder than the last, followed by a desperate shout. Her breath caught in her throat. No. She couldn't run. Not now. She took a shaky step forward, her feet heavy, as though made of stone. Her gaze locked onto the darkened doorway. She couldn't stand by while people she cared for fought for their lives. With a sharp breath, Josephine made her choice. Her heart hammered as determination surged through her, and she pushed forward.

A moment later, she crossed the threshold. Her chest heaved in short, ragged gasps as she ran down the corridor, shadows twisting after her. In the main hall, the battle raged. Blades clashed, men grunted and shouted, boots skidded across the wooden floors slick with broken glass and splintered debris. Her stomach turned when she nearly tripped over the leg of a prone man.

A flash of silver on the floor caught her eye. A cutlass. She snatched it up, her fingers trembling around the hilt, and pressed on. In the drawing room, she found Samantha locked in a deadly dance with a broad-shouldered pirate. Her friend's movements were swift and fluid, each parry and strike precise.

Then the door behind her slammed open.

Another pirate.

Josephine didn't think. She lunged, blade raised, a cry tearing from her throat—more fear than fury. Steel met steel with a jolt that rattled up her arms, but she held her ground. The pirate snarled and swung again, but Samantha turned, caught the blow mid-air, and drove him back. They worked together, Josephine cringing at her wild and clumsy strikes. Samantha's blade flashed alongside hers, and within moments, both attackers lay motionless on the floor.

Josephine stood over them, chest heaving, the sword trembling in her hands. Blood pounded in her ears, and she gave a shaky laugh. "We did it."

Samantha gave a nod, then raised her sword again. "Stay close. We're not done yet."

They eased from the room into the hallway. The sounds of fighting had grown distant and muffled. Outside. At the very end of the hall, the front door hung wide open. They moved that way, swords held at the ready.

Without a word, Samantha held her hand out, drawing to a stop. She took a deep breath and gazed down the hall. Her eyes widened. "Fire."

Josephine's chest tightened as she caught the faint scent of smoke.

"We need to get out of here." Samantha's words came out in an urgent whisper. Before Josephine could respond, a door to their side slammed open with a crash, and another pirate charged into the hallway.

Josephine leapt to the side as the man barreled into them. Samantha's rapier flashed in a blur of silver, the steel catching the low light. With a sharp twist of her body, she drove the blade toward the pirate's chest. He parried, and her sword moved in quick, decisive arcs. With each swipe, she pushed him farther toward the wall, her eyes focused, determined.

The pirate snarled and lunged, grazing Samantha's side. She stumbled and he swung again. *No.* Josephine gripped her sword tight and launched herself from the wall. She drove the blade forward with everything she had. For a heartbeat, time stood still. Then it came—the awful give of flesh, the jarring resistance of bone. It sank into his side with a sickening jolt. He let out a guttural scream, twisting violently. The hilt tore from her grip as he dropped to his knees, clutching at the steel buried in his flesh.

Josephine froze, her breath caught in her throat. Horror twisted through her, cold and biting—but beneath it burned something else. Something fierce. Wild.

Samantha grabbed her arm. "Well done. Now, let's get out."

Josephine nodded, swallowing hard. Her eyes watered as acrid fumes burned her nostrils. The thick, suffocating haze clung to the ceiling like a dark shroud. An ominous orange glow pulsed from the side of the foyer, where flames licked greedily at the wallpaper and thick smoke obscured the front door. Heat surged down the hall like a living thing, pressing against them in warning.

Their feet pounded against wooden floorboards as they raced down the hall. Smoke chased them, stinging and smothering. The house groaned around them, timbers popping behind them.

It seemed an eternity passed before she flung the back door open and the two of them stumbled into the night, gasping for breath. The door slammed behind them, muffling the growing chaos within. They rushed down the back steps, wood slick with humidity. The night air hit her like a slap, damp and heavy—but gloriously breathable. Josephine gulped it in, her lungs screaming as she doubled over, hands braced on her knees.

Samantha was already scanning the yard, sword still in hand, shoulders tense. "Let's get away from the house, into the shadows."

Josephine nodded, her heart slowing as the night began to calm her. The cool air. The sound of crickets still chirping beyond the edge of the chaos. The faint flicker of firelight reflecting in the windows.

And then—

Her eyes lifted toward the second floor. Abigail's room. The curtains billowed faintly, a thin wisp of smoke curling toward the sky.

A violent jolt struck through Josephine's chest.

"Lola!" Panic clawed at her gut. "She's still in there."

With a cry, she staggered back toward the house, but Samantha caught her arm. "Are you insane? Look how fast the fire is spreading. You can't go back in."

Flames already fanned from some of the bottom windows.

Josephine's eyes scanned the dark windows on the second floor. No flames. No glow. The fire hadn't spread upstairs yet.

With a jerk, she yanked her arm free and sprinted back up the steps.

Chapter Twenty-Six

"YOU AGAIN?" THORNE'S voice came in a growl, as he stepped forward, the blade of his sword gleaming in the moonlight. "You should really learn to back down."

Isaac deflected the blow just in time, the sharp clash of steel ringing through the air. The force of the impact reverberated through his arm, but he didn't falter. "You'll find backing down isn't in my nature."

"So you seem so eager to prove." The pirate's eyes darkened, the tip of his sword flicking dangerously close to Isaac's ribs. "Unfortunately for you, my patience has run out."

He jabbed with a low, slicing cut aimed at Isaac's legs. His chest heaved as he darted back and adjusted his position, sweat beading on his brow as they circled. Every muscle screamed for more speed, more precision, but Thorne's movements were smooth and fluid—a seasoned predator waiting for his moment. The pirate came at him with a series of quick, calculated slashes. Isaac parried each one, blade ringing, arms burning. They were evenly matched, each dodge, each block, a dangerous game of inches. Isaac's heart pounded as he found his rhythm, countering with a heavy thrust that made Thorne step back with narrowed eyes.

"Time to end this. I've more pressing business than you." With a sudden, deceptive shift, the captain brought his sword down in a wide arc.

Isaac threw all his strength into the block. The impact sent a shockwave of pain through his arms, his feet sliding in the dirt as he struggled to keep his balance. Thorne took advantage of the opening, stepping in close and driving forward with a swift thrust toward his ribs. Isaac deflected the blow at the last second, but the momentum left him exposed. The captain's sword danced around Isaac's guard, and with a precise flick of the wrist, he disarmed him, sending his blade clattering to the ground.

Thorne leveled his blade at him, drawing his arm back to deliver a death blow. Isaac didn't move. He had nothing left. Muscles trembling, lungs burning, he stared at the shining edge of the blade. So, this was it. He closed his eyes.

Steel rang against steel.

The strike never landed.

Christian lunged from the smoke with a roar, his blade driving Thorne's sword wide. Sparks flew as the weapons clashed, and the pirate staggered back a step, eyes darkening with sudden fury.

Isaac jumped back as father and son faced off.

The captain's lips curled into a snarl. "You think you can save Ross? You're only delaying the inevitable."

Christian's grip tightened on his weapon, his jaw clenched. "No need to save him," he growled. "I'm here for you."

Thorne's lips curled into a cruel smirk. "How touching,"

In one fluid motion, he brought his sword down in a vicious diagonal slash. Christian's blade glinted as he shifted, feet moving in a blur. He surged forward, forcing his father to take a step back. Thorne recovered with terrifying speed, lunging back in.

Christian parried the brutal swing and spun away. In that heartbeat of space, his eyes found Isaac's. "Go!" he shouted, voice sharp. "Get to Samantha and Josephine—now!"

Isaac ran. Boots pounding the ground, lungs burning, he rounded the house at a dead sprint. *Please still be out back.* Smoke billowed from broken windows, an eerie howling coming from the heart of the house as he rounded the first corner. No sign of them. He pushed harder.

He skidded around the next corner and nearly collapsed when

the smoke parted in the breeze. Two figures stood just beyond the reach of the fire's glow, silhouetted against the night. Samantha's arm was outstretched as if holding Josephine back while they watched the flames consume the house.

They were alive.

"Oh, thank God." He doubled over as the adrenaline of the fight began to seep from him, leaving his muscles shaky and weak. After a ragged breath, he started their way. A few steps in, Josephine broke away from Samantha and ran toward the house.

"What the…" He broke into a sprint. "Josephine!"

But it was too late. She'd disappeared through the door. He slid to a stop next to Samantha. "What the hell is she doing?"

She turned to him, her face pale in the moonlight. "She went back for her parrot."

"Son-of-a-bitch." They both flinched as a window blew out and new flames crackled into the air. "Where is the blasted bird?"

She shook her head. "I don't… Wait, it's in Abigail's room, I heard it while we packed." Her gaze locked with his. "Upstairs. Second room on the right."

It was all he needed to hear. His feet pounded the ground as he raced inside. Once in the door, he let out a curse. Thick, black smoke choked the hallway, curling in heavy coils that clung to his skin. It swallowed the world around him, turning every shape into shadow. A hellish orange glow punctuated the darkness, heat building with each step deeper into the house. The plaster above groaned and popped, and an angry shower of sparks rained onto his face. He raised an arm and pushed forward.

"Josephine!" He shouted into the inferno, but the fire's roar swallowed his words like dry tinder.

He reached blindly in front of him, as he desperately tried to remember the layout of Ross's home. He needed to get to the front, to the stairs. Fire burned through his lungs and he tore a strip from the bottom of his shirt, tying it tightly around his mouth. Barely better. But enough. A crash came from behind him, pushing a suffocating cloak of hot air around him. No turning back now.

Damn, how long was the hallway? His boots thudded over the scorched floorboards, heat searing through the soles. He stumbled, slipping on something slick and sharp beneath his heel. Glass. Jagged shards glittered faintly at his feet—the remains of the chandelier. The stairs loomed ahead, steep and wavering like a mirage. Each stair groaned under his weight, smoke swirling with every step. The haze clawed at his eyes as he made it to the top, and he pressed them shut as he ran his hand along the wall. One door. Two. He blindly entered, squinting his eyes. So much smoke.

"Josephine!" He bellowed into the darkness, her name tearing from the depths of his soul.

A cough came from the corner of the room. He stumbled over and found her huddled on the floor. Soot streaked her face and she clutched a cage in her arms. He bent, tearing another strip from his shirt. "Here." He tied it over her mouth.

One slender hand grasped toward him. "I can't see. My eyes."

His own stung like a swarm of a thousand bees had overtaken him. He caught her hand and pulled her to her feet. "It's alright. Hold onto me."

They crossed the room and eased back into the hallway. Again, he followed the wall. At the top of the stairs, he drew to a stop. "Shit."

Through the heavy black smoke, the bright flicker of flames licked up the staircase. He swallowed and guided her down one step. The next. Before he could take another, a terrible groan came from their side. Out of the rolling smoke a shape crashed toward them. A beam, enveloped in flames, smashed down, and the stairs gave way. They fell backward as fresh waves of black smoke billowed around them.

"Back up," he rasped, dragging her to her feet.

When they reached the top, a thunderous roar filled his ears as a terrible splintering cracked beneath their feet. He flung his arm out, throwing themselves back as the floor gave way, opening into a yawning pit. Josephine tumbled to the side, the cage rolling from sight toward the edge of the hellish abyss. Fire shot up, belching heat and smoke in a violent surge.

She crawled, grasping around her. "Lola!"

Isaac grabbed her arm. "There's no time—we need to get out."

With surprising strength, she yanked her arm free. "I'm not leaving her."

Damned bird was going to be the death of them both. "Stay here."

He eased toward the splintered floorboards. There. Just at the edge—the faint outline of the cage. He took a half step toward it and the boards beneath him flexed with a conspicuous crackle. Fire curled around the edges of the hole and he ground his teeth together—it wouldn't hold much longer. Another step. The entire floor shifted beneath him, tilting downward with a threatening creak. The cage began to roll.

"Damn it," he hissed.

With a burst of motion, he lunged forward, hooking a finger through the wire as the floor buckled. He threw himself toward the wall, clutching the cage to his chest as yet another crash split the air behind him. Flames erupted where he'd stood only seconds before. Behind him, a ragged cough cut through the roar of the fire.

Josephine sagged against the wainscoting. "I can't breathe."

His own vision swam as he darted across the hall, the fumes making every breath feel like a fight, and he braced his hand on the wall next to her. They had seconds left. "We need to get into a room. Find a window."

She coughed again, weaker. "Abigail's room has a tree next to the window. I climbed down it before."

Good.

With one arm around her waist, he shuffled backward through the smoke-filled corridor, the cage scraping against the wall. They reached a door frame. Was this the right room, or had they already gone too far? It no longer mattered. He shoved through the doorway, heart hammering in his chest.

He stumbled, nearly going down on one knee, but gritted his teeth and caught himself. "Come on."

But Josephine fell, her body going limp in his arms.

Pain flared behind his eyes, but he willed himself to stay conscious. *Almost there.* He shoved aside the fog that clouded his mind, the heat in his lungs burning like the fire itself. One foot in front of the other, he kept moving across the room, dragging her toward the faint outline of the window. His chest was tight, the weight of her in his arms almost unbearable, but he couldn't stop. Not when they were so close.

He leaned his head out, taking a gulp of precious air. "Samantha!" His voice came out in nothing more than a croak.

But blessedly, she answered. "I'm here."

He braced himself and heaved the suddenly heavy cage over the windowsill. "Catch."

It slipped from his weak fingers, falling into the darkness below. With a strangled grunt, he lifted Josephine into his arms. Her head lolled against his shoulder, her weight slack and terrifying in his grasp.

He climbed over the sill, smoke curling thick around them like a noose. The fire shrieked behind them in an otherworldly scream. Rough twigs scraped his palms as he reached for the nearest limb. He braced one foot onto a lower branch, then the next, easing down. Vision swimming, his boot slipped. He slammed into the trunk, gritting his teeth as the bark tore at his side.

He hit the ground hard, knees buckling as he collapsed. Josephine fell from his arms and he pressed his forehead into the damp grass next to her. The night air hit like ice, too cold, too sharp. His chest heaved as he tried to draw breath. Bile surged up, and he doubled over, retching onto the earth. The earth swayed beneath him as his stomach clenched, his throat raw.

Samantha's voice broke through the haze, sharp with worry,

and he jerked his head around to find her beside him, leaning over Josephine's prone form. She lay still and motionless. Too still. His hands trembled as they reached for her face, the soot and grime of the fire smearing beneath his fingertips as he cupped her cheeks.

"Josephine. No." He gave her a gentle shake, his fingers sliding down her neck, searching for any sign of life. Nothing. She didn't stir. Didn't breathe.

"Please." His voice cracked, the plea escaping in a raw whisper. The burn of tears stung his eyes as a tremor of something unspeakable surged through him.

Unable to stop himself, he dropped his head to her chest. The silence was deafening, his own raging pulse the only sound in the suffocating stillness. He held his breath, praying, begging for any sign. *There.* He pressed his eyes together as the faint beat of her heart fluttered against his cheek.

"Isaac?" Her eyes fluttered open, glazed. "Where am I?" A violent round of coughing overtook her and she curled forward with the force.

"Shhh." He held a finger to her lips. "You breathed in a lot of smoke. It's best if you don't talk right now. Try to take deep breaths."

She shook her head. "I thought… I thought I died—thought we died."

He dropped his head and pressed his lips to her sooty forehead. "You're safe."

She tried to sit, clawing at Isaac's shoulders for a grip as she struggled. "What about Lola?"

Samantha set the cage down next to them. "She's right here. She's alright. Though I'd say she's not very happy." More gray than green, the bird sat on a perch, feathers puffed out.

"Oh, thank goodness." The viselike grip of her fingers loosened and she slid back to the ground. Isaac kept his eyes on her chest as it rose and fell with each breath.

He glanced at Samantha. "The pirates?"

She nodded toward the front. "The rest of our men showed up. I think Thorne was more interested in pursuing Ross than staying to fight." She swiveled her gaze to the empty servant's road behind them. "I hope they got enough of a head start."

The thud of boots echoed around the corner of the burning house, and Christian emerged with a group of his men, still armed and on alert. He took one look at Isaac and grimaced. "Good God, you look like hell."

Isaac gave a hoarse laugh. "Thanks. I've just returned from it."

Christian crouched beside them, eyes scanning Josephine and the smoke-streaked bird in the cage. "Is everyone in one piece?"

"More or less," Samantha muttered, wiping a damp rag across Josephine's soot-streaked face. She met Isaac's eyes. "Why don't you come stay at our home tonight? Get cleaned up and you men can talk it out."

It.

As in, what happened between Christian and Thorne. And what would they do next with the new information they had.

THE BLESSED SLIP of cool water ran over Isaac's face.

Again.

And again.

Long gone murky and dark, the basin water swirled like ink—smoke and blood and ash clinging to every ripple. He leaned in and scrubbed harder. As if he could scour the soot from his skin. As if he could wipe away the memory of Thorne's blade flashing far too close, of fire licking at the walls. Of Josephine going limp in his arms.

Water splashed over the rim, pooling on the floor.

More frenzied scrubbing.

But the smell of smoke still clung to him.

He closed his eyes. All he saw was Josephine, motionless on the ground.

With a growl, he plunged his face into the basin, welcoming the deadening weight of water against his ears. Counted to ten. Twenty. Lost count and let the world go quiet around him.

He came up gasping, water streaming from his face. For a moment, he stayed there, hands gripping the basin, shoulders heaving. His reflection stared back at him in the mirror.

"Get yourself together." He wasn't sure who spoke, himself—or the reflection.

He dragged a towel across his face and grabbed the fresh shirt draped over the chair. The rest of his bathing could wait.

For now, there were questions to answer. Decisions to be made.

Once buttoned up, he strode from the room and descended the stairs. Light spilled from beneath Christian's study door, warm and steady. A thread of tension pulled tight in his chest as he pushed the door open.

His friend sat at his desk, feet propped up. He didn't look up, but picked up a bottle of bourbon and poured two glasses. Wordlessly, Isaac picked one up.

Christian took a hearty drink. "Hell of a night."

An understatement.

Isaac took a small sip, the warmth trailing down his raw throat. The burn didn't hurt, instead, it grounded him. A reminder he was still alive. He sank into the other chair. Took another drink.

Finally, he looked up. "Thanks."

Christian lifted a dark brow. "For what?"

"You know exactly what. For saving me."

The whisper of a smile played across Christian's face. "Well, I guess we can call ourselves even then."

"What happened?" Isaac glanced back at the closed door. "With Thorne? You two were fighting. And then—"

Christian met his eyes, unreadable. "He got away."

A fist of frustration twisted in Isaac's gut. He dragged a hand through his hair. "He was right there, Christian. We could've ended this."

"I know."

"We—you had him."

"I know."

Isaac ground his teeth together, frustration building. "Yet he slipped through our fingers. Again."

Christian's gaze darkened. "You think I don't know that?" He poured another drink. "We'll get him." His voice had gone quiet. "One way or another."

Would they?

Isaac wanted to believe it. Wanted to believe that after everything—after almost losing Josephine, after everything that had gone wrong—they could still bring Thorne down. But for the first time, doubt clung to him like the smoke in his clothes, and he didn't know how to shake it off.

Christian's soft voice brought him back. "I need to know what you found in Norfolk, Isaac."

He stared out the window. "What did Samantha tell you?"

"That it was an inside job. That the government is responsible for my mother's death."

Isaac nodded, his throat going dry.

Forest eyes found his, intense and searching. "Why? Why is Thorne after Ross?"

Isaac pressed his eyes closed for the space of a breath before turning to his friend. "Ross is the one who gave the orders for your mother to be kidnapped."

Christian stood and leaned over the desk, jaw tightened. "And we let him leave? Why?"

"Because Thorne would have killed him and his daughter. Would have tortured them."

Christian's eyes flickered with something sharp, something cold. "Maybe he deserved it."

Isaac pressed two fingers to his pounding temple. "I'm not

willing to see a man cut down based on one sheet of paper. Even if guilty, the law must be upheld."

Christian began to pace. "I don't understand. Ross worked with my father. Why would he betray him like that?"

"Thorne said… He said Ross approached him and tried to convince him to take part in a lucrative deal. He wouldn't tell him what, only that he would need to agree to look the other way and keep his mouth shut. He was offered a large sum of money. He declined." He took a slow breath. "Ross mentioned something about an investigation led by your father in the order."

Christian's hand tightened around the glass, the flickering light from the fire catching in his eyes. He didn't speak at first, his jaw set as he stared down into his drink, swirling it absentmindedly. Then he let out a long breath, shaking his head slowly.

"Ironic, isn't it? That such an honest man could become the monster he is today."

Isaac curled his hands into fists. "He had a choice. We all do. He could've stayed the honest man. But he chose the wrong path. He chose revenge."

"I didn't understand before." His friend's voice came whisper soft as he stared out the window. "But now that I have Samantha, it all makes sense. How losing my mother broke him, changed him."

"It's not the loss that makes a man a monster—it's what he does in response to it." Isaac pressed his lips together. "How deep do your sympathies go, exactly?"

Christian leaned forward, sharpness tightening his eyes. "It's easy to judge someone when you're not in their shoes. Easy to say you'd never let grief turn you into that monster. But you don't know. You don't know what it's like to lose everything."

Isaac set his jaw, thoughts racing as he fixed his eyes on Christian, trying to make sense of the words that didn't quite sit right. The pressure in his chest grew, each breath thinner than the last as his pulse quickened.

"Don't look at me like that." Christian raised his hands. "I'm not on his side."

Not yet.

Isaac exhaled sharply, shaking his head to clear the cloud of frustration. This wasn't the time to argue. He had bigger things to focus on. "I need to get to Washington and brief them about what happened."

"No."

Isaac pushed to his feet. "What do you mean, no?"

"If you tell them, you'll be in danger." Christian strode over and jabbed a finger toward the darkness outside. "Those men—Ross and whoever he was working with—think my father died. They think their secret is safe. If they find out you know, what makes you think they won't try to silence you?"

Isaac let out a growl. "They are not above the law. If we can find out who they are, we can have them arrested for treason."

His friend's gaze slid back to him. "And how high does it go? God only knows how many were involved, and who. Ross was a high-ranking commander."

"So, what would you have me do? I already might not have a job after all of this. I can't keep lying for your sake."

Christian shook his head. "You won't lose your job."

"I got a navy patrol schooner destroyed."

Christian snorted. "Not as bad as me getting a brand-new frigate sunk."

"You didn't abandon your own ship with half your men and steal it, *after* throwing a commander into the water."

His friend whistled. "Alright, you got me beat."

They shared a brief, reluctant grin, the weight of everything else still hanging between them. Isaac let out a long breath, the humor fading as reality settled back in.

"I'll hold off. Write a letter explaining what happened. Without bringing up Ross." He gave a nod, half to himself, half to Christian. His mind already poured through the next steps. It was all too much, but he had to keep moving forward.

Christian's voice broke through the silence. "What about

Miss Montclair?"

Isaac froze for a beat, then glanced at his friend. "What do you mean?"

Christian held his gaze, unwavering. "Are you going to marry her?"

He hesitated, rubbing the back of his neck. It seemed so long ago when he had so candidly thrown out similar words to Christian regarding Samantha. He'd thought it such a simple concept—a solution to a problem. He bit back a chuckle at how quickly things had changed. Christian's reaction back then made sense now.

"It's complicated."

Christian snorted. "You've ruined her. It's not that complicated."

Isaac's jaw clenched as his friends put it into words.

"I care about her," he admitted, voice low. "More than I should. But that doesn't matter." He raked a hand through his damp hair. "I have my entire career in front of me. I'll be at sea for most of it. She deserves better than that."

Christian shook his head. "And what about you, Isaac? What do you deserve?"

He didn't answer.

The fire cracked low in the hearth as he stared into the shadows, jaw tight.

What *did* he deserve? A ship. A commission. Orders that would take him farther from her with every tide. He'd always known the shape of his future. Had built his life around it— without softness, without entanglement.

Without her.

Now, suddenly, that future felt hollow.

"I chose this path a long time ago," he said at last.

"That doesn't mean you have to walk it alone." Christian tipped back the rest of his bourbon before locking eyes with him. "Duty and loneliness needn't go hand in hand."

Chapter Twenty-Seven

JOSEPHINE STOOD IN the quiet hallway, her hand half-raised toward the closed door. A single candle burned low on a side table, its light pooling gold across the worn floorboards, the flicker of the flame sending restless shadows along the walls. She stared at the door as though it might open on its own and relieve her of the choice.

The memory of his voice echoed in the back of her mind. *She's nothing. Not my woman. Never will be.* The words bit down like iron teeth, clamping tight around her heart. She clenched her jaw, but it didn't stop the sting that rose behind her eyes. She didn't want to care, didn't want *him* to matter. And yet...

Here she was.

She reached for the door once more, her fingers brushing the knob. At the last moment, she pulled back, her pulse stuttering in her throat.

He didn't deserve her thanks.

But he had *earned* it. Because whatever else he'd said or meant or believed, when the world went to hell, he'd gone straight into the fire for her. No hesitation.

Her heart gave an unsteady beat as she touched her knuckles gently to the wood. She closed her eyes, took a breath so deep it ached, then gave one light knock—a sound barely more than a breath in the dark.

Part of her hoped he wouldn't answer.

Was it horrible that the rest of her hoped he would?

She counted to ten. Let out a breath. Took a step back.

The door opened.

Isaac stood backlit by the glow of a lantern behind him. His half-buttoned nightshirt clung to damp skin, and wet hair curled loosely around his brow. Heat rose to her cheeks as water dripped to his collarbone, ran a trail over his chest, and disappeared beneath linen fabric. She'd interrupted his bath.

For a moment, neither of them moved.

The air between them fairly crackled—thick with everything unsaid. Confusion bloomed, twisting the lines between words like rescue and rejection until they were indistinguishable. Her breath caught as her heart pounded a furious rhythm against her ribs.

They spoke at the same time.

"I—"

"Thank you." The words escaped too fast, too loud, the moment unraveling before she could gather it. She flinched at the tremor in her voice, and dropped her gaze to the floorboards. "I just—I wanted to say thank you."

She didn't wait for a reply. She couldn't. The words had cost too much already, scraping raw places she hadn't known were still tender. With a hollow ache blooming in her chest, she turned and started down the hall.

"Josephine."

She froze as he whispered her name. Her shoulders rose and fell with uneven breaths. If she turned back, she might crumble. Might break in ways she didn't know how to mend. If she didn't, she might never forgive herself. With fists clenched, she swiveled, eyes on the floor. The silence pressed in, thick and unyielding, stretching the moment taut between them.

"Look at me."

Damn her, she did.

Her resolve to stay guarded fractured as the oceans within his eyes overtook her, crashing against the fragile walls she'd built until there was nothing left to hold onto.

He swallowed, then gave a subtle wave of his hand. "Join me?"

She could still walk away.

Except, she couldn't. Like a moth to a flame, she found herself stepping forward, unable to resist the pull. The door clicked shut behind her with a soft finality, sealing them both into the space.

He took a step forward, his hand hovering in the space between them. "Are you…" His voice faltered, then steadied. "I mean, you're not hurt, are you?" The question lingered, his worried eyes scanning her.

"If it weren't for you, I'd…" She took a shuddering breath. "I—"

The memory of it all crashed into her, the overwhelming rush of fear and helplessness hitting her like a physical blow. A sob broke free, the sound raw and jagged as it tore through her chest.

He closed the space between them and pulled her into his arms. One hand dropped to the small of her back, the other curled behind her head, cradling it against his shoulder. For a selfish moment, she soaked it in—his presence, his strength—letting the weight of everything melt away as she pressed her forehead against his chest.

Too soon, reality crept in. With a shaky breath, she stepped back.

His thumbs wiped tears from her cheeks. "It's over. Everything's going to be alright." The gentle weight of his lips pressed against her forehead.

If only it were so simple.

If only she could forget.

With a shuddering breath, she took a step back. "I—I should go."

A fresh wave of tears etched new paths from her eyes as she spun to the door. She reached out with trembling fingers, grasping for the knob through blurry sight, as though escape could offer her some relief.

"Josephine."

She stilled, her name echoing through the room—through her soul. It traveled into the darkest and furthest corners of her being, entwined with a longing she couldn't escape. Threatened to tear her apart.

"Before you go, there's something I need to say. This morning… What I mean to say is, what you heard…"

Her eyes widened. He wanted to talk about it. What he'd said to Thorne. She wasn't sure she could. She needed to leave. To start the process of forgetting this—all of this.

"I—" She had to take a breath. "I don't want to hear excuses."

"Fair enough. But I don't want you to walk out of this room thinking any of it was true."

Thump.

The thud of her heart drummed in her ears as the entire world narrowed to the charged space between them. A single footfall came from behind her, the soft pad of a bare foot on the floorboards. Moments later, his hands closed over her shoulders. Her throat went dry as he leaned in, his breath hot against her ear.

"The things you said…" She trailed off as his lips brushed her neck, sending a violent shiver through her.

"I lied to Thorne." Teeth grazed against her skin. "Don't you understand? Everything I said, I said to keep you safe."

Her heart crashed in her chest, each wild beat willing it to be true. Still, she shook her head. "It hurt." Tears pricked her eyes anew. "Worse than anything I've ever felt before."

"I'm sorry." His hands slipped down her sides. "I couldn't let him know how much you mean to me, couldn't let him use you against me. I would have never said it if I had known you would hear."

For a moment, his eyes burned into hers, raw with desire and desperation. He turned her, his grip firm on her hips. "I never meant to hurt you."

Something broke in her.

Not her resolve, but something deeper. Something primal.

"Isaac." His name came out in a whisper as her throat seized.

His mouth found hers, the soft crush of his lips sending a wave of heat rippling through her. Her knees began to tremble as he deepened the kiss. Searching. Tasting. As if his life depended on it.

His arms slid behind her, lifting her from the floor in one fluid movement. With a yelp, she clutched her hands behind his neck, her legs wrapping around him to stay steady. He groaned into her mouth as if the very act of holding her had set something wild loose inside him.

Staggering to the bed, he laid her down, his body following her with a kind of desperate precision. His weight settled over her, warm and steady, his mouth consuming her. She melted beneath him, her fingers clutching at his shoulders, pulling him closer.

His hands slid to the hem of her shift, lifting it slowly, deliberately. The cool air from the room met her skin, a sharp contrast to the heat of his body pressed against hers. His lips broke away, dark eyes finding hers with a raw intensity that nearly stole her breath. With one swift motion, he yanked the fabric higher, exposing her to him completely.

A fractured breath shuddered from him as he sat up, eyes blazing. "You're so damn beautiful."

Her breath hitched as his hands slid over her exposed skin, tracing the contours of her body with a mix of reverence and need. Each glide of his fingers set her nerves alight, the warmth of his hands leaving a trail of heat in its wake. He shifted above her, his body pressing down on hers with an urgency that left no room for hesitation. She could feel the hard press of him against her, a silent promise of what was to come.

His lips found the sensitive curve of her neck, his breath warm and uneven as he kissed his way downward, the gentle scrape of his teeth making her shiver. She moaned as he reached the swell of her breast, his lips and tongue coaxing, teasing. Every nerve in her body felt like it was alive, humming with anticipation, waiting for the next move, the next touch.

He paused, lifting his head to look down at her. His eyes were wild, burning with desire, but there was something else in them, something softer—tender, even.

"I need you." His voice came out in a rasp, thick with emotion. "More than I've ever needed anything."

The words sent a shudder through her, a deep, aching pull in her chest. She reached up, her hands finding the roughness of his jaw, the warmth of his face. With a tug, she tried to bring his face back to hers but he resisted. With a low groan, he shifted downward, his mouth grazing the curve of her belly. Farther down. Until he kissed the valley of her hip, brushed his fingers feather soft across her curls.

His breath puffed against the sensitive skin there, creating a trail of heat that flushed her skin. The aching pressure between her legs intensified, an unbearable pull that only he could ease. She tilted her hips, instinctively pressing herself closer to him, the need within her becoming almost desperate.

A low, reverent sound rumbled from his throat as if the offering of her body undid something inside him. And then his mouth was on her, hot and sure, and the world shattered. Her head fell back with a strangled cry, hands flying to the sheet, clutching it like a lifeline. The first sweep of his tongue was a revelation— tender, then demanding. She trembled beneath him, torn open by the shock of pleasure, the overwhelming sensation of too much. Too little.

He gripped her thighs, anchoring her. A tremor traveled through his hands, betraying the strain of his restraint. Every flick of his tongue, every kiss, sent her higher, a storm building behind her ribs. Her breath came in broken gasps, the heat spiraling, pressure mounting. She was unraveling, thread by thread, pulled apart by his mouth.

The pressure crested, then broke loose, flooding her in a rush of heat and helplessness. Pleasure burst through her like a bolt of blinding lightning. She arched her back, fingers twisting in his hair as she cried out his name, each pulse leaving her reeling in a dizzying storm of wild abandon.

As every muscle in her body slackened, he rose over her, his breath ragged, movements urgent and uneven. He fumbled with his nightshirt, then reached between her thighs, fingers slipping through the heat he'd drawn from her. A strained groan tore from his throat as he guided himself forward, the thick press of him finding her, testing her, needing her.

He stilled, his chest heaving against hers. "Tell me." His voice rasped with barely held control. "Tell me you want this."

She raised her hand and cupped his cheek, thumb tracing the rough outline of his jaw. "I want this—I want you."

With a growl, he surged forward. Her fingers curled into his skin as he took her in one desperate, consuming thrust. The force of it made her gasp, the sudden fullness sending a sharp shock of sensation through her body. She clung to him, her breath hitching at the aching stretch.

Every inch of him pressed deep, filling her with a hot, dizzying fullness. He withdrew slowly, sensation rippling through her before sinking back into her with a powerful, urgent motion. Her muscles tightened around him, instinctively meeting each slick plunge. He didn't stop, didn't slow, his hands dragging her hips to him as though he couldn't get close enough.

He grunted, his forehead pressing against hers as his rhythm grew frantic, desperate. The room seemed to close in around them, the sound of their bodies moving together filling the space. She gasped, pulling him closer, her legs wrapping around his waist, urging him deeper. A cry tore from her throat, but it was swallowed by his mouth as he kissed her fiercely, his thrusts erratic and wild. Her body tensed, a spark of heat shooting through her as she tumbled toward the edge once more.

"God, I want this to last forever." His groan echoed through the room. "But I can't. I'm already there."

He reached between them and began to pull free.

"Please." Her fingers dug into his back. "Don't."

His breath came out in a ragged gasp. "I can't hold off. If I finish in you…" His mouth went slack.

"I'll make sure to take precautions. Please. Isaac. I need this. I need you."

"Oh God. Josephine." His eyes pressed shut, head tipping back as a hoarse shout tore free.

He gripped her hips, driving deeper than ever. She cried out as he shuddered within her, heat exploding at her core. A blinding rush consumed her, the world exploding into white-hot waves of sensation. Her body arched beneath him, muscles taut with the force of her release, the air sucked from her lungs.

For a long moment, neither of them moved, both clinging to each other as the last tremors of their shared pleasure reverberated between them. After a shaky breath, he gently pulled free and settled at her side. Her gaze wandered over his face, flushed and glowing in the candlelight. He reached for her hand and brought it to his chest, holding it there like an anchor, like he never wanted to let go.

Josephine's fingers curled against his skin, the thud of his heartbeat fluttering beneath her palm. The air between them pulsed with something fragile and immense. Her heart swelled with emotion—full to bursting with everything she felt for him, with the sheer wonder of *him*. The words rose before she could stop them, as natural as breathing.

"I love you."

There. She'd said it. Laid her heart bare before him.

He locked his gaze on her, blue eyes churning. "Josephine, I—"

A frantic knock interrupted him. "Josephine, if you're in there, your father has just arrived and is demanding to see you." Samantha's hushed voice pressed through the crack.

Isaac leaped from the bed and snatched his trousers from where they hung over the chair. He shoved one leg in as Josephine's chest seized. Her father? *Oh God.* Her mouth dropped open and she swung her feet to the floor.

Blast it, where was her shift?

There, under the bed. She grabbed it and yanked it over her head. Her hair tangled around her face in a messy halo. She'd hardly had time to pull it over her shoulder when heavy footfalls echoed from the hallway.

Isaac stood still, his shirt half buttoned, eyes darting between her and the door.

"Quick." She pushed him between his shoulders. "Hide!"

He gave a curt nod and strode to the window, throwing it open. He grimaced when he looked down, but slung his leg over the sill and eased himself out. The door flew open and Josephine raised a hand to her eyes as bright light filled the room. Her father stormed in, nostrils flared. His eyes widened when he took in her rumpled appearance.

"Josephine Montclair, what have you done?" He ground out the words, the lantern in his hand trembling as his gaze flew around the room. His eyes narrowed when they settled on the open window. He took a step that way and her heart skipped a beat as she imagined Isaac hanging from the sill.

"It's not what it looks like."

A strangled laugh escaped him. "It couldn't be clearer than day, sweetheart." He pointed toward the boots on the floor, the tangled sheets.

A cold flush washed over her as her gaze dropped to the damning evidence. He strode to the window and flung the curtains open. She held her breath. Released it when all he found was empty space. But that moment of relief shattered when he turned, his face hard as stone. Before she could react, he crossed the room, his hand shooting out to seize her wrist with an iron grip.

"We're leaving. Now."

"Papa, no!" She dug her feet in but he yanked her from the room. She stumbled, struggling to keep up as he dragged her down the stairs, each step a jarring reminder of how little control she had. Her chest heaved with frantic breaths, and she tugged at her arm, trying to break free.

"Samantha, tell him I can stay! Please!" The words tumbled out in a rush, desperation flooding every syllable.

Her friend followed close behind them, lips drawn tight and hands clenched into fists. Josephine's heart sank as she realized Samantha was as powerless as she was. Just as they reached for the door, a figure stepped into their path, blocking the exit. Christian stood tall, his expression unreadable, but a steely resolve glinted in his eye. He didn't move as they came to a sudden halt in front of him.

"Governor Montclair, surely there's no need to rush out in the middle of the night. We've plenty of room. Why don't you stay and enjoy pleasant accommodations before your voyage?"

Her father raised his free hand to jab a finger in Christian's face. "I hardly call allowing my daughter to share a room with a man *pleasant accommodations*." Spittle flew from his mouth as his voice rose to a shout.

Christian lifted his hands, meeting Samantha's troubled gaze. "I understand your concerns, but I assure you, this is a house of propriety. Your daughter is welcome here as long as she likes. Perhaps it would be good for her to stay for a time, to settle her mind after everything that happened."

"Don't presume to tell me what's best for my daughter." Her father's eyes burned with fury. "My ship is waiting. And my daughter is getting married as soon as we get back."

Married?

Josephine's heart lurched to a stop. She tried to pull her arm free, but his grip only tightened. "No." The word came out ragged, defeated.

"Do not think about pleading your case. You lost that right the moment you stowed away on that lieutenant's ship."

"I won't. I can't." She took short desperate gasps as the room around her began to spin.

"You will." Her father's grip tightened, his face a mask of unyielding authority as he dragged her outside and down the steps. "You'll learn to become obedient, Josephine, if it's the last thing you do. I will not have you disrespecting my decisions any longer."

They reached the carriage, and without a word, her father yanked the door open, the sound of metal scraping against the wood echoing in the night.

"Governor!" Isaac's shout rang out over the courtyard as he limped around the corner. "A word, please."

Her father spun, color rising in his cheeks. "How dare you show your face to me? Don't think for a moment I'm unaware of what's happened between you and my daughter."

Isaac slid to a stop. "All the more reason to let me speak."

Josephine tried to pull away, but her father shoved her inside with a rough hand on her back. "Not another word, Lieutenant. I've heard enough already. I apologize for the trouble she caused. It won't happen again. Her soon-to-be husband will keep her in line, I'm sure of it."

Isaac lifted his hand as if to argue, but her father's voice lowered in warning. "Stay out of it. This is none of your business anymore."

Josephine leaned forward, Isaac's name upon her lips. But if she called for him, her father's fury would only deepen. So, she clamped her mouth shut and locked eyes with him as he stood there, his face a mask of raw frustration and helplessness. There was no hiding the anguish in his eyes, but there was also something else, something terrifying.

Resignation.

The moment stretched between them, suffocating in its weight—as if every unspoken word, every unspent promise, had been shattered by the finality of her father's declaration. His shoulders dropped in a silent acknowledgment that, for all their efforts, this was the end. There would be no rescue. There would be no stolen moments or whispered promises. There would be no more anything.

It was over.

In that stillness, something fractured inside her—a small, painful crack that reverberated through her entire being. Everything they'd fought for, everything they might have had slipped through her fingers, and there was nothing left to do but watch it disappear.

The door slammed shut, leaving nothing but the cold finality of unspoken words.

Chapter Twenty-Eight

HEAVY POUNDING SHATTERED the silence like cannon fire. Isaac flinched, the sound driving a spike through the base of his skull. He'd left the shutters closed, lamps unlit, hoping to escape daylight—and the suffocating weight on his chest.

Another round of knocking came from the door, louder.

He groaned and dragged a hand over his face, the movement making his stomach lurch. His coat lay discarded on the floor, boots still muddy near the hearth. The nearly empty bottle on the table mocked him, a cruel reminder of the sleepless night behind him.

Isaac forced himself up, swaying as blood rushed to his head. He frowned as the scent of ash filled his lungs. Would the God-forsaken smell ever go away? He unlatched the door.

Christian stood on the narrow stoop, the morning sun at his back. A dark brow arched as he looked Isaac up and down. "You still look like hell. I'd have thought a night's rest might've helped."

Isaac stepped back without a word, letting his friend into the dim confines of the rented house. Christian's gaze swept the room—past the rumpled coat on the floor, the half-dead hearth, settling on the bottle. His lips twitched. "You didn't sleep at all, did you?"

Isaac exhaled slowly, his voice rough. "Glad you find this amusing."

Christian shrugged and picked up the bottle, giving it a sniff before swirling the remaining finger's worth of whiskey. "You're the one who did this to yourself."

"What's that supposed to mean?"

With a heavy sigh, Christian turned to him. "You let her go. Stood there and watched him drag her away."

Fire burned through Isaac's veins and he staggered forward a step. "What else was I supposed to do? Pull a sword on the governor? Get myself court-martialed?"

Christian didn't blink. "You could've fought harder."

Isaac clenched his teeth. "I did." Silence stretched between them before he added, voice hollow, "She's better off without me."

A snort answered him. "You don't believe that."

His gaze drifted to the coat on the floor. "I *do*. Doesn't make it hurt less."

"Now what? You drink yourself to death in a rented room and call it duty?"

Isaac's laugh came dry. "I call it knowing my place."

Christian stepped closer, voice firm. "You love her."

Isaac nodded once, no fight left. "And that's exactly why I let her go."

Admitting it felt like tearing out a part of himself, the rawness nearly bringing him to his knees. He saw her there again lying beside him, felt the warmth of her hand against his chest, the wild beat of his heart slamming beneath her palm. Her words had trembled on the air, fragile and fierce at the same time. *I love you.* Even now, his reply hovered eager on his lips, ready to leap free. *"I love you, too."* But he hadn't told her and now the moment was gone, carried off like smoke in the night, impossible to call back.

Christian was quiet for a moment. "So that's it?"

Isaac blew out a breath. "What else is there? She's free. From me. From all of this. Whether I like it or not."

"Fate doesn't give up so easily. Sometimes it tests you."

"Fate?" A splintered laugh pressed from his chest. "The moment I realized I loved her... was the moment I had to give her up. I don't want to hear a damn thing about fate."

He scrubbed a hand over his face. "It was supposed to be simple, Christian. Orders. Strategy. The mission. Then she snuck into my life and everything I thought I knew—"

He broke off, the ache tightening in his chest.

Green eyes glinted in the dim light. "At least you're admitting it."

Isaac sank against the wall as Christian drained the remaining whiskey in a single swallow. He frowned as his friend coughed and set the bottle down with more force than necessary, fingers trembling before drawing into a fist. Beneath Christian's usual calm, a restless energy flowed. Something was off. He'd just been too damn preoccupied with his own misery to notice.

He straightened, eyes narrowed. "You didn't come here to talk about Josephine, did you?"

Christian didn't answer. He shifted his weight, then began to pace, boots thudding softly against the wood floor. His hands flexed at his sides, opening and closing as if itching to grab something and hold on.

Unease curled in Isaac's gut. The haze that had clung to him all morning, thick with whiskey and regret, thinned in an instant as his thoughts sharpened. "What is it? What's wrong?"

Christian stopped short at the window, staring out the gap between curtains for a breath. Then he turned back. "I'm leaving."

"What do you mean?"

His friend lifted his gaze, steady and unreadable. "To join my father."

Isaac's head snapped up. "The hell you are." The words burst out before he could temper them. He took a step closer, dropping his voice to a harsh whisper. "Have you lost your mind?"

"I have to know, Isaac."

He swallowed, his throat tight. "You know if you go, you will be an enemy of the United States of America?"

Christian gave him a tight smile. "What choice do I have? If the Navy finds out who Thorne really is, there will be no order to capture him. It will be to kill on sight. And then I'll never find the truth."

"What about Samantha? What does she have to say about that?"

"She doesn't know."

"Doesn't…" Isaac dragged a hand through his hair. "Christ, Christian, he killed her parents."

A muscle ticced in Christian's cheek. "I know."

"And what if our paths cross out there?" A growl rumbled through his throat. "What if you're killed in battle?"

Their gazes locked, Christian's going sharp. "Would you fight me?"

"Of course not." Isaac's jaw tensed. "But my men wouldn't know better."

Christian scoffed. "You think any of your men could best me?"

"That's not the point," Isaac snapped. "This has nothing to do with skill. You joining him… It changes everything."

Christian's smirk faded, the weight of the moment settling between them like a storm building at sea. Isaac stepped closer, eyes hard. "You're not some nameless sailor defecting to a rogue captain. You're *my* friend. And if you walk away now… if you stand beside Thorne—you're no longer just chasing answers. You're choosing your side. And God help us both if we end up on opposite ends of a cannon."

Christian held his ground, the edge of defiance in his posture tempered by the deep weariness in his eyes. "I know what I'm choosing." His voice was quiet, steady. "And I know what it might cost. So, don't lecture me."

Isaac shook his head, jaw clenched so tightly it ached. "Damn it, Christian. There's no coming back from this—not without consequences."

His friend's eyes darkened. "You think I don't understand that? Think it doesn't tear me up inside?" The words faltered at the edges, betraying something too heavy to hide.

Isaac stared at Christian, the weight of his declaration sinking in. His friend's determination—almost a quiet resignation—settled heavily between them. "I've known you long enough to know when you've already made up your mind. But this… you're playing with fire. You don't know what you're walking into."

Christian's mouth drew into a thin line, but he didn't back down. "I know exactly what I'm walking into."

Isaac's gaze flickered, the frustration brewing in his chest threatening to boil over. "And what? You think that's going to make it any easier? How exactly are you planning on finding him? We've had no luck the last few weeks."

"I won't have to." Christian adjusted his jacket. "Once he hears his son is looking for him, he'll find me *first*."

Isaac stared at him, heart thudding. "Samantha will never let you go."

Christian lifted his gaze. A shadow passed through his eyes, but a slow, crooked smile curved his lips. "She won't know. She's going to be too busy helping you rescue Miss Montclair."

THE SCENT OF salt and tar coiled around Isaac as his boots thudded against the wharf. He walked with purpose, but his thoughts churned like the tide. Christian's words echoed in his skull, each one more absurd than the last. Join his father? Madness. And yet he meant it.

Just as he meant Isaac to keep it from Samantha.

Bitterness burned up his throat at the thought. He swallowed it down and kept moving, though his pace slowed as the *Red Siren* came into view, moored at the end of the dock. Morning light glinted off the water, bright and blinding, and for a moment he paused beside a stack of crates. He stared across the river, eyes narrowed against the glare. A dark cloud hung low on the horizon, thick and swollen as if the sky itself conspired against him. The sun wouldn't last long. With a sigh he turned back toward the schooner.

Tortuga.

If he closed his eyes, he could almost see it. A speck of land so inconsequential from the deck of a ship, yet it had changed his life forever. And then, drawn up from the depths of his heart, came the curve of her smile, bright and wild beneath the waterfall, promising something he had never dared hope for. But the image was fragile, slipping through his fingers like smoke, replaced by her desperate struggle to escape her father, the look in her eyes that said he was worth more than orders and duty, the hope that had lit her face when he'd rounded the corner and called out.

God, that hope.

Watching it flicker, falter, then die had nearly undone him.

How could she trust him now? He'd stood there, trapped between duty and heartbreak, and let her father tear her away, force her into a marriage to a man she didn't want. The knowledge struck him hard, like a fist to the gut. Some cold, lifeless merchant with silver in his pocket and her father's approval. A man who'd take her hand, her freedom, her future.

A low growl escaped him. *No.*

The thought of another man touching her, claiming her, sent something ancient and possessive uncoiling in his chest. He'd sail to the island, tear through every gate, every man, every barrier standing between them. The wind shifted, pulling at his coat. He dropped his hand toward his sword without thinking, heart pounding—not from grief, but from the thrum of purpose rising in his blood.

A footstep came from behind him. Too soft. Too close.

Before he could turn, a cold blade kissed the hollow of his throat.

"A bit preoccupied, aren't you, Lieutenant?" The voice slid over him like oil over water.

Isaac froze, every muscle tightening. "Thorne."

The pirate's familiar laugh carried over the water. "I must

say, I'm surprised to catch you letting your guard down, Lieutenant. Not quite the Navy standard, is it?" He leaned in, breath brushing Isaac's ear. "Let me guess? Thinking of her?"

Isaac's fingers twisted around the hilt of his sword.

"Not so fast." Thorne's dagger pressed in just enough to bite. "Wouldn't want you making a scene."

"What do you want?" The words grated out between clenched teeth.

"I think you know exactly what I want." Thorne's voice came low and deadly.

"Where is Ross hiding?"

Isaac's body tensed, muscles coiling beneath the pressure, but his voice stayed steady.

"You're wasting time if you think you can get that from me."

The captain chuckled. "You know I can make things very unpleasant for you, very quickly."

Isaac took a steadying breath and squared his shoulders. "Your threats mean very little to me."

"I beg to differ." Thorne slid the blade upward and lifted Isaac's chin with the tip of it. "You forget, Lieutenant—I know exactly where your pretty little love lives. The whitewashed home on the hill, the one with the blue shutters, yes?"

A low growl rumbled deep in Isaac's throat. "Don't even think about it." His voice trembled with barely contained rage.

The dagger at his neck shifted. "A pity you let her leave here unprotected."

With a sudden twist, Isaac took advantage of the momentary slack and spun free. His sword flashed from its scabbard in one fluid motion, the blade gleaming in the morning light. Thorne's eyes flickered with amusement. In a heartbeat, his own blade was in hand, moving with deadly precision and parrying Isaac's strike before it fully formed.

"Impressive," he murmured. "But you'll have to do better than that."

Isaac lunged, steel flashing as he aimed for Thorne's side, but the pirate was faster, sidestepping with an ease honed from years at sea and countless battles.

The pirate's blade whipped forward in a ruthless counter-strike, slicing a shallow line along Isaac's forearm. Hot pain flared sharp and immediate, but Isaac clamped his jaw, refusing to falter. He twisted away, using the momentum to bring his sword in a wide arc, aiming to disarm. Thorne blocked, their blades clashing with a ringing clang that echoed off the water and wooden planks. Above, the sky shifted as the first cool drops splattered onto Isaac's face.

"What is it with you men and your women?" Thorne sneered. "Always risking everything for them. Love's a poison, Lieutenant. It'll be the death of you."

Isaac ignored the taunt and pressed forward, driving his opponent back with a series of sharp strikes. Each clang of steel against steel echoed his mounting fury. Lightning cracked and the heavens opened above, a torrent crashing down. The pirate gave ground, boots slipping as he neared the wharf's edge. But just as the advantage seemed certain, Thorne's eyes flickered with cold calculation.

With a sudden shift of weight and a twist of his wrist, the captain seized control as their weapons met in a grinding lock. With a snarl, he leaped inside Isaac's guard and slammed a shoulder into his chest. Isaac stumbled. Before he could recover, Thorne's blade hooked his, but Isaac twisted, and both swords slipped from their grips. The weapons clattered across the boards before plunging into the river below.

A fist crashed into Isaac's ribs, sharp and punishing, but Isaac didn't flinch. He drove forward with a shout, barreling into the pirate hard enough to send them slipping across the slick boards. They grappled, blows landing fast and vicious as the storm roared around them, wind whipping spray in their faces, but neither man faltered. Isaac's knuckles cracked into Thorne's jaw, blood smearing across his fingers.

The pirate lunged, seizing the front of Isaac's coat in a white-knuckled grip. "Let's see how well you fight underwater."

A moment later, they went over the edge of the dock, plunging toward the river in a tangle of limbs. At the last instant, Isaac's hand shot out, catching a coiled rope near the edge. The jolt tore through his shoulder as his body slammed against a post, boots dangling above the murky waves. With a grunt, he hauled himself onto the dock, chest heaving as he scanned the water below.

Thorne surfaced a few yards out and faced Isaac, blood streaming down his chin. "Do me a favor, Lieutenant: tell Ross he can't hide. I'll find him. And he will pay." He turned, arms cutting against the current and struck out into the river.

A muffled shout echoed across the water as a dark form materialized. The *Avenger* swept in from the mist, slicing toward the docks as if summoned from the depths themselves. Lines flew out. Hands reached. Thorne's crew hauled him aboard in a flurry of motion and shouted orders. Dripping and grinning, the captain climbed to his feet and gave a mocking salute. With a slap of sails, the ship vanished as fast as it had come, swallowed by the rain and swirling fog.

Boots thudded on the stairs behind him. Isaac didn't move. His chest still heaved from the fight, blood trailing warm and steady down his arm.

"Isaac!" Samantha's shout broke through the storm. She reached him first, boots splashing through a puddle. "You're hurt."

Christian followed close behind, his coat soaked through, face taut. "What happened?"

Isaac met his friend's eyes, the unspoken truth passing between them.

Christian's jaw clenched. "Where is he?"

Isaac's gaze flicked toward the dark horizon, water sluicing down his face. "He's gone. The ship came out of nowhere... and then vanished into the storm."

"Did you tell him where Ross went?"

"I told him he was going to Washington." The deception flowed smoothly off Isaac's tongue, though his heart clenched with every word. He hadn't breathed a word to Thorne. If Christian went to Washington, all the better. Unfortunately for the Rosses, Thorne was far too cunning to lose their trail for long—he would sail to New Orleans.

Christian held Isaac's gaze, eyes narrowing slightly as if weighing the shape of his response, testing its seams for weakness. The rain drummed steadily around them, muffling the world to a hush. Finally, he gave a single nod. "Good. What about Miss Montclair?"

Isaac wiped the blood from his chin, the sting in his bruised ribs sharpening with every breath. "I shouldn't go. Not with Thorne so close. This could be my best chance at getting him."

With a snort, Christian shook his head. "You have no ship. No crew. No plan. It'll take time to get all that." He turned to his wife. "Go with him. You two don't need me for this. We'll be better served if I stay behind and keep an ear to the ground for Thorne's next move."

A clean lie, as effortless as any Isaac had ever heard. He met his best friend's eyes, searching for something—conviction, hesitation, doubt—but found only steel. He truly meant to go through with his idiotic scheme. So be it. He swallowed the burn in his chest and gave a tight nod.

Samantha glanced between them, her smile faltering for just a heartbeat before she squared her shoulders. "Alright. Let's go get Josephine."

Chapter Twenty-Nine

A MOCKINGBIRD TRILLED.

Josephine's hand clenched into a fist as the last rays of sunrise filtered through the palm trees. Damn the bird. Damn destiny. Damn all of it. She stared into the pink-hued sky, eyes tight and dry. She'd already spilled all the tears she held. Now, only a bitter emptiness remained.

This morning, her life would be upended.

Mrs. Wentworth.

She shuddered at the thought. They'd arrived too late last night for her to meet her intended. Which meant she would have to face him for the first time at the altar. She pressed trembling fingers to her lips, as if she could hold in the rising panic.

The trip back had been spent locked in her cabin. Torture filled each day as she replayed all that had happened. Of Isaac's hands on her flesh. The way he's said her name, rough and reverent all at once. How he'd sent her soaring to heights she'd never known existed.

But mostly, the look in his eyes as the carriage left the drive. How they burned with quiet torment—a raw ache that tore through her chest even now. She hadn't even gotten to say goodbye.

If only her father had come *before*. Before she went to Isaac's room. Before he'd washed away all her anger and hurt with two simple words. *I lied.* Her fists curled in the morning air. If she hadn't gone to say thank you, she would still be upset.

And this wouldn't hurt so damn much.

She glanced down at the dark-haired head below and a fresh wave of indignation swept through her. Her father had the nerve to post a guard under her window. As if there were anywhere she could escape to on this God-forsaken island.

There was no space here for rebellion, no space for hope. She drew in a shuddering breath. If only she could go back in time. But she couldn't. The rest of her life, she'd be trapped by choices made for her. A hot trail crept down her cheek. She'd been wrong—there were more tears after all.

With an angry swipe of her hand, she stalked back into her room. Two crates lay open, packed with her belongings. Apparently, Mr. Wentworth had decided they would leave straight-away following the wedding. Her throat tightened. She didn't even know where he lived.

With everything she owned packed away, the room seemed hollow and bare. Her gaze settled on the empty cage in the corner and her heart squeezed. Her father had refused to bring Lola back with him. Said a respectable woman should never be allowed to own a parrot.

A soft knock came from her door and she spun. Colette stood there, arms crossed. "Looking awfully glum for a bride on her wedding day."

Bride. Josephine glanced at the dress laid across her bed and a stab of resentment shot through her. "How should I look? This is the worst day of my life."

With a cluck of her tongue and a shake of her head, Colette swooped into the room. "Don't say that. This is the very best type of marriage to have."

Josephine stared at her. "How could you ever say such a thing?"

"He's wealthy, yes?" When she nodded, Colette grinned. "See, you'll be well provided for and have everything you wish for."

Not everything.

Copper brows arched. "Won't you?"

Josephine gave a sad shake of her head and hugged her arms around herself. "But what about passion?"

"Ah, so you did find passion with your lieutenant?" Colette slanted a sly look at her.

Heat flamed to her cheeks and her friend gave a deep-throated laugh. "Your new husband will spend most of his time at sea. Which means you will have the freedom to do as you wish— no overbearing eyes on you. You'll find passion again, I promise you."

Josephine pressed her eyes closed. "That's not how I picture being married."

Colette picked up the dress and fluffed it out. "Josephine, the hard truth is, marriage isn't usually what you might have imagined. You can still find your own kind of freedom in a loveless match, and you should find no shame in it. I guarantee you, a man with his status has a woman in every port. It's how the world works, and it doesn't mean your happiness has to suffer because of it."

As usual Colette was only trying to make her feel better. But Josephine's insides twisted. There was only one person she wanted passion with. And she would never see him again.

"Come now, let's get you ready."

Josephine remained silent, only half listening to Colette as she went on about how to navigate the new life she was being forced into. Time passed in a blur of unshed tears and hollow words. She barely registered getting undressed, didn't feel the sharp tugs as Colette did her hair. Her mind was far away, lost in the hopeless-ness of it all.

"The most beautiful girl on the island." Colette's smile was wide and genuine when she pinned the last curl in place. "I sure will miss you."

A pang shot through Josephine's chest. She would likely never see Colette again. Despite the circumstances, she was glad to have her there.

"Thank you. For everything you've done for me. All of it."

Her voice cracked.

Colette pushed a tendril of hair back with a smile. "You've been like a daughter to me. Have faith in me when I say I know you will find happiness."

Josephine couldn't answer. Not when her entire body ached with despair. So, she turned down the stairs. Outside, the sun already beat down. They walked down the street to the little stone church on the hill. Any other day, she would smile at how picturesque it was, overlooking the azure sea. Today, it may as well be a prison.

Colette squeezed her hand as they walked through the door. "Go on now. Keep your chin up."

Mr. Wentworth stood next to her father, wearing a fine frock coat. Deep lines etched across his weathered face, his sparse hair combed over in a sad attempt to cover the balding crown of his head. Her stomach turned.

His eyes raked over her, sharp and greedy. Like she was a prized object he'd secured from a trading deal. "My dear Josephine, you look exquisite."

Her father smiled. "Ah, yes. That dress was her mother's. I knew it would suit her."

Father Bouchard stepped from behind the altar, beaming at her. "Our dear Josephine, finally all grown up and starting a new life. We're so proud of you."

He waved her forward and she approached with leaden feet. The scent of melted wax mingled with the cold, damp stone that surrounded her, pressing in from every side, suffocating. Her fingers itched to pull at the tight bodice of the gown, as if loosening the fabric might free the breath locked in her chest. The silk clung to her skin, every thread a reminder of the captivity she was about to be locked into.

Wentworth joined her, standing only inches away, his paunch pressing against the straining buttons of his coat. His fingers, heavy with rings, twitched as if itching to claim her already. Her skin prickled, not from the chill of the stone chapel, but from the sheer nearness of him. She kept her gaze fixed straight ahead, jaw clenched, but her body betrayed her. Her shoulders curled, angling herself away from him as her hands trembled at her sides, knuckles bloodless with tension.

Father Bouchard cleared his throat as he gave a worried look between them, the warm smile on his face faltering ever so slightly. His voice, too loud and too high, rang out across the silence, trying to fill the space with a sense of normalcy. "Dearly beloved…"

A vise tightened around her ribs with each word, until breathing became a struggle. She dared not glance at the open window, where the sea shimmered like a promise out of reach. A drop of sweat slid coldly down her spine. Her fingers twitched, grasping for something—anything—to hold herself together. Father Bouchard's voice had become distant, distorted, as if from underwater. The Latin echoes of his prayer rolled over her like surf on stone, grinding her down with every syllable. The room swam, flickering candlelight blurring into halos, carved saints along the nave bending into hollow-eyed spectators. Her knees weakened and she swayed, just enough for the priest to falter mid-phrase and glance up.

"Miss Montclair, are you quite alright?" His whisper barely penetrated the muffled roar rising in her ears.

"She'll be fine." Mr. Wentworth frowned. "I'm sure it's only nerves."

Her father gave a sharp nod from his seat in the front row. A silent command. Father Bouchard straightened and continued, his voice ringing through the chapel like a hammer striking cold iron. "If any among you know just cause why these two should not be lawfully joined together, let him speak now, or else forever hold his peace."

Mr. Wentworth kept his gaze fixed on Father Bouchard, but his hand, warm and heavy, slowly drifted toward hers. Josephine's breath caught in her throat as he closed the distance between them, his fingers curling around hers with eager possessiveness. She didn't dare look at him, her gaze fixed firmly on the floor, willing herself not to tremble under the weight of his touch.

Father Bouchard took one last glance over his spectacles at the quiet crowd and gave a satisfied grunt before turning back to them. "Now, let us proceed with the vow—"

Bang!

The door flew open, slamming against the wall. Everyone twisted and a flurry of gasps echoed through the room as a figure strode into the room. Tight breeches, a deeply cut blouse, and hair the color of fire.

Josephine blinked. "Samantha?"

Her friend met her gaze. "We're not too late, are we?"

A shadow fell across the floor and Josephine's heart seized. A pair of polished boots clicked across the stone as her eyes flew over his form. Could it be? No. A strangled laugh bubbled in her chest, bitter and soundless. Now her eyes were playing cruel tricks on her.

And yet, the mirage kept walking. Steady. Unshaken. He didn't vanish with the flicker of candlelight or the blink of her eye. He kept coming. Kept his blue gaze locked on her. Stopped in front of the altar. Josephine's heart pounded in her chest, each beat louder than the last as a wave of disbelief crashed through her.

"Lieutenant Caldwell of the US Navy. I would like to speak." The baritone of Isaac's voice cut through the heavy silence. It vibrated through her, each word a rough caress, and for a fleeting second, hope flickered within her.

Her father leapt to his feet. "It's too late. We've already passed that point. Continue, Father."

The ring of steel echoed through the room as Samantha drew her rapier. Father Bouchard's face went pale.

Isaac lifted his hand, signaling her to lower her blade. "It's alright," he said, voice steady but edged with something darker. "It's never too late to speak before God, is it, Father?"

An undercurrent of barely veiled warning ran through his words as the weight of his gaze turned to the priest. The poor man stuttered as he looked between Isaac and her father. "I—I—"

Isaac turned to face the crowd. "I have come to give just cause. In fact, I am the just cause. Josephine will not be marrying this man, because she will be marrying me."

Excited murmurs ran through the crowd, their whispers barely contained. Josephine's heart skipped, the impossible words ringing in her ears. *What was he doing?*

Her father stormed forward. "I told you to stay out of this, Lieutenant. My daughter's affairs are none of your concern."

Isaac stood unmoving, the flicker of something dangerous behind his calm exterior. His jaw tightened, but his voice remained even as stormy eyes met hers. "She's very much my concern at the moment."

Her pulse quickened, the world around her going momentarily still.

With a growl, her father spun to two guards. "Remove this man at once. He is not welcome on Tortuga."

The men strode forward, their steps heavy and menacing. Samantha whipped her blade up again, its sharp edge gleaming in the candlelight. The church seemed to hold its breath as the danger heightened. Josephine's heart beat wildly, her chest tight with panic. A full-on brawl was about to erupt right here, in the heart of the church.

She yanked her hand from Mr. Wentworth's. Without thinking, her feet were already moving, her legs carrying her toward Isaac. She barely registered the shocked gasps of the guests as she closed the distance between them and set a hand on his forearm.

He stepped between her and the approaching guards, his palm hovering over the hilt of his sword. "I'm not here to fight. But I will if I must."

Her father, face twisted with fury, stalked forward, each step a heavy echo in the stillness. "Are you going to risk straining relations between our countries over this?"

"Are you?" Isaac didn't flinch. He stood firm, unwavering, his eyes locked on her father with a steady defiance. "As governor, I would hope you'd be willing to reason."

The air crackled, thick with the impending violence. Isaac's hand closed around the worn leather grip of his sword, the motion slow and deliberate.

"Oh, for heaven's sake." Mr. Wentworth stepped from the altar and put a hand on her father's shoulder. "I've spent enough time on this earth to know when to admit defeat. Why not let these two have a chance?"

Her father's face twisted with disbelief. "She's been promised to you."

Mr. Wentworth locked eyes with Josephine. "And I thought she was willing. An unwilling woman is nothing but a liability."

Her father crossed his arms and faced Isaac, the fire in his eyes burning hotter than ever. "You truly want her, even after all the trouble she's caused?"

A slow smile spread across his face. "*Especially* because of it."

His words sent a thrill through Josephine, her pulse leaping at the heat behind them. Her breath caught as the intensity of his gaze locked with hers, his meaning clear.

After a long moment, her father threw up his hands. "This is madness."

Isaac turned to her and brushed a tendril of hair from her damp cheek. Was she crying again? She blinked up at him, barely breathing, the chaos around them fading. "Is this real?" The words left her in a strangled whisper.

With a smile, he closed his hands around hers, the warm weight anchoring her to the moment. "I sure hope so."

He turned to the crowd. "You've all gathered for a wedding, and I'd hate to disappoint you. What do you say, Josephine? Shall we get married?"

She stared into sparkling blue eyes, her heartbeat thrumming in her throat. "Are you sure?"

"Am I sure? What kind of question is that? Let me tell you

what I'm sure of. I'm sure I've never met anyone like you. I'm sure I fell in love with you long before I had the good sense to admit it. And I'm damn sure I don't want to face another day without you in it. So, Josephine Montclair, I will ask you one more time, will you marry me?"

"You love me?" The timid question tumbled forth before she could stop it.

His eyes softened as his thumbs swept slow circles over the backs of her hands. "More than you will ever know."

New tears welled in the corners of her eyes and she managed a smile.

His lips tugged into a crooked half-grin. "Is that a yes?"

A laugh, watery and disbelieving, bubbled up her throat. How could this be happening? How could she possibly say no? She nodded, breath catching, heart full to bursting.

He glanced toward the stunned priest, mischief dancing in his eyes. "Father? What do you think?"

The priest blinked. "Well… I mean…" With an exasperated look around the church, he waved them forward. He glanced at the book in his hand and the crowd. "I suppose we can start where we left off."

"Josephine Montclair," the priest began, his voice suddenly calm and serious, "do you take the lieutenant to be your lawfully wedded husband?" She nodded, her throat tight with emotion.

"And Lieutenant Caldwell, do you take Josephine to be your lawfully wedded wife?"

Isaac's voice came steady and firm. "I do."

There was a pause, and the priest lifted his hands in blessing. "Then by the power vested in me, I now pronounce you husband and wife."

The words barely reached her ears before Isaac was there, his hand sliding around her waist, pulling her closer. His lips found hers, soft and reassuring, a promise wrapped in the quiet heat of a thousand unsaid things. The crowd erupted into applause, but the steady thrum of her heartbeat in her chest drowned it out.

Colette surged forward through the onlookers and wrapped her in a warm embrace. "When I told you I knew you'd find your happiness, I never imagined it would come so quickly. Congratulations."

Josephine squeezed her back with a breathless laugh. "I didn't think I'd find it at all."

Samantha slipped in beside them, her smile warm. "Now that was an entrance. Hopefully our exit is a little more uneventful. My ship is prepped and ready—you'll have the captain's cabin on the way back to Savannah."

"Thank you. This…" Josephine's voice thickened. "This means more than you'll ever know."

The streets of Tortuga shimmered under the bright press of late morning sun as they made their way down toward the docks after gathering her belongings. Islanders paused to stare, a few offering cheers or well-wishes, as if news of the chaos at the church had already spread like wildfire.

At the gangplank, Isaac stopped and offered his hand with a crooked grin. "No stowaways this time."

Josephine slipped her fingers into his. "I make no promises."

With a chuckle, he led her onto the ship. Movement caught her eye the moment they stepped onto the deck. The cabin door creaked open, and Samantha stepped out with a warm smile. With a burst of color and the rustle of wings, Lola swooped from her extended hands and landed neatly on Josephine's shoulder.

"Lola!" she cried, turning to nuzzle soft green feathers.

Isaac grinned. "I thought you might like to see her again."

Josephine pressed a kiss to the bird's head, then reached for him. "Thank you."

His hands slid behind her back, pulling her close. "You're welcome, Wife."

She let out a quiet breath. "Husband." The word felt new and strange on her tongue, yet full of promise and possibility.

The shout to cast off the lines rang through the air and the crew jumped into motion. She glanced over her shoulder at the island—at the life she had known, and the one she was leaving behind. A thrill stirred deep within her, a mix of excitement and uncertainty as the future stretched out before her.

Isaac's arms tightened around her and he leaned in, the soft brush of his breath caressing her ear. "Will you miss it?"

She turned to him. "No."

He gazed at her, the oceans in his eyes calm and sure. "Looks like we've come full circle. Who knew all those nights ago when I showed up shipwrecked and desperate that fate would find us together?"

Her lips curved. "Maybe it wasn't fate. Maybe it was destiny."

Epilogue
Isaac

Savannah, GA
Two weeks later

THE SUN HUNG low, yet fierce, in the late afternoon sky, casting golden shafts across the deck and gilding the river's surface with light. Beneath Isaac's boots, the deck creaked with the quiet stretch of timber soaked in heat. Brine and tar mingled with the sweeter wafts of molasses and drying tobacco drifting up from the warehouses. Canvas snapped gently in the breeze, a familiar conversation between the wind and the rigging.

A commotion came from the main deck and he strode to the rail. Warmth bloomed in his chest as a broad smile curved across his face. Josephine stood next to Samantha, dressed in a sea-blue gown that caught the sunlight and shimmered like the tide. The color played against her dark hair, which spilled over her shoulders in loose waves. She scanned the deck, her gaze quick to find him—and when it did, her expression softened, eyes shining with something that pulled the air from his lungs.

His wife. His compass. And for the first time since their hasty wedding, he was leaving her behind.

A fresh gust lifted the edge of the flag behind him, snapping it with sudden force. He exhaled, slow and steady, willing the uncomfortable pressure in his chest to settle. This was duty. This was the life they both knew he'd return to. Still—knowing he'd set sail without her settled a lonely weight behind his ribs.

With a fluid grace, she moved toward the base of the stairs leading up to him. His eyes traced the sway of her hips, searing the picture into memory. She climbed the steps and came to stand beside him, her gaze flickering out over the water before meeting his eyes. "You seem so far away already, gazing out over the water like that."

Isaac gave a tight smile, trying to hide the unease in his gut. "Just thinking."

Josephine didn't press further. She simply stood beside him, her presence a balm for his frayed nerves, even if it made the ache of leaving that much harder to bear.

Her hand brushed lightly against his, a subtle touch that somehow seemed to convey more than words ever could. The noise of the ship, the murmurs of the crew, faded into the distance as the world narrowed to the space between them. For a long moment, they stood in silence, the steady breeze sweeping between them.

She stole a glance up at him. "Are you worried?"

He nuzzled into her hair, the already familiar scent anchoring him. "Would you think less of me if I said a little?"

"Not in this lifetime. Not in any."

"Good. Because I am worried. Worried what Thorne is going to do next. Worried about who else is involved. Worried about what was so important to hide that a whole group of men had no qualms killing someone's wife." He let out a long exhale. "Worried if I'll even have a job after I get to Washington."

Her palm settled over his with a soft squeeze. "You don't have to face any of that alone."

The simple words struck deeper than any oath and he rested his forehead against hers for a moment before drawing back. "God help me... leaving you feels impossible."

She offered him a small smile, though it didn't reach her eyes. "I'm rather glad you're going to Washington over chasing Thorne."

He pressed his jaw together. It would come soon enough.

Whether he—or she—liked it or not.

"I'll be waiting for you, Isaac." Her voice came steady but quiet, almost as though she were saying it more to herself than to him.

The words hit him like a blow to the chest, a rush of warmth and anguish flooding his veins. *Waiting.* She would wait for him. And that, perhaps, was the hardest part of all. That she would stand on the dock, watch him sail away, and trust that he would come back to her.

He turned his face toward the horizon, trying to steady his racing thoughts. There was a lump in his throat, a tightness in his chest that made it hard to breathe. "Don't wait too long," he finally managed, voice hoarse with the emotion he'd been holding back.

"I'll wait as long as it takes." Promise filled her words. She slanted her gaze to meet his with a wry smile. "But, don't make me wait longer than necessary."

His fingers laced through hers and he tugged her close, bending to meet her lips. She gasped, and he caught the sound with his mouth, deepening the kiss with a hunger tempered by restraint. One hand rose to cradle her cheek, his thumb brushing her skin, committing its smooth warmth to memory.

"I love you." He breathed the truth against the curve of her lips, his arms drawing her into an embrace that left no room for doubt.

"Forever." She leaned into him, the word wrapped in tenderness and promise.

Josephine

"GOODBYE."

The whispered word drifted on the breeze, swallowed by the murmur of the river. Josephine and Samantha lingered at the dock's edge, staring at the spot where the tall masts had vanished beyond the river bend.

With a sigh, she turned to her friend. "Does it ever get easier?"

A copper brow lifted. "To be honest, I don't know. Christian and I never sail without each other…" Her voice drifted off as her eyes pressed shut. "At least we haven't up until now."

The melancholy in Josephine's chest shifted, making room for a quiet sympathy. When they had arrived back from Tortuga, Samantha had been furious when she found her husband missing. Even more so when she discovered his note explaining he had gone to join his father—the same man who had murdered her parents.

Josephine twisted her hands together. "I'm sorry"

"Don't be. Christian is the one who's going to be sorry when I get my hands on him." She spun toward her ship, her jaunty red feather bouncing with each agitated step.

Josephine's gaze traveled from the polished rapier to the unconventional breeches, before falling in step beside her. Samantha was one of the fiercest women she'd ever met, let alone imagined. She could only imagine the type of set down her friend would give her husband.

"Don't people talk?" Josephine nodded toward Samantha's outfit.

Her friend chuckled, the sound skipping lightly off the water as they walked along the dock. "Of course they do."

"Does it bother you?"

The corner of Samantha's mouth twitched. "No. I feel sorry for them. They'll never taste the thrill of adventure." She gave a theatrical shudder. "What a dull life."

A dull life indeed. Josephine couldn't help her grin.

They climbed the *Siren's* gangplank. Onboard, Samantha ran her hand over a smooth rail and a wistful smile played across her face. "Soon, my beauty." The words came out in a barely-there whisper, as if she were talking to herself.

A flurry of activity filled the deck around them as the crew coiled ropes and fastened cargo in place. Several men climbed into the rigging, their movements sure and practiced, and she jerked her gaze down as a flutter ran through her stomach. The subtle rhythm of the ship under her feet sent her pulse quickening, as if the *Siren* herself were daring her to embrace this world.

Josephine frowned. "It looks like you're getting ready to sail."

Samantha didn't answer as they climbed to the quarterdeck. She examined the wheel, spinning it one way, then the next before meeting Josephine's eyes.

"I'm going after my wayward husband." She gave the wheel one last sharp turn. "And I need to check on Abigail."

"You're going to New Orleans?"

Her friend nodded.

Josephine blinked. "But won't Christian be going the opposite way, to Washington? I thought Isaac told Thorne the Rosses went there?"

Samantha set her jaw and stared out over the water. "I'm not sure he said anything of the sort. Thorne's too clever to fall for that kind of ruse, and Christian knows it—he's remarkably like his father in that regard. I'd almost guarantee he's headed for New Orleans."

A knot curled in Josephine's gut as the memory of Abigail's terrified face in the cart flashed before her. That knot turned to icy dread when she thought of the pirate captain's brutal tactics. If he got his hands on Abigail... She shivered.

"Do you think your uncle will be able to keep her safe?"

Samantha traced a finger over the carved wood of the wheel, eyes on the deck. "He's the best chance she has."

A sailor with a graying beard jogged up the steps. "We're ready, Captain."

"Very good. Tell the crew to stand by while I get Mrs. Caldwell back to shore."

He nodded and returned to the main deck, barking orders. Samantha and Josephine followed, making their way toward the gangplank.

"Goodbye for now. Try to keep yourself occupied; it will help the time go by faster." Samantha nodded a greeting to a passing sailor, her words falling flat.

"I'm sure I'll keep busy getting settled into the townhome." Josephine forced a smile and sighed. "Though I wish you didn't have to go."

"Hopefully, I won't be gone long. I'm excited to spend more time with you on my return."

Josephine's throat tightened, a lump forming as she swallowed. Though her friend hid it well behind her confident smile, the flicker in her eyes betrayed the quiet hurt she carried. She jerked to a stop at the top of the gangplank and spun.

"Let me come with you."

Samantha stilled. "No. It's too dangerous."

Josephine let out an unladylike snort, arms crossing over her chest. "More dangerous than anything I've faced the last month?"

"Yes, you've survived a great deal. Still, anytime Thorne is involved, nothing is ever simple or safe."

With a huff, Josephine squared her shoulders. "I'm not taking no for an answer. If you won't let me come, you'll have to drag me off the ship yourself." Her gaze flicked toward the water. "Or throw me overboard."

Samantha's brows drew together, a sly curve tugging at her lips. "Don't be so dramatic. Besides, I thought stowing away was more your suit."

A small thrill sparked in Josephine's chest. "Don't tempt me."

Her friend gave a worried glance back at the waiting crew. After a long moment, she let out a resigned exhale. "Very well. But it won't be easy. If you're to sail under my command, you'll need to be properly trained in sword fighting—and how to handle a ship."

The rush sliding through Josephine's veins made her breath catch. "I look forward to it." Somehow, her voice remained steady despite her pounding pulse.

"Oh." Samantha let the word hang for a beat. "You still have those breeches of yours?"

Josephine leveled a pointed look at her. "No. But I know who I can borrow some from."

Samantha's answering laugh rang out over the river. "I sure am glad I met you." Her grin faded as she straightened, eyes narrowing on the horizon. "We'll be sailing hard. Christian has at least a week's head start on us."

"Perhaps we'll reach him before he finds Thorne." Josephine's hopeful words made her friend stiffen.

"May it be so." Samantha's lips pressed together as her palm settled on the hilt of her rapier. "If not, God help us all."

The End

About the Author

Lauren Everly first discovered her love for historical romance at the age of twelve, when she stumbled upon a hidden box of Johanna Lindsey novels in her mom's closet—an accidental find that sparked a lifelong passion for dashing heroes and bold heroines. Now living in the heart of Middle Tennessee with her husband and three children, she's a flight attendant by day and a writer of sinfully delicious stories by night. When she's not jet setting around the country or putting steamy words to pages, you'll find her tending an expansive garden, baking something wonderfully sweet, or out exploring the beautiful scenery of TN. Her love for travel, both in real life and through the pages of history, continuously fuels her imagination. For Lauren, the best romances—like the best adventures—are the ones that leave you breathless and longing for more.

Instagram / Threads: laureneverlywrites
Facebook: laureneverlyauthor
Twitter / X: @lauren_everly
TikTok: @laureneverlywrites

www.ingramcontent.com/pod-product-compliance
Lightning Source LLC
Chambersburg PA
CBHW061308030726
47595CB00001B/262